Child of Storm by H. Rider Haggard

Sir Henry Rider Haggard, KBE was born on June 22nd, 1856 at Bradenham in Norfolk, England.

After his education he was pushed towards an Army career but failed the entrance exam. Next Haggard was positioned to work for the British Foreign Office but he seems not to have sat that exam. Using family connections, he was sent to Southern Africa by his father in search of a further opportunity of a career.

Haggard spent six years there before a return to England and marriage. He had begun to write and publish some non-fiction in Africa but it was only after studying Law in the hope it might prove to be the proper career his father wanted for him that Haggard began to write fiction, using his African experiences as the basis.

His first fiction was published in 1885 and the following year King Solomon's Mines was published. It was a phenomenal success. His career was set.

Haggard wrote well and wrote often. He managed to sympathise with the local populations even though they were exploited and manipulated by Europeans intent on amassing fortunes in money, people and resources. His writing career covered the great sprint to Empire of several European powers and both reflects and criticizes these events through his well-loved characters including Allan Quatermain and Ayesha.

In his later years Haggard pursued much in the way social reform as well as standing for Parliament and writing a great many letters to The Times.

Henry Rider Haggard died on May 14th, 1925 at the age of 68. His ashes were buried at Ditchingham Church.

Index of Contents

DEDICATION

Dear Mr. Stuart,

For twenty years, I believe I am right in saying, you, as Assistant Secretary for Native Affairs in Natal, and in other offices, have been intimately acquainted with the Zulu people. Moreover, you are one of the few living men who have made a deep and scientific study of their language, their customs and their history. So I confess that I was the more pleased after you were so good as to read this tale—the second book of the epic of the vengeance of Zikali, "the Thing-that-should-never-have-been-born," and of the fall of the House of Senzangakona—when you wrote to me that it was animated by the true Zulu spirit.

I must admit that my acquaintance with this people dates from a period which closed almost before your day. What I know of them I gathered at the time when Cetewayo, of whom my volume tells, was in his glory, previous to the evil hour in which he found himself driven by the clamour of his regiments, cut off, as they were, through the annexation of the Transvaal, from their hereditary trade of war, to match himself against the British strength. I learned it all by personal observation in the 'seventies, or from the lips of the great Shepstone, my chief and friend, and from my colleagues Osborn, Fynney, Clarke and others, every one of them long since "gone down."

Perhaps it may be as well that this is so, at any rate in the case of one who desires to write of the Zulus as a reigning nation, which now they have ceased to be, and to try to show them as they were, in all their superstitious madness and bloodstained grandeur.

Yet then they had virtues as well as vices. To serve their Country in arms, to die for it and for the King; such was their primitive ideal. If they were fierce they were loyal, and feared neither wounds nor doom; if they listened to the dark redes of the witch-doctor, the trumpet-call of duty sounded still louder in their ears; if, chanting their terrible "Ingoma," at the King's bidding they went forth to slay unsparingly, at least they were not mean or vulgar. From those who continually must face the last great issues of life or death meanness and vulgarity are far removed. These qualities belong to the safe and crowded haunts of civilised men, not to the kraals of Bantu savages, where, at any rate of old, they might be sought in vain.

Now everything is changed, or so I hear, and doubtless in the balance this is best. Still we may wonder what are the thoughts that pass through the mind of some ancient warrior of Chaka's or Dingaan's time, as he suns himself crouched on the ground, for example, where once stood the royal kraal, Duguza, and watches men and women of the Zulu blood passing homeward from the cities or the mines, bemused, some of them, with the white man's smuggled liquor, grotesque with the white man's cast-off garments, hiding, perhaps, in their blankets examples of the white man's doubtful photographs—and then shuts his sunken eyes and remembers the plumed and kilted regiments making that same ground shake as, with a thunder of salute, line upon line, company upon company, they rushed out to battle.

Well, because the latter does not attract me, it is of this former time that I have tried to write—the time of the Impis and the witch-finders and the rival princes of the royal House—as I am glad to learn from you, not quite in vain. Therefore, since you, so great an expert, approve of my labours in the seldom-travelled field of Zulu story, I ask you to allow me to set your name upon this page and subscribe myself,

Gratefully and sincerely yours,

H. RIDER HAGGARD.
Ditchingham, 12th October, 1912.

To James Stuart, Esq., Late Assistant Secretary for Native Affairs, Natal.

AUTHOR'S NOTE

Mr. Allan Quatermain's story of the wicked and fascinating Mameena, a kind of Zulu Helen, has, it should be stated, a broad foundation in historical fact. Leaving Mameena and her wiles on one side, the tale of the struggle between the Princes Cetewayo and Umbelazi for succession to the throne of Zululand is true.

When the differences between these sons of his became intolerable, because of the tumult which they were causing in his country, King Panda, their father, the son of Senzangakona, and the brother of the great Chaka and of Dingaan, who had ruled before him, did say that "when two young bulls quarrel they had better fight it out." So, at least, I was told by the late Mr. F. B. Fynney, my colleague at the time of the annexation of the Transvaal in 1877, who, as Zulu Border Agent, with the exceptions of the late Sir Theophilus Shepstone and the late Sir Melmoth Osborn, perhaps knew more of that land and people than anyone else of his period.

As a result of this hint given by a maddened king, the great battle of the Tugela was fought at Endondakusuka in December, 1856, between the Usutu party, commanded by Cetewayo, and the adherents of Umbelazi the Handsome, his brother, who was known among the Zulus as "Indhlovu-ene-Sihlonti," or the "Elephant with the tuft of hair," from a little lock of hair which grew low down upon his back.

My friend, Sir Melmoth Osborn, who died in or about the year 1897, was present at this battle, although not as a combatant. Well do I remember his thrilling story, told to me over thirty years ago, of the events of that awful day.

Early in the morning, or during the previous night, I forget which, he swam his horse across the Tugela and hid with it in a bush-clad kopje, blindfolding the animal with his coat lest it should betray him. As it chanced, the great fight of the day, that of the regiment of veterans, which Sir Melmoth informed me Panda had sent down at the last moment to the assistance of Umbelazi, his favourite son, took place almost at the foot of this kopje. Mr. Quatermain, in his narrative, calls this regiment the Amawombe, but my recollection is that the name Sir Melmoth Osborn gave them was "The Greys" or "Upunga."

Whatever their exact title may have been, however, they made a great stand. At least, he told me that when Umbelazi's impi, or army, began to give before the Usutu onslaught, these "Greys" moved forward above 3,000 strong, drawn up in a triple line, and were charged by one of Cetewayo's regiments.

The opposing forces met, and the noise of their clashing shields, said Sir Melmoth, was like the roll of heavy thunder. Then, while he watched, the veteran "Greys" passed over the opposing regiment "as a wave passes over a rock"—these were his exact words—and, leaving about a third of their number dead or wounded among the bodies of the annihilated foe, charged on to meet a second regiment sent against them by Cetewayo. With these the struggle was repeated, but again the "Greys" conquered. Only now there were not more than five or six hundred of them left upon their feet.

These survivors ran to a mound, round which they formed a ring, and here for a long while withstood the attack of a third regiment, until at length they perished almost to a man, buried beneath heaps of their slain assailants, the Usutu.

Truly they made a noble end fighting thus against tremendous odds!

As for the number who fell at this battle of Endondakusuka, Mr. Fynney, in a pamphlet which he wrote, says that six of Umbelazi's brothers died, "whilst it is estimated that upwards of 100,000 of the people—men, women and children—were slain"—a high and indeed an impossible estimate.

That curious personage named John Dunn, an Englishman who became a Zulu chief, and who actually fought in this battle, as narrated by Mr. Quatermain, however, puts the number much lower. What the true total was will never be known; but Sir Melmoth Osborn told me that when he swam his horse back across the Tugela that night it was black with bodies; and Sir Theophilus Shepstone also told me that when he visited the scene a day or two later the banks of the river were strewn with multitudes of them, male and female.

It was from Mr. Fynney that I heard the story of the execution by Cetewayo of the man who appeared before him with the ornaments of Umbelazi, announcing that he had killed the prince with his own hand. Of course, this tale, as Mr. Quatermain points out, bears a striking resemblance to that recorded in the Old Testament in connection with the death of King Saul.

It by no means follows, however, that it is therefore apocryphal; indeed, Mr. Fynney assured me that it was quite true, although, if he gave me his authorities, I cannot remember them after a lapse of more than thirty years.

The exact circumstances of Umbelazi's death are unknown, but the general report was that he died, not by the assegais of the Usutu, but of a broken heart. Another story declares that he was drowned. His body was never found, and it is therefore probable that it sank in the Tugela, as is suggested in the following pages.

I have only to add that it is quite in accordance with Zulu beliefs that a man should be haunted by the ghost of one whom he has murdered or betrayed, or, to be more accurate, that the spirit ("umoya") should enter into the slayer and drive him mad. Or, in such a case, that spirit might bring misfortune upon him, his family, or his tribe.

H. RIDER HAGGARD.

CHAPTER I

ALLAN QUATERMAIN HEARS OF MAMEENA

We white people think that we know everything. For instance, we think that we understand human nature. And so we do, as human nature appears to us, with all its trappings and accessories seen dimly through the glass of our conventions, leaving out those aspects of it which we have forgotten or do not think it polite to mention. But I, Allan Quatermain, reflecting upon these matters in my ignorant and uneducated fashion, have always held that no one really understands human nature who has not studied it in the rough. Well, that is the aspect of it with which I have been best acquainted.

For most of the years of my life I have handled the raw material, the virgin ore, not the finished ornament that is smelted out of it—if, indeed, it is finished yet, which I greatly doubt. I dare say that a time may come when the perfected generations—if Civilisation, as we understand it, really has a future and any such should be allowed to enjoy their hour on the World—will look back to us as crude, half-developed creatures whose only merit was that we handed on the flame of life.

Maybe, maybe, for everything goes by comparison; and at one end of the ladder is the ape-man, and at the other, as we hope, the angel. No, not the angel; he belongs to a different sphere, but that last expression of humanity upon which I will not speculate. While man is man—that is, before he suffers the magical death-change into spirit, if such should be his destiny—well, he will remain man. I mean that the same passions will sway him; he will aim at the same ambitions; he will know the same joys and be oppressed by the same fears, whether he lives in a Kafir hut or in a golden palace; whether he walks upon his two feet or, as for aught I know he may do one day, flies through the air. This is certain: that in the flesh he can never escape from our atmosphere, and while he breathes it, in the main with some variations prescribed by climate, local law and religion, he will do much as his forefathers did for countless ages.

That is why I have always found the savage so interesting, for in him, nakedly and forcibly expressed, we see those eternal principles which direct our human destiny.

To descend from these generalities, that is why also I, who hate writing, have thought it worth while, at the cost of some labour to myself, to occupy my leisure in what to me is a strange land—for although I was born in England, it is not my country—in setting down various experiences of my life that do, in my opinion, interpret this our universal nature. I dare say that no one will ever read them; still, perhaps they are worthy of record, and who knows? In days to come they may fall into the hands of others and prove of value. At any rate, they are true stories of interesting peoples, who, if they should survive in the savage competition of the nations, probably are doomed to undergo great changes. Therefore I tell of them before they began to change.

Now, although I take it out of its strict chronological order, the first of these histories that I wish to preserve is in the main that of an extremely beautiful woman—with the exception of a certain Nada, called "the Lily," of whom I hope to speak some day, I think the most beautiful that ever lived among the Zulus. Also she was, I think, the most able, the most wicked, and the most ambitious. Her attractive name—for it was very attractive as the Zulus said it, especially those of them who were in love with her—was Mameena, daughter of Umbezi. Her other name was Child of Storm (Ingane-ye-Sipepo, or, more freely and shortly, O-we-Zulu), but the word "Ma-mee-na" had its origin in the sound of the wind that wailed about the hut when she was born.[*]

[—The Zulu word "Meena"—or more correctly "Mina"—means "Come here," and would therefore be a name not unsuitable to one of the heroine's proclivities; but Mr. Quatermain does not seem to accept this interpretation.—EDITOR.]*

Since I have been settled in England I have read—of course in a translation—the story of Helen of Troy, as told by the Greek poet, Homer. Well, Mameena reminds me very much of Helen, or, rather, Helen reminds me of Mameena. At any rate, there was this in common between them, although one of them was black, or, rather, copper-coloured, and the other white—they both were lovely; moreover, they both were faithless, and brought men by hundreds to their deaths. There, perhaps, the resemblance ends, since Mameena had much more fire and grit than Helen could boast, who, unless Homer misrepresents her, must have been but a poor thing after all. Beauty Itself, which those old rascals of Greek gods made use of to bait their snares set for the lives and honour of men, such was Helen, no more; that is, as I understand her, who have not had the advantage of a classical education. Now, Mameena, although she was superstitious—a common weakness of great minds—acknowledging no gods in particular, as we understand them, set her own snares, with varying success but a very definite object, namely, that of becoming the first woman in the world as she knew it—the stormy, bloodstained world of the Zulus.

But the reader shall judge for himself, if ever such a person should chance to cast his eye upon this history.

It was in the year 1854 that I first met Mameena, and my acquaintance with her continued off and on until 1856, when it came to an end in a fashion that shall be told after the fearful battle of the Tugela in which Umbelazi, Panda's son and Cetewayo's brother—who, to his sorrow, had also met Mameena—lost his life. I was still a youngish man in those days, although I had already buried my second wife, as I have told elsewhere, after our brief but happy time of marriage.

Leaving my boy in charge of some kind people in Durban, I started into "the Zulu"—a land with which I had already become well acquainted as a youth, there to carry on my wild life of trading and hunting.

For the trading I never cared much, as may be guessed from the little that ever I made out of it, the art of traffic being in truth repugnant to me. But hunting was always the breath of my nostrils—not that I am fond of killing creatures, for any humane man soon wearies of slaughter. No, it is the excitement of sport, which, before breechloaders came in, was acute enough, I can assure you; the lonely existence in wild places, often with only the sun and the stars for companions; the continual adventures; the strange tribes with whom I came in contact; in short, the change, the danger, the hope always of finding something great and new, that attracted and still attracts me, even now when I have found the great and the new. There, I must not go on writing like this, or I shall throw down my pen and book a passage for Africa, and incidentally to the next world, no doubt—that world of the great and new!

It was, I think, in the month of May in the year 1854 that I went hunting in rough country between the White and Black Umvolosi Rivers, by permission of Panda—whom the Boers had made king of Zululand after the defeat and death of Dingaan his brother. The district was very feverish, and for this reason I had entered it in the winter months. There was so much bush that, in the total absence of roads, I thought it wise not to attempt to bring my wagons down, and as no horses would live in that veld I went on foot. My principal companions were a Kafir of mixed origin, called Sikauli, commonly abbreviated into Scowl, the Zulu chief Saduko, and a headman of the Undwandwe blood named Umbezi, at whose kraal on the high land about thirty miles away I left my wagon and certain of my men in charge of the goods and some ivory that I had traded.

This Umbezi was a stout and genial-mannered man of about sixty years of age, and, what is rare among these people, one who loved sport for its own sake. Being aware of his tastes, also that he knew the country and was skilled in finding game, I had promised him a gun if he would accompany me and bring a few hunters. It was a particularly bad gun that had seen much service, and one which had an unpleasing habit of going off at half-cock; but even after he had seen it, and I in my honesty had explained its weaknesses, he jumped at the offer.

"O Macumazana" (that is my native name, often abbreviated into Macumazahn, which means "One who stands out," or as many interpret it, I don't know how, "Watcher-by-Night")—"a gun that goes off sometimes when you do not expect it is much better than no gun at all, and you are a chief with a great heart to promise it to me, for when I own the White Man's weapon I shall be looked up to and feared by everyone between the two rivers."

Now, while he was speaking he handled the gun, that was loaded, observing which I moved behind him. Off it went in due course, its recoil knocking him backwards—for that gun was a devil to kick—and its bullet cutting the top off the ear of one of his wives. The lady fled screaming, leaving a little bit of her ear upon the ground.

"What does it matter?" said Umbezi, as he picked himself up, rubbing his shoulder with a rueful look. "Would that the evil spirit in the gun had cut off her tongue and not her ear! It is the Worn-out-Old-Cow's own fault; she is always peeping into everything like a monkey. Now she will have something to chatter about and leave my things alone for awhile. I thank my ancestral Spirit it was not Mameena, for then her looks would have been spoiled."

"Who is Mameena?" I asked. "Your last wife?"

"No, no, Macumazahn; I wish she were, for then I should have the most beautiful wife in the land. She is my daughter, though not that of the Worn-out-Old-Cow; her mother died when she was born, on the night of the Great Storm. You should ask Saduko there who Mameena is," he added with a broad grin, lifting his head from the gun, which he was examining gingerly, as though he thought it might go off again while unloaded, and nodding towards someone who stood behind him.

I turned, and for the first time saw Saduko, whom I recognised at once as a person quite out of the ordinary run of natives.

He was a tall and magnificently formed young man, who, although his breast was scarred with assegai wounds, showing that he was a warrior, had not yet attained to the honour of the "ring" of polished wax laid over strips of rush bound round with sinew and sewn to the hair, the "isicoco" which at a certain age or dignity, determined by the king, Zulus are allowed to assume. But his face struck me more even than his grace, strength and stature. Undoubtedly it was a very fine face, with little or nothing of the negroid type about it; indeed, he might have been a rather dark-coloured Arab, to which stock he probably threw back. The eyes, too, were large and rather melancholy, and in his reserved, dignified air there was something that showed him to be no common fellow, but one of breeding and intellect.

"Siyakubona" (that is, "we see you," anglice "good morrow") "Saduko," I said, eyeing him curiously. "Tell me, who is Mameena?"

"Inkoosi," he answered in his deep voice, lifting his delicately shaped hand in salutation, a courtesy that pleased me who, after all, was nothing but a white hunter, "Inkoosi, has not her father said that she is his daughter?"

"Aye," answered the jolly old Umbezi, "but what her father has not said is that Saduko is her lover, or, rather, would like to be. Wow! Saduko," he went on, shaking his fat finger at him, "are you mad, man, that you think a girl like that is for you? Give me a hundred cattle, not one less, and I will begin to think of it. Why, you have not ten, and Mameena is my eldest daughter, and must marry a rich man."

"She loves me, O Umbezi," answered Saduko, looking down, "and that is more than cattle."

"For you, perhaps, Saduko, but not for me who am poor and want cows. Also," he added, glancing at him shrewdly, "are you so sure that Mameena loves you though you be such a fine man? Now, I should have thought that whatever her eyes may say, her heart loves no one but herself, and that in the end she will follow her heart and not her eyes. Mameena the beautiful does not seek to be a poor man's wife and do all the hoeing. But bring me the hundred cattle and we will see, for, speaking truth from my heart, if you were a big chief there is no one I should like better as a son-in-law, unless it were Macumazahn here," he said, digging me in the ribs with his elbow, "who would lift up my House on his white back."

Now, at this speech Saduko shifted his feet uneasily; it seemed to me as though he felt there was truth in Umbezi's estimate of his daughter's character. But he only said:

"Cattle can be acquired."

"Or stolen," suggested Umbezi.

"Or taken in war," corrected Saduko. "When I have a hundred head I will hold you to your word, O father of Mameena."

"And then what would you live on, fool, if you gave all your beasts to me? There, there, cease talking wind. Before you have a hundred head of cattle Mameena will have six children who will not call you father. Ah, don't you like that? Are you going away?"

"Yes, I am going," he answered, with a flash of his quiet eyes; "only then let the man whom they do call father beware of Saduko."

"Beware of how you talk, young man," said Umbezi in a grave voice. "Would you travel your father's road? I hope not, for I like you well; but such words are apt to be remembered."

Saduko walked away as though he did not hear.

"Who is he?" I asked.

"One of high blood," answered Umbezi shortly. "He might be a chief to-day had not his father been a plotter and a wizard. Dingaan smelt him out"—and he made a sideways motion with his hand that among the Zulus means much. "Yes, they were killed, almost every one; the chief, his wives, his children and his headmen—every one except Chosa his brother and his son Saduko, whom Zikali the dwarf, the Smeller-out-of-evil-doers, the Ancient, who was old before Senzangakona became a father of kings, hid him. There, that is an evil tale to talk of," and he shivered. "Come, White Man, and doctor that old Cow of mine, or she will give me no peace for months."

So I went to see the Worn-out-Old-Cow—not because I had any particular interest in her, for, to tell the truth, she was a very disagreeable and antique person, the cast-off wife of some chief whom at an unknown date in the past the astute Umbezi had married from motives of policy—but because I hoped to hear more of Miss Mameena, in whom I had become interested.

Entering a large hut, I found the lady so impolitely named "the Old Cow" in a parlous state. There she lay upon the floor, an unpleasant object because of the blood that had escaped from her wound, surrounded by a crowd of other women and of children. At regular intervals she announced that she was dying, and emitted a fearful yell, whereupon all the audience yelled also; in short, the place was a perfect pandemonium.

Telling Umbezi to get the hut cleared, I said that I would go to fetch my medicines. Meanwhile I ordered my servant, Scowl, a humorous-looking fellow, light yellow in hue, for he had a strong dash of Hottentot in his composition, to cleanse the wound. When I returned from the wagon ten minutes later the screams were more terrible than before, although the chorus now stood without the hut. Nor was this altogether wonderful, for on entering the place I found Scowl trimming up "the Old Cow's" ear with a pair of blunt nail-scissors.

"O Macumazana," said Umbezi in a hoarse whisper, "might it not perhaps be as well to leave her alone? If she bled to death, at any rate she would be quieter."

"Are you a man or a hyena?" I answered sternly, and set about the job, Scowl holding the poor woman's head between his knees.

It was over at length; a simple operation in which I exhibited—I believe that is the medical term—a strong solution of caustic applied with a feather.

"There, Mother," I said, for now we were alone in the hut, whence Scowl had fled, badly bitten in the calf, "you won't die now."

"No, you vile White Man," she sobbed. "I shan't die, but how about my beauty?"

"It will be greater than ever," I answered; "no one else will have an ear with such a curve in it. But, talking of beauty, where is Mameena?"

"I don't know where she is," she replied with fury, "but I very well know where she would be if I had my way. That peeled willow-wand of a girl"—here she added certain descriptive epithets I will not repeat— "has brought this misfortune upon me. We had a slight quarrel yesterday, White Man, and, being a witch as she is, she prophesied evil. Yes, when by accident I scratched her ear, she said that before long mine should burn, and surely burn it does." (This, no doubt, was true, for the caustic had begun to bite.)

"O devil of a White Man," she went on, "you have bewitched me; you have filled my head with fire."

Then she seized an earthenware pot and hurled it at me, saying, "Take that for your doctor-fee. Go, crawl after Mameena like the others and get her to doctor you."

By this time I was half through the bee-hole of the hut, my movements being hastened by a vessel of hot water which landed on me behind.

"What is the matter, Macumazahn?" asked old Umbezi, who was waiting outside.

"Nothing at all, friend," I answered with a sweet smile, "except that your wife wants to see you at once. She is in pain, and wishes you to soothe her. Go in; do not hesitate."

After a moment's pause he went in—that is, half of him went in. Then came a fearful crash, and he emerged again with the rim of a pot about his neck and his countenance veiled in a coating of what I took to be honey.

"Where is Mameena?" I asked him as he sat up spluttering.

"Where I wish I was," he answered in a thick voice; "at a kraal five hours' journey away."

Well, that was the first I heard of Mameena.

That night as I sat smoking my pipe under the flap lean-to attached to the wagon, laughing to myself over the adventure of "the Old Cow," falsely described as "worn out," and wondering whether Umbezi had got the honey out of his hair, the canvas was lifted, and a Kafir wrapped in a kaross crept in and squatted before me.

"Who are you?" I asked, for it was too dark to see the man's face.

"Inkoosi," answered a deep voice, "I am Saduko."

"You are welcome," I answered, handing him a little gourd of snuff in token of hospitality. Then I waited while he poured some of the snuff into the palm of his hand and took it in the usual fashion.

"Inkoosi," he said, when he had scraped away the tears produced by the snuff, "I have come to ask you a favour. You heard Umbezi say to-day that he will not give me his daughter, Mameena, unless I give him a hundred head of cows. Now, I have not got the cattle, and I cannot earn them by work in many years. Therefore I must take them from a certain tribe I know which is at war with the Zulus. But this I cannot do unless I have a gun. If I had a good gun, Inkoosi—one that only goes off when it is asked, and not of its own fancy, I who have some name could persuade a number of men whom I know, who once were servants of my father, or their sons, to be my companions in this venture."

"Do I understand that you wish me to give you one of my good guns with two mouths to it (i.e. double-barrelled), a gun worth at least twelve oxen, for nothing, O Saduko?" I asked in a cold and scandalised voice.

"Not so, O Watcher-by-Night," he answered; "not so, O He-who-sleeps-with-one-eye-open" (another free and difficult rendering of my native name, Macumazahn, or more correctly, Macumazana)—"I should never dream of offering such an insult to your high-born intelligence." He paused and took another pinch of snuff, then went on in a meditative voice: "Where I propose to get those hundred cattle there are many more; I am told not less than a thousand head in all. Now, Inkoosi," he added, looking at me sideways, "suppose you gave me the gun I ask for, and suppose you accompanied me with your own gun and your armed hunters, it would be fair that you should have half the cattle, would it not?"

"That's cool," I said. "So, young man, you want to turn me into a cow-thief and get my throat cut by Panda for breaking the peace of his country?"

"Neither, Macumazahn, for these are my own cattle. Listen, now, and I will tell you a story. You have heard of Matiwane, the chief of the Amangwane?"

"Yes," I answered. "His tribe lived near the head of the Umzinyati, did they not? Then they were beaten by the Boers or the English, and Matiwane came under the Zulus. But afterwards Dingaan wiped him out, with his House, and now his people are killed or scattered."

"Yes, his people are killed and scattered, but his House still lives. Macumazahn, I am his House, I, the only son of his chief wife, for Zikali the Wise Little One, the Ancient, who is of the Amangwane blood, and who hated Chaka and Dingaan—yes, and Senzangakona their father before them, but whom none of them could kill because he is so great and has such mighty spirits for his servants, saved and sheltered me."

"If he is so great, why, then, did he not save your father also, Saduko?" I asked, as though I knew nothing of this Zikali.

"I cannot say, Macumazahn. Perhaps the spirits plant a tree for themselves, and to do so cut down many other trees. At least, so it happened. It happened thus: Bangu, chief of the Amakoba, whispered into Dingaan's ear that Matiwane, my father, was a wizard; also that he was very rich. Dingaan listened because he thought a sickness that he had came from Matiwane's witchcraft. He said: 'Go, Bangu, and take a company with you and pay Matiwane a visit of honour, and in the night, O in the night! Afterwards, Bangu, we will divide the cattle, for Matiwane is strong and clever, and you shall not risk your life for nothing.'"

Saduko paused and looked down at the ground, brooding heavily.

"Macumazahn, it was done," he said presently. "They ate my father's meat, they drank his beer; they gave him a present from the king, they praised him with high names; yes, Bangu took snuff with him and called him brother. Then in the night, O in the night—!

"My father was in the hut with my mother, and I, so big only"—and he held his hand at the height of a boy of ten—"was with them. The cry arose, the flames began to eat; my father looked out and saw.

'Break through the fence and away, woman,' he said; 'away with Saduko, that he may live to avenge me. Begone while I hold the gate! Begone to Zikali, for whose witchcrafts I pay with my blood.'

"Then he kissed me on the brow, saying but one word, 'Remember,' and thrust us from the hut.

"My mother broke a way through the fence; yes, she tore at it with her nails and teeth like a hyena. I looked back out of the shadow of the hut and saw Matiwane my father fighting like a buffalo. Men went down before him, one, two, three, although he had no shield: only his spear. Then Bangu crept behind him and stabbed him in the back and he threw up his arms and fell. I saw no more, for by now we were through the fence. We ran, but they perceived us. They hunted us as wild dogs hunt a buck. They killed my mother with a throwing assegai; it entered at her back and came out at her heart. I went mad, I drew it from her body, I ran at them. I dived beneath the shield of the first, a very tall man, and held the spear, so, in both my little hands. His weight came upon its point and it went through him as though he were but a bowl of buttermilk. Yes, he rolled over, quite dead, and the handle of the spear broke upon the ground. Now the others stopped astonished, for never had they seen such a thing. That a child should kill a tall warrior, oh! that tale had not been told. Some of them would have let me go, but just then Bangu came up and saw the dead man, who was his brother.

"'Wow!' he said when he knew how the man had died. 'This lion's cub is a wizard also, for how else could he have killed a soldier who has known war? Hold out his arms that I may finish him slowly.'

"So two of them held out my arms, and Bangu came up with his spear."

Saduko ceased speaking, not that his tale was done, but because his voice choked in his throat. Indeed, seldom have I seen a man so moved. He breathed in great gasps, the sweat poured from him, and his muscles worked convulsively. I gave him a pannikin of water and he drank, then he went on:

"Already the spear had begun to prick—look, here is the mark of it"—and opening his kaross he pointed to a little white line just below the breast-bone—"when a strange shadow thrown by the fire of the burning huts came between Bangu and me, a shadow as that of a toad standing on its hind legs. I looked round and saw that it was the shadow of Zikali, whom I had seen once or twice. There he stood, though whence he came I know not, wagging his great white head that sits on the top of his body like a pumpkin on an ant-heap, rolling his big eyes and laughing loudly.

"'A merry sight,' he cried in his deep voice that sounded like water in a hollow cave. 'A merry sight, O Bangu, Chief of the Amakoba! Blood, blood, plenty of blood! Fire, fire, plenty of fire! Wizards dead here, there, and everywhere! Oh, a merry sight! I have seen many such; one at the kraal of your grandmother, for instance—your grandmother the great Inkosikazi, when myself I escaped with my life because I was so old; but never do I remember a merrier than that which this moon shines on,' and he pointed to the White Lady who just then broke through the clouds. 'But, great Chief Bangu, lord loved by the son of Senzangakona, brother of the Black One (Chaka) who has ridden hence on the assegai, what is the meaning of this play?' and he pointed to me and to the two soldiers who held out my little arms.

"'I kill the wizard's cub, Zikali, that is all,' answered Bangu.

"'I see, I see,' laughed Zikali. 'A gallant deed! You have butchered the father and the mother, and now you would butcher the child who has slain one of your grown warriors in fair fight. A very gallant deed, well worthy of the chief of the Amakoba! Well, loose his spirit—only—' He stopped and took a pinch of snuff from a box which he drew from a slit in the lobe of his great ear.

"'Only what?' asked Bangu, hesitating.

"'Only I wonder, Bangu, what you will think of the world in which you will find yourself before to-morrow's moon arises. Come back thence and tell me, Bangu, for there are so many worlds beyond the sun, and I would learn for certain which of them such a one as you inhabits: a man who for hatred and for gain murders the father and the mother and then butchers the child—the child that could slay a warrior who has seen war—with the spear hot from his mother's heart.'

"'Do you mean that I shall die if I kill this lad?' shouted Bangu in a great voice.

"'What else?' answered Zikali, taking another pinch of snuff.

"'This, Wizard; that we will go together.'

"'Good, good!' laughed the dwarf. 'Let us go together. Long have I wished to die, and what better companion could I find than Bangu, Chief of the Amakoba, Slayer of Children, to guard me on a dark and terrible road. Come, brave Bangu, come; kill me if you can,' and again he laughed at him.

"Now, Macumazahn, the people of Bangu fell back muttering, for they found this business horrible. Yes, even those who held my arms let go of them.

"'What will happen to me, Wizard, if I spare the boy?' asked Bangu.

"Zikali stretched out his hand and touched the scratch that the assegai had made in me here. Then he held up his finger red with my blood, and looked at it in the light of the moon; yes, and tasted it with his tongue.

"'I think this will happen to you, Bangu,' he said. 'If you spare this boy he will grow into a man who will kill you and many others one day. But if you do not spare him I think that his spirit, working as spirits can do, will kill you to-morrow. Therefore the question is, will you live a while or will you die at once, taking me with you as your companion? For you must not leave me behind, brother Bangu.'

"Now Bangu turned and walked away, stepping over the body of my mother, and all his people walked away after him, so that presently Zikali the Wise and Little and I were left alone.

"'What! have they gone?' said Zikali, lifting up his eyes from the ground. 'Then we had better be going also, Son of Matiwane, lest he should change his mind and come back. Live on, Son of Matiwane, that you may avenge Matiwane.'"

"A nice tale," I said. "But what happened afterwards?"

"Zikali took me away and nurtured me at his kraal in the Black Kloof, where he lived alone save for his servants, for in that kraal he would suffer no woman to set foot, Macumazahn. He taught me much wisdom and many secret things, and would have made a great doctor of me had I so willed. But I willed it not who find spirits ill company, and there are many of them about the Black Kloof, Macumazahn. So in the end he said: 'Go where your heart calls, and be a warrior, Saduko. But know this: You have opened a door that can never be shut again, and across the threshold of that door spirits will pass in and out for all your life, whether you seek them or seek them not.'

"'It was you who opened the door, Zikali,' I answered angrily.

"'Mayhap,' said Zikali, laughing after his fashion, 'for I open when I must and shut when I must. Indeed, in my youth, before the Zulus were a people, they named me Opener of Doors; and now, looking through one of those doors, I see something about you, O Son of Matiwane.'

"'What do you see, my father?' I asked.

"'I see two roads, Saduko: the Road of Medicine, that is the spirit road, and the Road of Spears, that is the blood road. I see you travelling on the Road of Medicine, that is my own road, Saduko, and growing wise and great, till at last, far, far away, you vanish over the precipice to which it leads, full of years and honour and wealth, feared by all men, white and black. Only that road you must travel alone, since such wisdom may have no friends, and, above all, no woman to share its secrets. Then I look at the Road of Spears and see you, Saduko, travelling on that road, and your feet are red with blood, and women wind their arms about your neck, and one by one your enemies go down before you. You love much, and sin much for the sake of the love, and she for whom you sin comes and goes and comes again. And the road is short, Saduko, and near the end of it are many spirits; and though you shut your eyes you see them, and though you fill your ears with clay you hear them, for they are the ghosts of your slain. But the end of your journeying I see not. Now choose which road you will, Son of Matiwane, and choose swiftly, for I speak no more of this matter.'

"Then, Macumazahn, I thought a while of the safe and lonely path of wisdom, also of the blood-red path of spears where I should find love and war, and my youth rose up in me and—I chose the path of spears and the love and the sin and the unknown death."

"A foolish choice, Saduko, supposing that there is any truth in this tale of roads, which there is not."

"Nay, a wise one, Macumazahn, for since then I have seen Mameena and know why I chose that path."

"Ah!" I said. "Mameena—I forgot her. Well, after all, perhaps there is some truth in your tale of roads. When I have seen Mameena I will tell you what I think."

"When you have seen Mameena, Macumazahn, you will say that the choice was very wise. Well, Zikali, Opener of Doors, laughed loudly when he heard it. 'The ox seeks the fat pasture, but the young bull the rough mountainside where the heifers graze,' he said; 'and after all, a bull is better than an ox. Now begin to travel your own road, Son of Matiwane, and from time to time return to the Black Kloof and tell me how it fares with you. I will promise you not to die before I know the end of it.'

"Now, Macumazahn, I have told you things that hitherto have lived in my own heart only. And, Macumazahn, Bangu is in ill favour with Panda, whom he defies in his mountain, and I have a promise—never mind how—that he who kills him will be called to no account and may keep his cattle. Will you come with me and share those cattle, O Watcher-by-Night?"

"Get thee behind me, Satan," I said in English, then added in Zulu: "I don't know. If your story is true I should have no objection to helping to kill Bangu; but I must learn lots more about this business first. Meanwhile I am going on a shooting trip to-morrow with Umbezi the Fat, and I like you, O Chooser of the Road of Spears and Blood. Will you be my companion and earn the gun with two mouths in payment?"

"Inkoosi," he said, lifting his hand in salute with a flash of his dark eyes, "you are generous, you honour me. What is there that I should love better? Yet," he added, and his face fell, "first I must ask Zikali the Little, Zikali my foster-father."

"Oh!" I said, "so you are still tied to the Wizard's girdle, are you?"

"Not so, Macumazahn; but I promised him not long ago that I would undertake no enterprise, save that you know of, until I had spoken with him."

"How far off does Zikali live?" I asked Saduko.

"One day's journeying. Starting at sunrise I can be there by sunset."

"Good! Then I will put off the shooting for three days and come with you if you think that this wonderful old dwarf will receive me."

"I believe that he will, Macumazahn, for this reason—he told me that I should meet you and love you, and that you would be mixed up in my fortunes."

"Then he poured moonshine into your gourd instead of beer," I answered. "Would you keep me here till midnight listening to such foolishness when we must start at dawn? Begone now and let me sleep."

"I go," he answered with a little smile. "But if this is so, O Macumazana, why do you also wish to drink of the moonshine of Zikali?" and he went.

Yet I did not sleep very well that night, for Saduko and his strange and terrible story had taken a hold of my imagination. Also, for reasons of my own, I greatly wished to see this Zikali, of whom I had heard a great deal in past years. I wished further to find out if he was a common humbug, like so many witch-doctors, this dwarf who announced that my fortunes were mixed up with those of his foster-son, and who at least could tell me something true or false about the history and position of Bangu, a person for whom I had conceived a strong dislike, possibly quite unjustified by the facts. But more than all did I wish to see Mameena, whose beauty or talents produced so much impression upon the native mind. Perhaps if I went to see Zikali she would be back at her father's kraal before we started on our shooting trip.

Thus it was then that fate wove me and my doings into the web of some very strange events; terrible, tragic and complete indeed as those of a Greek play, as it has often done both before and since those days.

CHAPTER II

On the following morning I awoke, as a good hunter always should do, just at that time when, on looking out of the wagon, nothing can be seen but a little grey glint of light which he knows is reflected from the horns of the cattle tied to the trek-tow. Presently, however, I saw another glint of light which I guessed came from the spear of Saduko, who was seated by the ashes of the cooking fire wrapped in his kaross of wildcat skins. Slipping from the voorkisse, or driving-box, I came behind him softly and touched him on the shoulder. He leapt up with a start which revealed his nervous nature, then recognising me through the soft grey gloom, said:

"You are early, Macumazahn."

"Of course," I answered; "am I not named Watcher-by-Night? Now let us go to Umbezi and tell him that I shall be ready to start on our hunting trip on the third morning from to-day."

So we went, to find that Umbezi was in a hut with his last wife and asleep. Fortunately enough, however, as under the circumstances I did not wish to disturb him, outside the hut we found the Old Cow, whose sore ear had kept her very wide awake, who, for purposes of her own, although etiquette did not allow her to enter the hut, was waiting for her husband to emerge.

Having examined her wound and rubbed some ointment on it, with her I left my message. Next I woke up my servant Scowl, and told him that I was going on a short journey, and that he must guard all things until my return; and while I did so, took a nip of raw rum and made ready a bag of biltong, that is sun-dried flesh, and biscuits.

Then, taking with me a single-barrelled gun, that same little Purdey rifle with which I shot the vultures on the Hill of Slaughter at Dingaan's Kraal,[*] we started on foot, for I would not risk my only horse on such a journey.

[*—For the story of this shooting of the vultures by Allan Quatermain, see the book called "Marie."— EDITOR.]

A rough journey it proved to be indeed, over a series of bush-clad hills that at their crests were covered with rugged stones among which no horse could have travelled. Up and down these hills we went, and across the valleys that divided them, following some path which I could not see, for all that live-long day. I have always been held a good walker, being by nature very light and active; but I am bound to say that my companion taxed my powers to the utmost, for on he marched for hour after hour, striding ahead of me at such a rate that at times I was forced to break into a run to keep up with him. Although my pride would not suffer me to complain, since as a matter of principle I would never admit to a Kafir that he was my master at anything, glad enough was I when, towards evening, Saduko sat himself down on a stone at the top of a hill and said:

"Behold the Black Kloof, Macumazahn," which were almost the first words he had uttered since we started.

Truly the spot was well named, for there, cut out by water from the heart of a mountain in some primeval age, lay one of the most gloomy places that ever I had beheld. It was a vast cleft in which granite boulders were piled up fantastically, perched one upon another in great columns, and upon its sides grew dark trees set sparsely among the rocks. It faced towards the west, but the light of the sinking sun that flowed up it served only to accentuate its vast loneliness, for it was a big cleft, the best part of a mile wide at its mouth.

Up this dreary gorge we marched, mocked at by chattering baboons and following a little path not a foot wide that led us at length to a large hut and several smaller ones set within a reed fence and overhung by a gigantic mass of rock that looked as though it might fall at any moment. At the gate of the fence two natives of I know not what tribe, men of fierce and forbidding appearance, suddenly sprang out and thrust their spears towards my breast.

"Whom bring you here, Saduko?" asked one of them sternly.

"A white man that I vouch for," he answered. "Tell Zikali that we wait on him."

"What need to tell Zikali that which he knows already?" said the sentry. "Your food and that of your companion is already cooked in yonder hut. Enter, Saduko, with him for whom you vouch."

So we went into the hut and ate, also I washed myself, for it was a beautifully clean hut, and the stools, wooden bowls, etc., were finely carved out of red ivory wood, this work, Saduko informed me, being done by Zikali's own hand. Just as we were finishing our meal a messenger came to tell us that Zikali waited our presence. We followed him across an open space to a kind of door in the tall reed fence, passing which I set eyes for the first time upon the famous old witch-doctor of whom so many tales were told.

Certainly he was a curious sight in those strange surroundings, for they were very strange, and I think their complete simplicity added to the effect. In front of us was a kind of courtyard with a black floor made of polished ant-heap earth and cow-dung, two-thirds of which at least was practically roofed in by the huge over-hanging mass of rock whereof I have spoken, its arch bending above at a height of not less than sixty or seventy feet from the ground. Into this great, precipice-backed cavity poured the fierce light of the setting sun, turning it and all within it, even the large straw hut in the background, to the deep hue of blood. Seeing the wonderful effect of the sunset in that dark and forbidding place, it occurred to me at once that the old wizard must have chosen this moment to receive us because of its impressiveness.

Then I forgot these scenic accessories in the sight of the man himself. There he sat on a stool in front of his hut, quite unattended, and wearing only a cloak of leopard skins open in front, for he was unadorned with the usual hideous trappings of a witch-doctor, such as snake-skins, human bones, bladders full of unholy compounds, and so forth.

What a man he was, if indeed he could be called quite human. His stature, though stout, was only that of a child; his head was enormous, and from it plaited white hair fell down on to his shoulders. His eyes were deep and sunken, his face was broad and very stern. Except for this snow-white hair, however, he did not look ancient, for his flesh was firm and plump, and the skin on his cheeks and neck unwrinkled, which suggested to me that the story of his great antiquity was false. A man who was over a hundred years old, for instance, surely could not boast such a beautiful set of teeth, for even at that distance I could see them gleaming. On the other hand, evidently middle age was far behind him; indeed, from his appearance it was quite impossible to guess even approximately the number of his years. There he sat, red in the red light, perfectly still, and staring without a blink of his eyes at the furious ball of the setting sun, as an eagle is said to be able to do.

Saduko advanced, and I walked after him. My stature is not great, and I have never considered myself an imposing person, but somehow I do not think that I ever felt more insignificant than on this occasion. The tall and splendid native beside, or rather behind whom I walked, the gloomy magnificence of the place, the blood-red light in which it was bathed, and the solemn, solitary, little figure with wisdom stamped upon its face before me, all tended to induce humility in a man not naturally vain. I felt myself growing smaller and smaller, both in a moral and a physical sense; I wished that my curiosity had not prompted me to seek an interview with yonder uncanny being.

Well, it was too late to retreat; indeed, Saduko was already standing before the dwarf and lifting his right arm above his head as he gave him the salute of "Makosi!"[*] whereon, feeling that something was expected of me, I took off my shabby cloth hat and bowed, then, remembering my white man's pride, replaced it on my head.

[*—"Makosi", the plural of "Inkoosi", is the salute given to Zulu wizards, because they are not one but many, since in them (as in the possessed demoniac in the Bible) dwell an unnumbered horde of spirits.—EDITOR.]

The wizard suddenly seemed to become aware of our presence, for, ceasing his contemplation of the sinking sun, he scanned us both with his slow, thoughtful eyes, which somehow reminded me of those of a chameleon, although they were not prominent, but, as I have said, sunken.

"Greeting, son Saduko!" he said in a deep, rumbling voice. "Why are you back here so soon, and why do you bring this flea of a white man with you?"

Now this was more than I could bear, so without waiting for my companion's answer I broke in:

"You give me a poor name, O Zikali. What would you think of me if I called you a beetle of a wizard?"

"I should think you clever," he answered after reflection, "for after all I must look something like a beetle with a white head. But why should you mind being compared to a flea? A flea works by night and so do you, Macumazahn; a flea is active and so are you; a flea is very hard to catch and kill and so are you; and lastly a flea drinks its fill of that which it desires, the blood of man and beast, and so you have done, do, and will, Macumazahn," and he broke into a great laugh that rolled and echoed about the rocky roof above.

Once, long years before, I had heard that laugh, when I was a prisoner in Dingaan's kraal, after the massacre of Retief and his company, and I recognised it again.

While I was searching for some answer in the same vein, and not finding it, though I thought of plenty afterwards, ceasing of a sudden from his unseemly mirth, he went on:

"Do not let us waste time in jests, for it is a precious thing, and there is but little of it left for any one of us. Your business, son Saduko?"

"Baba!" (that is the Zulu for father), said Saduko, "this white Inkoosi, for, as you know well enough, he is a chief by nature, a man of a great heart and doubtless of high blood [this, I believe, is true, for I have been told that my ancestors were more or less distinguished, although, if this is so, their talents did not lie in the direction of money-making], has offered to take me upon a shooting expedition and to give me a good gun with two mouths in payment of my services. But I told him I could not engage in any fresh venture without your leave, and—he is come to see whether you will grant it, my father."

"Indeed," answered the dwarf, nodding his great head. "This clever white man has taken the trouble of a long walk in the sun to come here to ask me whether he may be allowed the privilege of presenting you with a weapon of great value in return for a service that any man of your years in Zululand would love to give for nothing in such company?

"Son Saduko, because my eye-holes are hollow, do you think it your part to try to fill them up with dust? Nay, the white man has come because he desires to see him who is named Opener-of-Roads, of whom he heard a great deal when he was but a lad, and to judge whether in truth he has wisdom, or is but a common cheat. And you have come to learn whether or no your friendship with him will be fortunate; whether or no he will aid you in a certain enterprise that you have in your mind."

"True, O Zikali," I said. "That is so far as I am concerned."

But Saduko answered nothing.

"Well," went on the dwarf, "since I am in the mood I will try to answer both your questions, for I should be a poor Nyanga" [that is doctor] "if I did not when you have travelled so far to ask them. Moreover, O Macumazana, be happy, for I seek no fee who, having made such fortune as I need long ago, before your father was born across the Black Water, Macumazahn, no longer work for a reward—unless it be from the hand of one of the House of Senzangakona—and therefore, as you may guess, work but seldom."

Then he clapped his hands, and a servant appeared from somewhere behind the hut, one of those fierce-looking men who had stopped us at the gate. He saluted the dwarf and stood before him in silence and with bowed head.

"Make two fires," said Zikali, "and give me my medicine."

The man fetched wood, which he built into two little piles in front of Zikali. These piles he fired with a brand brought from behind the hut. Then he handed his master a catskin bag.

"Withdraw," said Zikali, "and return no more till I summon you, for I am about to prophesy. If, however, I should seem to die, bury me to-morrow in the place you know of and give this white man a safe-conduct from my kraal."

The man saluted again and went without a word.

When he had gone the dwarf drew from the bag a bundle of twisted roots, also some pebbles, from which he selected two, one white and the other black.

"Into this stone," he said, holding up the white pebble so that the light from the fire shone on it—since, save for the lingering red glow, it was now growing dark—"into this stone I am about to draw your spirit,

O Macumazana; and into this one"—and he held up the black pebble—"yours, O Son of Matiwane. Why do you look frightened, O brave White Man, who keep saying in your heart, 'He is nothing but an ugly old Kafir cheat'? If I am a cheat, why do you look frightened? Is your spirit already in your throat, and does it choke you, as this little stone might do if you tried to swallow it?" and he burst into one of his great, uncanny laughs.

I tried to protest that I was not in the least frightened, but failed, for, in fact, I suppose my nerves were acted on by his suggestion, and I did feel exactly as though that stone were in my throat, only coming upwards, not going downwards. "Hysteria," thought I to myself, "the result of being overtired," and as I could not speak, sat still as though I treated his gibes with silent contempt.

"Now," went on the dwarf, "perhaps I shall seem to die; and if so do not touch me lest you should really die. Wait till I wake up again and tell you what your spirits have told me. Or if I do not wake up—for a time must come when I shall go on sleeping—well—for as long as I have lived—after the fires are quite out, not before, lay your hands upon my breast; and if you find me turning cold, get you gone to some other Nyanga as fast as the spirits of this place will let you, O ye who would peep into the future."

As he spoke he threw a big handful of the roots that I have mentioned on to each of the fires, whereon tall flames leapt up from them, very unholy-looking flames which were followed by columns of dense, white smoke that emitted a most powerful and choking odour quite unlike anything that I had ever smelt before. It seemed to penetrate all through me, and that accursed stone in my throat grew as large as an apple and felt as though someone were poking it upwards with a stick.

Next he threw the white pebble into the right-hand fire, that which was opposite to me, saying:

"Enter, Macumazahn, and look," and the black pebble he threw into the left-hand fire saying: "Enter, Son of Matiwane, and look. Then come back both of you and make report to me, your master."

Now it is a fact that as he said these words I experienced a sensation as though a stone had come out of my throat; so readily do our nerves deceive us that I even thought it grated against my teeth as I opened my mouth to give it passage. At any rate the choking was gone, only now I felt as though I were quite empty and floating on air, as though I were not I, in short, but a mere shell of a thing, all of which doubtless was caused by the stench of those burning roots. Still I could look and take note, for I distinctly saw Zikali thrust his huge head, first into the smoke of what I will call my fire, next into that of Saduko's fire, and then lean back, blowing the stuff in clouds from his mouth and nostrils. Afterwards I saw him roll over on to his side and lie quite still with his arms outstretched; indeed, I noticed that one of his fingers seemed to be in the left-hand fire and reflected that it would be burnt off. In this, however, I must have been mistaken, since I observed subsequently that it was not even scorched.

Thus Zikali lay for a long while till I began to wonder whether he were not really dead. Dead enough he seemed to be, for no corpse could have stayed more stirless. But that night I could not keep my thoughts fixed on Zikali or anything. I merely noted these circumstances in a mechanical way, as might one with whom they had nothing whatsoever to do. They did not interest me at all, for there appeared to be nothing in me to be interested, as I gathered according to Zikali, because I was not there, but in a warmer place than I hope ever to occupy, namely, in the stone in that unpleasant-looking, little right-hand fire.

So matters went as they might in a dream. The sun had sunk completely, not even an after-glow was left. The only light remaining was that from the smouldering fires, which just sufficed to illumine the bulk of Zikali, lying on his side, his squat shape looking like that of a dead hippopotamus calf. What was left of my consciousness grew heartily sick of the whole affair; I was tired of being so empty.

At length the dwarf stirred. He sat up, yawned, sneezed, shook himself, and began to rake among the burning embers of my fire with his naked hand. Presently he found the white stone, which was now red-hot—at any rate it glowed as though it were—and after examining it for a moment finally popped it into his mouth! Then he hunted in the other fire for the black stone, which he treated in a similar fashion. The next thing I remember was that the fires, which had died away almost to nothing, were burning very brightly again, I suppose because someone had put fuel on them, and Zikali was speaking.

"Come here, O Macumazana and O Son of Matiwane," he said, "and I will repeat to you what your spirits have been telling me."

We drew near into the light of the fires, which for some reason or other was extremely vivid. Then he spat the white stone from his mouth into his big hand, and I saw that now it was covered with lines and patches like a bird's egg.

"You cannot read the signs?" he said, holding it towards me; and when I shook my head went on: "Well, I can, as you white men read a book. All your history is written here, Macumazahn; but there is no need to tell you that, since you know it, as I do well enough, having learned it in other days, the days of Dingaan, Macumazahn. All your future, also, a very strange future," and he scanned the stone with interest. "Yes, yes; a wonderful life, and a noble death far away. But of these matters you have not asked me, and therefore I may not tell them even if I wished, nor would you believe if I did. It is of your hunting trip that you have asked me, and my answer is that if you seek your own comfort you will do well not to go. A pool in a dry river-bed; a buffalo bull with the tip of one horn shattered. Yourself and the bull in the pool. Saduko, yonder, also in the pool, and a little half-bred man with a gun jumping about upon the bank. Then a litter made of boughs and you in it, and the father of Mameena walking lamely at your side. Then a hut and you in it, and the maiden called Mameena sitting at your side.

"Macumazahn, your spirit has written on this stone that you should beware of Mameena, since she is more dangerous than any buffalo. If you are wise you will not go out hunting with Umbezi, although it is true that hunt will not cost you your life. There, away, Stone, and take your writings with you!" and as he spoke he jerked his arm and I heard something whiz past my face.

Next he spat out the black stone and examined it in similar fashion.

"Your expedition will be successful, Son of Matiwane," he said. "Together with Macumazahn you will win many cattle at the cost of sundry lives. But for the rest—well, you did not ask me of it, did you? Also, I have told you something of that story before to-day. Away, Stone!" and the black pebble followed the white out into the surrounding gloom.

We sat quite still until the dwarf broke the deep silence with one of his great laughs.

"My witchcraft is done," he said. "A poor tale, was it not? Well, hunt for those stones to-morrow and read the rest of it if you can. Why did you not ask me to tell you everything while I was about it, White Man? It would have interested you more, but now it has all gone from me back into your spirit with the stones. Saduko, get you to sleep. Macumazahn, you who are a Watcher-by-Night, come and sit with me awhile in my hut, and we will talk of other things. All this business of the stones is nothing more than a Kafir trick, is it, Macumazahn? When you meet the buffalo with the split horn in the pool of a dried river, remember it is but a cheating trick, and now come into my hut and drink a kamba [bowl] of beer and let us talk of other things more interesting."

So he took me into the hut, which was a fine one, very well lighted by a fire in its centre, and gave me Kafir beer to drink, that I swallowed gratefully, for my throat was dry and still felt as though it had been scraped.

"Who are you, Father?" I asked point-blank when I had taken my seat upon a low stool, with my back resting against the wall of the hut, and lit my pipe.

He lifted his big head from the pile of karosses on which he was lying and peered at me across the fire.

"My name is Zikali, which means 'Weapons,' White Man. You know as much as that, don't you?" he answered. "My father 'went down' so long ago that his does not matter. I am a dwarf, very ugly, with some learning, as we of the Black House understand it, and very old. Is there anything else you would like to learn?"

"Yes, Zikali; how old?"

"There, there, Macumazahn, as you know, we poor Kafirs cannot count very well. How old? Well, when I was young I came down towards the coast from the Great River, you call it the Zambesi, I think, with Undwandwe, who lived in the north in those days. They have forgotten it now because it is some time ago, and if I could write I would set down the history of that march, for we fought some great battles with the people who used to live in this country. Afterwards I was the friend of the Father of the Zulus, he whom they still call Inkoosi Umkulu—the mighty chief—you may have heard tell of him. I carved that stool on which you sit for him and he left it back to me when he died."

"Inkoosi Umkulu!" I exclaimed. "Why, they say he lived hundreds of years ago."

"Do they, Macumazahn? If so, have I not told you that we black people cannot count as well as you do? Really it was only the other day. Anyhow, after his death the Zulus began to maltreat us Undwandwe and the Quabies and the Tetwas with us—you may remember that they called us the Amatefula, making a mock of us. So I quarrelled with the Zulus and especially with Chaka, he whom they named 'Uhlanya' [the Mad One]. You see, Macumazahn, it pleased him to laugh at me because I am not as other men are. He gave me a name which means 'The-thing-which-should-never-have-been-born.' I will not speak that name, it is secret to me, it may not pass my lips. Yet at times he sought my wisdom, and I paid him back for his names, for I gave him very ill counsel, and he took it, and I brought him to his death, although none ever saw my finger in that business. But when he was dead at the hands of his brothers Dingaan and Umhlangana and of Umbopa, Umbopa who also had a score to settle with him, and his body was cast out of the kraal like that of an evil-doer, why I, who because I was a dwarf was not sent with the men against Sotshangana, went and sat on it at night and laughed thus," and he broke into one of his hideous peals of merriment.

"I laughed thrice: once for my wives whom he had taken; once for my children whom he had slain; and once for the mocking name that he had given me. Then I became the counsellor of Dingaan, whom I hated worse than I had hated Chaka, for he was Chaka again without his greatness, and you know the end of Dingaan, for you had a share in that war, and of Umhlangana, his brother and fellow-murderer, whom I counselled Dingaan to slay. This I did through the lips of the old Princess Menkabayi, Jama's daughter, Senzangakona's sister, the Oracle before whom all men bowed, causing her to say that 'This land of the Zulus cannot be ruled by a crimson assegai.' For, Macumazahn, it was Umhlangana who first struck Chaka with the spear. Now Panda reigns, the last of the sons of Senzangakona, my enemy, Panda the Fool, and I hold my hand from Panda because he tried to save the life of a child of mine whom Chaka slew. But Panda has sons who are as Chaka was, and against them I work as I worked against those who went before them."

"Why?" I asked.

"Why? Oh! if I were to tell you all my story you would understand why, Macumazahn. Well, perhaps I will one day." (Here I may state that as a matter of fact he did, and a very wonderful tale it is, but as it has nothing to do with this history I will not write it here.)

"I dare say," I answered. "Chaka and Dingaan and Umhlangana and the others were not nice people. But another question. Why do you tell me all this, O Zikali, seeing that were I but to repeat it to a talking-bird you would be smelt out and a single moon would not die before you do?"

"Oh! I should be smelt out and killed before one moon dies, should I? Then I wonder that this has not happened during all the moons that are gone. Well, I tell the story to you, Macumazahn, who have had so much to do with the tale of the Zulus since the days of Dingaan, because I wish that someone should know it and perhaps write it down when everything is finished. Because, too, I have just been reading your spirit and see that it is still a white spirit, and that you will not whisper it to a 'talking-bird.'"

Now I leant forward and looked at him.

"What is the end at which you aim, O Zikali?" I asked. "You are not one who beats the air with a stick; on whom do you wish the stick to fall at last?"

"On whom?" he answered in a new voice, a low, hissing voice. "Why, on these proud Zulus, this little family of men who call themselves the 'People of Heaven,' and swallow other tribes as the great tree-snake swallows kids and small bucks, and when it is fat with them cries to the world, 'See how big I am! Everything is inside of me.' I am a Ndwande, one of those peoples whom it pleases the Zulus to call 'Amatefula'—poor hangers-on who talk with an accent, nothing but bush swine. Therefore I would see the swine tusk the hunter. Or, if that may not be, I would see the black hunter laid low by the rhinoceros, the white rhinoceros of your race, Macumazahn, yes, even if it sets its foot upon the Ndwande boar as well. There, I have told you, and this is the reason that I live so long, for I will not die until these things have come to pass, as come to pass they will. What did Chaka, Senzangakona's son, say when the little red assegai, the assegai with which he slew his mother, aye and others, some of whom were near to me, was in his liver? What did he say to Mbopa and the princes? Did he not say that he heard the feet of a great white people running, of a people who should stamp the Zulus flat? Well, I, 'The-thing-who-should-not-have-been-born,' live on until that day comes, and when it comes I think that you and I, Macumazahn, shall not be far apart, and that is why I have opened out my heart to you, I who have knowledge of the future. There, I speak no more of these things that are to be, who perchance have already said too much of them. Yet do not forget my words. Or forget them if you will, for I shall remind you of them, Macumazahn, when the feet of your people have avenged the Ndwandes and others whom it pleases the Zulus to treat as dirt."

Now, this strange man, who had sat up in his excitement, shook his long white hair which, after the fashion of wizards, he wore plaited into thin ropes, till it hung like a veil about him, hiding his broad face and deep eyes. Presently he spoke again through this veil of hair, saying:

"You are wondering, Macumazahn, what Saduko has to do with all these great events that are to be. I answer that he must play his part in them; not a very great part, but still a part, and it is for this purpose that I saved him as a child from Bangu, Dingaan's man, and reared him up to be a warrior, although, since I cannot lie, I warned him that he would do well to leave spears alone and follow after wisdom. Well, he will slay Bangu, who now has quarrelled with Panda, and a woman will come into the story, one Mameena, and that woman will bring about war between the sons of Panda, and from this war shall spring the ruin of the Zulus, for he who wins will be an evil king to them and bring down on them the wrath of a mightier race. And so 'The-thing-that-should-not-have-been-born' and the Ndwandes and the Quabies and Twetwas, whom it has pleased the conquering Zulus to name 'Amatefula,' shall be avenged. Yes, yes, my Spirit tells me all these things, and they are true."

"And what of Saduko, my friend and your fosterling?"

"Saduko, your friend and my fosterling, will take his appointed road, Macumazahn, as I shall and you will. What more could he desire, seeing it is that which he has chosen? He will take his road and he will play the part which the Great-Great has prepared for him. Seek not to know more. Why should you, since Time will tell you the story? And now go to rest, Macumazahn, as I must who am old and feeble. And when it pleases you to visit me again, we will talk further. Meanwhile, remember always that I am nothing but an old Kafir cheat who pretends to a knowledge that belongs to no man. Remember it especially, Macumazahn, when you meet a buffalo with a split horn in the pool of a dried-up river, and afterwards, when a woman named Mameena makes a certain offer to you, which you may be tempted to accept. Good night to you, Watcher-by-Night with the white heart and the strange destiny, good night to you, and try not to think too hardly of the old Kafir cheat who just now is called 'Opener-of-Roads.' My servant waits without to lead you to your hut, and if you wish to be back at Umbezi's kraal by nightfall to-morrow, you will do well to start ere sunrise, since, as you found in coming, Saduko, although he may be a fool, is a very good walker, and you do not like to be left behind, Macumazahn, do you?"

So I rose to go, but as I went some impulse seemed to take him and he called me back and made me sit down again.

"Macumazahn," he said, "I would add a word. When you were quite a lad you came into this country with Retief, did you not?"

"Yes," I answered slowly, for this matter of the massacre of Retief is one of which I have seldom cared to speak, for sundry reasons, although I have made a record of it in writing.[*] Even my friends Sir Henry Curtis and Captain Good have heard little of the part I played in that tragedy. "But what do you know of that business, Zikali?"

[*—Published under the title of "Marie."—EDITOR.]

"All that there is to know, I think, Macumazahn, seeing that I was at the bottom of it, and that Dingaan killed those Boers on my advice—just as he killed Chaka and Umhlangana."

"You cold-blooded old murderer—" I began, but he interrupted me at once.

"Why do you throw evil names at me, Macumazahn, as I threw the stone of your fate at you just now? Why am I a murderer because I brought about the death of some white men that chanced to be your friends, who had come here to cheat us black folk of our country?"

"Was it for this reason that you brought about their deaths, Zikali?" I asked, staring him in the face, for I felt that he was lying to me.

"Not altogether, Macumazahn," he answered, letting his eyes, those strange eyes that could look at the sun without blinking, fall before my gaze. "Have I not told you that I hate the House of Senzangakona? And when Retief and his companions were killed, did not the spilling of their blood mean war to the end between the Zulus and the White Men? Did it not mean the death of Dingaan and of thousands of his people, which is but a beginning of deaths? Now do you understand?"

"I understand that you are a very wicked man," I answered with indignation.

"At least you should not say so, Macumazahn," he replied in a new voice, one with the ring of truth in it.

"Why not?"

"Because I saved your life on that day. You escaped alone of the White Men, did you not? And you never could understand why, could you?"

"No, I could not, Zikali. I put it down to what you would call 'the spirits.'"

"Well, I will tell you. Those spirits of yours wore my kaross," and he laughed. "I saw you with the Boers, and saw, too, that you were of another people—the people of the English. You may have heard at the time that I was doctoring at the Great Place, although I kept out of the way and we did not meet, or at least you never knew that we met, for you were—asleep. Also I pitied your youth, for, although you do not believe it, I had a little bit of heart left in those days. Also I knew that we should come together again in the after years, as you see we have done to-day and shall often do until the end. So I told Dingaan that whoever died you must be spared, or he would bring up the 'people of George' [i.e. the English] to avenge you, and your ghost would enter into him and pour out a curse upon him. He believed me who did not understand that already so many curses were gathered about his head that one more or less made no matter. So you see you were spared, Macumazahn, and afterwards you helped to pour out a curse upon Dingaan without becoming a ghost, which is the reason why Panda likes you so well to-day, Panda, the enemy of Dingaan, his brother. You remember the woman who helped you? Well, I made her do so. How did it go with you afterwards, Macumazahn, with you and the Boer maiden across the Buffalo River, to whom you were making love in those days?"

"Never mind how it went," I replied, springing up, for the old wizard's talk had stirred sad and bitter memories in my heart. "That time is dead, Zikali."

"Is it, Macumazahn? Now, from the look upon your face I should have said that it was still very much alive, as things that happened in our youth have a way of keeping alive. But doubtless I am mistaken, and it is all as dead as Dingaan, and as Retief, and as the others, your companions. At least, although you do not believe it, I saved your life on that red day, for my own purposes, of course, not because one white life was anything among so many in my count. And now go to rest, Macumazahn, go to rest, for although your heart has been awakened by memories this evening, I promise that you shall sleep well to-night," and throwing the long hair back off his eyes he looked at me keenly, wagging his big head to and fro, and burst into another of his great laughs.

So I went. But, ah! as I went I wept.

Anyone who knew all that story would understand why. But this is not the place to tell it, that tale of my first love and of the terrible events which befell us in the time of Dingaan. Still, as I say, I have written it down, and perhaps one day it will be read.

CHAPTER III

THE BUFFALO WITH THE CLEFT HORN

I slept very well that night, I suppose because I was so dog-tired I could not help it; but next day, on our long walk back to Umbezi's kraal, I thought a great deal.

Without doubt I had seen and heard very strange things, both of the past and the present—things that I could not in the least understand. Moreover, they were mixed up with all sorts of questions of high Zulu policy, and threw a new light upon events that happened to me and others in my youth.

Now, in the clear sunlight, was the time to analyse these things, and this I did in the most logical fashion I could command, although without the slightest assistance from Saduko, who, when I asked him questions, merely shrugged his shoulders.

These questions, he said, did not interest him; I had wished to see the magic of Zikali, and Zikali had been pleased to show me some very good magic, quite of his best indeed. Also he had conversed alone with me afterwards, doubtless on high matters—so high that he, Saduko, was not admitted to share the conversation—which was an honour he accorded to very few. I could form my own conclusions in the light of the White Man's wisdom, which everyone knew was great.

I replied shortly that I could, for Saduko's tone irritated me. Of course, the truth was that he felt aggrieved at being sent off to bed like a little boy while his foster-father, the old dwarf, made confidences to me. One of Saduko's faults was that he had always a very good opinion of himself. Also he was by nature terribly jealous, even in little things, as the readers of his history, if any, will learn.

We trudged on for several hours in silence, broken at length by my companion.

"Do you still mean to go on a shooting expedition with Umbezi, Inkoosi?" he asked, "or are you afraid?"

"Of what should I be afraid?" I answered tartly.

"Of the buffalo with the split horn, of which Zikali told you. What else?"

Now, I fear I used strong language about the buffalo with the split horn, a beast in which I declared I had no belief whatsoever, either with or without its accessories of dried river-beds and water-holes.

"If all this old woman's talk has made you afraid, however," I added, "you can stop at the kraal with Mameena."

"Why should the talk make me afraid, Macumazahn? Zikali did not say that this evil spirit of a buffalo would hurt me. If I fear, it is for you, seeing that if you are hurt you may not be able to go with me to look for Bangu's cattle."

"Oh!" I replied sarcastically; "it seems that you are somewhat selfish, friend Saduko, since it is of your welfare and not of my safety that you are thinking."

"If I were as selfish as you seem to believe, Inkoosi, should I advise you to stop with your wagons, and thereby lose the good gun with two mouths that you have promised me? Still, it is true that I should like well enough to stay at Umbezi's kraal with Mameena, especially if Umbezi were away."

Now, as there is nothing more uninteresting than to listen to other people's love affairs, and as I saw that with the slightest encouragement Saduko was ready to tell me all the history of his courtship over again, I did not continue the argument. So we finished our journey in silence, and arrived at Umbezi's kraal a little after sundown, to find, to the disappointment of both of us, that Mameena was still away.

Upon the following morning we started on our shooting expedition, the party consisting of myself, my servant Scowl, who, as I think I said, hailed from the Cape and was half a Hottentot; Saduko; the merry old Zulu, Umbezi, and a number of his men to serve as bearers and beaters. It proved a very successful trip—that is, until the end of it—for in those days the game in this part of the country was extremely plentiful. Before the end of the second week I killed four elephants, two of them with large tusks, while Saduko, who soon developed into a very fair shot, bagged another with the double-barrelled gun that I had promised him. Also, Umbezi—how, I have never discovered, for the thing partook of the nature of a miracle—managed to slay an elephant cow with fair ivories, using the old rifle that went off at half-cock.

Never have I seen a man, black or white, so delighted as was that vainglorious Kafir. For whole hours he danced and sang and took snuff and saluted with his hand, telling me the story of his deed over and over again, no single version of which tale agreed with the other. He took a new title also, that meant "Eater-up-of-Elephants"; he allowed one of his men to "bonga"—that is, praise—him all through the night, preventing us from getting a wink of sleep, until at last the poor fellow dropped in a kind of fit from exhaustion, and so forth. It really was very amusing until it became a bore.

Besides the elephants we killed lots of other things, including two lions, which I got almost with a right and left, and three white rhinoceroses, that now, alas! are nearly extinct. At last, towards the end of the third week, we had as much as our men could carry in the shape of ivory, rhinoceros horns, skins and sun-dried buckflesh, or biltong, and determined to start back for Umbezi's kraal next day. Indeed, this could not be long delayed, as our powder and lead were running low; for in those days, it will be remembered, breechloaders had not come in, and ammunition, therefore, had to be carried in bulk.

To tell the truth, I was very glad that our trip had come to such a satisfactory conclusion, for, although I would not admit it even to myself, I could not get rid of a kind of sneaking dread lest after all there might be something in the old dwarf's prophecy about a disagreeable adventure with a buffalo which was in store for me. Well, as it chanced, we had not so much as seen a buffalo, and as the road which we were going to take back to the kraal ran over high, bare country that these animals did not frequent, there was now little prospect of our doing so—all of which, of course, showed what I already knew, that only weak-headed superstitious idiots would put the slightest faith in the drivelling nonsense of deceiving or self-deceived Kafir medicine-men. These things, indeed, I pointed out with much vigour to Saduko before we turned in on the last night of the hunt.

Saduko listened in silence and said nothing at all, except that he would not keep me up any longer, as I must be tired.

Now, whatever may be the reason for it, my experience in life is that it is never wise to brag about anything. At any rate, on a hunting trip, to come to a particular instance, wait until you are safe at home till you begin to do so. Of the truth of this ancient adage I was now destined to experience a particularly fine and concrete example.

The place where we had camped was in scattered bush overlooking a great extent of dry reeds, that in the wet season was doubtless a swamp fed by a small river which ran into it on the side opposite to our camp. During the night I woke up, thinking that I heard some big beasts moving in these reeds; but as no further sounds reached my ears I went to sleep again.

Shortly after dawn I was awakened by a voice calling me, which in a hazy fashion I recognised as that of Umbezi.

"Macumazahn," said the voice in a hoarse whisper, "the reeds below us are full of buffalo. Get up. Get up at once."

"What for?" I answered. "If the buffalo came into the reeds they will go out of them. We do not want meat."

"No, Macumazahn; but I want their hides. Panda, the King, has demanded fifty shields of me, and without killing oxen that I can ill spare I have not the skins whereof to make them. Now, these buffalo are in a trap. This swamp is like a dish with one mouth. They cannot get out at the sides of the dish, and the mouth by which they came in is very narrow. If we station ourselves at either side of it we can kill many of them."

By this time I was thoroughly awake and had arisen from my blankets. Throwing a kaross over my shoulders, I left the hut, made of boughs, in which I was sleeping and walked a few paces to the crest of a rocky ridge, whence I could see the dry vlei below. Here the mists of dawn still clung, but from it rose sounds of grunts, bellows and tramplings which I, an old hunter, could not mistake. Evidently a herd of buffalo, one or two hundred of them, had established themselves in those reeds.

Just then my bastard servant, Scowl, and Saduko joined us, both of them full of excitement.

It appeared that Scowl, who never seemed to sleep at any natural time, had seen the buffalo entering the reeds, and estimated their number at two or three hundred. Saduko had examined the cleft through which they passed, and reported it to be so narrow that we could kill any number of them as they rushed out to escape.

"Quite so. I understand," I said. "Well, my opinion is that we had better let them escape. Only four of us, counting Umbezi, are armed with guns, and assegais are not of much use against buffalo. Let them go, I say."

Umbezi, thinking of a cheap raw material for the shields which had been requisitioned by the King, who would surely be pleased if they were made of such a rare and tough hide as that of buffalo, protested violently, and Saduko, either to please one whom he hoped might be his father-in-law or from sheer love of sport, for which he always had a positive passion, backed him up. Only Scowl—whose dash of Hottentot blood made him cunning and cautious—took my side, pointing out that we were very short of powder and that buffalo "ate up much lead." At last Saduko said:

"The lord Macumazana is our captain; we must obey him, although it is a pity. But doubtless the prophesying of Zikali weighs upon his mind, so there is nothing to be done."

"Zikali!" exclaimed Umbezi. "What has the old dwarf to do with this matter?"

"Never mind what he has or has not to do with it," I broke in, for although I do not think that he meant them as a taunt, but merely as a statement of fact, Saduko's words stung me to the quick, especially as my conscience told me that they were not altogether without foundation.

"We will try to kill some of these buffalo," I went on, "although, unless the herd should get bogged, which is not likely, as the swamp is very dry, I do not think that we can hope for more than eight or ten at the most, which won't be of much use for shields. Come, let us make a plan. We have no time to lose, for I think they will begin to move again before the sun is well up."

Half an hour later the four of us who were armed with guns were posted behind rocks on either side of the steep, natural roadway cut by water, which led down to the vlei, and with us some of Umbezi's men. That chief himself was at my side—a post of honour which he had insisted upon taking. To tell the truth, I did not dissuade him, for I thought that I should be safer so than if he were opposite to me, since, even if the old rifle did not go off of its own accord, Umbezi, when excited, was a most uncertain shot. The herd of buffalo appeared to have lain down in the reeds, so, being careful to post ourselves first, we sent three of the native bearers to the farther side of the vlei, with instructions to rouse the beasts by shouting. The remainder of the Zulus—there were ten or a dozen of them armed with stabbing spears—we kept with us.

But what did these scoundrels do? Instead of disturbing the herd by making a noise, as we told them, for some reason best known to themselves—I expect it was because they were afraid to go into the vlei, where they might meet the horn of a buffalo at any moment—they fired the dry reeds in three or four places at once, and this, if you please, with a strong wind blowing from them to us. In a minute or two the farther side of the swamp was a sheet of crackling flame that gave off clouds of dense white smoke. Then pandemonium began.

The sleeping buffalo leapt to their feet, and, after a few moments of indecision, crashed towards us, the whole huge herd of them, snorting and bellowing like mad things. Seeing what was about to happen, I nipped behind a big boulder, while Scowl shinned up a mimosa with the swiftness of a cat and, heedless of its thorns, sat himself in an eagle's nest at the top. The Zulus with the spears bolted to take cover where they could. What became of Saduko I did not see, but old Umbezi, bewildered with excitement, jumped into the exact middle of the roadway, shouting:

"They come! They come! Charge, buffalo folk, if you will. The Eater-up-of-Elephants awaits you!"

"You etceterad old fool!" I shouted, but got no farther, for just at this moment the first of the buffalo, which I could see was an enormous bull, probably the leader of the herd, accepted Umbezi's invitation and came, with its nose stuck straight out in front of it. Umbezi's gun went off, and next instant he went up. Through the smoke I saw his black bulk in the air, and then heard it alight with a thud on the top of the rock behind which I was crouching.

"Exit Umbezi," I said to myself, and by way of a requiem let the bull which had hoisted him, as I thought to heaven, have an ounce of lead in the ribs as it passed me. After that I did not fire any more, for it occurred to me that it was as well not to further advertise my presence.

In all my hunting experience I cannot remember ever seeing such a sight as that which followed. Out of the vlei rushed the buffalo by dozens, every one of them making remarks in its own language as it came. They jammed in the narrow roadway, they leapt on to each other's backs. They squealed, they kicked, they bellowed. They charged my friendly rock till I felt it shake. They knocked over Scowl's mimosa thorn, and would have shot him out of his eagle's nest had not its flat top fortunately caught in that of another and less accessible tree. And with them came clouds of pungent smoke, mixed with bits of burning reed and puffs of hot air.

It was over at last. With the exception of some calves, which had been trampled to death in the rush, the herd had gone. Now, like the Roman emperor—I think he was an emperor—I began to wonder what had become of my legions.

"Umbezi," I shouted, or, rather, sneezed through the smoke, "are you dead, Umbezi?"

"Yes, yes, Macumazahn," replied a choking and melancholy voice from the top of the rock, "I am dead, quite dead. That evil spirit of a silwana [i.e. wild beast] has killed me. Oh! why did I think I was a hunter; why did I not stop at my kraal and count my cattle?"

"I am sure I don't know, you old lunatic," I answered, as I scrambled up the rock to bid him good-bye.

It was a rock with a razor top like the ridge of a house, and there, hanging across this ridge like a pair of nether garments on a clothes-line, I found the "Eater-up-of-Elephants."

"Where did he get you, Umbezi?" I asked, for I could not see his wounds because of the smoke.

"Behind, Macumazahn, behind!" he groaned, "for I had turned to fly, but, alas! too late."

"On the contrary," I replied, "for one so heavy you flew very well; like a bird, Umbezi, like a bird."

"Look and see what the evil beast has done to me, Macumazahn. It will be easy, for my moocha has gone."

So I looked, examining Umbezi's ample proportions with care, but could discover nothing except a large smudge of black mud, as though he had sat down in a half-dried puddle. Then I guessed the truth. The buffalo's horns had missed him. He had been struck only with its muddy nose, which, being almost as broad as that portion of Umbezi with which it came in contact, had inflicted nothing worse than a bruise. When I was sure he had received no serious injury, my temper, already sorely tried, gave out, and I administered to him the soundest smacking—his position being very convenient—that he had ever received since he was a little boy.

"Get up, you idiot!" I shouted, "and let us look for the others. This is the end of your folly in making me attack a herd of buffalo in reeds. Get up. Am I to stop here till I choke?"

"Do you mean to tell me that I have no mortal wound, Macumazahn?" he asked, with a return of cheerfulness, accepting the castigation in good part, for he was not one who bore malice. "Oh, I am glad to hear it, for now I shall live to make those cowards who fired the reeds sorry that they are not dead; also to finish off that wild beast, for I hit him, Macumazahn, I hit him."

"I don't know whether you hit him; I know he hit you," I replied, as I shoved him off the rock and ran towards the tilted tree where I had last seen Scowl.

Here I beheld another strange sight. Scowl was still seated in the eagle's nest that he shared with two nearly fledged young birds, one of which, having been injured, was uttering piteous cries. Nor did it cry in vain, for its parents, which were of that great variety of kite that the Boers call "lammefange", or lamb-lifters, had just arrived to its assistance, and were giving their new nestling, Scowl, the best doing that man ever received at the beak and claws of feathered kind. Seen through those rushing smoke wreaths, the combat looked perfectly titanic; also it was one of the noisiest to which I ever listened, for I don't know which shrieked the more loudly, the infuriated eagles or their victim.

Seeing how things stood, I burst into a roar of laughter, and just then Scowl grabbed the leg of the male bird, that was planted in his breast while it removed tufts of his wool with its hooked beak, and leapt boldly from the nest, which had become too hot to hold him. The eagle's outspread wings broke his fall, for they acted as a parachute; and so did Umbezi, upon whom he chanced to land. Springing from the prostrate shape of the chief, who now had a bruise in front to match that behind, Scowl, covered with pecks and scratches, ran like a lamp-lighter, leaving me to collect my second gun, which he had dropped at the bottom of the tree, but fortunately without injuring it. The Kafirs gave him another name after that encounter, which meant "He-who-fights-birds-and-gets-the-worst-of-it."

Well, we escaped from the line of the smoke, a dishevelled trio—indeed, Umbezi had nothing left on him except his head ring—and shouted for the others, if perchance they had not been trodden to death in the rush. The first to arrive was Saduko, who looked quite calm and untroubled, but stared at us in astonishment, and asked coolly what we had been doing to get in such a state. I replied in appropriate language, and asked in turn how he had managed to remain so nicely dressed.

He did not answer, but I believe the truth was that he had crept into a large ant-bear's hole—small blame to him, to be frank. Then the remainder of our party turned up one by one, some of them looking very blown, as though they had run a long way. None were missing, except those who had fired the reeds, and they thought it well to keep clear for a good many hours. I believe that afterwards they regretted not having taken a longer leave of absence; but when they finally did arrive I was in no condition to note what passed between them and their outraged chief.

Being collected, the question arose what we should do. Of course, I wished to return to camp and get out of this ill-omened place as soon as possible. But I had reckoned without the vanity of Umbezi. Umbezi stretched over the edge of a sharp rock, whither he had been hoisted by the nose of a buffalo, and imagining himself to be mortally wounded, was one thing; but Umbezi in a borrowed moocha, although, because of his bruises, he supported his person with one hand in front and with the other behind, knowing his injuries to be purely superficial, was quite another.

"I am a hunter," he said; "I am named 'Eater-up-of-Elephants';" and he rolled his eyes, looking about for someone to contradict him, which nobody did. Indeed, his "praiser," a thin, tired-looking person, whose voice was worn out with his previous exertions, repeated in a feeble way:

"Yes, Black One, 'Eater-up-of-Elephants' is your name; 'Lifted-up-by-Buffalo' is your name."

"Be silent, idiot," roared Umbezi. "As I said, I am a hunter; I have wounded the wild beast that subsequently dared to assault me. [As a matter of fact, it was I, Allan Quatermain, who had wounded it.] I would make it bite the dust, for it cannot be far away. Let us follow it."

He glared round him, whereon his obsequious people, or one of them, echoed:

"Yes, by all means let us follow it, 'Eater-up-of-Elephants.' Macumazahn, the clever white man, will show us how, for where is the buffalo that he fears!"

Of course, after this there was nothing else to be done, so, having summoned the scratched Scowl, who seemed to have no heart in the business, we started on the spoor of the herd, which was as easy to track as a wagon road.

"Never mind, Baas," said Scowl, "they are two hours' march off by now."

"I hope so," I answered; but, as it happened, luck was against me, for before we had covered half a mile some over-zealous fellow struck a blood spoor.

I marched on that spoor for twenty minutes or so, till we came to a patch of bush that sloped downwards to a river-bed. Right to this river I followed it, till I reached the edge of a big pool that was still full of water, although the river itself had gone dry. Here I stood looking at the spoor and consulting with Saduko as to whether the beast could have swum the pool, for the tracks that went to its very verge had become confused and uncertain. Suddenly our doubts were ended, since out of a patch of dense bush which we had passed—for it had played the common trick of doubling back on its own spoor—appeared the buffalo, a huge bull, that halted on three legs, my bullet having broken one of its thighs. As to its identity there was no doubt, since on, or rather from, its right horn, which was cleft apart at the top, hung the remains of Umbezi's moocha.

"Oh, beware, Inkoosi," cried Saduko in a frightened voice. "It is the buffalo with the cleft horn!"

I heard him; I saw. All the scene in the hut of Zikali rose before me—the old dwarf, his words, everything. I lifted my rifle and fired at the charging beast, but knew that the bullet glanced from its skull. I threw down the gun—for the buffalo was right on me—and tried to jump aside.

Almost I did so, but that cleft horn, to which hung the remains of Umbezi's moocha, scooped me up and hurled me off the river bank backwards and sideways into the deep pool below. As I departed thither I saw Saduko spring forward and heard a shot fired that caused the bull to collapse for a moment. Then with a slow, sliding motion it followed me into the pool.

Now we were together, and there was no room for both, so after a certain amount of dodging I went under, as the lighter dog always does in a fight. That buffalo seemed to do everything to me which a buffalo could do under the circumstances. It tried to horn me, and partially succeeded, although I ducked at each swoop. Then it struck me with its nose and drove me to the bottom of the pool, although I got hold of its lip and twisted it. Then it calmly knelt on me and sank me deeper and deeper into the mud. I remember kicking it in the stomach. After this I remember no more, except a kind of wild dream in which I rehearsed all the scene in the dwarf's hut, and his request that when I met the buffalo with the cleft horn in the pool of a dried river, I should remember that he was nothing but a "poor old Kafir cheat."

After this I saw my mother bending over a little child in my bed in the old house in Oxfordshire where I was born, and then—blackness!

I came to myself again and saw, instead of my mother, the stately figure of Saduko bending over me upon one side, and on the other that of Scowl, the half-bred Hottentot, who was weeping, for his hot tears fell upon my face.

"He is gone," said poor Scowl; "that bewitched beast with the split horn has killed him. He is gone who was the best white man in all South Africa, whom I loved better than my father and all my relatives."

"That you might easily do, Bastard," answered Saduko, "seeing that you do not know who they are. But he is not gone, for the 'Opener-of-Roads' said that he would live; also I got my spear into the heart of that buffalo before he had kneaded the life out of him, as fortunately the mud was soft. Yet I fear that his ribs are broken"; and he poked me with his finger on the breast.

"Take your clumsy hand off me," I gasped.

"There!" said Saduko, "I have made him feel. Did I not tell you that he would live?"

After this I remember little more, except some confused dreams, till I found myself lying in a great hut, which I discovered subsequently was Umbezi's own, the same, indeed, wherein I had doctored the ear of that wife of his who was called "Worn-out-old-Cow."

CHAPTER IV

MAMEENA

For a while I contemplated the roof and sides of the hut by the light which entered it through the smoke-vent and the door-hole, wondering whose it might be and how I came there.

Then I tried to sit up, and instantly was seized with agony in the region of the ribs, which I found were bound about with broad strips of soft tanned hide. Clearly they, or some of them, were broken.

What had broken them? I asked myself, and in a flash everything came back to me. So I had escaped with my life, as the old dwarf, "Opener-of-Roads," had told me that I should. Certainly he was an excellent prophet; and if he spoke truth in this matter, why not in others? What was I to make of it all? How could a black savage, however ancient, foresee the future?

By induction from the past, I supposed; and yet what amount of induction would suffice to show him the details of a forthcoming accident that was to happen to me through the agency of a wild beast with a peculiarly shaped horn? I gave it up, as before and since that day I have found it necessary to do in the case of many other events in life. Indeed, the question is one that I often have had cause to ask where Kafir "witch-doctors" or prophets are concerned, notably in the instance of a certain Mavovo, of whom I hope to tell one day, whose predictions saved my life and those of my companions.

Just then I heard the sound of someone creeping through the bee-hole of the hut, and half-closed my eyes, as I did not feel inclined for conversation. The person came and stood over me, and somehow—by instinct, I suppose—I became aware that my visitor was a woman. Very slowly I lifted my eyelids, just enough to enable me to see her.

There, standing in a beam of golden light that, passing through the smoke-hole, pierced the soft gloom of the hut, stood the most beautiful creature that I had ever seen—that is, if it be admitted that a person who is black, or rather copper-coloured, can be beautiful.

She was a little above the medium height, not more, with a figure that, so far as I am a judge of such matters, was absolutely perfect—that of a Greek statue indeed. On this point I had an opportunity of forming an opinion, since, except for her little bead apron and a single string of large blue beads about her throat, her costume was—well, that of a Greek statue. Her features showed no trace of the negro type; on the contrary, they were singularly well cut, the nose being straight and fine and the pouting mouth that just showed the ivory teeth between, very small. Then the eyes, large, dark and liquid, like those of a buck, set beneath a smooth, broad forehead on which the curling, but not woolly, hair grew low. This hair, by the way, was not dressed up in any of the eccentric native fashions, but simply parted in the middle and tied in a big knot over the nape of the neck, the little ears peeping out through its tresses. The hands, like the feet, were very small and delicate, and the curves of the bust soft and full without being coarse, or even showing the promise of coarseness.

A lovely woman, truly; and yet there was something not quite pleasing about that beautiful face; something, notwithstanding its childlike outline, which reminded me of a flower breaking into bloom, that one does not associate with youth and innocence. I tried to analyse what this might be, and came to the conclusion that without being hard, it was too clever and, in a sense, too reflective. I felt even then that the brain within the shapely head was keen and bright as polished steel; that this woman was one made to rule, not to be man's toy, or even his loving companion, but to use him for her ends.

She dropped her chin till it hid the little, dimple-like depression below her throat, which was one of her charms, and began not to look at, but to study me, seeing which I shut my eyes tight and waited. Evidently she thought that I was still in my swoon, for now she spoke to herself in a low voice that was soft and sweet as honey.

"A small man," she said; "Saduko would make two of him, and the other"—who was he, I wondered—"three. His hair, too, is ugly; he cuts it short and it sticks up like that on a cat's back. Iya!" (i.e. Piff!), and she moved her hand contemptuously, "a feather of a man. But white—white, one of those who rule. Why, they all of them know that he is their master. They call him 'He-who-never-Sleeps.' They say that he has the courage of a lioness with young—he who got away when Dingaan killed Piti [Retief] and the Boers; they say that he is quick and cunning as a snake, and that Panda and his great indunas think more of him than of any white man they know. He is unmarried also, though they say, too, that twice he had a wife, who died, and now he does not turn to look at women, which is strange in any man, and shows that he will escape trouble and succeed. Still, it must be remembered that they are all ugly down here in Zululand, cows, or heifers who will be cows. Piff! no more."

She paused for a little while, then went on in her dreamy, reflective voice:

"Now, if he met a woman who is not merely a cow or a heifer, a woman cleverer than himself, even if she were not white, I wonder—"

At this point I thought it well to wake up. Turning my head I yawned, opened my eyes and looked at her vaguely, seeing which her expression changed in a flash from that of brooding power to one of moved and anxious girlhood; in short, it became most sweetly feminine.

"You are Mameena?" I said; "is it not so?"

"Oh, yes, Inkoosi," she answered, "that is my poor name. But how did you hear it, and how do you know me?"

"I heard it from one Saduko"—here she frowned a little—"and others, and I knew you because you are so beautiful"—an incautious speech at which she broke into a dazzling smile and tossed her deer-like head.

"Am I?" she asked. "I never knew it, who am only a common Zulu girl to whom it pleases the great white chief to say kind things, for which I thank him"; and she made a graceful little reverence, just bending one knee. "But," she went on quickly, "whatever else I be, I am of no knowledge, not fit to tend you who are hurt. Shall I go and send my oldest mother?"

"Do you mean her whom your father calls the 'Worn-out-old-Cow,' and whose ear he shot off?"

"Yes, it must be she from the description," she answered with a little shake of laughter, "though I never heard him give her that name."

"Or if you did, you have forgotten it," I said dryly. "Well, I think not, thank you. Why trouble her, when you will do quite as well? If there is milk in that gourd, perhaps you will give me a drink of it."

She flew to the bowl like a swallow, and next moment was kneeling at my side and holding it to my lips with one hand, while with the other she supported my head.

"I am honoured," she said. "I only came to the hut the moment before you woke, and seeing you still lost in swoon, I wept—look, my eyes are still wet [they were, though how she made them so I do not know]—for I feared lest that sleep should be but the beginning of the last."

"Quite so," I said; "it is very good of you. And now, since your fears are groundless—thanks be to the heavens—sit down, if you will, and tell me the story of how I came here."

She sat down, not, I noted, as a Kafir woman ordinarily does, in a kind of kneeling position, but on a stool.

"You were carried into the kraal, Inkoosi," she said, "on a litter of boughs. My heart stood still when I saw that litter coming; it was no more heart; it was cold iron, because I thought the dead or injured man was—" And she paused.

"Saduko?" I suggested.

"Not at all, Inkoosi—my father."

"Well, it wasn't either of them," I said, "so you must have felt happy."

"Happy! Inkoosi, when the guest of our house had been wounded, perhaps to death—the guest of whom I have heard so much, although by misfortune I was absent when he arrived."

"A difference of opinion with your eldest mother?" I suggested.

"Yes, Inkoosi; my own is dead, and I am not too well treated here. She called me a witch."

"Did she?" I answered. "Well, I do not altogether wonder at it; but please continue your story."

"There is none, Inkoosi. They brought you here, they told me how the evil brute of a buffalo had nearly killed you in the pool; that is all."

"Yes, yes, Mameena; but how did I get out of the pool?"

"Oh, it seems that your servant, Sikauli, the bastard, leapt into the water and engaged the attention of the buffalo which was kneading you into the mud, while Saduko got on to its back and drove his assegai down between its shoulders to the heart, so that it died. Then they pulled you out of the mud, crushed and almost drowned with water, and brought you to life again. But afterwards you became senseless, and so lay wandering in your speech until this hour."

"Ah, he is a brave man, is Saduko."

"Like others, neither more nor less," she replied with a shrug of her rounded shoulders. "Would you have had him let you die? I think the brave man was he who got in front of the bull and twisted its nose, not he who sat on its back and poked at it with a spear."

At this period in our conversation I became suddenly faint and lost count of things, even of the interesting Mameena. When I awoke again she was gone, and in her place was old Umbezi, who, I noticed, took down a mat from the side of the hut and folded it up to serve as a cushion before he sat himself upon the stool.

"Greeting, Macumazahn," he said when he saw that I was awake; "how are you?"

"As well as can be hoped," I answered; "and how are you, Umbezi?"

"Oh, bad, Macumazahn; even now I can scarcely sit down, for that bull had a very hard nose; also I am swollen up in front where Sikauli struck me when he tumbled out of the tree. Also my heart is cut in two because of our losses."

"What losses, Umbezi?"

"Wow! Macumazahn, the fire that those low fellows of mine lit got to our camp and burned up nearly everything—the meat, the skins, and even the ivory, which it cracked so that it is useless. That was an unlucky hunt, for although it began so well, we have come out of it quite naked; yes, with nothing at all except the head of the bull with the cleft horn, that I thought you might like to keep."

"Well, Umbezi, let us be thankful that we have come out with our lives—that is, if I am going to live," I added.

"Oh, Macumazahn, you will live without doubt, and be none the worse. Two of our doctors—very clever men—have looked at you and said so. One of them tied you up in all those skins, and I promised him a heifer for the business, if he cured you, and gave him a goat on account. But you must lie here for a month or more, so he says. Meanwhile Panda has sent for the hides which he demanded of me to be made into shields, and I have been obliged to kill twenty-five of my beasts to provide them—that is, of my own and of those of my headmen."

"Then I wish you and your headmen had killed them before we met those buffalo, Umbezi," I groaned, for my ribs were paining me very much. "Send Saduko and Sikauli here; I would thank them for saving my life."

So they came, next morning, I think, and I thanked them warmly enough.

"There, there, Baas," said Scowl, who was literally weeping tears of joy at my return from delirium and coma to the light of life and reason; not tears of Mameena's sort, but real ones, for I saw them running down his snub nose, that still bore marks of the eagle's claws. "There, there, say no more, I beseech you. If you were going to die, I wished to die, too, who, if you had left it, should only have wandered through the world without a heart. That is why I jumped into the pool, not because I am brave."

When I heard this my own eyes grew moist. Oh, it is the fashion to abuse natives, but from whom do we meet with more fidelity and love than from these poor wild Kafirs that so many of us talk of as black dirt which chances to be fashioned to the shape of man?

"As for myself, Inkoosi," added Saduko, "I only did my duty. How could I have held up my head again if the bull had killed you while I walked away alive? Why, the very girls would have mocked at me. But, oh, his skin was tough. I thought that assegai would never get through it."

Observe the difference between these two men's characters. The one, although no hero in daily life, imperils himself from sheer, dog-like fidelity to a master who had given him many hard words and sometimes a flogging in punishment for drunkenness, and the other to gratify his pride, also perhaps because my death would have interfered with his plans and ambitions in which I had a part to play. No, that is a hard saying; still, there is no doubt that Saduko always first took his own interests into consideration, and how what he did would reflect upon his prospects and repute, or influence the attainment of his desires. I think this was so even when Mameena was concerned—at any rate, in the beginning—although certainly he always loved her with a single-hearted passion that is very rare among Zulus.

Presently Scowl left the hut to prepare me some broth, whereon Saduko at once turned the talk to this subject of Mameena.

He understood that I had seen her. Did I not think her very beautiful?

"Yes, very beautiful," I answered; "indeed, the most beautiful Zulu woman I have ever seen."

And very clever—almost as clever as a white?

"Yes, and very clever—much cleverer than most whites."

And—anything else?

"Yes; very dangerous, and one who could turn like the wind and blow hot and blow cold."

"Ah!" he said, thought a while, then added: "Well, what do I care how she blows to others, so long as she blows hot to me."

"Well, Saduko, and does she blow hot for you?"

"Not altogether, Macumazahn." Another pause. "I think she blows rather like the wind before a great storm."

"That is a biting wind, Saduko, and when we feel it we know that the storm will follow."

"I dare say that the storm will follow, Inkoosi, for she was born in a storm and storm goes with her; but what of that, if she and I stand it out together? I love her, and I had rather die with her than live with any other woman."

"The question is, Saduko, whether she would rather die with you than live with any other man. Does she say so?"

"Inkoosi, Mameena's thought works in the dark; it is like a white ant in its tunnel of mud. You see the tunnel which shows that she is thinking, but you do not see the thought within. Still, sometimes, when she believes that no one beholds or hears her"—here I bethought me of the young lady's soliloquy over my apparently senseless self—"or when she is surprised, the true thought peeps out of its tunnel. It did so the other day, when I pleaded with her after she had heard that I killed the buffalo with the cleft horn.

"'Do I love you?' she said. 'I know not for sure. How can I tell? It is not our custom that a maiden should love before she is married, for if she did so most marriages would be things of the heart and not of cattle, and then half the fathers of Zululand would grow poor and refuse to rear girl-children who would bring them nothing. You are brave, you are handsome, you are well-born; I would sooner live with you than with any other man I know—that is, if you were rich and, better still, powerful. Become rich and powerful, Saduko, and I think that I shall love you.'

"'I will, Mameena,' I answered; 'but you must wait. The Zulu nation was not fashioned from nothing in a day. First Chaka had to come.'

"'Ah!' she said, and, my father, her eyes flashed. 'Ah! Chaka! There was a man! Be another Chaka, Saduko, and I will love you more—more than you can dream of—thus and thus,' and she flung her arms about me and kissed me as I was never kissed before, which, as you know, among us is a strange thing for a girl to do. Then she thrust me from her with a laugh, and added: 'As for the waiting, you must ask my father of that. Am I not his heifer, to be sold, and can I disobey my father?' And she was gone, leaving me empty, for it seemed as though she took my vitals with her. Nor will she talk thus any more, the white ant who has gone back into its tunnel."

"And did you speak to her father?"

"Yes, I spoke to him, but in an evil moment, for he had but just killed the cattle to furnish Panda's shields. He answered me very roughly. He said: 'You see these dead beasts which I and my people must slay for the king, or fall under his displeasure? Well, bring me five times their number, and we will talk of your marriage with my daughter, who is a maid in some request.'

"I answered that I understood and would try my best, whereon he became more gentle, for Umbezi has a kindly heart.

"'My son,' he said, 'I like you well, and since I saw you save Macumazahn, my friend, from that mad wild beast of a buffalo I like you better than before. Yet you know my case. I have an old name and am called the chief of a tribe, and many live on me. But I am poor, and this daughter of mine is worth much. Such a woman few men have bred. Well, I must make the best of her. My son-in-law must be one who will prop up my old age, one to whom, in my need or trouble, I could always go as to a dry log,[*] to break off some of its bark to make a fire to comfort me, not one who treads me into the mire as the buffalo did to Macumazahn. Now I have spoken, and I do not love such talk. Come back with the cattle, and I will listen to you, but meanwhile understand that I am not bound to you or to anyone; I shall take what my spirit sends me, which, if I may judge the future by the past, will not be much. One word more: Do not linger about this kraal too long, lest it should be said that you are the accepted suitor of Mameena. Go hence and do a man's work, and return with a man's reward, or not at all.'"

[*—In Zululand a son-in-law is known as "isigodo so mkwenyana", the "son-in-law log," for the reason stated in the text.—EDITOR.]

"Well, Saduko, that spear has an edge on it, has it not?" I answered. "And now, what is your plan?"

"My plan is, Macumazahn," he said, rising from his seat, "to go hence and gather those who are friendly to me because I am my father's son and still the chief of the Amangwane, or those who are left of them, although I have no kraal and no hoof of kine. Then, within a moon, I hope, I shall return here to find you strong again and once more a man, and we will start out against Bangu, as I have whispered to you, with the leave of a High One, who has said that, if I can take any cattle, I may keep them for my pains."

"I don't know about that, Saduko. I never promised you that I would make war upon Bangu—with or without the king's leave."

"No, you never promised, but Zikali the Dwarf, the Wise Little One, said that you would—and does Zikali lie? Ask yourself, who will remember a certain saying of his about a buffalo with a cleft horn, a pool and a dry river-bed. Farewell, O my father Macumazahn; I walk with the dawn, and I leave Mameena in your keeping."

"You mean that you leave me in Mameena's keeping," I began, but already he was crawling through the hole in the hut.

Well, Mameena kept me very comfortably. She was always in evidence, yet not too much so.

Heedless of her malice and abuse, she headed off the "Worn-out-old-Cow," whom she knew I detested, from my presence. She saw personally to my bandages, as well as to the cooking of my food, over which matter she had several quarrels with the bastard, Scowl, who did not like her, for on him she never wasted any of her sweet looks. Also, as I grew stronger, she sat with me a good deal, talking, since, by common consent, Mameena the fair was exempted from all the field, and even the ordinary household labours that fall to the lot of Kafir women. Her place was to be the ornament and, I may add, the advertisement of her father's kraal. Others might do the work, and she saw that they did it.

We discussed all sorts of things, from the Christian and other religions and European policy down, for her thirst for knowledge seemed to be insatiable. But what really interested her was the state of affairs in Zululand, with which she knew I was well acquainted, as a person who had played a part in its history and who was received and trusted at the Great House, and as a white man who understood the designs and plans of the Boers and of the Governor of Natal.

Now, if the old king, Panda, should chance to die, she would ask me, which of his sons did I think would succeed him—Umbelazi or Cetewayo, or another? Or, if he did not chance to die, which of them would he name his heir?

I replied that I was not a prophet, and that she had better ask Zikali the Wise.

"That is a very good idea," she said, "only I have no one to take me to him, since my father would not allow me to go with Saduko, his ward." Then she clapped her hands and added: "Oh, Macumazahn, will you take me? My father would trust me with you."

"Yes, I dare say," I answered; "but the question is, could I trust myself with you?"

"What do you mean?" she asked. "Oh, I understand. Then, after all, I am more to you than a black stone to play with?"

I think it was that unlucky joke of mine which first set Mameena thinking, "like a white ant in its tunnel," as Saduko said. At least, after it her manner towards me changed; she became very deferential; she listened to my words as though they were all wisdom; I caught her looking at me with her soft eyes as though I were quite an admirable object. She began to talk to me of her difficulties, her troubles and her ambitions. She asked me for my advice as to Saduko. On this point I replied to her that, if she loved him, and her father would allow it, presumably she had better marry him.

"I like him well enough, Macumazahn, although he wearies me at times; but love— Oh, tell me, what is love?" Then she clasped her slim hands and gazed at me like a fawn.

"Upon my word, young woman," I replied, "that is a matter upon which I should have thought you more competent to instruct me."

"Oh, Macumazahn," she said almost in a whisper, and letting her head droop like a fading lily, "you have never given me the chance, have you?" And she laughed a little, looking extremely attractive.

"Good gracious!"—or, rather, its Zulu equivalent—I answered, for I began to feel nervous. "What do you mean, Mameena? How could I—" There I stopped.

"I do not know what I mean, Macumazahn," she exclaimed wildly, "but I know well enough what you mean—that you are white as snow and I am black as soot, and that snow and soot don't mix well together."

"No," I answered gravely, "snow is good to look at, and so is soot, but mingled they make an ugly colour. Not that you are like soot," I added hastily, fearing to hurt her feelings. "That is your hue"—and I touched a copper bangle she was wearing—"a very lovely hue, Mameena, like everything else about you."

"Lovely," she said, beginning to weep a little, which upset me very much, for if there is one thing I hate, it is to see a woman cry. "How can a poor Zulu girl be lovely? Oh, Macumazahn, the spirits have dealt hardly with me, who have given me the colour of my people and the heart of yours. If I were white, now, what you are pleased to call this loveliness of mine would be of some use to me, for then— then— Oh, cannot you guess, Macumazahn?"

I shook my head and said that I could not, and next moment was sorry, for she proceeded to explain.

Sinking to her knees—for we were quite alone in the big hut and there was no one else about, all the other women being engaged on rural or domestic tasks, for which Mameena declared she had no time, as her business was to look after me—she rested her shapely head upon my knees and began to talk in a low, sweet voice that sometimes broke into a sob.

"Then I will tell you—I will tell you; yes, even if you hate me afterwards. I could teach you what love is very well, Macumazahn; you are quite right—because I love you." (Sob.) "No, you shall not stir till you have heard me out." Here she flung her arms about my legs and held them tight, so that without using great violence it was absolutely impossible for me to move. "When I saw you first, all shattered and senseless, snow seemed to fall upon my heart, and it stopped for a little while and has never been the same since. I think that something is growing in it, Macumazahn, that makes it big." (Sob.) "I used to like Saduko before that, but afterwards I did not like him at all—no, nor Masapo either—you know, he is the big chief who lives over the mountain, a very rich and powerful man, who, I believe, would like to marry me. Well, as I went on nursing you my heart grew bigger and bigger, and now you see it has burst." (Sob.) "Nay, stay still and do not try to speak. You shall hear me out. It is the least you can do, seeing that you have caused me all this pain. If you did not want me to love you, why did you not curse at me and strike me, as I am told white men do to Kafir girls?" She rose and went on:

"Now, hearken. Although I am the colour of copper, I am comely. I am well-bred also; there is no higher blood than ours in Zululand, both on my father's and my mother's side, and, Macumazahn, I have a fire in me that shows me things. I can be great, and I long for greatness. Take me to wife, Macumazahn, and I swear to you that in ten years I will make you king of the Zulus. Forget your pale white women and wed yourself to that fire which burns in me, and it shall eat up all that stands between you and the Crown, as flame eats up dry grass. More, I will make you happy. If you choose to take other wives, I will not be jealous, because I know that I should hold your spirit, and that, compared to me, they would be nothing in your thought—"

"But, Mameena," I broke in, "I don't want to be king of the Zulus."

"Oh, yes, yes, you do, for every man wants power, and it is better to rule over a brave, black people—thousands and thousands of them—than to be no one among the whites. Think, think! There is wealth in the land. By your skill and knowledge the amabuto [regiments] could be improved; with the wealth you would arm them with guns—yes, and 'by-and-byes' also with the throat of thunder" (that is, or was, the Kafir name for cannon).[*] "They would be invincible. Chaka's kingdom would be nothing to ours, for a hundred thousand warriors would sleep on their spears, waiting for your word. If you wished it even you could sweep out Natal and make the whites there your subjects, too. Or perhaps it would be safer to let them be, lest others should come across the green water to help them, and to strike northwards, where I am told there are great lands as rich and fair, in which none would dispute our sovereignty—"

[*—Cannon were called "by-and-byes" by the natives, because when field-pieces first arrived in Natal inquisitive Kafirs pestered the soldiers to show them how they were fired. The answer given was always "By-and-bye!" Hence the name.— EDITOR]

"But, Mameena," I gasped, for this girl's titanic ambition literally overwhelmed me, "surely you are mad! How would you do all these things?"

"I am not mad," she answered; "I am only what is called great, and you know well enough that I can do them, not by myself, who am but a woman and tied with the ropes that bind women, but with you to cut those ropes and help me. I have a plan which will not fail. But, Macumazahn," she added in a changed voice, "until I know that you will be my partner in it I will not tell it even to you, for perhaps you might talk—in your sleep, and then the fire in my breast would soon go out—for ever."

"I might talk now, for the matter of that, Mameena."

"No; for men like you do not tell tales of foolish girls who chance to love them. But if that plan began to work, and you heard say that kings or princes died, it might be otherwise. You might say, 'I think I know where the witch lives who causes these evils'—in your sleep, Macumazahn."

"Mameena," I said, "tell me no more. Setting your dreams on one side, can I be false to my friend, Saduko, who talks to me day and night of you?"

"Saduko! Piff!" she exclaimed, with that expressive gesture of her hand.

"And can I be false," I continued, seeing that Saduko was no good card to play, "to my friend, Umbezi, your father?"

"My father!" she laughed. "Why, would it not please him to grow great in your shadow? Only yesterday he told me to marry you, if I could, for then he would find a stick indeed to lean on, and be rid of Saduko's troubling."

Evidently Umbezi was a worse card even than Saduko, so I played another.

"And can I help you, Mameena, to tread a road that at the best must be red with blood?"

"Why not," she asked, "since with or without you I am destined to tread that road, the only difference being that with you it will lead to glory and without you perhaps to the jackals and the vultures? Blood! Piff! What is blood in Zululand?"

This card also having failed, I tabled my last.

"Glory or no glory, I do not wish to share it, Mameena. I will not make war among a people who have entertained me hospitably, or plot the downfall of their Great Ones. As you told me just now, I am nobody—just one grain of sand upon a white shore—but I had rather be that than a haunted rock which draws the heavens' lightnings and is drenched with sacrifice. I seek no throne over white or black, Mameena, who walk my own path to a quiet grave that shall perhaps not be without honour of its own, though other than you seek. I will keep your counsel, Mameena, but, because you are so beautiful and so wise, and because you say you are fond of me—for which I thank you—I pray you put away these fearful dreams of yours that in the end, whether they succeed or fail, will send you shivering from the world to give account of them to the Watcher-on-high."

"Not so, O Macumazana," she said, with a proud little laugh. "When your Watcher sowed my seed—if thus he did—he sowed the dreams that are a part of me also, and I shall only bring him back his own, with the flower and the fruit by way of interest. But that is finished. You refuse the greatness. Now, tell me, if I sink those dreams in a great water, tying about them the stone of forgetfulness and saying: 'Sleep there, O dreams; it is not your hour'—if I do this, and stand before you just a woman who loves and who swears by the spirits of her fathers never to think or do that which has not your blessing—will you love me a little, Macumazahn?"

Now I was silent, for she had driven me to the last ditch, and I knew not what to say. Moreover, I will confess my weakness—I was strangely moved. This beautiful girl with the "fire in her heart," this woman who was different from all other women that I had ever known, seemed to have twisted her slender fingers into my heart-strings and to be drawing me towards her. It was a great temptation, and I bethought me of old Zikali's saying in the Black Kloof, and seemed to hear his giant laugh.

She glided up to me, she threw her arms about me and kissed me on the lips, and I think I kissed her back, but really I am not sure what I did or said, for my head swam. When it cleared again she was standing in front of me, looking at me reflectively.

"Now, Macumazahn," she said, with a little smile that both mocked and dazzled, "the poor black girl has you, the wise, experienced white man, in her net, and I will show you that she can be generous. Do you think that I do not read your heart, that I do not know that you believe I am dragging you down to shame and ruin? Well, I spare you, Macumazahn, since you have kissed me and spoken words which already you may have forgotten, but which I do not forget. Go your road, Macumazahn, and I go mine, since the proud white man shall not be stained with my black touch. Go your road; but one thing I forbid you—to believe that you have been listening to lies, and that I have merely played off a woman's arts upon you for my own ends. I love you, Macumazahn, as you will never be loved till you die, and I shall never love any other man, however many I may marry. Moreover, you shall promise me one thing—that once in my life, and once only, if I wish it, you shall kiss me again before all men. And now, lest you should be moved to folly and forget your white man's pride, I bid you farewell, O Macumazana. When we meet again it will be as friends only."

Then she went, leaving me feeling smaller than ever I felt in my life, before or since—even smaller than when I walked into the presence of old Zikali the Wise. Why, I wondered, had she first made a fool of me, and then thrown away the fruits of my folly? To this hour I cannot quite answer the question, though I believe the explanation to be that she did really care for me, and was anxious not to involve me in trouble and her plottings; also she may have been wise enough to see that our natures were as oil and water and would never blend.

CHAPTER V

TWO BUCKS AND THE DOE

It may be thought that, as a sequel to this somewhat remarkable scene in which I was absolutely bowled over—perhaps bowled out would be a better term—by a Kafir girl who, after bending me to her will, had the genius to drop me before I repented, as she knew I would do so soon as her back was turned, thereby making me look the worst of fools, that my relations with that young lady would have been strained. But not a bit of it. When next we met, which was on the following morning, she was just her easy, natural self, attending to my hurts, which by now were almost well, joking about this and that, inquiring as to the contents of certain letters which I had received from Natal, and of some newspapers that came with them—for on all such matters she was very curious—and so forth.

Impossible, the clever critic will say—impossible that a savage could act with such finish. Well, friend critic, that is just where you are wrong. When you come to add it up there's very little difference in all main and essential matters between the savage and yourself.

To begin with, by what exact right do we call people like the Zulus savages? Setting aside the habit of polygamy, which, after all, is common among very highly civilised peoples in the East, they have a social system not unlike our own. They have, or had, their king, their nobles, and their commons. They have an ancient and elaborate law, and a system of morality in some ways as high as our own, and certainly more generally obeyed. They have their priests and their doctors; they are strictly upright, and observe the rites of hospitality.

Where they differ from us mainly is that they do not get drunk until the white man teaches them so to do, they wear less clothing, the climate being more genial, their towns at night are not disgraced by the sights that distinguish ours, they cherish and are never cruel to their children, although they may occasionally put a deformed infant or a twin out of the way, and when they go to war, which is often, they carry out the business with a terrible thoroughness, almost as terrible as that which prevailed in every nation in Europe a few generations ago.

Of course, there remain their witchcraft and the cruelties which result from their almost universal belief in the power and efficiency of magic. Well, since I lived in England I have been reading up this subject, and I find that quite recently similar cruelties were practised throughout Europe—that is in a part of the world which for over a thousand years has enjoyed the advantages of the knowledge and profession of the Christian faith.

Now, let him who is highly cultured take up a stone to throw at the poor, untaught Zulu, which I notice the most dissolute and drunken wretch of a white man is often ready to do, generally because he covets his land, his labour, or whatever else may be his.

But I wander from my point, which is that a clever man or woman among the people whom we call savages is in all essentials very much the same as a clever man or woman anywhere else.

Here in England every child is educated at the expense of the Country, but I have not observed that the system results in the production of more really able individuals. Ability is the gift of Nature, and that universal mother sheds her favours impartially over all who breathe. No, not quite impartially, perhaps, for the old Greeks and others were examples to the contrary. Still, the general rule obtains.

To return. Mameena was a very able person, as she chanced to be a very lovely one, a person who, had she been favoured by opportunity, would doubtless have played the part of a Cleopatra with equal or greater success, since she shared the beauty and the unscrupulousness of that famous lady and was, I believe, capable of her passion.

I scarcely like to mention the matter since it affects myself, and the natural vanity of man makes him prone to conclude that he is the particular object of sole and undying devotion. Could he know all the facts of the case, or cases, probably he would be much undeceived, and feel about as small as I did when Mameena walked, or rather crawled, out of the hut (she could even crawl gracefully). Still, to be honest—and why should I not, since all this business "went beyond" so long ago?—I do believe that there was a certain amount of truth in what she said—that, for Heaven knows what reason, she did take a fancy to me, which fancy continued during her short and stormy life. But the reader of her story may judge for himself.

Within a fortnight of the day of my discomfiture in the hut I was quite well and strong again, my ribs, or whatever part of me it was that the buffalo had injured with his iron knees, having mended up. Also, I was anxious to be going, having business to attend to in Natal, and, as no more had been seen or heard of Saduko, I determined to trek homewards, leaving a message that he knew where to find me if he wanted me. The truth is that I was by no means keen on being involved in his private war with Bangu. Indeed, I wished to wash my hands of the whole matter, including the fair Mameena and her mocking eyes.

So one morning, having already got up my oxen, I told Scowl to inspan them—an order which he received with joy, for he and the other boys wished to be off to civilisation and its delights. Just as the operation was beginning, however, a message came to me from old Umbezi, who begged me to delay my departure till after noon, as a friend of his, a big chief, had come to visit him who wished much to have the honour of making my acquaintance. Now, I wished the big chief farther off, but, as it seemed rude to refuse the request of one who had been so kind to me, I ordered the oxen to be unyoked but kept at hand, and in an irritable frame of mind walked up to the kraal. This was about half a mile from my place of outspan, for as soon as I was sufficiently recovered I had begun to sleep in my wagon, leaving the big hut to the "Worn-out-Old-Cow."

There was no particular reason why I should be irritated, since time in those days was of no great account in Zululand, and it did not much matter to me whether I trekked in the morning or the afternoon. But the fact was that I could not get over the prophecy of Zikali, "the Little and Wise," that I was destined to share Saduko's expedition against Bangu, and, although he had been right about the buffalo and Mameena, I was determined to prove him wrong in this particular.

If I had left the country, obviously I could not go against Bangu, at any rate at present. But while I remained in it Saduko might return at any moment, and then, doubtless, I should find it hard to escape from the kind of half-promise that I had given to him.

Well, as soon as I reached the kraal I saw that some kind of festivity was in progress, for an ox had been killed and was being cooked, some of it in pots and some by roasting; also there were several strange Zulus present. Within the fence of the kraal, seated in its shadow, I found Umbezi and some of his headmen, and with them a great, brawny "ringed" native, who wore a tiger-skin moocha as a mark of rank, and some of his headmen. Also Mameena was standing near the gate, dressed in her best beads and holding a gourd of Kafir beer which, evidently, she had just been handing to the guests.

"Would you have run away without saying good-bye to me, Macumazahn?" she whispered to me as I came abreast of her. "That is unkind of you, and I should have wept much. However, it was not so fated."

"I was going to ride up and bid farewell when the oxen were inspanned," I answered. "But who is that man?"

"You will find out presently, Macumazahn. Look, my father is beckoning to us."

So I went on to the circle, and as I advanced Umbezi rose and, taking me by the hand, led me to the big man, saying:

"This is Masapo, chief of the Amansomi, of the Quabe race, who desires to know you, Macumazahn."

"Very kind of him, I am sure," I replied coolly, as I threw my eye over Masapo. He was, as I have said, a big man, and of about fifty years of age, for his hair was tinged with grey. To be frank, I took a great dislike to him at once, for there was something in his strong, coarse face, and his air of insolent pride, which repelled me. Then I was silent, since among the Zulus, when two strangers of more or less equal rank meet, he who speaks first acknowledges inferiority to the other. Therefore I stood and contemplated this new suitor of Mameena, waiting on events.

Masapo also contemplated me, then made some remark to one of his attendants, that I did not catch, which caused the fellow to laugh.

"He has heard that you are an ipisi" (a great hunter), broke in Umbezi, who evidently felt that the situation was growing strained, and that it was necessary to say something.

"Has he?" I answered. "Then he is more fortunate than I am, for I have never heard of him or what he is." This, I am sorry to say, was a fib, for it will be remembered that Mameena had mentioned him in the hut as one of her suitors, but among natives one must keep up one's dignity somehow. "Friend Umbezi," I went on, "I have come to bid you farewell, as I am about to trek for Durban."

At this juncture Masapo stretched out his great hand to me, but without rising, and said:

"Siyakubona [that is, good-day], White Man."

"Siyakubona, Black Man," I answered, just touching his fingers, while Mameena, who had come up again with her beer, and was facing me, made a little grimace and tittered.

Now I turned on my heel to go, whereon Masapo said in a coarse, growling voice:

"O Macumazana, before you leave us I wish to speak with you on a certain matter. Will it please you to sit aside with me for a while?"

"Certainly, O Masapo." And I walked away a few yards out of hearing, whither he followed me.

"Macumazahn," he said (I give the gist of his remarks, for he did not come to the point at once), "I need guns, and I am told that you can provide them, being a trader."

"Yes, Masapo, I dare say that I can, at a price, though it is a risky business smuggling guns into Zululand. But might I ask what you need them for? is it to shoot elephants?"

"Yes, to shoot elephants," he replied, rolling his big eyes round him. "Macumazahn, I am told that you are discreet, that you do not shout from the top of a hut what you hear within it. Now, hearken to me. Our country is disturbed; we do not all of us love the seed of Senzangakona, of whom the present king, Panda, is one. For instance, you may know that we Quabies—for my tribe, the Amansomi, are of that race—suffered at the spear of Chaka. Well, we think that a time may come when we who live on shrubs like goats may again browse on tree-tops like giraffes, for Panda is no strong king, and he has sons who hate each other, one of whom may need our spears. Do you understand?"

"I understand that you want guns, O Masapo," I answered dryly. "Now, as to the price and place of delivery."

Then we bargained for a while, but the details of that business transaction of long ago will interest no one. Indeed, I only mention the matter to show that Masapo was plotting to bring trouble on the ruling house, whereof Panda was the representative at that time.

When we had concluded our rather nefarious negotiations, which were to the effect that I was to receive so many cattle in return for so many guns, if I could deliver them at a certain spot, namely, Umbezi's kraal, I returned to the circle where Umbezi, his followers and guests were sitting, purposing to bid him farewell. By now, however, meat had been served, and as I was hungry, having had little breakfast that morning, I stayed to eat. When I had finished my meal, and washed it down with a draught of tshwala (that is, Kafir beer), I rose to go, but just at that moment who should walk through the gate but Saduko?

"Piff!" said Mameena, who was standing near me, speaking in a voice that none but I could hear. "When two bucks meet, what happens, Macumazahn?"

"Sometimes they fight and sometimes one runs away. It depends very much on the doe," I answered in the same low voice, looking at her.

She shrugged her shoulders, folded her arms beneath her breast, nodded to Saduko as he passed, then leaned gracefully against the fence and awaited events.

"Greeting, Umbezi," said Saduko in his proud manner. "I see that you feast. Am I welcome here?"

"Of course you are always welcome, Saduko," replied Umbezi uneasily, "although, as it happens, I am entertaining a great man." And he looked towards Masapo.

"I see," said Saduko, eyeing the strangers. "But which of these may be the great man? I ask that I may salute him."

"You know well enough, umfokazana" (that is, low fellow), exclaimed Masapo angrily.

"I know that if you were outside this fence, Masapo, I would cram that word down your throat at the point of my assegai," replied Saduko in a fierce voice. "Oh, I can guess your business here, Masapo, and you can guess mine," and he glanced towards Mameena. "Tell me, Umbezi, is this little chief of the Amansomi your daughter's accepted suitor?"

"Nay, nay, Saduko," said Umbezi; "no one is her accepted suitor. Will you not sit down and take food with us? Tell us where you have been, and why you return here thus suddenly, and—uninvited?"

"I return here, O Umbezi, to speak with the white chief, Macumazahn. As to where I have been, that is my affair, and not yours or Masapo's."

"Now, if I were chief of this kraal," said Masapo, "I would hunt out of it this hyena with a mangy coat and without a hole who comes to devour your meat and, perhaps," he added with meaning, "to steal away your child."

"Did I not tell you, Macumazahn, that when two bucks met they would fight?" whispered Mameena suavely into my ear.

"Yes, Mameena, you did—or rather I told you. But you did not tell me what the doe would do."

"The doe, Macumazahn, will crouch in her form and see what happens—as is the fashion of does," and again she laughed softly.

"Why not do your own hunting, Masapo?" asked Saduko. "Come, now, I will promise you good sport. Outside this kraal there are other hyenas waiting who call me chief—a hundred or two of them—assembled for a certain purpose by the royal leave of King Panda, whose House, as we all know, you hate. Come, leave that beef and beer and begin your hunting of hyenas, O Masapo."

Now Masapo sat silent, for he saw that he who thought to snare a baboon had caught a tiger.

"You do not speak, O Chief of the little Amansomi," went on Saduko, who was beside himself with rage and jealousy. "You will not leave your beef and beer to hunt the hyenas who are captained by an umfokazana! Well, then, the umfokazana will speak," and, stepping up to Masapo, with the spear he carried poised in his right hand, Saduko grasped his rival's short beard with his left.

"Listen, Chief," he said. "You and I are enemies. You seek the woman I seek, and, mayhap, being rich, you will buy her. But if so, I tell you that I will kill you and all your House, you sneaking, half-bred dog!"

With these fierce words he spat in his face and tumbled him backwards. Then, before anyone could stop him, for Umbezi, and even Masapo's headmen, seemed paralysed with surprise, he stalked through the kraal gate, saying as he passed me:

"Inkoosi, I have words for you when you are at liberty."

"You shall pay for this," roared Umbezi after him, turning almost green with rage, for Masapo still lay upon his broad back, speechless, "you who dare to insult my guest in my own house."

"Somebody must pay," cried back Saduko from the gate, "but who it is only the unborn moons will see."

"Mameena," I said as I followed him, "you have set fire to the grass, and men will be burned in it."

"I meant to, Macumazahn," she answered calmly. "Did I not tell you that there was a flame in me, and it will break out sometimes? But, Macumazahn, it is you who have set fire to the grass, not I. Remember that when half Zululand is in ashes. Farewell, O Macumazana, till we meet again, and," she added softly, "whoever else must burn, may the spirits have you in their keeping."

At the gate, remembering my manners, I turned to bid that company a polite farewell. By now Masapo had gained his feet, and was roaring out like a bull:

"Kill him! Kill the hyena! Umbezi, will you sit still and see me, your guest—me, Masapo—struck and insulted under the shadow of your own hut? Go forth and kill him, I say!"

"Why not kill him yourself, Masapo," asked the agitated Umbezi, "or bid your headmen kill him? Who am I that I should take precedence of so great a chief in a matter of the spear?" Then he turned towards me, saying: "Oh, Macumazahn the crafty, if I have dealt well by you, come here and give me your counsel."

"I come, Eater-up-of-Elephants," I answered, and I did.

"What shall I do—what shall I do?" went on Umbezi, brushing the perspiration off his brow with one hand, while he wrung the other in his agitation. "There stands a friend of mine"—he pointed to the infuriated Masapo—"who wishes me to kill another friend of mine," and he jerked his thumb towards the kraal gate. "If I refuse I offend one friend, and if I consent I bring blood upon my hands which will call for blood, since, although Saduko is poor, without doubt he has those who love him."

"Yes," I answered, "and perhaps you will bring blood upon other parts of yourself besides your hands, since Saduko is not one to sit still like a sheep while his throat is cut. Also did he not say that he is not quite alone? Umbezi, if you will take my advice, you will leave Masapo to do his own killing."

"It is good; it is wise!" exclaimed Umbezi. "Masapo," he called to that warrior, "if you wish to fight, pray do not think of me. I see nothing, I hear nothing, and I promise proper burial to any who fall. Only you had best be swift, for Saduko is walking away all this time. Come, you and your people have spears, and the gate stands open."

"Am I to go without my meat in order to knock that hyena on the head?" asked Masapo in a brave voice. "No, he can wait my leisure. Sit still, my people. I tell you, sit still. Tell him, you Macumazahn, that I am coming for him presently, and be warned to keep yourself away from him, lest you should tumble into his hole."

"I will tell him," I answered, "though I know not who made me your messenger. But listen to me, you Speaker of big words and Doer of small deeds, if you dare to lift a finger against me I will teach you something about holes, for there shall be one or more through that great carcass of yours."

Then, walking up to him, I looked him in the face, and at the same time tapped the handle of the big double-barrelled pistol I carried.

He shrank back muttering something.

"Oh, don't apologise," I said, "only be more careful in future. And now I wish you a good dinner, Chief Masapo, and peace upon your kraal, friend Umbezi."

After this speech I marched off, followed by the clamour of Masapo's furious attendants and the sound of Mameena's light and mocking laughter.

"I wonder which of them she will marry?" I thought to myself, as I set out for the wagons.

As I approached my camp I saw that the oxen were being inspanned, as I supposed by the order of Scowl, who must have heard that there was a row up at the kraal, and thought it well to be ready to bolt. In this I was mistaken, however, for just then Saduko strolled out of a patch of bush and said:

"I ordered your boys to yoke up the oxen, Inkoosi."

"Have you? That's cool!" I answered. "Perhaps you will tell me why."

"Because we must make a good trek to the northward before night, Inkoosi."

"Indeed! I thought that I was heading south-east."

"Bangu does not live in the south or the east," he replied slowly.

"Oh, I had almost forgotten about Bangu," I said, with a rather feeble attempt at evasion.

"Is it so?" he answered in his haughty voice. "I never knew before that Macumazahn was a man who broke a promise to his friend."

"Would you be so kind as to explain your meaning, Saduko?"

"Is it needful?" he answered, shrugging his shoulders. "Unless my ears played me tricks, you agreed to go up with me against Bangu. Well, I have gathered the necessary men—with the king's leave—they await us yonder," and he pointed with his spear towards a dense patch of bush that lay some miles beneath us. "But," he added, "if you desire to change your mind I will go alone. Only then, I think, we had better bid each other good-bye, since I love not friends who change their minds when the assegais begin to shake."

Now, whether Saduko spoke thus by design I do not know. Certainly, however, he could have found no better way to ensure my companionship for what it was worth, since, although I had made no actual promise in this case, I have always prided myself on keeping even a half-bargain with a native.

"I will go with you," I said quietly, "and I hope that, when it comes to the pinch, your spear will be as sharp as your tongue, Saduko. Only do not speak to me again like that, lest we should quarrel."

As I said this I saw a look of relief appear on his face, of very great relief.

"I pray your pardon, my lord Macumazahn," he said, seizing my hand, "but, oh! there is a hole in my heart. I think that Mameena means to play me false, and now that has happened with yonder dog, Masapo, which will make her father hate me."

"If you will take my advice, Saduko," I replied earnestly, "you will let this Mameena fall out of the hole in your heart; you will forget her name; you will have done with her. Ask me not why."

"Perhaps there is no need, O Macumazana. Perhaps she has been making love to you, and you have turned her away, as, being what you are, and my friend, of course you would do." (It is rather inconvenient to be set upon such a pedestal at times, but I did not attempt to assent or to deny anything, much less to enter into explanations.)

"Perhaps all this has happened," he continued, "or perhaps it is she who has sent for Masapo the Hog. I do not ask, because if you know you will not tell me. Moreover, it matters nothing. While I have a heart, Mameena will never drop out of it; while I can remember names, hers will never be forgotten by me. Moreover, I mean that she shall be my wife. Now, I am minded to take a few men and spear this hog, Masapo, before we go up against Bangu, for then he, at any rate, will be out of my road."

"If you do anything of the sort, Saduko, you will go up against Bangu alone, for I trek east at once, who will not be mixed up with murder."

"Then let it be, Inkoosi; unless he attacks me, as my Snake send that he may, the Hog can wait. After all, he will only be growing a little fatter. Now, if it pleases you order the wagons to trek. I will show the road, for we must camp in that bush to-night where my people wait me, and there I will tell you my plans; also you will find one with a message for you."

CHAPTER VI

THE AMBUSH

We had reached the bush after six hours' downhill trek over a pretty bad track made by cattle—of course, there were no roads in Zululand at this date. I remember the place well. It was a kind of spreading woodland on a flat bottom, where trees of no great size grew sparsely. Some were mimosa thorns, others had deep green leaves and bore a kind of plum with an acid taste and a huge stone, and others silver-coloured leaves in their season. A river, too, low at this time of the year, wound through it, and in the scrub upon its banks were many guinea-fowl and other birds. It was a pleasing, lonely place, with lots of game in it, that came here in the winter to eat the grass, which was lacking on the higher veld. Also it gave the idea of vastness, since wherever one looked there was nothing to be seen except a sea of trees.

Well, we outspanned by the river, of which I forget the name, at a spot that Saduko showed us, and set to work to cook our food, that consisted of venison from a blue wildebeest, one of a herd of these wild-looking animals which I had been fortunate enough to shoot as they whisked past us, gambolling in and out between the trees.

While we were eating I observed that armed Zulus arrived continually in parties of from six to a score of men, and as they arrived lifted their spears, though whether in salutation to Saduko or to myself I did not know, and sat themselves down on an open space between us and the river-bank. Although it was difficult to say whence they came, for they appeared like ghosts out of the bush, I thought it well to take no notice of them, since I guessed that their coming was prearranged.

"Who are they?" I whispered to Scowl, as he brought me my tot of "squareface."

"Saduko's wild men," he answered in the same low voice, "outlaws of his tribe who live among the rocks."

Now I scanned them sideways, while pretending to light my pipe and so forth, and certainly they seemed a remarkably savage set of people. Great, gaunt fellows with tangled hair, who wore tattered skins upon their shoulders and seemed to have no possessions save some snuff, a few sleeping-mats, and an ample supply of large fighting shields, hardwood kerries or knob-sticks, and broad ixwas, or stabbing assegais. Such was the look of them as they sat round us in silent semicircles, like aas-vŏgels— as the Dutch call vultures—sit round a dying ox.

Still I smoked on and took no notice.

At length, as I expected, Saduko grew weary of my silence and spoke. "These are men of the Amangwane tribe, Macumazahn; three hundred of them, all that Bangu left alive, for when their fathers were killed, the women escaped with some of the children, especially those of the outlying kraals. I have gathered them to be revenged upon Bangu, I who am their chief by right of blood."

"Quite so," I answered. "I see that you have gathered them; but do they wish to be revenged on Bangu at the risk of their own lives?"

"We do, white Inkoosi," came the deep-throated answer from the three hundred.

"And do they acknowledge you, Saduko, to be their chief?"

"We do," again came the answer. Then a spokesman stepped forward, one of the few grey-haired men among them, for most of these Amangwane were of the age of Saduko, or even younger.

"O Watcher-by-Night," he said, "I am Tshoza, the brother of Matiwane, Saduko's father, the only one of his brothers that escaped the slaughter on the night of the Great Killing. Is it not so?"

"It is so," exclaimed the serried ranks behind him.

"I acknowledge Saduko as my chief, and so do we all," went on Tshoza.

"So do we all," echoed the ranks.

"Since Matiwane died we have lived as we could, O Macumazana; like baboons among the rocks, without cattle, often without a hut to shelter us; here one, there one. Still, we have lived, awaiting the hour of vengeance upon Bangu, that hour which Zikali the Wise, who is of our blood, has promised to us. Now we believe that it has come, and one and all, from here, from there, from everywhere, we have gathered at the summons of Saduko to be led against Bangu and to conquer him or to die. Is it not so, Amangwane?"

"It is, it is so!" came the deep, unanimous answer, that caused the stirless leaves to shake in the still air.

"I understand, O Tshoza, brother of Matiwane and uncle of Saduko the chief," I replied. "But Bangu is a strong man, living, I am told, in a strong place. Still, let that go; for have you not said that you come out to conquer or to die, you who have nothing to lose; and if you conquer, you conquer; and if you die, you die and the tale is told. But supposing that you conquer. What will Panda, King of the Zulus, say to you, and to me also, who stir up war in his country?"

Now the Amangwane looked behind them, and Saduko cried out:

"Appear, messenger from Panda the King!"

Before his words had ceased to echo I saw a little, withered man threading his way between the tall, gaunt forms of the Amangwane. He came and stood before me, saying:

"Hail, Macumazahn. Do you remember me?"

"Aye," I answered, "I remember you as Maputa, one of Panda's indunas."

"Quite so, Macumazahn; I am Maputa, one of his indunas, a member of his Council, a captain of his impis [that is, armies], as I was to his brothers who are gone, whose names it is not lawful that I should name. Well, Panda the King has sent me to you, at the request of Saduko there, with a message."

"How do I know that you are a true messenger?" I asked. "Have you brought me any token?"

"Aye," he answered, and, fumbling under his cloak, he produced something wrapped in dried leaves, which he undid and handed to me, saying:

"This is the token that Panda sends to you, Macumazahn, bidding me to tell you that you will certainly know it again; also that you are welcome to it, since the two little bullets which he swallowed as you directed made him very ill, and he needs no more of them."

I took the token, and, examining it in the moonlight, recognised it at once.

It was a cardboard box of strong calomel pills, on the top of which was written: "Allan Quatermain, Esq.: One only to be taken as directed." Without entering into explanations, I may state that I had taken "one as directed," and subsequently presented the rest of the box to King Panda, who was very anxious to "taste the white man's medicine."

"Do you recognise the token, Macumazahn?" asked the induna.

"Yes," I replied gravely; "and let the King return thanks to the spirits of his ancestors that he did not swallow three of the balls, for if he had done so, by now there would have been another Head in Zululand. Well, speak on, Messenger."

But to myself I reflected, not for the first time, how strangely these natives could mix up the sublime with the ridiculous. Here was a matter that must involve the death of many men, and the token sent to me by the autocrat who stood at the back of it all, to prove the good faith of his messenger, was a box of calomel pills! However, it served the purpose as well as anything else.

Maputa and I drew aside, for I saw that he wished to speak with me alone.

"O Macumazana," he said, when we were out of hearing of the others, "these are the words of Panda to you: 'I understand that you, Macumazahn, have promised to accompany Saduko, son of Matiwane, on an expedition of his against Bangu, chief of the Amakoba. Now, were anyone else concerned, I should forbid this expedition, and especially should I forbid you, a white man in my country, to share therein. But this dog of a Bangu is an evil-doer. Many years ago he worked on the Black One who went before me to send him to destroy Matiwane, my friend, filling the Black One's ears with false accusations; and thereafter he did treacherously destroy him and all his tribe save Saduko, his son, and some of the people and children who escaped. Moreover, of late he has been working against me, the King, striving to stir up rebellion against me, because he knows that I hate him for his crimes. Now I, Panda, unlike those who went before me, am a man of peace who do not wish to light the fire of civil war in the land, for who knows where such fires will stop, or whose kraals they will consume? Yet I do wish to see Bangu punished for his wickedness, and his pride abated. Therefore I give Saduko leave, and those people of the Amangwane who remain to him, to avenge their private wrongs upon Bangu if they can; and I give you leave, Macumazahn, to be of his party. Moreover, if any cattle are taken, I shall ask no account of them; you and Saduko may divide them as you wish. But understand, O Macumazana, that if you or your people are killed or wounded, or robbed of your goods, I know nothing of the matter, and am not responsible to you or to the white House of Natal; it is your own matter. These are my words. I have spoken.'"

"I see," I answered. "I am to pull Panda's hot iron out of the fire and to extinguish the fire. If I succeed I may keep a piece of the iron when it gets cool, and if I burn my fingers it is my own fault, and I or my House must not come crying to Panda."

"O Watcher-by-Night, you have speared the bull in the heart," replied Maputa, the messenger, nodding his shrewd old head. "Well, will you go up with Saduko?"

"Say to the King, O Messenger, that I will go up with Saduko because I promised him that I would, being moved by the tale of his wrongs, and not for the sake of the cattle, although it is true that if I hear any of them lowing in my camp I may keep them. Say to Panda also that if aught of ill befalls me he shall hear nothing of it, nor will I bring his high name into this business; but that he, on his part, must not blame me for anything that may happen afterwards. Have you the message?"

"I have it word for word; and may your Spirit be with you, Macumazahn, when you attack the strong mountain of Bangu, which, were I you," Maputa added reflectively, "I think I should do just at the dawn, since the Amakoba drink much beer and are heavy sleepers."

Then we took a pinch of snuff together, and he departed at once for Nodwengu, Panda's Great Place.

Fourteen days had gone by, and Saduko and I, with our ragged band of Amangwane, sat one morning, after a long night march, in the hilly country looking across a broad vale, which was sprinkled with trees like an English park, at that mountain on the side of which Bangu, chief of the Amakoba, had his kraal.

It was a very formidable mountain, and, as we had already observed, the paths leading up to the kraal were amply protected with stone walls in which the openings were quite narrow, only just big enough to allow one ox to pass through them at a time. Moreover, all these walls had been strengthened recently, perhaps because Bangu was aware that Panda looked upon him, a northern chief dwelling on the confines of his dominions, with suspicion and even active enmity, as he was also no doubt aware Panda had good cause to do.

Here in a dense patch of bush that grew in a kloof of the hills we held a council of war.

So far as we knew our advance had been unobserved, for I had left my wagons in the low veld thirty miles away, giving it out among the local natives that I was hunting game there, and bringing on with me only Scowl and four of my best hunters, all well-armed natives who could shoot. The three hundred Amangwane also had advanced in small parties, separated from each other, pretending to be Kafirs marching towards Delagoa Bay. Now, however, we had all met in this bush. Among our number were three Amangwane who, on the slaughter of their tribe, had fled with their mothers to this district and been brought up among the people of Bangu, but who at his summons had come back to Saduko. It was on these men that we relied at this juncture, for they alone knew the country. Long and anxiously did we consult with them. First they explained, and, so far as the moonlight would allow, for as yet the dawn had not broken, pointed out to us the various paths that led to Bangu's kraal.

"How many men are there in the town?" I asked.

"About seven hundred who carry spears," they answered, "together with others in outlying kraals. Moreover, watchmen are always set at the gateways in the walls."

"And where are the cattle?" I asked again.

"Here, in the valley beneath, Macumazahn," answered the spokesman. "If you listen you will hear them lowing. Fifty men, not less, watch them at night—two thousand head of them, or more."

"Then it would not be difficult to get round these cattle and drive them off, leaving Bangu to breed up a new herd?"

"It might not be difficult," interrupted Saduko, "but I came here to kill Bangu, as well as to seize his cattle, since with him I have a blood feud."

"Very good," I answered; "but that mountain cannot be stormed with three hundred men, fortified as it is with walls and schanzes. Our band would be destroyed before ever we came to the kraal, since, owing to the sentries who are set everywhere, it would be impossible to surprise the place. Also you have forgotten the dogs, Saduko. Moreover, even if it were possible, I will have nothing to do with the massacre of women and children, which must happen in an assault. Now, listen to me, O Saduko. I say let us leave the kraal of Bangu alone, and this coming night send fifty of our men, under the leadership of the guides, down to yonder bush, where they will lie hid. Then, after moonrise, when all are asleep, these fifty must rush the cattle kraal, killing any who may oppose them, should they be seen, and driving the herd out through yonder great pass by which we have entered the land. Bangu and his people, thinking that those who have taken the cattle are but common thieves of some wild tribe, will gather and follow the beasts to recapture them. But we, with the rest of the Amangwane, can set an ambush in the narrowest part of the pass among the rocks, where the grass is high and the euphorbia trees grow thick, and there, when they have passed the Nek, which I and my hunters will hold with our guns, we will give them battle. What say you?"

Now, Saduko answered that he would rather attack the kraal, which he wished to burn. But the old Amangwane, Tshoza, brother of the dead Matiwane, said:

"No, Macumazahn, Watcher-by-Night, is wise. Why should we waste our strength on stone walls, of which none know the number or can find the gates in the darkness, and thereby leave our skulls to be set up as ornaments on the fences of the accursed Amakoba? Let us draw the Amakoba out into the pass of the mountains, where they have no walls to protect them, and there fall on them when they are bewildered and settle the matter with them man to man. As for the women and children, with Macumazahn I say let them go; afterwards, perhaps, they will become our women and children."

"Aye," answered the Amangwane, "the plan of the white Inkoosi is good; he is clever as a weasel; we will have his plan and no other."

So Saduko was overruled and my counsel adopted.

All that day we rested, lighting no fires and remaining still as the dead in the dense bush. It was a very anxious day, for although the place was so wild and lonely, there was always the fear lest we should be discovered. It was true that we had travelled mostly by night in small parties, to avoid leaving a spoor, and avoided all kraals; still, some rumour of our approach might have reached the Amakoba, or a party of hunters might stumble on us, or those who sought for lost cattle.

Indeed, something of this sort did happen, for about midday we heard a footfall, and perceived the figure of a man, whom by his head-dress we knew for an Amakoba, threading his way through the bush. Before he saw us he was in our midst. For a moment he hesitated ere he turned to fly, and that moment was his last, for three of the Amangwane leapt on him silently as leopards leap upon a buck, and where he stood there he died. Poor fellow! Evidently he had been on a visit to some witch-doctor, for in his blanket we found medicine and love charms. This doctor cannot have been one of the stamp of Zikali the Dwarf, I thought to myself; at least, he had not warned him that he would never live to dose his beloved with that foolish medicine.

Meanwhile a few of us who had the quickest eyes climbed trees, and thence watched the town of Bangu and the valley that lay between us and it. Soon we saw that so far, at any rate, Fortune was playing into our hands, since herd after herd of kine were driven into the valley during the afternoon and enclosed in the stock-kraals. Doubtless Bangu intended on the morrow to make his half-yearly inspection of all the cattle of the tribe, many of which were herded at a distance from his town.

At length the long day drew to its close and the shadows of the evening thickened. Then we made ready for our dreadful game, of which the stake was the lives of all of us, since, should we fail, we could expect no mercy. The fifty picked men were gathered and ate food in silence. These men were placed under the command of Tshoza, for he was the most experienced of the Amangwane, and led by the three guides who had dwelt among the Amakoba, and who "knew every ant-heap in the land," or so they swore. Their duty, it will be remembered, was to cross the valley, separate themselves into small parties, unbar the various cattle kraals, kill or hunt off the herdsmen, and drive the beasts back across the valley into the pass. A second fifty men, under the command of Saduko, were to be left just at the end of this pass where it opened out into the valley, in order to help and reinforce the cattle-lifters, or, if need be, to check the following Amakoba while the great herds of beasts were got away, and then fall back on the rest of us in our ambush nearly two miles distant. The management of this ambush was to be my charge—a heavy one indeed.

Now, the moon would not be up till midnight. But two hours before that time we began our moves, since the cattle must be driven out of the kraals as soon as she appeared and gave the needful light. Otherwise the fight in the pass would in all probability be delayed till after sunrise, when the Amakoba would see how small was the number of their foes. Terror, doubt, darkness—these must be our allies if our desperate venture was to succeed.

All was arranged at last and the time had come. We, the three captains of our divided force, bade each other farewell, and passed the word down the ranks that, should we be separated by the accidents of war, my wagons were the meeting-place of any who survived.

Tshoza and his fifty glided away into the shadow silently as ghosts and were gone. Presently the fierce-faced Saduko departed also with his fifty. He carried the double-barrelled gun I had given him, and was accompanied by one of my best hunters, a Natal native, who was also armed with a heavy smooth-bore loaded with slugs. Our hope was that the sound of these guns might terrify the foe, should there be occasion to use them before our forces joined up again, and make them think they had to do with a body of raiding Dutch white men, of whose roers—as the heavy elephant guns of that day were called— all natives were much afraid.

So Saduko went with his fifty, leaving me wondering whether I should ever see his face again. Then I, my bearer Scowl, the two remaining hunters, and the ten score Amangwane who were left turned and soon were following the road by which we had come down the rugged pass. I call it a road, but, in fact, it was nothing but a water-washed gully strewn with boulders, through which we must pick our way as best we could in the darkness, having first removed the percussion cap from the nipple of every gun, for fear lest the accidental discharge of one of them should warn the Amakoba, confuse our other parties, and bring all our deep-laid plans to nothing.

Well, we accomplished that march somehow, walking in three long lines, so that each man might keep touch with him in front, and just as the moon began to rise reached the spot that I had chosen for the ambush.

Certainly it was well suited to that purpose. Here the track or gully bed narrowed to a width of not more than a hundred feet, while the steep slopes of the kloof on either side were clothed with scattered bushes and finger-like euphorbias which grew among stones. Behind these stones and bushes we hid ourselves, a hundred men on one side and a hundred on the other, whilst I and my three hunters, who were armed with guns, took up a position under shelter of a great boulder nearly five feet thick that lay but a little to the right of the gully itself, up which we expected the cattle would come. This place I chose for two reasons: first, that I might keep touch with both wings of my force, and, secondly, that we might be able to fire straight down the path on the pursuing Amakoba.

These were the orders that I gave to the Amangwane, warning them that he who disobeyed would be punished with death. They were not to stir until I, or, if I should be killed, one of my hunters, fired a shot; for my fear was lest, growing excited, they might leap out before the time and kill some of our own people, who very likely would be mixed up with the first of the pursuing Amakoba. Secondly, when the cattle had passed and the signal had been given, they were to rush on the Amakoba, throwing themselves across the gully, so that the enemy would have to fight upwards on a steep slope.

That was all I told them, since it is not wise to confuse natives by giving too many orders. One thing I added, however—that they must conquer or they must die. There was no mercy for them; it was a case of death or victory. Their spokesman—for these people always find a spokesman—answered that they thanked me for my advice; that they understood, and that they would do their best. Then they lifted their spears to me in salute. A wild lot of men they looked in the moonlight as they departed to take shelter behind the rocks and trees and wait.

That waiting was long, and I confess that before the end it got upon my nerves. I began to think of all sorts of things, such as whether I should live to see the sun rise again; also I reflected upon the legitimacy of this remarkable enterprise. What right had I to involve myself in a quarrel between these savages?

Why had I come here? To gain cattle as a trader? No, for I was not at all sure that I would take them if gained. Because Saduko had twitted me with faithlessness to my words? Yes, to a certain extent; but that was by no means the whole reason. I had been moved by the recital of the cruel wrongs inflicted upon Saduko and his tribe by this Bangu, and therefore had not been loath to associate myself with his attempted vengeance upon a wicked murderer. Well, that was sound enough so far as it went; but now a new consideration suggested itself to me. Those wrongs had been worked many years ago; probably most of the men who had aided and abetted them by now were dead or very aged, and it was their sons upon whom the vengeance would be wreaked.

What right had I to assist in visiting the sins of the fathers upon the sons? Frankly I could not say. The thing seemed to me to be a part of the problem of life, neither less nor more. So I shrugged my shoulders sadly and consoled myself by reflecting that very likely the issue would go against me, and that my own existence would pay the price of the venture and expound its moral. This consideration soothed my conscience somewhat, for when a man backs his actions with the risk of his life, right or wrong, at any rate he plays no coward's part.

The time went by very slowly and nothing happened. The waning moon shone brightly in a clear sky, and as there was no wind the silence seemed peculiarly intense. Save for the laugh of an occasional hyena and now and again for a sound which I took for the coughing of a distant lion, there was no stir between sleeping earth and moonlit heaven in which little clouds floated beneath the pale stars.

At length I thought that I heard a noise, a kind of murmur far away. It grew, it developed.

It sounded like a thousand sticks tapping upon something hard, very faintly. It continued to grow, and I knew the sound for that of the beating hoofs of animals galloping. Then there were isolated noises, very faint and thin; they might be shouts; then something that I could not mistake—shots fired at a distance. So the business was afoot; the cattle were moving, Saduko and my hunter were firing. There was nothing for it but to wait.

The excitement was very fierce; it seemed to consume me, to eat into my brain. The sound of the tapping upon the rocks grew louder until it merged into a kind of rumble, mixed with an echo as of that of very distant thunder, which presently I knew to be not thunder, but the bellowing of a thousand frightened beasts.

Nearer and nearer came the galloping hoofs and the rumble of bellowings; nearer and nearer the shouts of men, affronting the stillness of the solemn night. At length a single animal appeared, a koodoo buck that somehow had got mixed up with the cattle. It went past us like a flash, and was followed a minute or so later by a bull that, being young and light, had outrun its companions. That, too, went by, foam on its lips and its tongue hanging from its jaws.

Then the herd appeared—a countless herd it seemed to me—plunging up the incline—cows, heifers, calves, bulls, and oxen, all mixed together in one inextricable mass, and every one of them snorting, bellowing, or making some other kind of sound. The din was fearful, the sight bewildering, for the beasts were of all colours, and their long horns flashed like ivory in the moonlight. Indeed, the only thing in the least like it which I have ever seen was the rush of the buffaloes from the reed camp on that day when I got my injury.

They were streaming past us now, a mighty and moving mass so closely packed that a man might have walked upon their backs. In fact, some of the calves which had been thrust up by the pressure were being carried along in this fashion. Glad was I that none of us were in their path, for their advance seemed irresistible. No fence or wall could have saved us, and even stout trees that grew in the gully were snapped or thrust over.

At length the long line began to thin, for now it was composed of stragglers and weak or injured beasts, of which there were many. Other sounds, too, began to dominate the bellowings of the animals, those of the excited cries of men. The first of our companions, the cattle-lifters, appeared, weary and gasping, but waving their spears in triumph. Among them was old Tshoza. I stepped upon my rock, calling to him by name. He heard me, and presently was lying at my side panting.

"We have got them all!" he gasped. "Not a hoof is left save those that are trodden down. Saduko is not far behind with the rest of our brothers, except some that have been killed. All the Amakoba tribe are after us. He holds them back to give the cattle time to get away."

"Well done!" I answered. "It is very good. Now make your men hide among the others that they may find their breath before the fight."

So he stopped them as they came. Scarcely had the last of them vanished into the bushes when the gathering volume of shouts, amongst which I heard a gun go off, told us that Saduko and his band and the pursuing Amakoba were not far away. Presently they, too, appeared—that is the handful of Amangwane did—not fighting now, but running as hard as they could, for they knew they were approaching the ambush and wished to pass it so as not to be mixed up with the Amakoba. We let them go through us. Among the last of them came Saduko, who was wounded, for the blood ran down his side, supporting my hunter, who was also wounded, more severely as I feared.

I called to him.

"Saduko," I said, "halt at the crest of the path and rest there so that you may be able to help us presently."

He waved the gun in answer, for he was too breathless to speak, and went on with those who were left of his following—perhaps thirty men in all—in the track of the cattle. Before he was out of sight the Amakoba arrived, a mob of five or six hundred men mixed up together and advancing without order or discipline, for they seemed to have lost their heads as well as their cattle. Some of them had shields and some had none, some broad and some throwing assegais, while many were quite naked, not having stayed to put on their moochas and much less their war finery. Evidently they were mad with rage, for the sounds that issued from them seemed to concentrate into one mighty curse.

The moment had come, though to tell the truth I heartily wished that it had not. I wasn't exactly afraid, although I never set up for great courage, but I did not quite like the business. After all we were stealing these people's cattle, and now were going to kill as many of them as we could. I had to recall Saduko's dreadful story of the massacre of his tribe before I could make up my mind to give the signal. That hardened me, and so did the reflection that after all they outnumbered us enormously and very likely would prove victors in the end. Anyhow it was too late to repent. What a tricky and uncomfortable thing is conscience, that nearly always begins to trouble us at the moment of, or after, the event, not before, when it might be of some use.

I raised myself upon the rock and fired both barrels of my gun into the advancing horde, though whether I killed anyone or no I cannot say. I have always hoped that I did not; but as the mark was large and I am a fair shot, I fear that is scarcely possible. Next moment, with a howl that sounded like that of wild beasts, from either side of the gorge the fierce Amangwane free-spears—for that is what they were—leapt out of their hiding-places and hurled themselves upon their hereditary foes. They were fighting for more than cattle; they were fighting for hate and for revenge since these Amakoba had slaughtered their fathers and their mothers, their sisters and their brothers, and they alone remained to pay them back blood for blood.

Great heaven! how they did fight, more like devils than human beings. After that first howl which shaped itself to the word "Saduko," they were silent as bulldogs. Though they were so few, at first their terrible rush drove back the Amakoba. Then, as these recovered from their surprise, the weight of numbers began to tell, for they, too, were brave men who did not give way to panic. Scores of them went down at once, but the remainder pushed the Amangwane before them up the hill. I took little share in the fight, but was thrust backward with the others, only firing when I was obliged to save my own life. Foot by foot we were pushed back till at length we drew near to the crest of the pass.

Then, while the issue hung in the balance, there was another shout of "Saduko!" and that chief himself, followed by his thirty, rushed upon the Amakoba.

This charge decided the battle, for not knowing how many more were coming, those who were left of the Amakoba turned and fled, nor did we pursue them far.

We mustered on the hill-top, not more than two hundred of us now, the rest were fallen or desperately wounded, my poor hunter, whom I had lent to Saduko, being among the dead. Although wounded, he died fighting to the last, then fell down, shouting to me:

"Chief, have I done well?" and expired.

I was breathless and spent, but as in a dream I saw some Amangwane drag up a gaunt old savage, crying:

"Here is Bangu, Bangu the Butcher, whom we have caught alive."

Saduko stepped up to him.

"Ah! Bangu," he said, "now say, why should I not kill you as you would have killed the little lad Saduko long ago, had not Zikali saved him? See, here is the mark of your spear."

"Kill," said Bangu. "Your Spirit is stronger than mine. Did not Zikali foretell it? Kill, Saduko."

"Nay," answered Saduko. "If you are weary I am weary, too, and wounded as well. Take a spear, Bangu, and we will fight."

So they fought there in the moonlight, man to man; fought fiercely while all watched, till presently I saw Bangu throw his arms wide and fall backwards.

Saduko was avenged. I have always been glad that he slew his enemy thus, and not as it might have been expected that he would do.

CHAPTER VII

SADUKO BRINGS THE MARRIAGE GIFT

We reached my wagons in the early morning of the following day, bringing with us the cattle and our wounded. Thus encumbered it was a most toilsome march, and an anxious one also, for it was always possible that the remnant of the Amakoba might attempt pursuit. This, however, they did not do, for very many of them were dead or wounded, and those who remained had no heart left in them. They went back to their mountain home and lived there in shame and wretchedness, for I do not believe there were fifty head of cattle left among the tribe, and Kafirs without cattle are nothing. Still, they did not starve, since there were plenty of women to work the fields, and we had not touched their corn. The end of them was that Panda gave them to their conqueror, Saduko, and he incorporated them with the Amangwane. But that did not happen until some time afterwards.

When we had rested a while at the wagons the captured beasts were mustered, and on being counted were found to number a little over twelve hundred head, not reckoning animals that had been badly hurt in the flight, which we killed for beef. It was a noble prize, truly, and, notwithstanding the wound in his thigh, which hurt him a good deal now that it had stiffened, Saduko stood up and surveyed them with glistening eyes. No wonder, for he who had been so poor was now rich, and would remain so even after he had paid over whatever number of cows Umbezi chose to demand as the price of Mameena's hand. Moreover, he was sure, and I shared his confidence, that in these changed circumstances both that young woman and her father would look upon his suit with very favourable eyes. He had, so to speak, succeeded to the title and the family estates by means of a lawsuit brought in the "Court of the Assegai," and therefore there was hardly a father in Zululand who would shut his kraal gate upon him. We forgot, both of us, the proverb that points out how numerous are the slips between the cup and the lip, which, by the way, is one that has its Zulu equivalents. One of them, if I remember right at the moment, is: "However loud the hen cackles, the housewife does not always get the egg."

As it chanced, although Saduko's hen was cackling very loudly just at this time, he was not destined to find the coveted egg. But of that matter I will speak in its place.

I, too, looked at those cattle, wondering whether Saduko would remember our bargain, under which some six hundred head of them belonged to me. Six hundred head! Why, putting them at £5 apiece all round—and as oxen were very scarce just at that time, they were worth quite as much, if not more—that meant £3,000, a larger sum of money than I had ever owned at one time in all my life. Truly the paths of violence were profitable! But would he remember? On the whole I thought probably not, since Kafirs are not fond of parting with cattle.

Well, I did him an injustice, for presently he turned and said, with something of an effort:

"Macumazahn, half of all these belong to you, and truly you have earned them, for it was your cunning and good counsel that gained us the victory. Now we will choose them beast by beast."

So I chose a fine ox, then Saduko chose one; and so it went on till I had eight of my number driven out. As the eighth was taken I turned to Saduko and said:

"There, that will do. These oxen I must have to replace those in my teams which died on the trek, but I want no more."

"Wow!" said Saduko, and all those who stood with him, while one of them added—I think it was old Tshoza:

"He refuses six hundred cattle which are fairly his! He must be mad!"

"No friends," I answered, "I am not mad, but neither am I bad. I accompanied Saduko on this raid because he is dear to me and stood by me once in the hour of danger. But I do not love killing men with whom I have no quarrel, and I will not take the price of blood."

"Wow!" said old Tshoza again, for Saduko seemed too astonished to speak, "he is a spirit, not a man. He is holy!"

"Not a bit of it," I answered. "If you think that, ask Mameena"—a dark saying which they did not understand. "Now, listen. I will not take those cattle because I do not think as you Kafirs think. But as they are mine, according to your law, I am going to dispose of them. I give ten head to each of my hunters, and fifteen head to the relations of him who was killed. The rest I give to Tshoza and to the other men of the Amangwane who fought with us, to be divided among them in such proportions as they may agree, I being the judge in the event of any quarrel arising."

Now these men raised a great cry of "Inkoosi!" and, running up, old Tshoza seized my hand and kissed it.

"Your heart is big," he cried; "you drop fatness! Although you are so small, the spirit of a king lives in you, and the wisdom of the heavens."

Thus he praised me, while all the others joined in, till the din was awful. Saduko thanked me also in his magnificent manner. Yet I do not think that he was altogether pleased, although my great gift relieved him from the necessity of sharing up the spoil with his companions. The truth was, or so I believe, that he understood that henceforth the Amangwane would love me better than they loved him. This, indeed, proved to be the case, for I am sure that there was no man among all those wild fellows who would not have served me to the death, and to this day my name is a power among them and their descendants. Also it has grown into something of a proverb among all those Kafirs who know the story. They talk of any great act of liberality in an idiom as "a gift of Macumazana," and in the same way of one who makes any remarkable renunciation, as "a wearer of Macumazana's blanket," or as "he who has stolen Macumazana's shadow."

Thus did I earn a great reputation very cheaply, for really I could not have taken those cattle; also I am sure that had I done so they would have brought me bad luck. Indeed, one of the regrets of my life is that I had anything whatsoever to do with the business.

Our journey back to Umbezi's kraal—for thither we were heading—was very slow, hampered as we were with wounded and by a vast herd of cattle. Of the latter, indeed, we got rid after a while, for, except those which I had given to my men, and a hundred or so of the best beasts that Saduko took with him for a certain purpose, they were sent away to a place which he had chosen, in charge of about half of his people, under the command of his uncle, Tshoza, there to await his coming.

Over a month had gone by since the night of the ambush when at last we outspanned quite close to Umbezi's, in that bush where first I had met the Amangwane free-spears. A very different set of men they looked on this triumphant day to those fierce fellows who had slipped out of the trees at the call of their chief. As we went through the country Saduko had bought fine moochas and blankets for them; also head-dresses had been made with the long black feathers of the sakabuli finch, and shields and leglets of the hides and tails of oxen. Moreover, having fed plentifully and travelled easily, they were fat and well-favoured, as, given good food, natives soon become after a period of abstinence.

The plan of Saduko was to lie quiet in the bush that night, and on the following morning to advance in all his grandeur, accompanied by his spears, present the hundred head of cattle that had been demanded, and formally ask his daughter's hand from Umbezi. As the reader may have gathered already, there was a certain histrionic vein in Saduko; also when he was in feather he liked to show off his plumage.

Well, this plan was carried out to the letter. On the following morning, after the sun was well up, Saduko, as a great chief does, sent forward two bedizened heralds to announce his approach to Umbezi, after whom followed two other men to sing his deeds and praises. (By the way, I observed that they had clearly been instructed to avoid any mention of a person called Macumazahn.) Then we advanced in force. First went Saduko, splendidly apparelled as a chief, carrying a small assegai and adorned with plumes, leglets and a leopard-skin kilt. He was attended by about half a dozen of the best-looking of his followers, who posed as "indunas" or councillors. Behind these I walked, a dusty, insignificant little fellow, attended by the ugly, snub-nosed Scowl in a very greasy pair of trousers, worn-out European boots through which his toes peeped, and nothing else, and by my three surviving hunters, whose appearance was even more disreputable. After us marched about four score of the transformed Amangwane, and after them came the hundred picked cattle driven by a few herdsmen.

In due course we arrived at the gate of the kraal, where we found the heralds and the praisers prancing and shouting.

"Have you seen Umbezi?" asked Saduko of them.

"No," they answered; "he was asleep when we got here, but his people say that he is coming out presently."

"Then tell his people that he had better be quick about it, or I shall turn him out," replied the proud Saduko.

Just at this moment the kraal gate opened and through it appeared Umbezi, looking extremely fat and foolish; also, it struck me, frightened, although this he tried to conceal.

"Who visits me here," he said, "with so much—um—ceremony?" and with the carved dancing-stick he carried he pointed doubtfully at the lines of armed men. "Oh, it is you, is it, Saduko?" and he looked him up and down, adding: "How grand you are to be sure. Have you been robbing anybody? And you, too, Macumazahn. Well, you do not look grand. You look like an old cow that has been suckling two calves on the winter veld. But tell me, what are all these warriors for? I ask because I have not food for so many, especially as we have just had a feast here."

"Fear nothing, Umbezi," answered Saduko in his grandest manner. "I have brought food for my own men. As for my business, it is simple. You asked a hundred head of cattle as the lobola [that is, the marriage gift] of your daughter, Mameena. They are there. Go send your servants to the kraal and count them."

"Oh, with pleasure," Umbezi replied nervously, and he gave some orders to certain men behind him. "I am glad to see that you have become rich in this sudden fashion, Saduko, though how you have done so I cannot understand."

"Never mind how I have become rich," answered Saduko. "I am rich; that is enough for the present. Be pleased to send for Mameena, for I would talk with her."

"Yes, yes, Saduko, I understand that you would talk with Mameena; but"—and he looked round him desperately—"I fear that she is still asleep. As you know, Mameena was always a late riser, and, what is more, she hates to be disturbed. Don't you think that you could come back, say, to-morrow morning? She will be sure to be up by then; or, better still, the day after?"

"In which hut is Mameena?" asked Saduko sternly, while I, smelling a rat, began to chuckle to myself.

"I really do not know, Saduko," replied Umbezi. "Sometimes she sleeps in one, sometimes in another, and sometimes she goes several hours' journey away to her aunt's kraal for a change. I should not be in the least surprised if she had done so last night. I have no control over Mameena."

Before Saduko could answer, a shrill, rasping voice broke upon our ears, which after some search I saw proceeded from an ugly and ancient female seated in the shadow, in whom I recognised the lady who was known by the pleasing name of "Worn-out-Old-Cow."

"He lies!" screeched the voice. "He lies. Thanks be to the spirit of my ancestors that wild cat Mameena has left this kraal for good. She slept last night, not with her aunt, but with her husband, Masapo, to whom Umbezi gave her in marriage two days ago, receiving in payment a hundred and twenty head of cattle, which was twenty more than you bid, Saduko."

Now when Saduko heard these words I thought that he would really go mad with rage. He turned quite grey under his dark skin and for a while trembled like a leaf, looking as though he were about to fall to the ground. Then he leapt as a lion leaps, and seizing Umbezi by the throat, hurled him backwards, standing over him with raised spear.

"You dog!" he cried in a terrible voice. "Tell me the truth or I will rip you up. What have you done with Mameena?"

"Oh! Saduko," answered Umbezi in choking tones, "Mameena has chosen to get married. It was no fault of mine; she would have her way."

He got no farther, and had I not intervened by throwing my arms about Saduko and dragging him back, that moment would have been Umbezi's last, for Saduko was about to pin him to the earth with his spear. As it proved, I was just in time, and Saduko, being weak with emotion, for I felt his heart going like a sledge-hammer, could not break from my grasp before his reason returned to him.

At length he recovered himself a little and threw down his spear as though to put himself out of temptation. Then he spoke, always in the same terrible voice, asking:

"Have you more to say about this business, Umbezi? I would hear all before I answer you."

"Only this, Saduko," replied Umbezi, who had risen to his feet and was shaking like a reed. "I did no more than any other father would have done. Masapo is a very powerful chief, one who will be a good stick for me to lean on in my old age. Mameena declared that she wished to marry him—"

"He lies!" screeched the "Old Cow." "What Mameena said was that she had no will towards marriage with any Zulu in the land, so I suppose she is looking after a white man," and she leered in my direction. "She said, however, that if her father wished to marry her to Masapo, she must be a dutiful daughter and obey him, but that if blood and trouble came of that marriage, let it be on his head and not on hers."

"Would you also stick your claws into me, cat?" shouted Umbezi, catching the old woman a savage cut across the back with the light dancing-stick which he still held in his hand, whereon she fled away screeching and cursing him.

"Oh, Saduko," he went on, "let not your ears be poisoned by these falsehoods. Mameena never said anything of the sort, or if she did it was not to me. Well, the moment that my daughter had consented to take Masapo as her husband his people drove a hundred and twenty of the most beautiful cattle over the hill, and would you have had me refuse them, Saduko? I am sure that when you have seen them you will say that I was quite right to accept such a splendid lobola in return for one sharp-tongued girl. Remember, Saduko, that although you had promised a hundred head, that is less by twenty, at the time you did not own one, and where you were to get them from I could not guess. Moreover," he added with a last, desperate, imaginative effort, for I think he saw that his arguments were making no impression, "some strangers who called here told me that both you and Macumazahn had been killed by certain evil-doers in the mountains. There, I have spoken, and, Saduko, if you now have cattle, why, on my part, I have another daughter, not quite so good-looking perhaps, but a much better worker in the field. Come and drink a sup of beer, and I will send for her."

"Stop talking about your other daughter and your beer and listen to me," replied Saduko, looking at the assegai which he had thrown to the ground so ominously that I set my foot on it. "I am now a greater chief than the boar Masapo. Has Masapo such a bodyguard as these Eaters-up-of-Enemies?" and he jerked his thumb backwards towards the serried lines of fierce-faced Amangwane who stood listening behind us. "Has Masapo as many cattle as I have, whereof those which you see are but a tithe brought as a lobola gift to the father of her who had been promised to me as wife? Is Masapo Panda's friend? I think that I have heard otherwise. Has Masapo just conquered a countless tribe by his courage and his wit? Is Masapo young and of high blood, or is he but an old, low-born boar of the mountains?

"You do not answer, Umbezi, and perhaps you do well to be silent. Now listen again. Were it not for Macumazahn here, whom I do not desire to mix up with my quarrels, I would bid my men take you and beat you to death with the handles of their spears, and then go on and serve the Boar in the same fashion in his mountain sty. As it is, these things must wait a little while, especially as I have other matters to attend to first. Yet the day is not far off when I will attend to them also. Therefore my counsel to you, Cheat, is to make haste to die or to find courage to fall upon a spear, unless you would learn how it feels to be brayed with sticks like a green hide until none can know that you were once a man. Send now and tell my words to Masapo the Boar. And to Mameena say that soon I will come to take her with spears and not with cattle. Do you understand? Oh! I see that you do, since already you weep with fear like a woman. Then farewell to you till that day when I return with the sticks, O Umbezi the cheat and the liar, Umbezi, 'Eater-up-of-Elephants,'" and turning, Saduko stalked away.

I was about to follow in a great hurry, having had enough of this very unpleasant scene, when poor old Umbezi sprang at me and clasped me by the arm.

"O Macumazana," he exclaimed, weeping in his terror, "O Macumazana, if ever I have been a friend to you, help me out of this deep pit into which I have fallen through the tricks of that monkey of a daughter of mine, who I think is a witch born to bring trouble upon men. Macumazahn, if she had been your daughter and a powerful chief had appeared with a hundred and twenty head of such beautiful cattle, you would have given her to him, would you not, although he is of mixed blood and not very young, especially as she did not mind who only cares for place and wealth?"

"I think not," I answered; "but then it is not our custom to sell women in that fashion."

"No, no, I forgot; in this as in other matters you white men are mad and, Macumazahn, to tell you the truth, I believe it is you she really cares for; she said as much to me once or twice. Well, why did you not take her away when I was not looking? We could have settled matters afterwards, and I should have been free of her witcheries and not up to my neck in this hole as I am now."

"Because some people don't do that kind of thing, Umbezi."

"No, no, I forgot. Oh! why can I not remember that you are quite mad and therefore that it must not be expected of you to act as though you were sane. Well, at least you are that tiger Saduko's friend, which again shows that you must be very mad, for most people would sooner try to milk a cow buffalo than walk hand in hand with him. Don't you see, Macumazahn, that he means to kill me, Macumazahn, to bray me like a green hide? Ugh! to beat me to death with sticks. Ugh! And what is more, that unless you prevent him, he will certainly do it, perhaps to-morrow or the next day. Ugh! Ugh! Ugh!"

"Yes, I see, Umbezi, and I think that he will do it. But what I do not see is how I am to prevent him. Remember that you let Mameena grow into his heart and behaved badly to him, Umbezi."

"I never promised her to him, Macumazahn. I only said that if he brought a hundred cattle, then I might promise."

"Well, he has wiped out the Amakoba, the enemies of his House, and there are the hundred cattle whereof he has many more, and now it is too late for you to keep your share of the bargain. So I think you must make yourself as comfortable as you can in the hole that your hands dug, Umbezi, which I would not share for all the cattle in Zululand."

"Truly you are not one from whom to seek comfort in the hour of distress," groaned poor Umbezi, then added, brightening up: "But perhaps Panda will kill him because he has wiped out Bangu in a time of peace. Oh Macumazahn, can you not persuade Panda to kill him? If so, I now have more cattle than I really want—"

"Impossible," I answered. "Panda is his friend, and between ourselves I may tell you that he ate up the Amakoba by his especial wish. When the King hears of it he will call to Saduko to sit in his shadow and make him great, one of his councillors, probably with power of life and death over little people like you and Masapo."

"Then it is finished," said Umbezi faintly, "and I will try to die like a man. But to be brayed like a hide! And with thin sticks! Oh!" he added, grinding his teeth, "if only I can get hold of Mameena I will not leave much of that pretty hair of hers upon her head. I will tie her hands and shut her up with the 'Old Cow,' who loves her as a meer-cat loves a mouse. No; I will kill her. There—do you hear, Macumazahn, unless you do something to help me, I will kill Mameena, and you won't like that, for I am sure she is dear to you, although you were not man enough to run away with her as she wished."

"If you touch Mameena," I said, "be certain, my friend, that Saduko's sticks and your skin will not be far apart, for I will report you to Panda myself as an unnatural evil-doer. Now hearken to me, you old fool. Saduko is so fond of your daughter, on this point being mad, as you say I am, that if only he could get her I think he might overlook the fact of her having been married before. What you have to do is to try to buy her back from Masapo. Mind you, I say buy her back—not get her by bloodshed—which you might do by persuading Masapo to put her away. Then, if he knew that you were trying to do this, I think that Saduko might leave his sticks uncut for a while."

"I will try. I will indeed, Macumazahn. I will try very hard. It is true Masapo is an obstinate pig; still, if he knows that his own life is at stake, he might give way. Moreover, when she learns that Saduko has grown rich and great, Mameena might help me. Oh, I thank you, Macumazahn; you are indeed the prop of my hut, and it and all in it are yours. Farewell, farewell, Macumazahn, if you must go. But why—why did you not run away with Mameena, and save me all this fear and trouble?"

So I and that old humbug, Umbezi, "Eater-up-of-Elephants," parted for a while, and never did I know him in a more chastened frame of mind, except once, as I shall tell.

CHAPTER VIII

THE KING'S DAUGHTER

When I got back to my wagons after this semi-tragical interview with that bombastic and self-seeking old windbag, Umbezi, it was to find that Saduko and his warriors had already marched for the King's kraal, Nodwengu. A message awaited me, however, to the effect that it was hoped that I would follow, in order to make report of the affair of the destruction of the Amakoba. This, after reflection, I determined to do, really, I think, because of the intense human interest of the whole business. I wanted to see how it would work out.

Also, in a way, I read Saduko's mind and understood that at the moment he did not wish to discuss the matter of his hideous disappointment. Whatever else may have been false in this man's nature, one thing rang true, namely, his love or his infatuation for the girl Mameena. Throughout his life she was his guiding star—about as evil a star as could have arisen upon any man's horizon; the fatal star that was to light him down to doom. Let me thank Providence, as I do, that I was so fortunate as to escape its baneful influences, although I admit that they attracted me not a little.

So, seduced thither by my curiosity, which has so often led me into trouble, I trekked to Nodwengu, full of many doubts not unmingled with amusement, for I could not rid my mind of recollections of the utter terror of the "Eater-up-of-Elephants" when he was brought face to face with the dreadful and concentrated rage of the robbed Saduko and the promise of his vengeance. Ultimately I arrived at the

Great Place without experiencing any adventure that is worthy of record, and camped in a spot that was appointed to me by some induna whose name I forget, but who evidently knew of my approach, for I found him awaiting me at some distance from the town. Here I sat for quite a long while, two or three days, if I remember right, amusing myself with killing or missing turtle-doves with a shotgun, and similar pastimes, until something should happen, or I grew tired and started for Natal.

In the end, just as I was about to trek seawards, an old friend, Maputa, turned up at my wagons—that same man who had brought me the message from Panda before we started to attack Bangu.

"Greeting, Macumazahn," he said. "What of the Amakoba? I see they did not kill you."

"No," I answered, handing him some snuff, "they did not quite kill me, for here I am. What is your pleasure with me?"

"O Macumazana, only that the King wishes to know whether you have any of those little balls left in the box which I brought back to you, since, if so, he thinks he would like to swallow one of them in this hot weather."

I proffered him the whole box, but he would not take it, saying that the King would like me to give it to him myself. Now I understood that this was a summons to an audience, and asked when it would please Panda to receive me and "the-little-black-stones-that-work-wonders." He answered—at once.

So we started, and within an hour I stood, or rather sat, before Panda.

Like all his family, the King was an enormous man, but, unlike Chaka and those of his brothers whom I had known, one of a kindly countenance. I saluted him by lifting my cap, and took my place upon a wooden stool that had been provided for me outside the great hut, in the shadow of which he sat within his isi-gohlo, or private enclosure.

"Greeting, O Macumazana," he said. "I am glad to see you safe and well, for I understand that you have been engaged upon a perilous adventure since last we met."

"Yes, King," I answered; "but to which adventure do you refer—that of the buffalo, when Saduko helped me, or that of the Amakoba, when I helped Saduko?"

"The latter, Macumazahn, of which I desire to hear all the story."

So I told it to him, he and I being alone, for he commanded his councillors and servants to retire out of hearing.

"Wow!" he said, when I had finished, "you are clever as a baboon, Macumazahn. That was a fine trick to set a trap for Bangu and his Amakoba dogs and bait it with his own cattle. But they tell me that you refused your share of those cattle. Now, why was that, Macumazahn?"

By way of answer I repeated to Panda my reasons, which I have set out already.

"Ah!" he exclaimed, when I had finished. "Every one seeks greatness in his own way, and perhaps yours is better than ours. Well, the White man walks one road—or some of them do—and the Black man another. They both end at the same place, and none will know which is the right road till the journey is done. Meanwhile, what you lose Saduko and his people gain. He is a wise man, Saduko, who knows how to choose his friends, and his wisdom has brought him victory and gifts. But to you, Macumazahn, it has brought nothing but honour, on which, if a man feeds only, he will grow thin."

"I like to be thin, O Panda," I answered slowly.

"Yes, yes, I understand," replied the King, who, in common with most natives, was quick enough to seize a point, "and I, too, like people who keep thin on such food as yours, people, also, whose hands are always clean. We Zulus trust you, Macumazahn, as we trust few white men, for we have known for years that your lips say what your heart thinks, and that your heart always thinks the thing which is good. You may be named Watcher-by-Night, but you love light, not darkness."

Now, at these somewhat unusual compliments I bowed, and felt myself colouring a little as I did so, even through my sunburn, but I made no answer to them, since to do so would have involved a discussion of the past and its tragical events, into which I had no wish to enter. Panda, too, remained silent for a while. Then he called to a messenger to summon the princes, Cetewayo and Umbelazi, and to bid Saduko, the son of Matiwane, to wait without, in case he should wish to speak with him.

A few minutes later the two princes arrived. I watched their coming with interest, for they were the most important men in Zululand, and already the nation debated fiercely which of them would succeed to the throne. I will try to describe them a little.

They were both of much the same age—it is always difficult to arrive at a Zulu's exact years—and both fine young men. Cetewayo, however, had the stronger countenance. It was said that he resembled that fierce and able monster, Chaka the Wild Beast, his uncle, and certainly I perceived in him a likeness to his other uncle, Dingaan, Umpanda's predecessor, whom I had known but too well when I was a lad. He had the same surly eyes and haughty bearing; also, when he was angry his mouth shut itself in the same iron fashion.

Of Umbelazi it is difficult for me to speak without enthusiasm. As Mameena was the most beautiful woman I ever saw in Zululand—although it is true that old war-dog, Umslopogaas, a friend of mine who does not come into this story, used to tell me that Nada the Lily, whom I have mentioned, was even lovelier—so Umbelazi was by far the most splendid man. Indeed, the Zulus named him "Umbelazi the Handsome," and no wonder. To begin with, he stood at least three inches above the tallest of them; from a quarter of a mile away I have recognised him by his great height, even through the dust of a desperate battle, and his breadth was proportionate to his stature. Then he was perfectly made, his great, shapely limbs ending, like Saduko's, in small hands and feet. His face, too, was well-cut and open, his colour lighter than Cetewayo's, and his eyes, which always seemed to smile, were large and dark.

Even before they passed the small gate of the inner fence it was easy for me to see that this royal pair were not upon the best of terms, for each of them tried to get through it first, to show his right of precedence. The result was somewhat ludicrous, for they jammed in the gateway. Here, however, Umbelazi's greater weight told, for, putting out his strength, he squeezed his brother into the reeds of the fence, and won through a foot or so in front of him.

"You grow too fat, my brother," I heard Cetewayo say, and saw him scowl as he spoke. "If I had held an assegai in my hand you would have been cut."

"I know it, my brother," answered Umbelazi, with a good-humoured laugh, "but I knew also that none may appear before the King armed. Had it been otherwise, I would rather have followed after you."

Now, at this hint of Umbelazi's, that he would not trust his brother behind his back with a spear, although it seemed to be conveyed in jest, I saw Panda shift uneasily on his seat, while Cetewayo scowled even more ominously than before. However, no further words passed between them, and, walking up to the King side by side, they saluted him with raised hands, calling out "Baba!"—that is, Father.

"Greeting, my children," said Panda, adding hastily, for he foresaw a quarrel as to which of them should take the seat of honour on his right: "Sit there in front of me, both of you, and, Macumazahn, do you come hither," and he pointed to the coveted place. "I am a little deaf in my left ear this morning."

So these brothers sat themselves down in front of the King; nor were they, I think, grieved to find this way out of their rivalry; but first they shook hands with me, for I knew them both, though not well, and even in this small matter the old trouble arose, since there was some difficulty as to which of them should first offer me his hand. Ultimately, I remember, Cetewayo won this trick.

When these preliminaries were finished, Panda addressed the princes, saying:

"My sons, I have sent for you to ask your counsel upon a certain matter—not a large matter, but one that may grow." And he paused to take snuff, whereon both of them ejaculated:

"We hear you, Father."

"Well, my sons, the matter is that of Saduko, the son of Matiwane, chief of the Amangwane, whom Bangu, chief of the Amakoba, ate up years ago by leave of Him who went before me. Now, this Bangu, as you know, has for some time been a thorn in my foot—a thorn that caused it to fester—and yet I did not wish to make war on him. So I spoke a word in the ear of Saduko, saying, 'He is yours, if you can kill him; and his cattle are yours.' Well, Saduko is not dull. With the help of this white man, Macumazahn, our friend from of old, he has killed Bangu and taken his cattle, and already my foot is beginning to heal."

"We have heard it," said Cetewayo.

"It was a great deed," added Umbelazi, a more generous critic.

"Yes," continued Panda, "I, too, think it was a great deed, seeing that Saduko had but a small regiment of wanderers to back him—"

"Nay," interrupted Cetewayo, "it was not those eaters of rats who won him the day, it was the wisdom of this Macumazahn."

"Macumazahn's wisdom would have been of little use without the courage of Saduko and his rats," commented Umbelazi, and from this moment I saw that the two brothers were taking sides for and against Saduko, as they did upon every other matter, not because they cared for the right of whatever was in question, but because they wished to oppose each other.

"Quite so," went on the King; "I agree with both of you, my sons. But the point is this: I think Saduko a man of promise, and one who should be advanced that he may learn to love us all, especially as his House has suffered wrong from our House, since He-who-is-gone listened to the evil counsel of Bangu, and allowed him to kill out Matiwane's tribe without just cause. Therefore, in order to wipe away this stain and bind Saduko to us, I think it well to re-establish Saduko in the chieftainship of the Amangwane, with the lands that his father held, and to give him also the chieftainship of the Amakoba, of whom it seems that the women and children, with some of the men, remain, although he already holds their cattle which he has captured in war."

"As the King pleases," said Umbelazi, with a yawn, for he was growing weary of listening to the case of Saduko.

But Cetewayo said nothing, for he appeared to be thinking of something else.

"I think also," went on Panda in a rather uncertain voice, "in order to bind him so close that the bonds may never be broken, it would be wise to give him a woman of our family in marriage."

"Why should this little Amangwane be allowed to marry into the royal House?" asked Cetewayo, looking up. "If he is dangerous, why not kill him, and have done?"

"For this reason, my son. There is trouble ahead in Zululand, and I do not wish to kill those who may help us in that hour, nor do I wish them to become our enemies. I wish that they may be our friends; and therefore it seems to me wise, when we find a seed of greatness, to water it, and not to dig it up or plant it in a neighbour's garden. From his deeds I believe that this Saduko is such a seed."

"Our father has spoken," said Umbelazi; "and I like Saduko, who is a man of mettle and good blood. Which of our sisters does our father propose to give to him?"

"She who is named after the mother of our race, O Umbelazi; she whom your own mother bore—your sister Nandie" (in English, "The Sweet").

"A great gift, O my Father, since Nandie is both fair and wise. Also, what does she think of this matter?"

"She thinks well of it, Umbelazi, for she has seen Saduko and taken a liking to him. She told me herself that she wishes no other husband."

"Is it so?" replied Umbelazi indifferently. "Then if the King commands, and the King's daughter desires, what more is there to be said?"

"Much, I think," broke in Cetewayo. "I hold that it is out of place that this little man, who has but conquered a little tribe by borrowing the wit of Macumazahn here, should be rewarded not only with a chieftainship, but with the hand of the wisest and most beautiful of the King's daughters, even though Umbelazi," he added, with a sneer, "should be willing to throw him his own sister like a bone to a passing dog."

"Who threw the bone, Cetewayo?" asked Umbelazi, awaking out of his indifference. "Was it the King, or was it I, who never heard of the matter till this moment? And who are we that we should question the King's decrees? Is it our business to judge or to obey?"

"Has Saduko perchance made you a present of some of those cattle which he stole from the Amakoba, Umbelazi?" asked Cetewayo. "As our father asks no lobola, perhaps you have taken the gift instead."

"The only gift that I have taken from Saduko," said Umbelazi, who, I could see, was hard pressed to keep his temper, "is that of his service. He is my friend, which is why you hate him, as you hate all my friends."

"Must I then love every stray cur that licks your hand, Umbelazi? Oh, no need to tell me he is your friend, for I know it was you who put it into our father's heart to allow him to kill Bangu and steal his cattle, which I hold to be an ill deed, for now the Great House is thatched with his reeds and Bangu's blood is on its doorposts. Moreover, he who wrought the wrong is to come and dwell therein, and for aught I know to be called a prince, like you and me. Why should he not, since the Princess Nandie is to be given to him in marriage? Certainly, Umbelazi, you would do well to take the cattle which this white trader has refused, for all men know that you have earned them."

Now Umbelazi sprang up, straightening himself to the full of his great height, and spoke in a voice that was thick with passion.

"I pray your leave to withdraw, O King," he said, "since if I stay here longer I shall grow sorry that I have no spear in my hand. Yet before I go I will tell the truth. Cetewayo hates Saduko, because, knowing him to be a chief of wit and courage, who will grow great, he sought him for his man, saying, 'Sit you in my shadow,' after he had promised to sit in mine. Therefore it is that he heaps these taunts upon me. Let him deny it if he can."

"That I shall not trouble to do, Umbelazi," answered Cetewayo, with a scowl. "Who are you that spy upon my doings, and with a mouth full of lies call me to account before the King? I will hear no more of it. Do you bide here and pay Saduko his price with the person of our sister. For, as the King has promised her, his word cannot be changed. Only let your dog know that I keep a stick for him, if he should snarl at me. Farewell, my Father. I go upon a journey to my own lordship, the land of Gikazi, and there you will find me when you want me, which I pray may not be till after this marriage is finished, for on that I will not trust my eyes to look."

Then, with a salute, he turned and departed, bidding no good-bye to his brother.

My hand, however, he shook in farewell, for Cetewayo was always friendly to me, perhaps because he thought I might be useful to him. Also, as I learned afterwards, he was very pleased with me for the reason that I had refused my share of the Amakoba cattle, and that he knew I had no part in this proposed marriage between Saduko and Nandie, of which, indeed, I now heard for the first time.

"My Father," said Umbelazi, when Cetewayo had gone, "is this to be borne? Am I to blame in the matter? You have heard and seen—answer me, my Father."

"No, you are not to blame this time, Umbelazi," replied the King, with a heavy sigh. "But oh! my sons, my sons, where will your quarrelling end? I think that only a river of blood can quench so fierce a fire, and then which of you will live to reach its bank?"

For a while he looked at Umbelazi, and I saw love and fear in his eye, for towards him Panda always had more affection than for any of his other children.

"Cetewayo has behaved ill," he said at length; "and before a white man, who will report the matter, which makes it worse. He has no right to dictate to me to whom I shall or shall not give my daughters in marriage. Moreover, I have spoken; nor do I change my word because he threatens me. It is known throughout the land that I never change my word; and the white men know it also, do they not, O Macumazana?"

I answered yes, they did. Also, this was true, for, like most weak men, Panda was very obstinate, and honest, too, in his own fashion.

He waved his hand, to show that the subject was ended, then bade Umbelazi go to the gate and send a messenger to bring in "the son of Matiwane."

Presently Saduko arrived, looking very stately and composed as he lifted his right hand and gave Panda the "Bayéte"—the royal salute.

"Be seated," said the King. "I have words for your ear."

Thereon, with the most perfect grace, without hurrying and without undue delay, Saduko crouched himself down upon his knees, with one of his elbows resting on the ground, as only a native knows how to do without looking absurd, and waited.

"Son of Matiwane," said the King, "I have heard all the story of how, with a small company, you destroyed Bangu and most of the men of the Amakoba, and ate up their cattle every one."

"Your pardon, Black One," interrupted Saduko. "I am but a boy, I did nothing. It was Macumazahn, Watcher-by-Night, who sits yonder. His wisdom taught me how to snare the Amakoba, after they were decoyed from their mountain, and it was Tshoza, my uncle, who loosed the cattle from the kraals. I say that I did nothing, except to strike a blow or two with a spear when I must, just as a baboon throws stones at those who would steal its young."

"I am glad to see that you are no boaster, Saduko," said Panda. "Would that more of the Zulus were like you in that matter, for then I must not listen to so many loud songs about little things. At least, Bangu was killed and his proud tribe humbled, and, for reasons of state, I am glad that this happened without my moving a regiment or being mixed up with the business, for I tell you that there are some of my family who loved Bangu. But I—I loved your father, Matiwane, whom Bangu butchered, for we were brought up together as boys—yes, and served together in the same regiment, the Amawombe, when the Wild One, my brother, ruled" (he meant Chaka, for among the Zulus the names of dead kings are hlonipa—that is, they must not be spoken if it can be avoided). "Therefore," went on Panda, "for this reason, and for others, I am glad that Bangu has been punished, and that, although vengeance has crawled after him like a footsore bull, at length he has been tossed with its horns and crushed with its knees."

"Yebo, Ngonyama!" (Yes, O Lion!) said Saduko.

"Now, Saduko," went on Panda, "because you are your father's son, and because you have shown yourself a man, although you are still little in the land, I am minded to advance you. Therefore I give to you the chieftainship over those who remain of the Amakoba and over all of the Amangwane blood whom you can gather."

"Bayéte! As the King pleases," said Saduko.

"And I give you leave to become a kehla—a wearer of the head-ring—although, as you have said, you are still but a boy, and with it a place upon my Council."

"Bayéte! As the King pleases," said Saduko, still apparently unmoved by the honours that were being heaped upon him.

"And, Son of Matiwane," went on Panda, "you are still unmarried, are you not?"

Now, for the first time, Saduko's face changed. "Yes, Black One," he said hurriedly, "but—"

Here he caught my eye, and, reading some warning in it, was silent.

"But," repeated Panda after him, "doubtless you would like to be? Well, it is natural in a young man who wishes to found a House, and therefore I give you leave to marry."

"Yebo, Silo!" (Yes, O Wild Beast!) "I thank the King, but—"

Here I sneezed loudly, and he ceased.

"But," repeated Panda, "of course, you do not know where to find a wife between the time the hawk stoops and the rat squeaks in its claws. How should you who have never thought of the matter? Also," he continued, with a smile, "it is well that you have not thought of it, since she whom I shall give to you could not live in the second hut in your kraal and call another 'Inkosikazi' [that is, head lady or chieftainess]. Umbelazi, my son, go fetch her of whom we have thought as a bride for this boy."

Now Umbelazi rose, and went with a broad smile upon his face, while Panda, somewhat fatigued with all his speech-making—for he was very fat and the day was very hot—leaned his head back against the hut and closed his eyes.

"O Black One! O thou who consumeth with rage! [Dhlangamandhla]" broke out Saduko, who, I could see, was much disturbed. "I have something to say to you."

"No doubt, no doubt," answered Panda drowsily, "but save up your thanks till you have seen, or you will have none left afterwards," and he snored slightly.

Now I, perceiving that Saduko was about to ruin himself, thought it well to interfere, though what business of mine it was to do so I cannot say. At any rate, if only I had held my tongue at this moment, and allowed Saduko to make a fool of himself, as he wished to do—for where Mameena was concerned he never could be wise—I verily believe that all the history of Zululand would have run a different course, and that many thousands of men, white and black, who are now dead would be alive to-day. But Fate ordered it otherwise. Yes, it was not I who spoke, but Fate. The Angel of Doom used my throat as his trumpet.

Seeing that Panda dozed, I slipped behind Saduko and gripped him by the arm.

"Are you mad?" I whispered into his ear. "Will you throw away your fortune, and your life also?"

"But Mameena," he whispered back. "I would marry none save Mameena."

"Fool!" I answered. "Mameena has betrayed and spat upon you. Take what the Heavens send you and give thanks. Would you wear Masapo's soiled blanket?"

"Macumazahn," he said in a hollow voice, "I will follow your head, and not my own heart. Yet you sow a strange seed, Macumazahn, or so you may think when you see its fruit." And he gave me a wild look—a look that frightened me.

There was something in this look which caused me to reflect that I might do well to go away and leave Saduko, Mameena, Nandie, and the rest of them to "dree their weirds," as the Scotch say, for, after all, what was my finger doing in that very hot stew? Getting burnt, I thought, and not collecting any stew.

Yet, looking back on these events, how could I foresee what would be the end of the madness of Saduko, of the fearful machinations of Mameena, and of the weakness of Umbelazi when she snared him in the net of her beauty, thus bringing about his ruin, through the hate of Saduko and the ambition of Cetewayo? How could I know that, at the back of all these events, stood the old dwarf, Zikali the Wise, working night and day to slake the enmity and fulfil the vengeance which long ago he had conceived and planned against the royal House of Senzangakona and the Zulu people over whom it ruled?

Yes, he stood there like a man behind a great stone upon the brow of a mountain, slowly, remorselessly, with infinite skill, labour, and patience, pushing that stone to the edge of the cliff, whence at length, in the appointed hour, it would thunder down upon those who dwelt beneath, to leave them crushed and no more a people. How could I guess that we, the actors in this play, were all the while helping him to push that stone, and that he cared nothing how many of us were carried with it into the abyss, if only we brought about the triumph of his secret, unutterable rage and hate?

Now I see and understand all these things, as it is easy to do, but then I was blind; nor did the Voices reach my dull ears to warn me, as, how or why I cannot tell, they did, I believe, reach those of Zikali.

Oh, what was the sum of it? Just this, I think, and nothing more—that, as Saduko and the others were Mameena's tools, and as all of them and their passions were Zikali's tools, so he himself was the tool of some unseen Power that used him and us to accomplish its design. Which, I suppose, is fatalism, or, in other words, all these things happened because they must happen. A poor conclusion to reach after so much thought and striving, and not complimentary to man and his boasted powers of free will; still, one to which many of us are often driven, especially if we have lived among savages, where such dramas work themselves out openly and swiftly, unhidden from our eyes by the veils and subterfuges of civilisation. At least, there is this comfort about it—that, if we are but feathers blown by the wind, how can the individual feather be blamed because it did not travel against, turn or keep back the wind?

Well, let me return from these speculations to the history of the facts that caused them.

Just as—a little too late—I had made up my mind that I would go after my own business, and leave Saduko to manage his, through the fence gateway appeared the great, tall Umbelazi leading by the hand a woman. As I saw in a moment, it did not need certain bangles of copper, ornaments of ivory and of very rare pink beads, called infibinga, which only those of the royal House were permitted to wear, to proclaim her a person of rank, for dignity and high blood were apparent in her face, her carriage, her gestures, and all that had to do with her.

Nandie the Sweet was not a great beauty, as was Mameena, although her figure was fine, and her stature like that of all the race of Senzangakona—considerably above the average. To begin with, she was darker in hue, and her lips were rather thick, as was her nose; nor were her eyes large and liquid like those of an antelope. Further, she lacked the informing mystery of Mameena's face, that at times was broken and lit up by flashes of alluring light and quick, sympathetic perception, as a heavy evening sky, that seems to join the dim earth to the dimmer heavens, is illuminated by pulsings of fire, soft and many-hued, suggesting, but not revealing, the strength and splendour that it veils. Nandie had none of these attractions, which, after all, anywhere upon the earth belong only to a few women in each generation. She was a simple, honest-natured, kindly, affectionate young woman of high birth, no more; that is, as these qualities are understood and expressed among her people.

Umbelazi led her forward into the presence of the King, to whom she bowed gracefully enough. Then, after casting a swift, sidelong glance at Saduko, which I found it difficult to interpret, and another of inquiry at me, she folded her hands upon her breast and stood silent, with bent head, waiting to be addressed.

The address was brief enough, for Panda was still sleepy.

"My daughter," he said, with a yawn, "there stands your husband," and he jerked his thumb towards Saduko. "He is a young man and a brave, and unmarried; also one who should grow great in the shadow of our House, especially as he is a friend of your brother, Umbelazi. I understand also that you have seen him and like him. Unless you have anything to say against it, for as, not being a common father, the King receives no cattle—at least in this case—I am not prejudiced, but will listen to your words," and he chuckled in a drowsy fashion. "I propose that the marriage should take place to-morrow. Now, my daughter, have you anything to say? For if so, please say it at once, as I am tired. The eternal wranglings between your brethren, Cetewayo and Umbelazi, have worn me out."

Now Nandie looked about her in her open, honest fashion, her gaze resting first on Saduko, then on Umbelazi, and lastly upon me.

"My Father," she said at length, in her soft, steady voice, "tell me, I beseech you, who proposes this marriage? Is it the Chief Saduko, is it the Prince Umbelazi, or is it the white lord whose true name I do not know, but who is called Macumazahn, Watcher-by-Night?"

"I can't remember which of them proposed it," yawned Panda. "Who can keep on talking about things from night till morning? At any rate, I propose it, and I will make your husband a big man among our people. Have you anything to say against it?"

"I have nothing to say, my Father. I have met Saduko, and like him well—for the rest, you are the judge. But," she added slowly, "does Saduko like me? When he speaks my name, does he feel it here?" and she pointed to her throat.

"I am sure I do not know what he feels in his throat," Panda replied testily, "but I feel that mine is dry. Well, as no one says anything, the matter is settled. To-morrow Saduko shall give the umqoliso [the Ox of the Girl], that makes marriage—if he has not got one here I will lend it to him, and you can take the new, big hut that I have built in the outer kraal to dwell in for the present. There will be a dance, if you wish it; if not, I do not care, for I have no wish for ceremony just now, who am too troubled with great matters. Now I am going to sleep."

Then sinking from his stool on to his knees, Panda crawled through the doorway of his great hut, which was close to him, and vanished.

Umbelazi and I departed also through the gateway of the fence, leaving Saduko and the Princess Nandie alone together, for there were no attendants present. What happened between them I am sure I do not know, but I gather that, in one way or another, Saduko made himself sufficiently agreeable to the princess to persuade her to take him to husband. Perhaps, being already enamoured of him, she was not difficult to persuade. At any rate, on the morrow, without any great feasting or fuss, except the customary dance, the umqoliso, the "Ox of the Girl," was slaughtered, and Saduko became the husband of a royal maiden of the House of Senzangakona.

Certainly, as I remember reflecting, it was a remarkable rise in life for one who, but a few months before, had been without possessions or a home.

I may add that, after our brief talk in the King's kraal, while Panda was dozing, I had no further words with Saduko on this matter of his marriage, for between its proposal and the event he avoided me, nor did I seek him out. On the day of the marriage also, I trekked for Natal, and for a whole year heard no more of Saduko, Nandie, and Mameena; although, to be frank, I must admit I thought of the last of these persons more often, perhaps, than I should have done.

The truth is that Mameena was one of those women who sticks in a man's mind even more closely than a "Wait-a-bit" thorn does in his coat.

CHAPTER IX

ALLAN RETURNS TO ZULULAND

A whole year had gone by, in which I did, or tried to do, various things that have no connection with this story, when once more I found myself in Zululand—at Umbezi's kraal indeed. Hither I had trekked in fulfilment of a certain bargain, already alluded to, that was concerned with ivory and guns, which I had made with the old fellow, or, rather, with Masapo, his son-in-law, whom he represented in this matter.

Into the exact circumstances of that bargain I do not enter, since at the moment I cannot recall whether I ever obtained the necessary permit to import those guns into Zululand, although now that I am older I earnestly hope that I did so, since it is wrong to sell weapons to natives that may be put to all sorts of unforeseen uses.

At any rate, there I was, sitting alone with the Headman in his hut discussing a dram of "squareface" that I had given to him, for the "trade" was finished to our mutual satisfaction, and Scowl, my body servant, with the hunters, had just carried off the ivory—a fine lot of tusks—to my wagons.

"Well, Umbezi," I said, "and how has it fared with you since we parted a year ago? Have you seen anything of Saduko, who, you may remember, left you in some wrath?"

"Thanks be to my Spirit, I have seen nothing of that wild man, Macumazahn," answered Umbezi, shaking his fat old head in a fashion which showed great anxiety. "Yet I have heard of him, for he sent me a message the other day to tell me that he had not forgotten what he owed me."

"Did he mean the sticks with which he promised to bray you like a green hide?" I inquired innocently.

"I think so, Macumazahn—I think so, for certainly he owes me nothing else. And the worst of it is that, there at Panda's kraal, he has grown like a pumpkin on a dung heap—great, great!"

"And therefore is now one who can pay any debt that he owes, Umbezi," I said, taking a pull at the "squareface" and looking at him over the top of the pannikin.

"Doubtless he can, Macumazahn, and, between you and me, that is the real reason why I—or rather Masapo—was so anxious to get those guns. They were not for hunting, as he told you by the messenger, or for war, but to protect us against Saduko, in case he should attack. Well, now I hope we shall be able to hold our own."

"You and Masapo must teach your people to use them first, Umbezi. But I expect Saduko has forgotten all about both of you now that he is the husband of a princess of the royal blood. Tell me, how goes it with Mameena?"

"Oh, well, well, Macumazahn. For is she not the head lady of the Amasomi? There is nothing wrong with her—nothing at all, except that as yet she has no child; also that—," and he paused.

"That what?" I asked.

"That she hates the very sight of her husband, Masapo, and says that she would rather be married to a baboon—yes, to a baboon—than to him, which gives him offence, after he has paid so many cattle for her. But what of this, Macumazahn? There is always a grain missing upon the finest head of corn. Nothing is quite perfect in the world, Macumazahn, and if Mameena does not chance to love her husband—" and he shrugged his shoulders and drank some "squareface."

"Of course it does not matter in the least, Umbezi, except to Mameena and her husband, who no doubt will settle down in time, now that Saduko is married to a princess of the Zulu House."

"I hope so, Macumazahn, but, to tell the truth, I wish you had brought more guns, for I live amongst a terrible lot of people. Masapo, who is furious with Mameena because she will have none of him, and therefore with me, as though I could control Mameena; Mameena, who is mad with Masapo, and therefore with me, because I gave her in marriage to him; Saduko, who foams at the mouth at the name of Masapo, because he has married Mameena, whom, it is said, he still loves, and therefore at me, because I am her father and did my best to settle her in the world. Oh, give me some more of that fire-water, Macumazahn, for it makes me forget all these things, and especially that my guardian spirit made me the father of Mameena, with whom you would not run away when you might have done so. Oh, Macumazahn, why did you not run away with Mameena, and turn her into a quiet white woman who ties herself up in sacks, sings songs to the 'Great-Great' in the sky—[that is, hymns to the Power above us]—and never thinks of any man who is not her husband?"

"Because if I had done so, Umbezi, I should have ceased to be a quiet white man. Yes, yes, my friend, I should have been in some such place as yours to-day, and that is the last thing that I wish. And now, Umbezi, you have had quite enough 'squareface,' so I will take the bottle away with me. Good-night."

On the following morning I trekked very early from Umbezi's kraal—before he was up indeed, for the "squareface" made him sleep sound. My destination was Nodwengu, Panda's Great Place, where I hoped to do some trading, but, as I was in no particular hurry, my plan was to go round by Masapo's, and see for myself how it fared between him and Mameena. Indeed, I reached the borders of the Amasomi territory, whereof Masapo was chief, by evening, and camped there. But with the night came reflection, and reflection told me that I should do well to keep clear of Mameena and her domestic complications, if she had any. So I changed my mind, and next morning trekked on to Nodwengu by the only route that my guides reported to be practicable, one which took me a long way round.

That day, owing to the roughness of the road—if road it could be called—and an accident to one of the wagons, we only covered about fifteen miles, and as night fell were obliged to outspan at the first spot where we could find water. When the oxen had been unyoked I looked about me, and saw that we were in a place that, although I had approached it from a somewhat different direction, I recognised at once as the mouth of the Black Kloof, in which, over a year before, I had interviewed Zikali the Little and Wise. There was no mistaking the spot; that blasted valley, with the piled-up columns of boulders and the overhanging cliff at the end of it, have, so far as I am aware, no exact counterparts in Africa.

I sat upon the box of the first wagon, eating my food, which consisted of some biltong and biscuit, for I had not bothered to shoot any game that day, which was very hot, and wondering whether Zikali were still alive, also whether I should take the trouble to walk up the kloof and find out. On the whole I thought that I would not, as the place repelled me, and I did not particularly wish to hear any more of his prophecies and fierce, ill-omened talk. So I just sat there studying the wonderful effect of the red evening light pouring up between those walls of fantastic rocks.

Presently I perceived, far away, a single human figure—whether it were man or woman I could not tell—walking towards me along the path which ran at the bottom of the cleft. In those gigantic surroundings it looked extraordinarily small and lonely, although perhaps because of the intense red light in which it was bathed, or perhaps just because it was human, a living thing in the midst of all that still, inanimate grandeur, it caught and focused my attention. I grew greatly interested in it; I wondered if it were that of man or woman, and what it was doing here in this haunted valley.

The figure drew nearer, and now I saw it was slender and tall, like that of a lad or of a well-grown woman, but to which sex it belonged I could not see, because it was draped in a cloak of beautiful grey fur. Just then Scowl came to the other side of the wagon to speak to me about something, which took off my attention for the next two minutes. When I looked round again it was to see the figure standing within three yards of me, its face hidden by a kind of hood which was attached to the fur cloak.

"Who are you, and what is your business?" I asked, whereon a gentle voice answered:

"Do you not know me, O Macumazana?"

"How can I know one who is tied up like a gourd in a mat? Yet is it not—is it not—"

"Yes, it is Mameena, and I am very pleased that you should remember my voice, Macumazahn, after we have been separated for such a long, long time," and, with a sudden movement, she threw back the kaross, hood and all, revealing herself in all her strange beauty.

I jumped down off the wagon-box and took her hand.

"O Macumazana," she said, while I still held it—or, to be accurate, while she still held mine—"indeed my heart is glad to see a friend again," and she looked at me with her appealing eyes, which, in the red light, I could see appeared to float in tears.

"A friend, Mameena!" I exclaimed. "Why, now you are so rich, and the wife of a big chief, you must have plenty of friends."

"Alas! Macumazahn, I am rich in nothing except trouble, for my husband saves, like the ants for winter. Why, he even grudged me this poor kaross; and as for friends, he is so jealous that he will not allow me any."

"He cannot be jealous of women, Mameena!"

"Oh, women! Piff! I do not care for women; they are very unkind to me, because—because—well, perhaps you can guess why, Macumazahn," she answered, glancing at her own reflection in a little travelling looking-glass that hung from the woodwork of the wagon, for I had been using it to brush my hair, and smiled very sweetly.

"At least you have your husband, Mameena, and I thought that perhaps by this time—"

She held up her hand.

"My husband! Oh, I would that I had him not, for I hate him, Macumazahn; and as for the rest—never! The truth is that I never cared for any man except one whose name you may chance to remember, Macumazahn."

"I suppose you mean Saduko—" I began.

"Tell me, Macumazahn," she inquired innocently, "are white people very stupid? I ask because you do not seem as clever as you used to be. Or have you perhaps a bad memory?"

Now I felt myself turning red as the sky behind me, and broke in hurriedly:

"If you did not like your husband, Mameena, you should not have married him. You know you need not unless you wished."

"When one has only two thorn bushes to sit on, Macumazahn, one chooses that which seems to have the fewest prickles, to discover sometimes that they are still there in hundreds, although one did not see them. You know that at length everyone gets tired of standing."

"Is that why you have taken to walking, Mameena? I mean, what are you doing here alone?"

"I? Oh, I heard that you were passing this way, and came to have a talk with you. No, from you I cannot hide even the least bit of the truth. I came to talk with you, but also I came to see Zikali and ask him what a wife should do who hates her husband."

"Indeed! And what did he answer you?"

"He answered that he thought she had better run away with another man, if there were one whom she did not hate—out of Zululand, of course," she replied, looking first at me and then at my wagon and the two horses that were tied to it.

"Is that all he said, Mameena?"

"No. Have I not told you that I cannot hide one grain of the truth from you? He added that the only other thing to be done was to sit still and drink my sour milk, pretending that it is sweet, until my Spirit gives me a new cow. He seemed to think that my Spirit would be bountiful in the matter of new cows— one day."

"Anything more?" I inquired.

"One little thing. Have I not told you that you shall have all—all the truth? Zikali seemed to think also that at last every one of my herd of cows, old and new, would come to a bad end. He did not tell me to what end."

She turned her head aside, and when she looked up again I saw that she was weeping, really weeping this time, not just making her eyes swim, as she did before.

"Of course they will come to a bad end, Macumazahn," she went on in a soft, thick voice, "for I and all with whom I have to do were 'torn out of the reeds' [i.e. created] that way. And that's why I won't tempt you to run away with me any more, as I meant to do when I saw you, because it is true, Macumazahn you are the only man I ever liked or ever shall like; and you know I could make you run away with me if I chose, although I am black and you are white—oh, yes, before to-morrow morning. But I won't do it; for why should I catch you in my unlucky web and bring you into all sorts of trouble among my people and your own? Go you your road, Macumazahn, and I will go mine as the wind blows me. And now give me a cup of water and let me be away—a cup of water, no more. Oh, do not be afraid for me, or melt too much, lest I should melt also. I have an escort waiting over yonder hill. There, thank you for your water, Macumazahn, and good night. Doubtless we shall meet again ere long, and— I forgot; the Little Wise

One said he would like to have a talk with you. Good night, Macumazahn, good night. I trust that you did a profitable trade with Umbezi my father and Masapo my husband. I wonder why such men as these should have been chosen to be my father and my husband. Think it over, Macumazahn, and tell me when next we meet. Give me that pretty mirror, Macumazahn; when I look in it I shall see you as well as myself, and that will please me—you don't know how much. I thank you. Good night."

In another minute I was watching her solitary little figure, now wrapped again in the hooded kaross, as it vanished over the brow of the rise behind us, and really, as she went, I felt a lump rising in my throat. Notwithstanding all her wickedness—and I suppose she was wicked—there was something horribly attractive about Mameena.

When she had gone, taking my only looking-glass with her, and the lump in my throat had gone also, I began to wonder how much fact there was in her story. She had protested so earnestly that she told me all the truth that I felt sure there must be something left behind. Also I remembered she had said Zikali wanted to see me. Well, the end of it was I took a moonlight walk up that dreadful gorge, into which not even Scowl would accompany me, because he declared that the place was well known to be haunted by imikovu, or spectres who have been raised from the dead by wizards.

It was a long and disagreeable walk, and somehow I felt very depressed and insignificant as I trudged on between those gigantic cliffs, passing now through patches of bright moonlight and now through deep pools of shadow, threading my way among clumps of bush or round the bases of tall pillars of piled-up stones, till at length I came to the overhanging cliffs at the end, which frowned down on me like the brows of some titanic demon.

Well, I got to the end at last, and at the gate of the kraal fence was met by one of those fierce and huge men who served the dwarf as guards. Suddenly he emerged from behind a stone, and having scanned me for a moment in silence, beckoned to me to follow him, as though I were expected. A minute later I found myself face to face with Zikali, who was seated in the clear moonlight just outside the shadow of his hut, and engaged, apparently, in his favourite occupation of carving wood with a rough native knife of curious shape.

For a while he took no notice of me; then suddenly looked up, shaking back his braided grey locks, and broke into one of his great laughs.

"So it is you, Macumazahn," he said. "Well, I knew you were passing my way and that Mameena would send you here. But why do you come to see the 'Thing-that-should-not-have-been-born'? To tell me how you fared with the buffalo with the split horn, eh?"

"No, Zikali, for why should I tell you what you know already? Mameena said you wished to talk with me, that was all."

"Then Mameena lied," he answered, "as is her nature, in whose throat live four false words for every one of truth. Still, sit down, Macumazahn. There is beer made ready for you by that stool; and give me the knife and a pinch of the white man's snuff that you have brought for me as a present."

I produced these articles, though how he knew that I had them with me I cannot tell, nor did I think it worth while to inquire. The snuff, I remember, pleased him very much, but of the knife he said that it was a pretty toy, but he would not know how to use it. Then we fell to talking.

"What was Mameena doing here?" I asked boldly.

"What was she doing at your wagons?" he asked. "Oh, do not stop to tell me; I know, I know. That is a very good Snake of yours, Macumazahn, which always just lets you slip through her fingers, when, if she chose to close her hand— Well, well, I do not betray the secrets of my clients; but I say this to you—go on to the kraal of the son of Senzangakona, and you will see things happen that will make you laugh, for Mameena will be there, and the mongrel Masapo, her husband. Truly she hates him well, and, after all, I would rather be loved than hated by Mameena, though both are dangerous. Poor Mongrel! Soon the jackals will be chewing his bones."

"Why do you say that?" I asked.

"Only because Mameena tells me that he is a great wizard, and the jackals eat many wizards in Zululand. Also he is an enemy of Panda's House, is he not?"

"You have been giving her some bad counsel, Zikali," I said, blurting out the thought in my mind.

"Perhaps, perhaps, Macumazahn; only I may call it good counsel. I have my own road to walk, and if I can find some to clear away the thorns that would prick my feet, what of it? Also she will get her pay, who finds life dull up there among the Amasomi, with one she hates for a hut-fellow. Go you and watch, and afterwards, when you have an hour to spare, come and tell me what happens—that is, if I do not chance to be there to see for myself."

"Is Saduko well?" I asked to change the subject, for I did not wish to become privy to the plots that filled the air.

"I am told that his tree grows great, that it overshadows all the royal kraal. I think that Mameena wishes to sleep in the shade of it. And now you are weary, and so am I. Go back to your wagons, Macumazahn, for I have nothing more to say to you to-night. But be sure to return and tell me what chances at Panda's kraal. Or, as I have said, perhaps I shall meet you there. Who knows, who knows?"

Now, it will be observed that there was nothing very remarkable in this conversation between Zikali and myself. He did not tell me any deep secrets or make any great prophecy. It may be wondered, indeed, when there is so much to record, why I set it down at all.

My answer is, because of the extraordinary impression that it produced upon me. Although so little was said, I felt all the while that those few words were a veil hiding terrible events to be. I was sure that some dreadful scheme had been hatched between the old dwarf and Mameena whereof the issue would soon become apparent, and that he had sent me away in a hurry after he learned that she had told me nothing, because he feared lest I should stumble on its cue and perhaps cause it to fail.

At any rate, as I walked back to my wagons by moonlight down that dreadful gorge, the hot, thick air seemed to me to have a physical taste and smell of blood, and the dank foliage of the tropical trees that grew there, when now and again a puff of wind stirred them, moaned like the fabled imikovu, or as men might do in their last faint agony. The effect upon my nerves was quite strange, for when at last I reached my wagons I was shaking like a reed, and a cold perspiration, unnatural enough upon that hot night, poured from my face and body.

Well, I took a couple of stiff tots of "squareface" to pull myself together, and at length went to sleep, to awake before dawn with a headache. Looking out of the wagon, to my surprise I saw Scowl and the hunters, who should have been snoring, standing in a group and talking to each other in frightened whispers. I called Scowl to me and asked what was the matter.

"Nothing, Baas," he said with a shamefaced air; "only there are so many spooks about this place. They have been passing in and out of it all night."

"Spooks, you idiot!" I answered. "Probably they were people going to visit the Nyanga, Zikali."

"Perhaps, Baas; only then we do not know why they should all look like dead people—princes, some of them, by their dress—and walk upon the air a man's height from the ground."

"Pooh!" I replied. "Do you not know the difference between owls in the mist and dead kings? Make ready, for we trek at once; the air here is full of fever."

"Certainly, Baas," he said, springing off to obey; and I do not think I ever remember two wagons being got under way quicker than they were that morning.

I merely mention this nonsense to show that the Black Kloof could affect other people's nerves as well as my own.

In due course I reached Nodwengu without accident, having sent forward one of my hunters to report my approach to Panda. When my wagons arrived outside the Great Place they were met by none other than my old friend, Maputa, he who had brought me back the pills before our attack upon Bangu.

"Greeting, Macumazahn," he said. "I am sent by the King to say that you are welcome and to point you out a good place to outspan; also to give you permission to trade as much as you will in this town, since he knows that your dealings are always fair."

I returned my thanks in the usual fashion, adding that I had brought a little present for the King which I would deliver when it pleased him to receive me. Then I invited Maputa, to whom I also offered some trifle which delighted him very much, to ride with me on the wagon-box till we came to the selected outspan.

This, by the way, proved, to be a very good place indeed, a little valley full of grass for the cattle—for by the King's order it had not been grazed—with a stream of beautiful water running down it. Moreover it overlooked a great open space immediately in front of the main gate of the town, so that I could see everything that went on and all who arrived or departed.

"You will be comfortable here, Macumazahn," said Maputa, "during your stay, which we hope will be long, since, although there will soon be a mighty crowd at Nodwengu, the King has given orders that none except your own servants are to enter this valley."

"I thank the King; but why will there be a crowd, Maputa?"

"Oh!" he answered with a shrug of the shoulders, "because of a new thing. All the tribes of the Zulus are to come up to be reviewed. Some say that Cetewayo has brought this about, and some say that it is Umbelazi. But I am sure that it is the work of neither of these, but of Saduko, your old friend, though what his object is I cannot tell you. I only trust," he added uneasily, "that it will not end in bloodshed between the Great Brothers."

"So Saduko has grown tall, Maputa?"

"Tall as a tree, Macumazahn. His whisper in the King's ear is louder than the shouts of others. Moreover, he has become a 'self-eater' [that is a Zulu term which means one who is very haughty]. You will have to wait on him, Macumazahn; he will not wait on you."

"Is it so?" I answered. "Well, tall trees are blown down sometimes."

He nodded his wise old head. "Yes, Macumazahn; I have seen plenty grow and fall in my time, for at last the swimmer goes with the stream. Anyhow, you will be able to do a good trade among so many, and, whatever happens, none will harm you whom all love. And now farewell; I bear your messages to the King, who sends an ox for you to kill lest you should grow hungry in his house."

That same evening I saw Saduko and the others, as I shall tell. I had been up to visit the King and give him my present, a case of English table-knives with bone handles, which pleased him greatly, although he did not in the least know how to use them. Indeed, without their accompanying forks these are somewhat futile articles. I found the old fellow very tired and anxious, but as he was surrounded by indunas, I had no private talk with him. Seeing that he was busy, I took my leave as soon as I could, and when I walked away whom should I meet but Saduko.

I saw him while he was a good way off, advancing towards the inner gate with a train of attendants like a royal personage, and knew very well that he saw me. Making up my mind what to do at once, I walked straight on to him, forcing him to give me the path, which he did not wish to do before so many people, and brushed past him as though he were a stranger. As I expected, this treatment had the desired effect, for after we had passed each other he turned and said:

"Do you not know me, Macumazahn?"

"Who calls?" I asked. "Why, friend, your face is familiar to me. How are you named?"

"Have you forgotten Saduko?" he said in a pained voice.

"No, no, of course not," I answered. "I know you now, although you seem somewhat changed since we went out hunting and fighting together—I suppose because you are fatter. I trust that you are well, Saduko? Good-bye. I must be going back to my wagons. If you wish to see me you will find me there."

These remarks, I may add, seemed to take Saduko very much aback. At any rate, he found no reply to them, even when old Maputa, with whom I was walking, and some others sniggered aloud. There is nothing that Zulus enjoy so much as seeing one whom they consider an upstart set in his place.

Well, a couple of hours afterwards, just as the sun was sinking, who should walk up to my wagons but Saduko himself, accompanied by a woman whom I recognised at once as his wife, the Princess Nandie, who carried a fine baby boy in her arms. Rising, I saluted Nandie and offered her my camp-stool, which she looked at suspiciously and declined, preferring to seat herself on the ground after the native fashion. So I took it back again, and after I had sat down on it, not before, stretched out my hand to Saduko, who by this time was quite humble and polite.

Well, we talked away, and by degrees, without seeming too much interested in them, I was furnished with a list of all the advancements which it had pleased Panda to heap upon Saduko during the past year. In their way they were remarkable enough, for it was much as though some penniless country gentleman in England had been promoted in that short space of time to be one of the premier peers of the kingdom and endowed with great offices and estates. When he had finished the count of them he paused, evidently waiting for me to congratulate him. But all I said was:

"By the Heavens above I am sorry for you, Saduko! How many enemies you must have made! What a long way there will be for you to fall one night!"—a remark at which the quiet Nandie broke into a low laugh that I think pleased her husband even less than my sarcasm. "Well," I went on, "I see that you have got a baby, which is much better than all these titles. May I look at it, Inkosazana?"

Of course she was delighted, and we proceeded to inspect the baby, which evidently she loved more than anything on earth. Whilst we were examining the child and chatting about it, Saduko sitting by meanwhile in the sulks, who on earth should appear but Mameena and her fat and sullen-looking husband, the chief Masapo.

"Oh, Macumazahn," she said, appearing to notice no one else, "how pleased I am to see you after a whole long year!"

I stared at her and my jaw dropped. Then I recovered myself, thinking she must have made a mistake and meant to say "week."

"Twelve moons," she went on, "and, Macumazahn, not one of them has gone by but I have thought of you several times and wondered if we should ever meet again. Where have you been all this while?"

"In many places," I answered; "amongst others at the Black Kloof, where I called upon the dwarf, Zikali, and lost my looking-glass."

"The Nyanga, Zikali! Oh, how often have I wished to see him. But, of course, I cannot, for I am told he will not receive any women."

"I don't know, I am sure," I replied, "but you might try; perhaps he would make an exception in your favour."

"I think I will, Macumazahn," she murmured, whereon I collapsed into silence, feeling that things were getting beyond me.

When I recovered myself a little it was to hear Mameena greeting Saduko with much effusion, and complimenting him on his rise in life, which she said she had always foreseen. This remark seemed to bowl out Saduko also, for he made no answer to it, although I noticed that he could not take his eyes off Mameena's beautiful face. Presently, however, he seemed to become aware of Masapo, and instantly his whole demeanour changed, for it grew proud and even terrible. Masapo tendered him some greeting; whereon Saduko turned upon him and said:

"What, chief of the Amasomi, do you give the good-day to an umfokazana and a mangy hyena? Why do you do this? Is it because the low umfokazana has become a noble and the mangy hyena has put on a tiger's coat?" And he glared at him like a veritable tiger.

Masapo made no answer that I could catch. Muttering some inaudible words, he turned to depart, and in doing so—quite innocently, I think—struck Nandie, knocking her over on to her back and causing the child to fall out of her arms in such fashion that its tender head struck against a pebble with sufficient force to cause it to bleed.

Saduko leapt at him, smiting him across the shoulders with the little stick that he carried. For a moment Masapo paused, and I thought that he was going to show fight. If he had any such intention, however, he changed his mind, for without a word, or showing any resentment at the insult which he had received, he broke into a heavy run and vanished among the evening shadows. Mameena, who had observed all, broke into something else, namely, a laugh.

"Piff! My husband is big yet not brave," she said, "but I do not think he meant to hurt you, woman."

"Do you speak to me, wife of Masapo?" asked Nandie with gentle dignity, as she gained her feet and picked up the stunned child. "If so, my name and titles are the Inkosazana Nandie, daughter of the Black One and wife of the lord Saduko."

"Your pardon," replied Mameena humbly, for she was cowed at once. "I did not know who you were, Inkosazana."

"It is granted, wife of Masapo. Macumazahn, give me water, I pray you, that I may bathe the head of my child."

The water was brought, and presently, when the little one seemed all right again, for it had only received a scratch, Nandie thanked me and departed to her own huts, saying with a smile to her husband as she passed that there was no need for him to accompany her, as she had servants waiting at the kraal gate. So Saduko stayed behind, and Mameena stayed also. He talked with me for quite a long while, for he had much to tell me, although all the time I felt that his heart was not in his talk. His heart was with Mameena, who sat there and smiled continually in her mysterious way, only putting in a word now and again, as though to excuse her presence.

At length she rose and said with a sigh that she must be going back to where the Amasomi were in camp, as Masapo would need her to see to his food. By now it was quite dark, although I remember that from time to time the sky was lit up by sheet lightning, for a storm was brewing. As I expected, Saduko rose also, saying that he would see me on the morrow, and went away with Mameena, walking like one who dreams.

A few minutes later I had occasion to leave the wagons in order to inspect one of the oxen which was tied up by itself at a distance, because it had shown signs of some sickness that might or might not be catching. Moving quietly, as I always do from a hunter's habit, I walked alone to the place where the beast was tethered behind some mimosa thorns. Just as I reached these thorns the broad lightning shone out vividly, and showed me Saduko holding the unresisting shape of Mameena in his arms and kissing her passionately.

Then I turned and went back to the wagons even more quietly than I had come.

I should add that on the morrow I found out that, after all, there was nothing serious the matter with my ox.

CHAPTER X

THE SMELLING-OUT

After these events matters went on quietly for some time. I visited Saduko's huts—very fine huts—about the doors of which sat quite a number of his tribesmen, who seemed glad to see me again. Here I learned from the Lady Nandie that her babe, whom she loved dearly, was none the worse for its little accident. Also I learned from Saduko himself, who came in before I left, attended like a prince by several notable men, that he had made up his quarrel with Masapo, and, indeed, apologised to him, as he found that he had not really meant to insult the princess, his wife, having only thrust her over by accident. Saduko added indeed that now they were good friends, which was well for Masapo, a man whom the King had no cause to like. I said that I was glad to hear it, and went on to call upon Masapo, who received me with enthusiasm, as also did Mameena.

Here I noted with pleasure that this pair seemed to be on much better terms than I understood had been the case in the past, for Mameena even addressed her husband on two separate occasions in very affectionate language, and fetched something that he wanted without waiting to be asked. Masapo, too, was in excellent spirits, because, as he told me, the old quarrel between him and Saduko was thoroughly made up, their reconciliation having been sealed by an interchange of gifts. He added that he was very glad that this was the case, since Saduko was now one of the most powerful men in the country, who could harm him much if he chose, especially as some secret enemy had put it about of late that he, Masapo, was an enemy of the King's House, and an evil-doer who practised witchcraft. In proof of his new friendship, however, Saduko had promised that these slanders should be looked into and their originator punished, if he or she could be found.

Well, I congratulated him and took my departure, "thinking furiously," as the Frenchman says. That there was a tragedy pending I was sure; this weather was too calm to last; the water ran so still because it was preparing to leap down some hidden precipice.

Yet what could I do? Tell Masapo I had seen his wife being embraced by another man? Surely that was not my business; it was Masapo's business to attend to her conduct. Also they would both deny it, and I had no witness. Tell him that Saduko's reconciliation with him was not sincere, and that he had better look to himself? How did I know it was not sincere? It might suit Saduko's book to make friends with Masapo, and if I interfered I should only make enemies and be called a liar who was working for some secret end.

Go to Panda and confide my suspicions to him? He was far too anxious and busy about great matters to listen to me, and if he did, would only laugh at this tale of a petty flirtation. No, there was nothing to be done except sit still and wait. Very possibly I was mistaken, after all, and things would smooth themselves out, as they generally do.

Meanwhile the "reviewing," or whatever it may have been, was in progress, and I was busy with my own affairs, making hay while the sun shone. So great were the crowds of people who came up to Nodwengu that in a week I had sold everything I had to sell in the two wagons, that were mostly laden with cloth, beads, knives and so forth. Moreover, the prices I got were splendid, since the buyers bid against each other, and before I was cleared out I had collected quite a herd of cattle, also a quantity of ivory. These I sent on to Natal with one of the wagons, remaining behind myself with the other, partly because Panda asked me to do so—for now and again he would seek my advice on sundry questions—and partly from curiosity.

There was plenty to be curious about up at Nodwengu just then, since no one was sure that civil war would not break out between the princes Cetewayo and Umbelazi, whose factions were present in force.

It was averted for the time, however, by Umbelazi keeping away from the great gathering under pretext of being sick, and leaving Saduko and some others to watch his interests. Also the rival regiments were not allowed to approach the town at the same time. So that public cloud passed over, to the enormous relief of everyone, especially of Panda the King. As to the private cloud whereof this history tells, it was otherwise.

As the tribes came up to the Great Place they were reviewed and sent away, since it was impossible to feed so vast a multitude as would have collected had they all remained. Thus the Amasomi, a small people who were amongst the first to arrive, soon left. Only, for some reason which I never quite understood, Masapo, Mameena and a few of Masapo's children and headmen were detained there; though perhaps, if she had chosen, Mameena could have given an explanation.

Well, things began to happen. Sundry personages were taken ill, and some of them died suddenly; and soon it was noted that all these people either lived near to where Masapo's family was lodged or had at some time or other been on bad terms with him. Thus Saduko himself was taken ill, or said he was; at any rate, he vanished from public gaze for three days, and reappeared looking very sorry for himself, though I could not observe that he had lost strength or weight. These catastrophes I pass over, however, in order to come to the greatest of them, which is one of the turning points of this chronicle.

After recovering from his alleged sickness Saduko gave a kind of thanksgiving feast, at which several oxen were killed. I was present at this feast, or rather at the last part of it, for I only put in what may be called a complimentary appearance, having no taste for such native gorgings. As it drew near its close Saduko sent for Nandie, who at first refused to come as there were no women present—I think because he wished to show his friends that he had a princess of the royal blood for his wife, who had borne him a son that one day would be great in the land. For Saduko, as I have said, had become a "self-eater," and this day his pride was inflamed by the adulation of the company and by the beer that he had drunk.

At length Nandie did come, carrying her babe, from which she never would be parted. In her dignified, ladylike fashion (although it seems an odd term to apply to a savage, I know none that describes her better) she greeted first me and then sundry of the other guests, saying a few words to each of them. At length she came opposite to Masapo, who had dined not wisely but too well, and to him, out of her natural courtesy, spoke rather longer than to the others, inquiring after his wife, Mameena, and others.

At the moment it occurred to me that she did this in order to assure him that she bore no malice because of the accident of a while before, and was a party to her husband's reconciliation with him.

Masapo, in a hazy way, tried to reciprocate these kind intentions. Rising to his feet, his fat, coarse body swaying to and fro because of the beer that he had drunk, he expressed satisfaction at the feast that had been prepared in her house. Then, his eyes falling on the child, he began to declaim about its size and beauty, until he was stopped by the murmured protests of others, since among natives it is held to be not fortunate to praise a young child. Indeed, the person who does so is apt to be called an "umtakati", or bewitcher, who will bring evil upon its head, a word that I heard murmured by several near to me. Not satisfied with this serious breach of etiquette, the intoxicated Masapo snatched the infant from its mother's arms under pretext of looking for the hurt that had been caused to its brow when it fell to the ground at my camp, and finding none, proceeded to kiss it with his thick lips.

Nandie dragged it from him, saying:

"Would you bring death upon my son, O Chief of the Amasomi?"

Then, turning, she walked away from the feasters, upon whom there fell a certain hush.

Fearing lest something unpleasant should ensue, for I saw Saduko biting his lips with rage not unmixed with fear, and remembering Masapo's reputation as a wizard, I took advantage of this pause to bid a general good night to the company and retire to my camp.

What happened immediately after I left I do not know, but just before dawn on the following morning I was awakened from sleep in my wagon by my servant Scowl, who said that a messenger had come from the huts of Saduko, begging that I would proceed there at once and bring the white man's medicines, as his child was very ill. Of course I got up and went, taking with me some ipecacuanha and a few other remedies that I thought might be suitable for infantile ailments.

Outside the huts, which I reached just as the sun began to rise, I was met by Saduko himself, who was coming to seek me, as I saw at once, in a state of terrible grief.

"What is the matter?" I asked.

"O Macumazana," he answered, "that dog Masapo has bewitched my boy, and unless you can save him he dies."

"Nonsense," I said, "why do you utter wind? If the babe is sick, it is from some natural cause."

"Wait till you see it," he replied.

Well, I went into the big hut, and there found Nandie and some other women, also a native doctor or two. Nandie was seated on the floor looking like a stone image of grief, for she made no sound, only pointed with her finger to the infant that lay upon a mat in front of her.

A single glance showed me that it was dying of some disease of which I had no knowledge, for its dusky little body was covered with red blotches and its tiny face twisted all awry. I told the women to heat water, thinking that possibly this might be a case of convulsions, which a hot bath would mitigate; but before it was ready the poor babe uttered a thin wail and died.

Then, when she saw that her child was gone, Nandie spoke for the first time.

"The wizard has done his work well," she said, and flung herself face downwards on the floor of the hut.

As I did not know what to answer, I went out, followed by Saduko.

"What has killed my son, Macumazahn?" he asked in a hollow voice, the tears running down his handsome face, for he had loved his firstborn.

"I cannot tell," I replied; "but had he been older I should have thought he had eaten something poisonous, which seems impossible."

"Yes, Macumazahn, and the poison that he has eaten came from the breath of a wizard whom you may chance to have seen kiss him last night. Well, his life shall be avenged."

"Saduko," I exclaimed, "do not be unjust. There are many sicknesses that may have killed your son of which I have no knowledge, who am not a trained doctor."

"I will not be unjust, Macumazahn. The babe has died by witchcraft, like others in this town of late, but the evil-doer may not be he whom I suspect. That is for the smellers-out to decide," and without more words he turned and left me.

Next day Masapo was put upon his trial before a Court of Councillors, over which the King himself presided, a very unusual thing for him to do, and one which showed the great interest he took in the case.

At this court I was summoned to give evidence, and, of course, confined myself to answering such questions as were put to me. Practically these were but two. What had passed at my wagons when Masapo had knocked over Nandie and her child, and Saduko had struck him, and what had I seen at Saduko's feast when Masapo had kissed the infant? I told them in as few words as I could, and after some slight cross-examination by Masapo, made with a view to prove that the upsetting of Nandie was an accident and that he was drunk at Saduko's feast, to both of which suggestions I assented, I rose to go. Panda, however, stopped me and bade me describe the aspect of the child when I was called in to give it medicine.

I did so as accurately as possible, and could see that my account made a deep impression on the mind of the court. Then Panda asked me if I had ever seen any similar case, to which I was obliged to reply:

"No, I have not."

After this the Councillors consulted privately, and when we were called back the King gave his judgment, which was very brief. It was evident, he said, that there had been events which might have caused enmity to arise in the mind of Masapo against Saduko, by whom Masapo had been struck with a stick. Therefore, although a reconciliation had taken place, there seemed to be a possible motive for revenge. But if Masapo killed the child, there was no evidence to show how he had done so. Moreover, that infant, his own grandson, had not died of any known disease. He had, however, died of a similar disease to that which had carried off certain others with whom Masapo had been mixed up, whereas more, including Saduko himself, had been sick and recovered, all of which seemed to make a strong case against Masapo.

Still, he and his Councillors wished not to condemn without full proof. That being so, they had determined to call in the services of some great witch-doctor, one who lived at a distance and knew nothing of the circumstances. Who that doctor should be was not yet settled. When it was and he had arrived, the case would be re-opened, and meanwhile Masapo would be kept a close prisoner. Finally, he prayed that the white man, Macumazahn, would remain at his town until the matter was settled.

So Masapo was led off, looking very dejected, and, having saluted the King, we all went away.

I should add that, except for the remission of the case to the court of the witch-doctor, which, of course, was an instance of pure Kafir superstition, this judgment of the King's seemed to me well reasoned and just, very different indeed from what would have been given by Dingaan or Chaka, who were wont, on less evidence, to make a clean sweep not only of the accused, but of all his family and dependents.

About eight days later, during which time I had heard nothing of the matter and seen no one connected with it, for the whole thing seemed to have become Zila—that is, not to be talked about—I received a summons to attend the "smelling-out," and went, wondering what witch-doctor had been chosen for that bloody and barbarous ceremony. Indeed, I had not far to go, since the place selected for the occasion was outside the fence of the town of Nodwengu, on that great open stretch of ground which lay at the mouth of the valley where I was camped. Here, as I approached, I saw a vast multitude of people crowded together, fifty deep or more, round a little oval space not much larger than the pit of a theatre. On the inmost edge of this ring were seated many notable people, male and female, and as I was conducted to the side of it which was nearest to the gate of the town, I observed among them Saduko, Masapo, Mameena and others, and mixed up with them a number of soldiers, who were evidently on duty.

Scarcely had I seated myself on a camp-stool, carried by my servant Scowl, when through the gate of the kraal issued Panda and certain of his Council, whose appearance the multitude greeted with the royal salute of "Bayéte", that came from them in a deep and simultaneous roar of sound. When its echoes died away, in the midst of a deep silence Panda spoke, saying:

"Bring forth the Nyanga [doctor]. Let the umhlahlo [that is, the witch-trial] begin!"

There was a long pause, and then in the open gateway appeared a solitary figure that at first sight seemed to be scarcely human, the figure of a dwarf with a gigantic head, from which hung long, white hair, plaited into locks. It was Zikali, no other!

Quite unattended, and naked save for his moocha, for he had on him none of the ordinary paraphernalia of the witch-doctor, he waddled forward with a curious toad-like gait till he had passed through the Councillors and stood in the open space of the ring. Halting there, he looked about him slowly with his deep-set eyes, turning as he looked, till at length his glance fell upon the King.

"What would you have of me, Son of Senzangakona?" he asked. "Many years have passed since last we met. Why do you drag me from my hut, I who have visited the kraal of the King of the Zulus but twice since the 'Black One' [Chaka] sat upon the throne—once when the Boers were killed by him who went before you, and once when I was brought forth to see all who were left of my race, shoots of the royal Dwandwe stock, slain before my eyes. Do you bear me hither that I may follow them into the darkness, O Child of Senzangakona? If so I am ready; only then I have words to say that it may not please you to hear."

His deep, rumbling voice echoed into silence, while the great audience waited for the King's answer. I could see that they were all afraid of this man, yes, even Panda was afraid, for he shifted uneasily upon his stool. At length he spoke, saying:

"Not so, O Zikali. Who would wish to do hurt to the wisest and most ancient man in all the land, to him who touches the far past with one hand and the present with the other, to him who was old before our grandfathers began to be? Nay, you are safe, you on whom not even the 'Black One' dared to lay a finger, although you were his enemy and he hated you. As for the reason why you have been brought here, tell it to us, O Zikali. Who are we that we should instruct you in the ways of wisdom?"

When the dwarf heard this he broke into one of his great laughs.

"So at last the House of Senzangakona acknowledges that I have wisdom. Then before all is done they will think me wise indeed."

He laughed again in his ill-omened fashion and went on hurriedly, as though he feared that he should be called upon to explain his words:

"Where is the fee? Where is the fee? Is the King so poor that he expects an old Dwandwe doctor to divine for nothing, just as though he were working for a private friend?"

Panda made a motion with his hand, and ten fine heifers were driven into the circle from some place where they had been kept in waiting.

"Sorry beasts!" said Zikali contemptuously, "compared to those we used to breed before the time of Senzangakona"—a remark which caused a loud "Wow!" of astonishment to be uttered by the multitude that heard it. "Still, such as they are, let them be taken to my kraal, with a bull, for I have none."

The cattle were driven away, and the ancient dwarf squatted himself down and stared at the ground, looking like a great black toad. For a long while—quite ten minutes, I should think—he stared thus, till I, for one, watching him intently, began to feel as though I were mesmerised.

At length he looked up, tossing back his grey locks, and said:

"I see many things in the dust. Oh, yes, it is alive, it is alive, and tells me many things. Show that you are alive, O Dust. Look!"

As he spoke, throwing his hands upwards, there arose at his very feet one of those tiny and incomprehensible whirlwinds with which all who know South Africa will be familiar. It drove the dust together; it lifted it in a tall, spiral column that rose and rose to a height of fifty feet or more. Then it died away as suddenly as it had come, so that the dust fell down again over Zikali, over the King, and over three of his sons who sat behind him. Those three sons, I remember, were named Tshonkweni,

Dabulesinye, and Mantantashiya. As it chanced, by a strange coincidence all of these were killed at the great battle of the Tugela of which I have to tell.

Now again an exclamation of fear and wonder rose from the audience, who set down this lifting of the dust at Zikali's very feet not to natural causes, but to the power of his magic. Moreover, those on whom it had fallen, including the King, rose hurriedly and shook and brushed it from their persons with a zeal that was not, I think, inspired by a mere desire for cleanliness. But Zikali only laughed again in his terrible fashion and let it lie on his fresh-oiled body, which it turned to the dull, dead hue of a grey adder.

He rose and, stepping here and there, examined the new-fallen dust. Then he put his hand into a pouch he wore and produced from it a dried human finger, whereof the nail was so pink that I think it must have been coloured—a sight at which the circle shuddered.

"Be clever," he said, "O Finger of her I loved best; be clever and write in the dust as yonder Macumazana can write, and as some of the Dwandwe used to write before we became slaves and bowed ourselves down before the Great Heavens." (By this he meant the Zulus, whose name means the Heavens.) "Be clever, dear Finger which caressed me once, me, the 'Thing-that-should-not-have-been-born,' as more will think before I die, and write those matters that it pleases the House of Senzangakona to know this day."

Then he bent down, and with the dead finger at three separate spots made certain markings in the fallen dust, which to me seemed to consist of circles and dots; and a strange and horrid sight it was to see him do it.

"I thank you, dear Finger. Now sleep, sleep, your work is done," and slowly he wrapped the relic up in some soft material and restored it to his pouch.

Then he studied the first of the markings and asked: "What am I here for? What am I here for? Does he who sits upon the Throne desire to know how long he has to reign?"

Now, those of the inner circle of the spectators, who at these "smellings-out" act as a kind of chorus, looked at the King, and, seeing that he shook his head vigorously, stretched out their right hands, holding the thumb downwards, and said simultaneously in a cold, low voice:

"Izwa!" (That is, "We hear you.")

Zikali stamped upon this set of markings.

"It is well," he said. "He who sits upon the Throne does not desire to know how long he has to reign, and therefore the dust has forgotten and shows it not to me."

Then he walked to the next markings and studied them.

"Does the Child of Senzangakona desire to know which of his sons shall live and which shall die; aye, and which of them shall sleep in his hut when he is gone?"

Now a great roar of "Izwa!" accompanied by the clapping of hands, rose from all the outer multitude who heard, for there was no information that the Zulu people desired so earnestly as this at the time of which I write.

But again Panda, who, I saw, was thoroughly alarmed at the turn things were taking, shook his head vigorously, whereon the obedient chorus negatived the question in the same fashion as before.

Zikali stamped upon the second set of markings, saying:

"The people desire to know, but the Great Ones are afraid to learn, and therefore the dust has forgotten who in the days to come shall sleep in the hut of the King and who shall sleep in the bellies of the jackals and the crops of the vultures after they have 'gone beyond' by the bridge of spears."

Now, at this awful speech (which, both because of all that it implied of bloodshed and civil war and of the wild, wailing voice in which it was spoken, that seemed quite different from Zikali's, caused everyone who heard it, including myself, I am afraid, to gasp and shiver) the King sprang from his stool as though to put a stop to such doctoring. Then, after his fashion, he changed his mind and sat down again. But Zikali, taking no heed, went to the third set of marks and studied them.

"It would seem," he said, "that I am awakened from sleep in my Black House yonder to tell of a very little matter, that might well have been dealt with by any common Nyanga born but yesterday. Well, I have taken my fee, and I will earn it, although I thought that I was brought here to speak of great matters, such as the death of princes and the fortunes of peoples. Is it desired that my Spirit should speak of wizardries in this town of Nodwengu?"

"Izwa!" said the chorus in a loud voice.

Zikali nodded his great head and seemed to talk with the dust, waiting now and again for an answer.

"Good," he said; "they are many, and the dust has told them all to me. Oh, they are very many"—and he glared around him—"so many that if I spoke them all the hyenas of the hills would be full to-night—"

Here the audience began to show signs of great apprehension.

"But," looking down at the dust and turning his head sideways, "what do you say, what do you say? Speak more plainly, Little Voices, for you know I grow deaf. Oh! now I understand. The matter is even smaller than I thought. Just of one wizard—"

"Izwa!" (loudly).

"—just of a few deaths and some sicknesses."

"Izwa!"

"Just of one death, one principal death."

"Izwa!" (very loudly).

"Ah! So we have it—one death. Now, was it a man?"

"Izwa!" (very coldly).

"A woman?"

"Izwa!" (still more coldly).

"Then a child? It must be a child, unless indeed it is the death of a spirit. But what do you people know of spirits? A child! A child! Ah! you hear me—a child. A male child, I think. Do you not say so, O Dust?"

"Izwa!" (emphatically).

"A common child? A bastard? The son of nobody?"

"Izwa!" (very low).

"A well-born child? One who would have been great? O Dust, I hear, I hear; a royal child, a child in whom ran the blood of the Father of the Zulus, he who was my friend? The blood of Senzangakona, the blood of the 'Black One,' the blood of Panda."

He stopped, while both from the chorus and from the thousands of the circle gathered around went up one roar of "Izwa!" emphasised by a mighty movement of outstretched arms and down-pointing thumbs.

Then silence, during which Zikali stamped upon all the remaining markings, saying:

"I thank you, O Dust, though I am sorry to have troubled you for so small a matter. So, so," he went on presently, "a royal boy-child is dead, and you think by witchcraft. Let us find out if he died by witchcraft or as others die, by command of the Heavens that need them. What! Here is one mark which I have left. Look! It grows red, it is full of spots! The child died with a twisted face."

"Izwa! Izwa! Izwa!" (crescendo).

"This death was not natural. Now, was it witchcraft or was it poison? Both, I think, both. And whose was the child? Not that of a son of the King, I think. Oh, yes, you hear me, People, you hear me; but be silent; I do not need your help. No, not of a son; of a daughter, then." He turned and, looked about him till his eye fell upon a group of women, amongst whom sat Nandie, dressed like a common person. "Of a daughter, a daughter—" He walked to the group of women. "Why, none of these are royal; they are the children of low people. And yet—and yet I seem to smell the blood of Senzangakona."

He sniffed at the air as a dog does, and as he sniffed drew ever nearer to Nandie, till at last he laughed and pointed to her.

"Your child, Princess, whose name I do not know. Your firstborn child, whom you loved more than your own heart."

She rose.

"Yes, yes, Nyanga," she cried. "I am the Princess Nandie, and he was my child, whom I loved more than my own heart."

"Haha!" said Zikali. "Dust, you did not lie to me. My Spirit, you did not lie to me. But now, tell me, Dust—and tell me, my Spirit—who killed this child?"

He began to waddle round the circle, an extraordinary sight, covered as he was with grey grime, varied with streaks of black skin where the perspiration had washed the dust away.

Presently he came opposite to me, and, to my dismay, paused, sniffing at me as he had at Nandie.

"Ah! ah! O Macumazana," he said, "you have something to do with this matter," a saying at which all that audience pricked their ears.

Then I rose up in wrath and fear, knowing my position to be one of some danger.

"Wizard, or Smeller-out of Wizards, whichever you name yourself," I called in a loud voice, "if you mean that I killed Nandie's child, you lie!"

"No, no, Macumazahn," he answered, "but you tried to save it, and therefore you had something to do with the matter, had you not? Moreover, I think that you, who are wise like me, know who did kill it. Won't you tell me, Macumazahn? No? Then I must find out for myself. Be at peace. Does not all the land know that your hands are white as your heart?"

Then, to my great relief, he passed on, amidst a murmur of approbation, for, as I have said, the Zulus liked me. Round and round he wandered, to my surprise passing both Mameena and Masapo without taking any particular note of them, although he scanned them both, and I thought that I saw a swift glance of recognition pass between him and Mameena. It was curious to watch his progress, for as he went those in front of him swayed in their terror like corn before a puff of wind, and when he had passed they straightened themselves as the corn does when the wind has gone by.

At length he had finished his journey and returned to his starting-point, to all appearance completely puzzled.

"You keep so many wizards at your kraal, King," he said, addressing Panda, "that it is hard to say which of them wrought this deed. It would have been easier to tell you of greater matters. Yet I have taken your fee, and I must earn it—I must earn it. Dust, you are dumb. Now, my Idhlozi, my Spirit, do you speak?" and, holding his head sideways, he turned his left ear up towards the sky, then said presently, in a curious, matter-of-fact voice:

"Ah! I thank you, Spirit. Well, King, your grandchild was killed by the House of Masapo, your enemy, chief of the Amasomi."

Now a roar of approbation went up from the audience, among whom Masapo's guilt was a foregone conclusion.

When this had died down Panda spoke, saying:

"The House of Masapo is a large house; I believe that he has several wives and many children. It is not enough to smell out the House, since I am not as those who went before me were, nor will I slay the innocent with the guilty. Tell us, O Opener-of-Roads, who among the House of Masapo has wrought this deed?"

"That's just the question," grumbled Zikali in a deep voice. "All that I know is that it was done by poisoning, and I smell the poison. It is here."

Then he walked to where Mameena sat and cried out:

"Seize that woman and search her hair."

Executioners who were in waiting sprang forward, but Mameena waved them away.

"Friends," she said, with a little laugh, "there is no need to touch me," and, rising, she stepped forward to the centre of the ring. Here, with a few swift motions of her hands, she flung off first the cloak she wore, then the moocha about her middle, and lastly the fillet that bound her long hair, and stood before that audience in all her naked beauty—a wondrous and a lovely sight.

"Now," she said, "let women come and search me and my garments, and see if there is any poison hid there."

Two old crones stepped forward—though I do not know who sent them—and carried out a very thorough examination, finally reporting that they had found nothing. Thereon Mameena, with a shrug of her shoulders, resumed such clothes as she wore, and returned to her place.

Zikali appeared to grow angry. He stamped upon the ground with his big feet; he shook his braided grey locks and cried out:

"Is my wisdom to be defeated in such a little matter? One of you tie a bandage over my eyes."

Now a man—it was Maputa, the messenger—came out and did so, and I noted that he tied it well and tight. Zikali whirled round upon his heels, first one way and then another, and, crying aloud: "Guide me, my Spirit!" marched forward in a zigzag fashion, as a blindfolded man does, with his arms stretched out in front of him. First he went to the right, then to the left, and then straight forward, till at length, to my astonishment, he came exactly opposite the spot where Masapo sat and, stretching out his great, groping hands, seized the kaross with which he was covered and, with a jerk, tore it from him.

"Search this!" he cried, throwing it on the ground, and a woman searched.

Presently she uttered an exclamation, and from among the fur of one of the tails of the kaross produced a tiny bag that appeared to be made out of the bladder of a fish. This she handed to Zikali, whose eyes had now been unbandaged.

He looked at it, then gave it to Maputa, saying:

"There is the poison—there is the poison, but who gave it I do not say. I am weary. Let me go."

Then, none hindering him, he walked away through the gate of the kraal.

Soldiers seized upon Masapo, while the multitude roared: "Kill the wizard!"

Masapo sprang up, and, running to where the King sat, flung himself upon his knees, protesting his innocence and praying for mercy. I also, who had doubts as to all this business, ventured to rise and speak.

"O King," I said, "as one who has known this man in the past, I plead with you. How that powder came into his kaross I know not, but perchance it is not poison, only harmless dust."

"Yes, it is but wood dust which I use for the cleaning of my nails," cried Masapo, for he was so terrified I think he knew not what he said.

"So you own to knowledge of the medicine?" exclaimed Panda. "Therefore none hid it in your kaross through malice."

Masapo began to explain, but what he said was lost in a mighty roar of "Kill the wizard!"

Panda held up his hand and there was silence.

"Bring milk in a dish," commanded the King, and it, was brought, and, at a further word from him, dusted with the powder.

"Now, O Macumazana," said Panda to me, "if you still think that yonder man is innocent, will you drink this milk?"

"I do not like milk, O King," I answered, shaking my head, whereon all who heard me laughed.

"Will Mameena, his wife, drink it, then?" asked Panda.

She also shook her head, saying:

"O King, I drink no milk that is mixed with dust."

Just then a lean, white dog, one of those homeless, mangy beasts that stray about kraals and live upon carrion, wandered into the ring. Panda made a sign, and a servant, going to where the poor beast stood staring about it hungrily, set down the wooden dish of milk in front of it. Instantly the dog lapped it up, for it was starving, and as it finished the last drop the man slipped a leathern thong about its neck and held it fast.

Now all eyes were fixed upon the dog, mine among them. Presently the beast uttered a long and melancholy howl which thrilled me through, for I knew it to be Masapo's death warrant, then began to scratch the ground and foam at the mouth. Guessing what would follow, I rose, bowed to the King, and walked away to my camp, which, it will be remembered, was set up in a little kloof commanding this place, at a distance only of a few hundred yards. So intent was all the multitude upon watching the dog that I doubt whether anyone saw me go. As for that poor beast, Scowl, who stayed behind, told me that it did not die for about ten minutes, since before its end a red rash appeared upon it similar to that which I had seen upon Saduko's child, and it was seized with convulsions.

Well, I reached my tent unmolested, and, having lit my pipe, engaged myself in making business entries in my note-book, in order to divert my mind as much as I could, when suddenly I heard a most devilish clamour. Looking up, I saw Masapo running towards me with a speed that I should have thought impossible in so fat a man, while after him raced the fierce-faced executioners, and behind came the mob.

"Kill the evil-doer!" they shouted.

Masapo reached me. He flung himself on his knees before me, gasping:

"Save me, Macumazahn! I am innocent. Mameena, the witch! Mameena—"

He got no farther, for the slayers had leapt on him like hounds upon a buck and dragged him from me.

Then I turned and covered up my eyes.

Next morning I left Nodwengu without saying good-bye to anyone, for what had happened there made me desire a change. My servant, Scowl, and one of my hunters remained, however, to collect some cattle that were still due to me.

A month or more later, when they joined me in Natal, bringing the cattle, they told me that Mameena, the widow of Masapo, had entered the house of Saduko as his second wife. In answer to a question which I put to them, they added that it was said that the Princess Nandie did not approve of this choice of Saduko, which she thought would not be fortunate for him or bring him happiness. As her husband seemed to be much enamoured of Mameena, however, she had waived her objections, and when Panda asked if she gave her consent had told him that, although she would prefer that Saduko should choose some other woman who had not been mixed up with the wizard who killed her child, she was prepared to take Mameena as her sister, and would know how to keep her in her place.

CHAPTER XI

THE SIN OF UMBELAZI

About eighteen months had gone by, and once again, in the autumn of the year 1856, I found myself at old Umbezi's kraal, where there seemed to be an extraordinary market for any kind of gas-pipe that could be called a gun. Well, as a trader who could not afford to neglect profitable markets, which are hard things to find, there I was.

Now, in eighteen months many things become a little obscured in one's memory, especially if they have to do with savages, in whom, after all, one takes only a philosophical and a business interest. Therefore I may perhaps be excused if I had more or less forgotten a good many of the details of what I may call the Mameena affair. These, however, came back to me very vividly when the first person that I met—at some distance from the kraal, where I suppose she had been taking a country walk—was the beautiful

Mameena herself. There she was, looking quite unchanged and as lovely as ever, sitting under the shade of a wild fig-tree and fanning herself with a handful of its leaves.

Of course I jumped off my wagon-box and greeted her.

"Siyakubona [that is, good morrow], Macumazahn," she said. "My heart is glad to see you."

"Siyakubona, Mameena," I answered, leaving out all reference to my heart. Then I added, looking at her: "Is it true that you have a new husband?"

"Yes, Macumazahn, an old lover of mine has become a new husband. You know whom I mean—Saduko. After the death of that evil-doer, Masapo, he grew very urgent, and the King, also the Inkosazana Nandie, pressed it on me, and so I yielded. Also, to be honest, Saduko was a good match, or seemed to be so."

By now we were walking side by side, for the train of wagons had gone ahead to the old outspan. So I stopped and looked her in the face.

"'Seemed to be,'" I repeated. "What do you mean by 'seemed to be'? Are you not happy this time?"

"Not altogether, Macumazahn," she answered, with a shrug of her shoulders. "Saduko is very fond of me—fonder than I like indeed, since it causes him to neglect Nandie, who, by the way, has another son, and, although she says little, that makes Nandie cross. In short," she added, with a burst of truth, "I am the plaything, Nandie is the great lady, and that place suits me ill."

"If you love Saduko, you should not mind, Mameena."

"Love," she said bitterly. "Piff! What is love? But I have asked you that question once before."

"Why are you here, Mameena?" I inquired, leaving it unanswered.

"Because Saduko is here, and, of course, Nandie, for she never leaves him, and he will not leave me; because the Prince Umbelazi is coming; because there are plots afoot and the great war draws near—that war in which so many must die."

"Between Cetewayo and Umbelazi, Mameena?"

"Aye, between Cetewayo and Umbelazi. Why do you suppose those wagons of yours are loaded with guns for which so many cattle must be paid? Not to shoot game with, I think. Well, this little kraal of my father's is just now the headquarters of the Umbelazi faction, the Isigqosa, as the princedom of Gikazi is that of Cetewayo. My poor father!" she added, with her characteristic shrug, "he thinks himself very great to-day, as he did after he had shot the elephant—before I nursed you, Macumazahn—but often I wonder what will be the end of it—for him and for all of us, Macumazahn, including yourself."

"I!" I answered. "What have I to do with your Zulu quarrels?"

"That you will know when you have done with them, Macumazahn. But here is the kraal, and before we enter it I wish to thank you for trying to protect that unlucky husband of mine, Masapo."

"I only did so, Mameena, because I thought him innocent."

"I know, Macumazahn; and so did I, although, as I always told you, I hated him, the man with whom my father forced me to marry. But I am afraid, from what I have learned since, that he was not altogether innocent. You see, Saduko had struck him, which he could not forget. Also, he was jealous of Saduko, who had been my suitor, and wished to injure him. But what I do not understand," she added, with a burst of confidence, "is why he did not kill Saduko instead of his child."

"Well, Mameena, you may remember it was said he tried to do so."

"Yes, Macumazahn; I had forgotten that. I suppose that he did try, and failed. Oh, now I see things with both eyes. Look, yonder is my father. I will go away. But come and talk to me sometimes, Macumazahn, for otherwise Nandie will be careful that I should hear nothing—I who am the plaything, the beautiful woman of the House, who must sit and smile, but must not think."

So she departed, and I went on to meet old Umbezi, who came gambolling towards me like an obese goat, reflecting that, whatever might be the truth or otherwise of her story, her advancement in the world did not seem to have brought Mameena greater happiness and contentment.

Umbezi, who greeted me warmly, was in high spirits and full of importance. He informed me that the marriage of Mameena to Saduko, after the death of the wizard, her husband, whose tribe and cattle had been given to Saduko in compensation for the loss of his son, was a most fortunate thing for him.

I asked why.

"Because as Saduko grows great so I, his father-in-law, grow great with him, Macumazahn, especially as he has been liberal to me in the matter of cattle, passing on to me a share of the herds of Masapo, so that I, who have been poor so long, am getting rich at last. Moreover, my kraal is to be honoured with a visit from Umbelazi and some of his brothers to-morrow, and Saduko has promised to lift me up high when the Prince is declared heir to the throne."

"Which prince?" I asked.

"Umbelazi, Macumazahn. Who else? Umbelazi, who without doubt will conquer Cetewayo."

"Why without doubt, Umbezi? Cetewayo has a great following, and if he should conquer I think that you will only be lifted up in the crops of the vultures."

At this rough suggestion Umbezi's fat face fell.

"O Macumazana," he said, "if I thought that, I would go over to Cetewayo, although Saduko is my son-in-law. But it is not possible, since the King loves Umbelazi's mother most of all his wives, and, as I chance to know, has sworn to her that he favours Umbelazi's cause, since he is the dearest to him of all his sons, and will do everything that he can to help him, even to the sending of his own regiment to his assistance, if there should be need. Also, it is said that Zikali, Opener-of-Roads, who has all wisdom, has prophesied that Umbelazi will win more than he ever hoped for."

"The King!" I said, "a straw blown hither and thither between two great winds, waiting to be wafted to rest by that which is strongest! The prophecy of Zikali! It seems to me that it can be read two ways, if, indeed, he ever made one. Well, Umbezi, I hope that you are right, for, although it is no affair of mine, who am but a white trader in your country, I like Umbelazi better than Cetewayo, and think that he has a kinder heart. Also, as you have chosen his side, I advise you to stick to it, since traitors to a cause seldom come to any good, whether it wins or loses. And now, will you take count of the guns and powder which I have brought with me?"

Ah! better would it have been for Umbezi if he had listened to my advice and remained faithful to the leader he had chosen, for then, even if he had lost his life, at least he would have kept his good name. But of him presently, as they say in pedigrees.

Next day I went to pay my respects to Nandie, whom I found engaged in nursing her new baby and as quiet and stately in her demeanour as ever. Still, I think that she was very glad to see me, because I had tried to save the life of her first child, whom she could not forget, if for no other reason. Whilst I was talking to her of that sad matter, also of the political state of the country, as to which I think she wished to say something to me, Mameena entered the hut, without waiting to be asked, and sat down, whereon Nandie became suddenly silent.

This, however, did not trouble Mameena, who talked away about anything and everything, completely ignoring the head-wife. For a while Nandie bore it with patience, but at length she took advantage of a pause in the conversation to say in her firm, low voice:

"This is my hut, daughter of Umbezi, a thing which you remember well enough when it is a question whether Saduko, our husband, shall visit you or me. Can you not remember it now when I would speak with the white chief, Watcher-by-Night, who has been so good as to take the trouble to come to see me?"

On hearing these words Mameena leapt up in a rage, and I must say I never saw her look more lovely.

"You insult me, daughter of Panda, as you always try to do, because you are jealous of me."

"Your pardon, sister," replied Nandie. "Why should I, who am Saduko's Inkosikazi, and, as you say, daughter of Panda, the King, be jealous of the widow of the wizard, Masapo, and the daughter of the headman, Umbezi, whom it has pleased our husband to take into his house to be the companion of his leisure?"

"Why? Because you know that Saduko loves my little finger more than he does your whole body, although you are of the King's blood and have borne him brats," she answered, looking at the infant with no kindly eye.

"It may be so, daughter of Umbezi, for men have their fancies, and without doubt you are fair. Yet I would ask you one thing—if Saduko loves you so much, how comes it he trusts you so little that you must learn any matter of weight by listening at my door, as I found you doing the other day?"

"Because you teach him not to do so, O Nandie. Because you are ever telling him not to consult with me, since she who has betrayed one husband may betray another. Because you make him believe my place is that of his toy, not that of his companion, and this although I am cleverer than you and all your House tied into one bundle, as you may find out some day."

"Yes," answered Nandie, quite undisturbed, "I do teach him these things, and I am glad that in this matter Saduko has a thinking head and listens to me. Also I agree that it is likely I shall learn many more ill things through and of you one day, daughter of Umbezi. And now, as it is not good that we should wrangle before this white lord, again I say to you that this is my hut, in which I wish to speak alone with my guest."

"I go, I go!" gasped Mameena; "but I tell you that Saduko shall hear of this."

"Certainly he will hear of it, for I shall tell him when he comes to-night."

Another instant and Mameena was gone, having shot out of the hut like a rabbit from its burrow.

"I ask your pardon, Macumazahn, for what has happened," said Nandie, "but it had become necessary that I should teach my sister, Mameena, upon which stool she ought to sit. I do not trust her, Macumazahn. I think that she knows more of the death of my child than she chooses to say, she who wished to be rid of Masapo for a reason you can guess. I think also she will bring shame and trouble upon Saduko, whom she has bewitched with her beauty, as she bewitches all men—perhaps even yourself a little, Macumazahn. And now let us talk of other matters."

To this proposition I agreed cordially, since, to tell the truth, if I could have managed to do so with any decent grace, I should have been out of that hut long before Mameena. So we fell to conversing on the condition of Zululand and the dangers that lay ahead for all who were connected with the royal House— a state of affairs which troubled Nandie much, for she was a clear-headed woman, and one who feared the future.

"Ah! Macumazahn," she said to me as we parted, "I would that I were the wife of some man who did not desire to grow great, and that no royal blood ran in my veins."

On the next day the Prince Umbelazi arrived, and with him Saduko and a few other notable men. They came quite quietly and without any ostensible escort, although Scowl, my servant, told me he heard that the bush at a little distance was swarming with soldiers of the Isigqosa party. If I remember rightly, the excuse for the visit was that Umbezi had some of a certain rare breed of white cattle whereof the prince wished to secure young bulls and heifers to improve his herd.

Once inside the kraal, however, Umbelazi, who was a very open-natured man, threw off all pretence, and, after greeting me heartily enough, told me with plainness that he was there because this was a convenient spot on which to arrange the consolidation of his party.

Almost every hour during the next two weeks messengers—many of whom were chiefs disguised— came and went. I should have liked to follow their example—that is, so far as their departure was concerned—for I felt that I was being drawn into a very dangerous vortex. But, as a matter of fact, I could not escape, since I was obliged to wait to receive payment for my stuff, which, as usual, was made in cattle.

Umbelazi talked with me a good deal at that time, impressing upon me how friendly he was towards the English white men of Natal, as distinguished from the Boers, and what good treatment he was prepared to promise to them, should he ever attain to authority in Zululand. It was during one of the earliest of these conversations, which, of course, I saw had an ultimate object, that he met Mameena, I think, for the first time.

We were walking together in a little natural glade of the bush that bordered one side of the kraal, when, at the end of it, looking like some wood nymph of classic fable in the light of the setting sun, appeared the lovely Mameena, clothed only in her girdle of fur, her necklace of blue beads and some copper ornaments, and carrying upon her head a gourd.

Umbelazi noted her at once, and, ceasing his political talk, of which he was obviously tired, asked me who that beautiful intombi (that is, girl) might be.

"She is not an intombi, Prince," I answered. "She is a widow who is again a wife, the second wife of your friend and councillor, Saduko, and the daughter of your host, Umbezi."

"Is it so, Macumazahn? Oh, then I have heard of her, though, as it chances, I have never met her before. No wonder that my sister Nandie is jealous, for she is beautiful indeed."

"Yes," I answered, "she looks pretty against the red sky, does she not?"

By now we were drawing near to Mameena, and I greeted her, asking if she wanted anything.

"Nothing, Macumazahn," she answered in her delicate, modest way, for never did I know anyone who could seem quite so modest as Mameena, and with a swift glance of her shy eyes at the tall and splendid Umbelazi, "nothing. Only," she added, "I was passing with the milk of one of the few cows my father gave me, and saw you, and I thought that perhaps, as the day has been so hot, you might like a drink of it."

Then, lifting the gourd from her head, she held it out to me.

I thanked her, drank some—who could do less?—and returned it to her, whereon she made as though she would hasten to depart.

"May I not drink also, daughter of Umbezi?" asked Umbelazi, who could scarcely take his eyes off her.

"Certainly, sir, if you are a friend of Macumazahn," she replied, handing him the gourd.

"I am that, Lady, and more than that, since I am a friend of your husband, Saduko, also, as you will know when I tell you that my name is Umbelazi."

"I thought it must be so," she replied, "because of your—of your stature. Let the Prince accept the offering of his servant, who one day hopes to be his subject," and, dropping upon her knee, she held out the gourd to him. Over it I saw their eyes meet. He drank, and as he handed back the vessel she said:

"O Prince, may I be granted a word with you? I have that to tell which you would perhaps do well to hear, since news sometimes reaches the ears of humble women that escapes those of the men, our masters."

He bowed his head in assent, whereon, taking a hint which Mameena gave me with her eyes, I muttered something about business and made myself scarce. I may add that Mameena must have had a great deal to tell Umbelazi. Fully an hour and a half had gone by before, by the light of the moon, from a point of vantage on my wagon-box, whence, according to my custom, I was keeping a lookout on things in general, I saw her slip back to the kraal silently as a snake, followed at a little distance by the towering form of Umbelazi.

Apparently Mameena continued to be the recipient of information which she found it necessary to communicate in private to the prince. At any rate, on sundry subsequent evenings the dullness of my vigil on the wagon-box was relieved by the sight of her graceful figure gliding home from the kloof that Umbelazi seemed to find a very suitable spot for reflection after sunset. On one of the last of these occasions I remember that Nandie chanced to be with me, having come to my wagon for some medicine for her baby.

"What does it mean, Macumazahn?" she asked, when the pair had gone by, as they thought unobserved, since we were standing where they could not see us.

"I don't know, and I don't want to know," I answered sharply.

"Neither do I, Macumazahn; but without doubt we shall learn in time. If the crocodile is patient and silent the buck always drops into its jaws at last."

On the day after Nandie made this wise remark Saduko started on a mission, as I understood, to win over several doubtful chiefs to the cause of Indhlovu-ene-sihlonti (the Elephant-with-the-tuft-of-hair), as the Prince Umbelazi was called among the Zulus, though not to his face. This mission lasted ten days, and before it was concluded an important event happened at Umbezi's kraal.

One evening Mameena came to me in a great rage, and said that she could bear her present life no longer. Presuming on her rank and position as head-wife, Nandie treated her like a servant—nay, like a little dog, to be beaten with a stick. She wished that Nandie would die.

"It will be very unlucky for you if she does," I answered, "for then, perhaps, Zikali will be summoned to look into the matter, as he was before."

What was she to do, she went on, ignoring my remark.

"Eat the porridge that you have made in your own pot, or break the pot" (i.e. go away), I suggested. "There was no need for you to marry Saduko, any more than there was for you to marry Masapo."

"How can you talk to me like that, Macumazahn," she answered, stamping her foot, "when you know well it is your fault if I married anyone? Piff! I hate them all, and, since my father would only beat me if I took my troubles to him, I will run off, and live in the wilderness alone and become a witch-doctoress."

"I am afraid you will find it very dull, Mameena," I began in a bantering tone, for, to tell the truth, I did not think it wise to show her too much sympathy while she was so excited.

Mameena never waited for the end of the sentence, but, sobbing out that I was false and cruel, she turned and departed swiftly. Oh! little did I foresee how and where we should meet again.

Next morning I was awakened shortly after sunrise by Scowl, whom I had sent out with another man the night before to look for a lost ox.

"Well, have you found the ox?" I asked.

"Yes, Baas; but I did not waken you to tell you that. I have a message for you, Baas, from Mameena, wife of Saduko, whom I met about four hours ago upon the plain yonder."

I bade him set it out.

"These were the words of Mameena, Baas: 'Say to Macumazahn, your master, that Indhlovu-ene-sihlonti, taking pity on my wrongs and loving me with his heart, has offered to take me into his House and that I have accepted his offer, since I think it better to become the Inkosazana of the Zulus, as I shall one day, than to remain a servant in the house of Nandie. Say to Macumazahn that when Saduko returns he is to tell him that this is all his fault, since if he had kept Nandie in her place I would have died rather than leave him. Let him say to Saduko also that, although from henceforth we can be no more than friends, my heart is still tender towards him, and that by day and by night I will strive to water his greatness, so that it may grow into a tree that shall shade the land. Let Macumazahn bid him not to be angry with me, since what I do I do for his good, as he would have found no happiness while Nandie and I dwelt in one house. Above all, also let him not be angry with the Prince, who loves him more than any man, and does but travel whither the wind that I breathe blows him. Bid Macumazahn think of me kindly, as I shall of him while my eyes are open.'"

I listened to this amazing message in silence, then asked if Mameena was alone.

"No, Baas; Umbelazi and some soldiers were with her, but they did not hear her words, for she stepped aside to speak with me. Then she returned to them, and they walked away swiftly, and were swallowed up in the night."

"Very good, Sikauli," I said. "Make me some coffee, and make it strong."

I dressed and drank several cups of the coffee, all the while "thinking with my head," as the Zulus say. Then I walked up to the kraal to see Umbezi, whom I found just coming out of his hut, yawning.

"Why do you look so black upon this beautiful morning, Macumazahn?" asked the genial old scamp. "Have you lost your best cow, or what?"

"No, my friend," I answered; "but you and another have lost your best cow." And word for word I repeated to him Mameena's message. When I had finished really I thought that Umbezi was about to faint.

"Curses be on the head of this Mameena!" he exclaimed. "Surely some evil spirit must have been her father, not I, and well was she called Child of Storm.[*] What shall I do now, Macumazahn? Thanks be to my Spirit," he added, with an air of relief, "she is too far gone for me to try to catch her; also, if I did, Umbelazi and his soldiers would kill me."

[*—That, if I have not said so already, was the meaning which the Zulus gave to the word "Mameena", although as I know the language I cannot get any such interpretation out of the name, I believe that it was given to her, however, because she was born just before a terrible tempest, when the wind wailing round the hut made a sound like the word "Ma-mee-na". —A. Q.]

"And what will Saduko do if you don't?" I asked.

"Oh, of course he will be angry, for no doubt he is fond of her. But, after all, I am used to that. You remember how he went mad when she married Masapo. At least, he cannot say that I made her run away with Umbelazi. After all, it is a matter which they must settle between them."

"I think it may mean great trouble," I said, "at a time when trouble is not needed."

"Oh, why so, Macumazahn? My daughter did not get on with the Princess Nandie—we could all see that—for they would scarcely speak to each other. And if Saduko is fond of her—well, after all, there are other beautiful women in Zululand. I know one or two of them myself whom I will mention to Saduko—or rather to Nandie. Really, as things were, I am not sure but that he is well rid of her."

"But what do you think of the matter as her father?" I asked, for I wanted to see to what length his accommodating morality would stretch.

"As her father—well, of course, Macumazahn, as her father I am sorry, because it will mean talk, will it not, as the Masapo business did? Still, there is this to be said for Mameena," he added, with a brightening face, "she always runs away up the tree, not down. When she got rid of Masapo—I mean when Masapo was killed for his witchcraft—she married Saduko, who was a bigger man—Saduko, whom she would not marry when Masapo was the bigger man. And now, when she has got rid of Saduko, she enters the hut of Umbelazi, who will one day be King of the Zulus, the biggest man in all the world, which means that she will be the biggest woman, for remember, Macumazahn, she will walk round and round that great Umbelazi till whatever way he looks he will see her and no one else. Oh, she will grow great, and carry up her poor old father in the blanket on her back. Oh, the sun still shines behind the cloud, Macumazahn, so let us make the best of the cloud, since we know that it will break out presently."

"Yes, Umbezi; but other things besides the sun break out from clouds sometimes—lightning, for instance; lightning which kills."

"You speak ill-omened words, Macumazahn; words that take away my appetite, which is generally excellent at this hour. Well, if Mameena is bad it is not my fault, for I brought her up to be good. After all," he added with an outburst of petulance, "why do you scold me when it is your fault? If you had run away with the girl when you might have done so, there would have been none of this trouble."

"Perhaps not," I answered; "only then I am sure I should have been dead to-day, as I think that all who have to do with her will be ere long. And now, Umbezi, I wish you a good breakfast."

On the following morning, Saduko returned and was told the news by Nandie, whom I had carefully avoided. On this occasion, however, I was forced to be present, as the person to whom the sinful Mameena had sent her farewell message. It was a very painful experience, of which I do not remember all the details. For a while after he learned the truth Saduko sat still as a stone, staring in front of him, with a face that seemed to have become suddenly old. Then he turned upon Umbezi, and in a few terrible words accused him of having arranged the matter in order to advance his own fortunes at the price of his daughter's dishonour. Next, without listening to his ex-father-in-law's voluble explanations, he rose and said that he was going away to kill Umbelazi, the evil-doer who had robbed him of the wife he loved, with the connivance of all three of us, and by a sweep of his hand he indicated Umbezi, the Princess Nandie and myself.

This was more than I could stand, so I, too, rose and asked him what he meant, adding in the irritation of the moment that if I had wished to rob him of his beautiful Mameena, I thought I could have done so long ago—a remark that staggered him a little.

Then Nandie rose also, and spoke in her quiet voice.

"Saduko, my husband," she said, "I, a Princess of the Zulu House, married you who are not of royal blood because I loved you, and although Panda the King and Umbelazi the Prince wished it, for no other reason whatsoever. Well, I have been faithful to you through some trials, even when you set the widow of a wizard—if, indeed, as I have reason to suspect, she was not herself the wizard—before me, and although that wizard had killed our son, lived in her hut rather than in mine. Now this woman of whom you thought so much has deserted you for your friend and my brother, the Prince Umbelazi—Umbelazi who is called the Handsome, and who, if the fortune of war goes with him, as it may or may not, will succeed to Panda, my father. This she has done because she alleges that I, your Inkosikazi and the King's daughter, treated her as a servant, which is a lie. I kept her in her place, no more, who, if she could have had her will, would have ousted me from mine, perhaps by death, for the wives of wizards learn their arts. On this pretext she has left you; but that is not her real reason. She has left you because the Prince, my brother, whom she has befooled with her tricks and beauty, as she has befooled others, or tried to"—and she glanced at me—"is a bigger man than you are. You, Saduko, may become great, as my heart prays that you will, but my brother may become a king. She does not love him any more than she loved you, but she does love the place that may be his, and therefore hers—she who would be the first doe of the herd. My husband, I think that you are well rid of Mameena, for I think also that if she had stayed with us there would have been more deaths in our House; perhaps mine, which would not matter, and perhaps yours, which would matter much. All this I say to you, not from jealousy of one who is fairer than I, but because it is the truth. Therefore my counsel to you is to let this business pass over and keep silent. Above all, seek not to avenge yourself upon Umbelazi, since I am sure that he has taken vengeance to dwell with him in his own hut. I have spoken."

That this moderate and reasoned speech of Nandie's produced a great effect upon Saduko I could see, but at the time the only answer he made to it was:

"Let the name of Mameena be spoken no more within hearing of my ears. Mameena is dead."

So her name was heard no more in the Houses of Saduko and of Umbezi, and when it was necessary for any reason to refer to her, she was given a new name, a composite Zulu word, "O-we-Zulu", I think it was, which is "Storm-child" shortly translated, for "Zulu" means a storm as well as the sky.

I do not think that Saduko spoke of her to me again until towards the climax of this history, and certainly I did not mention her to him. But from that day forward I noted that he was a changed man. His pride and open pleasure in his great success, which had caused the Zulus to name him the "Self-eater," were no longer marked. He became cold and silent, like a man who is thinking deeply, but who shutters his thoughts lest some should read them through the windows of his eyes. Moreover, he paid a visit to Zikali the Little and Wise, as I found out by accident; but what advice that cunning old dwarf gave to him I did not find out—then.

The only other event which happened in connection with this elopement was that a message came from Umbelazi to Saduko, brought by one of the princes, a brother of Umbelazi, who was of his party. As I know, for I heard it delivered, it was a very humble message when the relative positions of the two men are considered—that of one who knew that he had done wrong, and, if not repentant, was heartily ashamed of himself.

"Saduko," it said, "I have stolen a cow of yours, and I hope you will forgive me, since that cow did not love the pasture in your kraal, but in mine she grows fat and is content. Moreover, in return I will give you many other cows. Everything that I have to give, I will give to you who are my friend and trusted councillor. Send me word, O Saduko, that this wall which I have built between us is broken down, since ere long you and I must stand together in war."

To this message Saduko's answer was:

"O Prince, you are troubled about a very little thing. That cow which you have taken was of no worth to me, for who wishes to keep a beast that is ever tearing and lowing at the gates of the kraal, disturbing those who would sleep inside with her noise? Had you asked her of me, I would have given her to you freely. I thank you for your offer, but I need no more cows, especially if, like this one, they have no calves. As for a wall between us, there is none, for how can two men who, if the battle is to be won, must stand shoulder to shoulder, fight if divided by a wall? O Son of the King, I am dreaming by day and night of the battle and the victory, and I have forgotten all about the barren cow that ran away after you, the great bull of the herd. Only do not be surprised if one day you find that this cow has a sharp horn."

CHAPTER XII

PANDA'S PRAYER

About six weeks later, in the month of November, 1856, I chanced to be at Nodwengu when the quarrel between the princes came to a head. Although none of the regiments was actually allowed to enter the town—that is, as a regiment—the place was full of people, all of them in a state of great excitement, who came in during the daytime and went to sleep in the neighbouring military kraals at night. One evening, as some of these soldiers—about a thousand of them, if I remember right—were returning to the Ukubaza kraal, a fight occurred between them, which led to the final outbreak.

As it happened, at that time there were two separate regiments stationed at this kraal. I think that they were the Imkulutshana and the Hlaba, one of which favoured Cetewayo and the other Umbelazi. As certain companies of each of these regiments marched along together in parallel lines, two of their captains got into dispute on the eternal subject of the succession to the throne. From words they came to blows, and the end of it was that he who favoured Umbelazi killed him who favoured Cetewayo with his kerry. Thereon the comrades of the slain man, raising a shout of "Usutu," which became the war-cry of Cetewayo's party, fell upon the others, and a dreadful combat ensued. Fortunately the soldiers were only armed with sticks, or the slaughter would have been very great; but as it was, after an indecisive engagement, about fifty men were killed and many more injured.

Now, with my usual bad luck, I, who had gone out to shoot a few birds for the pot—pauw, or bustard, I think they were—was returning across this very plain to my old encampment in the kloof where Masapo had been executed, and so ran into the fight just as it was beginning. I saw the captain killed and the subsequent engagement. Indeed, as it happened, I did more. Not knowing where to go or what to do, for I was quite alone, I pulled up my horse behind a tree and waited till I could escape the horrors about me; for I can assure anyone who may ever read these words that it is a very horrible sight to see a thousand men engaged in fierce and deadly combat. In truth, the fact that they had no spears, and could only batter each other to death with their heavy kerries, made it worse, since the duels were more desperate and prolonged.

Everywhere men were rolling on the ground, hitting at each other's heads, until at last some blow went home and one of them threw out his arms and lay still, either dead or senseless. Well, there I sat watching all this shocking business from the saddle of my trained shooting pony, which stood like a stone, till presently I became aware of two great fellows rushing at me with their eyes starting out of their heads and shouting as they came:

"Kill Umbelazi's white man! Kill! Kill!"

Then, seeing that the matter was urgent and that it was a question of my life or theirs, I came into action.

In my hand I held a double-barrelled shotgun loaded with what we used to call "loopers," or B.B. shot, of which but a few went to each charge, for I had hoped to meet with a small buck on my way to camp. So, as these soldiers came, I lifted the gun and fired, the right barrel at one of them and the left barrel at the other, aiming in each case at the centre of the small dancing shields, which from force of habit they held stretched out to protect their throats and breasts. At that distance, of course, the loopers sank through the soft hide of the shields and deep into the bodies of those who carried them, so that both of them dropped dead, the left-hand man being so close that he fell against my pony, his uplifted kerry striking me upon the thigh and bruising me.

When I saw what I had done, and that my danger was over for the moment, without waiting to reload I dug the spurs into my horse's sides and galloped off to Nodwengu, passing between the groups of struggling men. On arriving unharmed at the town, I went instantly to the royal huts and demanded to see the King, who sent word that I was to be admitted. On coming before him I told him exactly what had happened—that I had killed two of Cetewayo's men in order to save my own life, and on that account submitted myself to his justice.

"O Macumazana," said Panda in great distress, "I know well that you are not to blame, and already I have sent out a regiment to stop this fighting, with command that those who caused it should be brought before me to-morrow for judgment. I am glad indeed, Macumazahn, that you have escaped without harm, but I must tell you that I fear henceforth your life will be in danger, since all the Usutu party will hold it forfeit if they can catch you. While you are in my town I can protect you, for I will set a strong guard about your camp; but here you will have to stay until these troubles are done with, since if you leave you may be murdered on the road."

"I thank you for your kindness, King," I answered; "but all this is very awkward for me, who hoped to trek for Natal to-morrow."

"Well, there it is, Macumazahn, you will have to stay here unless you wish to be killed. He who walks into a storm must put up with the hailstones."

So it came about that once again Fate dragged me into the Zulu maelstrom.

On the morrow I was summoned to the trial, half as a witness and half as one of the offenders. Going to the head of the Nodwengu kraal, where Panda was sitting in state with his Council, I found the whole great space in front of him crowded with a dense concourse of fierce-faced partisans, those who favoured Cetewayo—the Usutu—sitting on the right, and those who favoured Umbelazi—the Isigqosa— sitting on the left. At the head of the right-hand section sat Cetewayo, his brethren and chief men. At the head of the left-hand section sat Umbelazi, his brethren and his chief men, amongst whom I saw Saduko take a place immediately behind the Prince, so that he could whisper into his ear.

To myself and my little band of eight hunters, who by Panda's express permission, came armed with their guns, as I did also, for I was determined that if the necessity arose we would sell our lives as dearly as we could, was appointed a place almost in front of the King and between the two factions. When everyone was seated the trial began, Panda demanding to know who had caused the tumult of the previous night.

I cannot set out what followed in all its details, for it would be too long; also I have forgotten many of them. I remember, however, that Cetewayo's people said that Umbelazi's men were the aggressors, and that Umbelazi's people said that Cetewayo's men were the aggressors, and that each of their parties backed up these statements, which were given at great length, with loud shouts.

"How am I to know the truth?" exclaimed Panda at last. "Macumazahn, you were there; step forward and tell it to me."

So I stood out and told the King what I had seen, namely that the captain who favoured Cetewayo had begun the quarrel by striking the captain who favoured Umbelazi, but that in the end Umbelazi's man had killed Cetewayo's man, after which the fighting commenced.

"Then it would seem that the Usutu are to blame," said Panda.

"Upon what grounds do you say so, my father?" asked Cetewayo, springing up. "Upon the testimony of this white man, who is well known to be the friend of Umbelazi and of his henchman Saduko, and who himself killed two of those who called me chief in the course of the fight?"

"Yes, Cetewayo," I broke in, "because I thought it better that I should kill them than that they should kill me, whom they attacked quite unprovoked."

"At any rate, you killed them, little White Man," shouted Cetewayo, "for which cause your blood is forfeit. Say, did Umbelazi give you leave to appear before the King accompanied by men armed with guns, when we who are his sons must come with sticks only? If so, let him protect you!"

"That I will do if there is need!" exclaimed Umbelazi.

"Thank you, Prince," I said; "but if there is need I will protect myself as I did yesterday," and, cocking my double-barrelled rifle, I looked full at Cetewayo.

"When you leave here, then at least I will come even with you, Macumazahn!" threatened Cetewayo, spitting through his teeth, as was his way when mad with passion.

For he was beside himself, and wished to vent his temper on someone, although in truth he and I were always good friends.

"If so I shall stop where I am," I answered coolly, "in the shadow of the King, your father. Moreover, are you so lost in folly, Cetewayo, that you should wish to bring the English about your ears? Know that if I am killed you will be asked to give account of my blood."

"Aye," interrupted Panda, "and know that if anyone lays a finger on Macumazana, who is my guest, he shall die, whether he be a common man or a prince and my son. Also, Cetewayo, I fine you twenty head of cattle, to be paid to Macumazana because of the unprovoked attack which your men made upon him when he rightly slew them."

"The fine shall be paid, my father," said Cetewayo more quietly, for he saw that in threatening me he had pushed matters too far.

Then, after some more talk, Panda gave judgment in the cause, which judgment really amounted to nothing. As it was impossible to decide which party was most to blame, he fined both an equal number of cattle, accompanying the fine with a lecture on their ill-behaviour, which was listened to indifferently.

After this matter was disposed of the real business of the meeting began.

Rising to his feet, Cetewayo addressed Panda.

"My father," he said, "the land wanders and wanders in darkness, and you alone can give light for its feet. I and my brother, Umbelazi, are at variance, and the quarrel is a great one, namely, as to which of us is to sit in your place when you are 'gone down,' when we call and you do not answer. Some of the nation favour one of us and some favour the other, but you, O King, and you alone, have the voice of judgment. Still, before you speak, I and those who stand with me would bring this to your mind. My mother, Umqumbazi, is your Inkosikazi, your head-wife, and therefore, according to our law, I, her eldest son, should be your heir. Moreover, when you fled to the Boers before the fall of him who sat in your place before you [Dingaan], did not they, the white Amabunu, ask you which amongst your sons was your heir, and did you not point me out to the white men? And thereon did not the Amabunu clothe me in a dress of honour because I was the King to be? But now of late the mother of Umbelazi has been whispering in your ear, as have others"—and he looked at Saduko and some of Umbelazi's brethren—"and your face has grown cold towards me, so cold that many say that you will point out

Umbelazi to be King after you and stamp on my name. If this is so, my father, tell me at once, that I may know what to do."

Having finished this speech, which certainly did not lack force and dignity, Cetewayo sat down again, awaiting the answer in sullen silence. But, making none, Panda looked at Umbelazi, who, on rising, was greeted with a great cheer, for although Cetewayo had the larger following in the land, especially among the distant chiefs, the Zulus individually loved Umbelazi more, perhaps because of his stature, beauty and kindly disposition—physical and moral qualities that naturally appeal to a savage nation.

"My father," he said, "like my brother, Cetewayo, I await your word. Whatever you may have said to the Amabunu in haste or fear, I do not admit that Cetewayo was ever proclaimed your heir in the hearing of the Zulu people. I say that my right to the succession is as good as his, and that it lies with you, and you alone, to declare which of us shall put on the royal kaross in days that my heart prays may be distant. Still, to save bloodshed, I am willing to divide the land with Cetewayo" (here both Panda and Cetewayo shook their heads and the audience roared "Nay"), "or, if that does not please him, I am willing to meet Cetewayo man to man and spear to spear and fight till one of us be slain."

"A safe offer!" sneered Cetewayo, "for is not my brother named 'Elephant,' and the strongest warrior among the Zulus? No, I will not set the fortunes of those who cling to me on the chance of a single stab, or on the might of a man's muscles. Decide, O father; say which of the two of us is to sit at the head of your kraal after you have gone over to the Spirits and are but an ancestor to be worshipped."

Now, Panda looked much disturbed, as was not wonderful, since, rushing out from the fence behind which they had been listening, Umqumbazi, Cetewayo's mother, whispered into one of his ears, while Umbelazi's mother whispered into the other. What advice each of them gave I do not know, although obviously it was not the same advice, since the poor man rolled his eyes first at one and then at the other, and finally put his hands over his ears that he might hear no more.

"Choose, choose, O King!" shouted the audience. "Who is to succeed you, Cetewayo or Umbelazi?"

Watching Panda, I saw that he fell into a kind of agony; his fat sides heaved, and, although the day was cold, sweat ran from his brow.

"What would the white men do in such a case?" he said to me in a hoarse, low voice, whereon I answered, looking at the ground and speaking so that few could hear me:

"I think, O King, that a white man would do nothing. He would say that others might settle the matter after he was dead."

"Would that I could say so, too," muttered Panda; "but it is not possible."

Then followed a long pause, during which all were silent, for every man there felt that the hour was big with doom. At length Panda rose with difficulty, because of his unwieldy weight, and uttered these fateful words, that were none the less ominous because of the homely idiom in which they were couched:

"When two young bulls quarrel they must fight it out."

Instantly in one tremendous roar volleyed forth the royal salute of "Bayéte", a signal of the acceptance of the King's word—the word that meant civil war and the death of many thousands.

Then Panda turned and, so feebly that I thought he would fall, walked through the gateway behind him, followed by the rival queens. Each of these ladies struggled to be first after him in the gate, thinking that it would be an omen of success for her son. Finally, however, to the disappointment of the multitude, they only succeeded in passing it side by side.

When they had gone the great audience began to break up, the men of each party marching away together as though by common consent, without offering any insult or molestation to their adversaries. I think that this peaceable attitude arose, however, from the knowledge that matters had now passed from the stage of private quarrel into that of public war. It was felt that their dispute awaited decision, not with sticks outside the Nodwengu kraal, but with spears upon some great battlefield, for which they went to prepare.

Within two days, except for those regiments which Panda kept to guard his person, scarcely a soldier was to be seen in the neighbourhood of Nodwengu. The princes also departed to muster their adherents, Cetewayo establishing himself among the Mandhlakazi that he commanded, and Umbelazi returning to the kraal of Umbezi, which happened to stand almost in the centre of that part of the nation which adhered to him.

Whether he took Mameena with him there I am not certain. I believe, however, that, fearing lest her welcome at her birthplace should be warmer than she wished, she settled herself at some retired and outlying kraal in the neighbourhood, and there awaited the crisis of her fortune. At any rate, I saw nothing of her, for she was careful to keep out of my way.

With Umbelazi and Saduko, however, I did have an interview. Before they left Nodwengu they called on me together, apparently on the best of terms, and said in effect that they hoped for my support in the coming war.

I answered that, however well I might like them personally, a Zulu civil war was no affair of mine, and that, indeed, for every reason, including the supreme one of my own safety, I had better get out of the way at once.

They argued with me for a long while, making great offers and promises of reward, till at length, when he saw that my determination could not be shaken, Umbelazi said:

"Come, Saduko, let us humble ourselves no more before this white man. After all, he is right; the business is none of his, and why should we ask him to risk his life in our quarrel, knowing as we do that white men are not like us; they think a great deal of their lives. Farewell, Macumazahn. If I conquer and grow great you will always be welcome in Zululand, whereas if I fail perhaps you will be best over the Tugela river."

Now, I felt the hidden taunt in this speech very keenly. Still, being determined that for once I would be wise and not allow my natural curiosity and love of adventure to drag me into more risks and trouble, I replied:

"The Prince says that I am not brave and love my life, and what he says is true. I fear fighting, who by nature am a trader with the heart of a trader, not a warrior with the heart of a warrior, like the great Indhlovu-ene-Sihlonti"—words at which I saw the grave Saduko smile faintly. "So farewell to you, Prince, and may good fortune attend you."

Of course, to call the Prince to his face by this nickname, which referred to a defect in his person, was something of an insult; but I had been insulted, and meant to give him "a Roland for his Oliver." However, he took it in good part.

"What is good fortune, Macumazahn?" Umbelazi replied as he grasped my hand. "Sometimes I think that to live and prosper is good fortune, and sometimes I think that to die and sleep is good fortune, for in sleep there is neither hunger nor thirst of body or of spirit. In sleep there come no cares; in sleep ambitions are at rest; nor do those who look no more upon the sun smart beneath the treacheries of false women or false friends. Should the battle turn against me, Macumazahn, at least that good fortune will be mine, for never will I live to be crushed beneath Cetewayo's heel."

Then he went. Saduko accompanied him for a little way, but, making some excuse to the Prince, came back and said to me:

"Macumazahn, my friend, I dare say that we part for the last time, and therefore I make a request to you. It is as to one who is dead to me. Macumazahn, I believe that Umbelazi the thief"—these words broke from his lips with a hiss—"has given her many cattle and hidden her away either in the kloof of Zikali the Wise, or near to it, under his care. Now, if the war should go against Umbelazi and I should be killed in it, I think evil will fall upon that woman's head, I who have grown sure that it was she who was the wizard and not Masapo the Boar. Also, as one connected with Umbelazi, who has helped him in his plots, she will be killed if she is caught. Macumazahn, hearken to me. I will tell you the truth. My heart is still on fire for that woman. She has bewitched me; her eyes haunt my sleep and I hear her voice in the wind. She is more to me than all the earth and all the sky, and although she has wronged me I do not wish that harm should come to her. Macumazahn, I pray you if I die, do your best to befriend her, even though it be only as a servant in your house, for I think that she cares more for you than for anyone, who only ran away with him"—and he pointed in the direction that Umbelazi had taken—"because he is a prince, who, in her folly, she believes will be a king. At least take her to Natal, Macumazahn, where, if you wish to be free of her, she can marry whom she will and will live safe until night comes. Panda loves you much, and, whoever conquers in the war, will give you her life if you ask it of him."

Then this strange man drew the back of his hand across his eyes, from which I saw the tears were running, and, muttering, "If you would have good fortune remember my prayer," turned and left me before I could answer a single word.

As for me, I sat down upon an ant-heap and whistled a whole hymn tune that my mother had taught me before I could think at all. To be left the guardian of Mameena! Talk of a "damnosa hereditas," a terrible and mischievous inheritance—why, this was the worst that ever I heard of. A servant in my house indeed, knowing what I did about her! Why, I had sooner share the "good fortune" which Umbelazi anticipated beneath the sod. However, that was not in the question, and without it the alternative of acting as her guardian was bad enough, though I comforted myself with the reflection that the circumstances in which this would become necessary might never arise. For, alas! I was sure that if they did arise I should have to live up to them. True, I had made no promise to Saduko with my lips, but I felt, as I knew he felt, that this promise had passed from my heart to his.

"That thief Umbelazi!" Strange words to be uttered by a great vassal of his lord, and both of them about to enter upon a desperate enterprise. "A prince whom in her folly she believes will be a king." Stranger words still. Then Saduko did not believe that he would be a king! And yet he was about to share the fortunes of his fight for the throne, he who said that his heart was still on fire for the woman whom "Umbelazi the thief" had stolen. Well, if I were Umbelazi, thought I to myself, I would rather that Saduko were not my chief councillor and general. But, thank Heaven! I was not Umbelazi, or Saduko, or any of them! And, thank Heaven still more, I was going to begin my trek from Zululand on the morrow!

Man proposes but God disposes. I did not trek from Zululand for many a long day. When I got back to my wagons it was to find that my oxen had mysteriously disappeared from the veld on which they were accustomed to graze. They were lost; or perhaps they had felt the urgent need of trekking from Zululand back to a more peaceful country. I sent all the hunters I had with me to look for them, only Scowl and I remaining at the wagons, which in those disturbed times I did not like to leave unguarded.

Four days went by, a week went by, and no sign of either hunters or oxen. Then at last a message, which reached me in some roundabout fashion, to the effect that the hunters had found the oxen a long way off, but on trying to return to Nodwengu had been driven by some of the Usutu—that is, by Cetewayo's party—across the Tugela into Natal, whence they dared not attempt to return.

For once in my life I went into a rage and cursed that nondescript kind of messenger, sent by I know not whom, in language that I think he will not forget. Then, realising the futility of swearing at a mere tool, I went up to the Great House and demanded an audience with Panda himself. Presently the inceku, or household servant, to whom I gave my message, returned, saying that I was to be admitted at once, and on entering the enclosure I found the King sitting at the head of the kraal quite alone, except for a man who was holding a large shield over him in order to keep off the sun.

He greeted me warmly, and I told him my trouble about the oxen, whereon he sent away the shield-holder, leaving us two together.

"Watcher-by-Night," he said, "why do you blame me for these events, when you know that I am nobody in my own House? I say that I am a dead man, whose sons fight for his inheritance. I cannot tell you for certain who it was that drove away your oxen. Still, I am glad that they are gone, since I believe that if you had attempted to trek to Natal just now you would have been killed on the road by the Usutu, who believe you to be a councillor of Umbelazi."

"I understand, O King," I answered, "and I dare say that the accident of the loss of my oxen is fortunate for me. But tell me now, what am I to do? I wish to follow the example of John Dunn [another white man in the country who was much mixed up with Zulu politics] and leave the land. Will you give me more oxen to draw my wagons?"

"I have none that are broken in, Macumazahn, for, as you know, we Zulus possess few wagons; and if I had I would not lend them to you, who do not desire that your blood should be upon my head."

"You are hiding something from me, O King," I said bluntly. "What is it that you want me to do? Stay here at Nodwengu?"

"No, Macumazahn. When the trouble begins I want you to go with a regiment of my own that I shall send to the assistance of my son, Umbelazi, so that he may have the benefit of your wisdom. O Macumazana, I will tell you the truth. My heart loves Umbelazi, and I fear me that he is overmatched by Cetewayo. If I could I would save his life, but I know not how to do so, since I must not seem to take sides too openly. But I can send down a regiment as your escort, if you choose to go to view the battle as my agent and make report to me. Say, will you not go?"

"Why should I go?" I answered, "seeing that whoever wins I may be killed, and that if Cetewayo wins I shall certainly be killed, and all for no reward."

"Nay, Macumazahn; I will give orders that whoever conquers, the man that dares to lift a spear against you shall die. In this matter, at least, I shall not be disobeyed. Oh! I pray you, do not desert me in my trouble. Go down with the regiment that I shall send and breathe your wisdom into the ear of my son, Umbelazi. As for your reward, I swear to you by the head of the Black One [Chaka] that it shall be great. I will see to it that you do not leave Zululand empty-handed, Macumazahn."

Still I hesitated, for I mistrusted me of this business.

"O Watcher-by-Night," exclaimed Panda, "you will not desert me, will you? I am afraid for the son of my heart, Umbelazi, whom I love above all my children; I am much afraid for Umbelazi," and he burst into tears before me.

It was foolish, no doubt, but the sight of the old King weeping for his best-beloved child, whom he believed to be doomed, moved me so much that I forgot my caution.

"If you wish it, O Panda," I said, "I will go down to the battle with your regiment and stand there by the side of the Prince Umbelazi."

CHAPTER XIII

UMBELAZI THE FALLEN

So I stayed on at Nodwengu, who, indeed, had no choice in the matter, and was very wretched and ill at ease. The place was almost deserted, except for a couple of regiments which were quartered there, the Sangqu and the Amawombe. This latter was the royal regiment, a kind of Household Guards, to which the Kings Chaka, Dingaan and Panda all belonged in turn. Most of the headmen had taken one side or the other, and were away raising forces to fight for Cetewayo or Umbelazi, and even the greater part of the women and children had gone to hide themselves in the bush or among the mountains, since none knew what would happen, or if the conquering army would not fall upon and destroy them.

A few councillors, however, remained with Panda, among whom was old Maputa, the general, who had once brought me the "message of the pills." Several times he visited me at night and told me the rumours that were flying about. From these I gathered that some skirmishes had taken place and the battle could not be long delayed; also that Umbelazi had chosen his fighting ground, a plain near the banks of the Tugela.

"Why has he done this," I asked, "seeing that then he will have a broad river behind him, and if he is defeated water can kill as well as spears?"

"I know not for certain," answered Maputa; "but it is said because of a dream that Saduko, his general, has dreamed thrice, which dream declares that there and there alone Umbelazi will find honour. At any rate, he has chosen this place; and I am told that all the women and children of his army, by thousands, are hidden in the bush along the banks of the river, so that they may fly into Natal if there is need."

"Have they wings," I asked, "wherewith to fly over the Tugela 'in wrath,' as it well may be after the rains? Oh, surely his Spirit has turned from Umbelazi!"

"Aye, Macumazahn," he answered, "I, too, think that ufulatewe idhlozi [that is, his own Spirit] has turned its back on him. Also I think that Saduko is no good councillor. Indeed, were I the prince," added the old fellow shrewdly, "I would not keep him whose wife I had stolen as the whisperer in my ear."

"Nor I, Maputa," I answered as I bade him good-bye.

Two days later, early in the morning, Maputa came to me again and said that Panda wished to see me. I went to the head of the kraal, where I found the King seated and before him the captains of the royal Amawombe regiment.

"Watcher-by-Night," he said, "I have news that the great battle between my sons will take place within a few days. Therefore I am sending down this, my own royal regiment, under the command of Maputa the skilled in war to spy out the battle, and I pray that you will go with it, that you may give to the General Maputa and to the captains the help of your wisdom. Now these are my orders to you, Maputa, and to you, O captains—that you take no part in the fight unless you should see that the Elephant, my son Umbelazi, is fallen into a pit, and that then you shall drag him out if you can and save him alive. Now repeat my words to me."

So they repeated the words, speaking with one voice.

"Your answer, O Macumazana," he said when they had spoken.

"O King, I have told you that I will go—though I do not like war—and I will keep my promise," I replied.

"Then make ready, Macumazahn, and be back here within an hour, for the regiment marches ere noon."

So I went up to my wagons and handed them over to the care of some men whom Panda had sent to take charge of them. Also Scowl and I saddled our horses, for this faithful fellow insisted upon accompanying me, although I advised him to stay behind, and got out our rifles and as much ammunition as we could possibly need, and with them a few other necessaries. These things done, we rode back to the gathering-place, taking farewell of the wagons with a sad heart, since I, for one, never expected to see them again.

As we went I saw that the regiment of the Amawombe, picked men every one of them, all fifty years of age or over, nearly four thousand strong, was marshalled on the dancing-ground, where they stood company by company. A magnificent sight they were, with their white fighting-shields, their gleaming spears, their otter-skin caps, their kilts and armlets of white bulls' tails, and the snowy egret plumes which they wore upon their brows. We rode to the head of them, where I saw Maputa, and as I came they greeted me with a cheer of welcome, for in those days a white man was a power in the land. Moreover, as I have said, the Zulus knew and liked me well. Also the fact that I was to watch, or perchance to fight with them, put a good heart into the Amawombe.

There we stood until the lads, several hundreds of them, who bore the mats and cooking vessels and drove the cattle that were to be our commissariat, had wended away in a long line. Then suddenly Panda appeared out of his hut, accompanied by a few servants, and seemed to utter some kind of prayer, as he did so throwing dust or powdered medicine towards us, though what this ceremony meant I did not understand.

When he had finished Maputa raised a spear, whereon the whole regiment, in perfect time, shouted out the royal salute, "Bayéte", with a sound like that of thunder. Thrice they repeated this tremendous and impressive salute, and then were silent. Again Maputa raised his spear, and all the four thousand voices broke out into the Ingoma, or national chant, to which deep, awe-inspiring music we began our march. As I do not think it has ever been written down, I will quote the words. They ran thus:

"Ba ya m'zonda,
Ba ya m'loyisa,
Izizwe zonke,
Ba zond', Inkoosi."[*]

[*—Literally translated, this famous chant, now, I think, published for the first time, which, I suppose, will never again pass the lips of a Zulu impi, means:

"They [i.e. the enemy] bear him [i.e. the King] hatred, They call down curses on his head, All of them throughout this land Abhor our King."

The Ingoma when sung by twenty or thirty thousand men rushing down to battle must, indeed, have been a song to hear.—EDITOR.]

The spirit of this fierce Ingoma, conveyed by sound, gesture and inflection of voice, not the exact words, remember, which are very rude and simple, leaving much to the imagination, may perhaps be rendered somewhat as follows. An exact translation into English verse is almost impossible—at any rate, to me:

"Loud on their lips is lying,
Rebels their King defying.
There shall be dead and dying,

Red are their eyes with hate;
Lo! where our impis wait
Vengeance insatiate!"

It was early on the morning of the 2nd of December, a cold, miserable morning that came with wind and driving mist, that I found myself with the Amawombe at the place known as Endondakusuka, a plain with some kopjes in it that lies within six miles of the Natal border, from which it is separated by the Tugela river.

As the orders of the Amawombe were to keep out of the fray if that were possible, we had taken up a position about a mile to the right of what proved to be the actual battlefield, choosing as our camping ground a rising knoll that looked like a huge tumulus, and was fronted at a distance of about five hundred yards by another smaller knoll. Behind us stretched bushland, or rather broken land, where mimosa thorns grew in scattered groups, sloping down to the banks of the Tugela about four miles away.

Shortly after dawn I was roused from the place where I slept, wrapped up in some blankets, under a mimosa tree—for, of course, we had no tents—by a messenger, who said that the Prince Umbelazi and the white man, John Dunn, wished to see me. I rose and tidied myself as best I could, since, if I can avoid it, I never like to appear before natives in a dishevelled condition. I remember that I had just finished brushing my hair when Umbelazi arrived.

I can see him now, looking a veritable giant in that morning mist. Indeed, there was something quite unearthly about his appearance as he arose out of those rolling vapours, such light as there was being concentrated upon the blade of his big spear, which was well known as the broadest carried by any warrior in Zululand, and a copper torque he wore about his throat.

There he stood, rolling his eyes and hugging his kaross around him because of the cold, and something in his anxious, indeterminate expression told me at once that he knew himself to be a man in terrible danger. Just behind him, dark and brooding, his arms folded on his breast, his eyes fixed upon the ground, looking, to my moved imagination, like an evil genius, stood the stately and graceful Saduko. On his left was a young and sturdy white man carrying a rifle and smoking a pipe, whom I guessed to be John Dunn, a gentleman whom, as it chanced, I had never met, while behind were a force of Natal Government Zulus, clad in some kind of uniform and armed with guns, and with them a number of natives, also from Natal—"kraal Kafirs," who carried stabbing assegais. One of these led John Dunn's horse.

Of those Government men there may have been thirty or forty, and of the "kraal Kafirs" anything between two and three hundred.

I shook Umbelazi's hand and gave him good-day.

"That is an ill day upon which no sun shines, O Macumazana," he answered—words that struck me as ominous. Then he introduced me to John Dunn, who seemed glad to meet another white man. Next, not knowing what to say, I asked the exact object of their visit, whereon Dunn began to talk. He said that he had been sent over on the previous afternoon by Captain Walmsley, who was an officer of the Natal Government stationed across the border, to try to make peace between the Zulu factions, but that when he spoke of peace one of Umbelazi's brothers—I think it was Mantantashiya—had mocked at him, saying that they were quite strong enough to cope with the Usutu—that was Cetewayo's party. Also, he added, that when he suggested that the thousands of women and children and the cattle should be got across the Tugela drift during the previous night into safety in Natal, Mantantashiya would not listen, and Umbelazi being absent, seeking the aid of the Natal Government, he could do nothing.

"Quem Deus vult perdere prius dementat" [whom God wishes to destroy, He first makes mad], quoted I to myself beneath my breath. This was one of the Latin tags that my old father, who was a scholar, had taught me, and at that moment it came back to my mind. But as I suspected that John Dunn knew no Latin, I only said aloud:

"What an infernal fool!" (We were talking in English.) "Can't you get Umbelazi to do it now?" (I meant, to send the women and children across the river.)

"I fear it is too late, Mr. Quatermain," he answered. "The Usutu are in sight. Look for yourself." And he handed me a telescope which he had with him.

I climbed on to some rocks and scanned the plain in front of us, from which just then a puff of wind rolled away the mist. It was black with advancing men! As yet they were a considerable distance away— quite two miles, I should think—and coming on very slowly in a great half-moon with thin horns and a deep breast; but a ray from the sun glittered upon their countless spears. It seemed to me that there must be quite twenty or thirty thousand of them in this breast, which was in three divisions, commanded, as I learned afterwards, by Cetewayo, Uzimela, and by a young Boer named Groening.

"There they are, right enough," I said, climbing down from my rocks. "What are you going to do, Mr. Dunn?"

"Obey orders and try to make peace, if I can find anyone to make peace with; and if I can't—well, fight, I suppose. And you, Mr. Quatermain?"

"Oh, obey orders and stop here, I suppose. Unless," I added doubtfully, "these Amawombe take the bit between their teeth and run away with me."

"They'll do that before nightfall, Mr. Quatermain, if I know anything of the Zulus. Look here, why don't you get on your horse and come off with me? This is a queer place for you."

"Because I promised not to," I answered with a groan, for really, as I looked at those savages round me, who were already fingering their spears in a disagreeable fashion, and those other thousands of savages advancing towards us, I felt such little courage as I possessed sinking into my boots.

"Very well, Mr. Quatermain, you know your own business best; but I hope you will come out of it safely, that is all."

"Same to you," I replied.

Then John Dunn turned, and in my hearing asked Umbelazi what he knew of the movements of the Usutu and of their plan of battle.

The Prince replied, with a shrug of his shoulders:

"Nothing at present, Son of Mr. Dunn, but doubtless before the sun is high I shall know much."

As he spoke a sudden gust of wind struck us, and tore the nodding ostrich plume from its fastening on Umbelazi's head-ring. Whilst a murmur of dismay rose from all who saw what they considered this very ill-omened accident, away it floated into the air, to fall gently to the ground at the feet of Saduko. He stooped, picked it up, and reset it in its place, saying as he did so, with that ready wit for which some Kafirs are remarkable:

"So may I live, O Prince, to set the crown upon the head of Panda's favoured son!"

This apt speech served to dispel the general gloom caused by the incident, for those who heard it cheered, while Umbelazi thanked his captain with a nod and a smile. Only I noted that Saduko did not mention the name of "Panda's favoured son" upon whose head he hoped to live to set the crown. Now, Panda had many sons, and that day would show which of them was favoured.

A minute or two later John Dunn and his following departed, as he said, to try to make peace with the advancing Usutu. Umbelazi, Saduko and their escort departed also towards the main body of the host of the Isigqosa, which was massed to our left, "sitting on their spears," as the natives say, and awaiting the attack. As for me, I remained alone with the Amawombe, drinking some coffee that Scowl had brewed for me, and forcing myself to swallow food.

I can say honestly that I do not ever remember partaking of a more unhappy meal. Not only did I believe that I was looking on the last sun I should ever see—though by the way, there was uncommonly little of that orb visible—but what made the matter worse was that, if so, I should be called upon to die alone among savages, with not a single white face near to comfort me. Oh, how I wished I had never allowed myself to be dragged into this dreadful business. Yes, and I was even mean enough to wish that I had broken my word to Panda and gone off with John Dunn when he invited me, although now I thank goodness that I did not yield to that temptation and thereby sacrifice my self-respect.

Soon, however, things grew so exciting that I forgot these and other melancholy reflections in watching the development of events from the summit of our tumulus-like knoll, whence I had a magnificent view of the whole battle. Here, after seeing that his regiment made a full meal, as a good general should, old Maputa joined me, whom I asked whether he thought there would be any fighting for him that day.

"I think so, I think so," he answered cheerfully. "It seems to me that the Usutu greatly outnumber Umbelazi and the Isigqosa, and, of course, as you know, Panda's orders are that if he is in danger we must help him. Oh, keep a good heart, Macumazahn, for I believe I can promise you that you will see our spears grow red to-day. You will not go hungry from this battle to tell the white people that the Amawombe are cowards whom you could not flog into the fight. No, no, Macumazahn, my Spirit looks towards me this morning, and I who am old and who thought that I should die at length like a cow, shall see one more great fight—my twentieth, Macumazahn; for I fought with this same Amawombe in all the Black One's big battles, and for Panda against Dingaan also."

"Perhaps it will be your last," I suggested.

"I dare say, Macumazahn; but what does that matter if only I and the royal regiment can make an end that shall be spoken of? Oh, cheer up, cheer up, Macumazahn; your Spirit, too, looks towards you, as I promise that we all will do when the shields meet; for know, Macumazahn, that we poor black soldiers expect that you will show us how to fight this day, and, if need be, how to fall hidden in a heap of the foe."

"Oh!" I replied, "so this is what you Zulus mean by the 'giving of counsel,' is it?—you infernal, bloodthirsty old scoundrel," I added in English.

But I think Maputa never heard me. At any rate, he only seized my arm and pointed in front, a little to the left, where the horn of the great Usutu army was coming up fast, a long, thin line alive with twinkling spears; their moving arms and legs causing them to look like spiders, of which the bodies were formed by the great war shields.

"See their plan?" he said. "They would close on Umbelazi and gore him with their horns and then charge with their head. The horn will pass between us and the right flank of the Isigqosa. Oh! awake, awake, Elephant! Are you asleep with Mameena in a hut? Unloose your spears, Child of the King, and at them as they mount the slope. Behold!" he went on, "it is the Son of Dunn that begins the battle! Did I not tell you that we must look to the white men to show us the way? Peep through your tube, Macumazahn, and tell me what passes."

So I "peeped," and, the telescope which John Dunn had kindly left with me being good though small, saw everything clearly enough. He rode up almost to the point of the left horn of the Usutu, waving a white handkerchief and followed by his small force of police and Natal Kafirs. Then from somewhere among the Usutu rose a puff of smoke. Dunn had been fired at.

He dropped the handkerchief and leapt to the ground. Now he and his police were firing rapidly in reply, and men fell fast among the Usutu. They raised their war shout and came on, though slowly, for they feared the bullets. Step by step John Dunn and his people were thrust back, fighting gallantly against overwhelming odds. They were level with us, not a quarter of a mile to our left. They were pushed past us. They vanished among the bush behind us, and a long while passed before ever I heard what became of them, for we met no more that day.

Now, the horns having done their work and wrapped themselves round Umbelazi's army as the nippers of a wasp close about a fly (why did not Umbelazi cut off those horns, I wondered), the Usutu bull began his charge. Twenty or thirty thousand strong, regiment after regiment, Cetewayo's men rushed up the slope, and there, near the crest of it, were met by Umbelazi's regiments springing forward to repel the onslaught and shouting their battle-cry of "Laba! Laba! Laba! Laba!"

The noise of their meeting shields came to our ears like that of the roll of thunder, and the sheen of their stabbing-spears shone as shines the broad summer lightning. They hung and wavered on the slope; then from the Amawombe ranks rose a roar of

"Umbelazi wins!"

Watching intently, we saw the Usutu giving back. Down the slope they went, leaving the ground in front of them covered with black spots which we knew to be dead or wounded men.

"Why does not the Elephant charge home?" said Maputa in a perplexed voice. "The Usutu bull is on his back! Why does he not trample him?"

"Because he is afraid, I suppose," I answered, and went on watching.

There was plenty to see, as it happened. Finding that they were not pursued, Cetewayo's impi reformed swiftly at the bottom of the slope, in preparation for another charge. Among that of Umbelazi, above them, rapid movements took place of which I could not guess the meaning, which movements were accompanied by much noise of angry shouting. Then suddenly, from the midst of the Isigqosa army, emerged a great body of men, thousands strong, which ran swiftly, but in open order, down the slope towards the Usutu, holding their spears reversed. At first I thought that they were charging independently, till I saw the Usutu ranks open to receive them with a shout of welcome.

"Treachery!" I said. "Who is it?"

"Saduko, with the Amakoba and Amangwane soldiers and others. I know them by their head-dresses," answered Maputa in a cold voice.

"Do you mean that Saduko has gone over to Cetewayo with all his following?" I asked excitedly.

"What else, Macumazahn? Saduko is a traitor: Umbelazi is finished," and he passed his hand swiftly across his mouth—a gesture that has only one meaning among the Zulus.

As for me, I sat down upon a stone and groaned, for now I understood everything.

Presently the Usutu raised fierce, triumphant shouts, and once again their impi, swelled with Saduko's power, began to advance up the slope. Umbelazi, and those of the Isigqosa party who clung to him—now, I should judge, not more than eight thousand men—never stayed to wait the onslaught. They broke! They fled in a hideous rout, crashing through the thin, left horn of the Usutu by mere weight of numbers, and passing behind us obliquely on their road to the banks of the Tugela. A messenger rushed up to us, panting.

"These are the words of Umbelazi," he gasped. "O Watcher-by-Night and O Maputa, Indhlovu-ene-sihlonti prays that you will hold back the Usutu, as the King bade you do in case of need, and so give to him and those who cling to him time to escape with the women and children into Natal. His general, Saduko, has betrayed him, and gone over with three regiments to Cetewayo, and therefore we can no longer stand against the thousands of the Usutu."

"Go tell the prince that Macumazahn, Maputa, and the Amawombe regiment will do their best," answered Maputa calmly. "Still, this is our advice to him, that he should cross the Tugela swiftly with the women and the children, seeing that we are few and Cetewayo is many."

The messenger leapt away, but, as I heard afterwards, he never found Umbelazi, since the poor man was killed within five hundred yards of where we stood.

Then Maputa gave an order, and the Amawombe formed themselves into a triple line, thirteen hundred men in the first line, thirteen hundred men in the second line, and about a thousand in the third, behind whom were the carrier boys, three or four hundred of them. The place assigned to me was in the exact centre of the second line, where, being mounted on a horse, it was thought, as I gathered, that I should serve as a convenient rallying-point.

In this formation we advanced a few hundred yards to our left, evidently with the object of interposing ourselves between the routed impi and the pursuing Usutu, or, if the latter should elect to go round us, with that of threatening their flank. Cetewayo's generals did not leave us long in doubt as to what they would do. The main body of their army bore away to the right in pursuit of the flying foe, but three regiments, each of about two thousand five hundred spears, halted. Five minutes passed perhaps while they marshalled, with a distance of some six hundred yards between them. Each regiment was in a triple line like our own.

To me that seemed a very long five minutes, but, reflecting that it was probably my last on earth, I tried to make the best of it in a fashion that can be guessed. Strange to say, however, I found it impossible to keep my mind fixed upon those matters with which it ought to have been filled. My eyes and thoughts would roam. I looked at the ranks of the veteran Amawombe, and noted that they were still and solemn as men about to die should be, although they showed no sign of fear. Indeed, I saw some of those near me passing their snuffboxes to each other. Two grey-haired men also, who evidently were old friends, shook hands as people do who are parting before a journey, while two others discussed in a low voice the possibility of our wiping out most of the Usutu before we were wiped out ourselves.

"It depends," said one of them, "whether they attack us regiment by regiment or all together, as they will do if they are wise."

Then an officer bade them be silent, and conversation ceased. Maputa passed through the ranks giving orders to the captains. From a distance his withered old body, with a fighting shield held in front of it, looked like that of a huge black ant carrying something in its mouth. He came to where Scowl and I sat upon our horses.

"Ah! I see that you are ready, Macumazahn," he said in a cheerful voice. "I told you that you should not go away hungry, did I not?"

"Maputa," I said in remonstrance, "what is the use of this? Umbelazi is defeated, you are not of his impi, why send all these"—and I waved my hand—"down into the darkness? Why not go to the river and try to save the women and children?"

"Because we shall take many of those down into the darkness with us, Macumazahn," and he pointed to the dense masses of the Usutu. "Yet," he added, with a touch of compunction, "this is not your quarrel. You and your servant have horses. Slip out, if you will, and gallop hard to the lower drift. You may get away with your lives."

Then my white man's pride came to my aid.

"Nay," I answered, "I will not run while others stay to fight."

"I never thought you would, Macumazahn, who, I am sure, do not wish to earn a new and ugly name. Well, neither will the Amawombe run to become a mock among their people. The King's orders were that we should try to help Umbelazi, if the battle went against him. We obey the King's orders by dying where we stand. Macumazahn, do you think that you could hit that big fellow who is shouting insults at us there? If so, I should be obliged to you, as I dislike him very much," and he showed me a captain who was swaggering about in front of the lines of the first of the Usutu regiments, about six hundred yards away.

"I will try," I answered, "but it's a long shot." Dismounting, I climbed a pile of stones and, resting my rifle on the topmost of them, took a very full sight, aimed, held my breath, and pressed the trigger. A second afterwards the shouter of insults threw his arms wide, letting fall his spear, and pitched forward on to his face.

A roar of delight rose from the watching Amawombe, while old Maputa clapped his thin brown hands and grinned from ear to ear.

"Thank you, Macumazahn. A very good omen! Now I am sure that, whatever those Isigqosa dogs of Umbelazi's may do, we King's men shall make an excellent end, which is all that we can hope. Oh, what a beautiful shot! It will be something to think of when I am an idhlozi, a spirit-snake, crawling about my own kraal. Farewell, Macumazahn," and he took my hand and pressed it. "The time has come. I go to lead the charge. The Amawombe have orders to defend you to the last, for I wish you to see the finish of this fight. Farewell."

Then off he hurried, followed by his orderlies and staff-officers.

I never saw him again alive, though I think that once in after years I did meet his idhlozi in his kraal under strange circumstances. But that has nothing to do with this history.

As for me, having reloaded, I mounted my horse again, being afraid lest, if I went on shooting, I should miss and spoil my reputation. Besides, what was the use of killing more men unless I was obliged? There were plenty ready to do that.

Another minute, and the regiment in front of us began to move, while the other two behind it ostentatiously sat themselves down in their ranks, to show that they did not mean to spoil sport. The fight was to begin with a duel between about six thousand men.

"Good!" muttered the warrior who was nearest me. "They are in our bag."

"Aye," answered another, "those little boys" (used as a term of contempt) "are going to learn their last lesson."

For a few seconds there was silence, while the long ranks leant forward between the hedges of lean and cruel spears. A whisper went down the line; it sounded like the noise of wind among trees, and was the signal to prepare. Next a far-off voice shouted some word, which was repeated again and again by other voices before and behind me. I became aware that we were moving, quite slowly at first, then more quickly. Being lifted above the ranks upon my horse I could see the whole advance, and the general aspect of it was that of a triple black wave, each wave crowned with foam—the white plumes and shields of the Amawombe were the foam—and alive with sparkles of light—their broad spears were the light.

We were charging now—and oh! the awful and glorious excitement of that charge! Oh, the rush of the bending plumes and the dull thudding of eight thousand feet! The Usutu came up the slope to meet us. In silence we went, and in silence they came. We drew near to each other. Now we could see their faces peering over the tops of their mottled shields, and now we could see their fierce and rolling eyes.

Then a roar—a rolling roar such as at that time I had never heard: the thunder of the roar of the meeting shields—and a flash—a swift, simultaneous flash, the flash of the lightning of the stabbing spears. Up went the cry of:

"Kill, Amawombe, kill!" answered by another cry of:

"Toss, Usutu, toss!"

After that, what happened? Heaven knows alone—or at least I do not. But in later years Mr. Osborn, afterwards the resident magistrate at Newcastle, in Natal, who, being young and foolish in those days, had swum his horse over the Tugela and hidden in a little kopje quite near to us in order to see the battle, told me that it looked as though some huge breaker—that breaker being the splendid Amawombe—rolling in towards the shore with the weight of the ocean behind it, had suddenly struck a ridge of rock and, rearing itself up, submerged and hidden it.

At least, within three minutes that Usutu regiment was no more. We had killed them every one, and from all along our lines rose a fierce hissing sound of "S'gee, S'gee" ("Zhi" in the Zulu) uttered as the spears went home in the bodies of the conquered.

That regiment had gone, taking nearly a third of our number with it, for in such a battle as this the wounded were as good as dead. Practically our first line had vanished in a fray that did not last more than a few minutes. Before it was well over the second Usutu regiment sprang up and charged. With a yell of victory we rushed down the slope towards them. Again there was the roar of the meeting shields, but this time the fight was more prolonged, and, being in the front rank now, I had my share of it. I remember shooting two Usutu who stabbed at me, after which my gun was wrenched from my hand. I remember the mêlée swinging backwards and forwards, the groans of the wounded, the shouts of victory and despair, and then Scowl's voice saying:

"We have beat them, Baas, but here come the others."

The third regiment was on our shattered lines. We closed up, we fought like devils, even the bearer boys rushed into the fray. From all sides they poured down upon us, for we had made a ring; every minute men died by hundreds, and, though their numbers grew few, not one of the Amawombe yielded. I was fighting with a spear now, though how it came into my hand I cannot remember for certain. I think, however, I wrenched it from a man who rushed at me and was stabbed before he could strike. I killed a captain with this spear, for as he fell I recognised his face. It was that of one of Cetewayo's companions to whom I had sold some cloth at Nodwengu. The fallen were piled up quite thick around me—we were using them as a breastwork, friend and foe together. I saw Scowl's horse rear into the air and fall. He slipped over its tail, and next instant was fighting at my side, also with a spear, muttering Dutch and English oaths as he struck.

"Beetje varm! [a little hot] Beetje varm, Baas!" I heard him say. Then my horse screamed aloud and something hit me hard upon the head—I suppose it was a thrown kerry—after which I remember nothing for a while, except a sensation of passing through the air.

I came to myself again, and found that I was still on the horse, which was ambling forward across the veld at a rate of about eight miles an hour, and that Scowl was clinging to my stirrup leather and running at my side. He was covered with blood, so was the horse, and so was I. It may have been our own blood, for all three were more or less wounded, or it may have been that of others; I am sure I do not know, but we were a terrible sight. I pulled upon the reins, and the horse stopped among some thorns. Scowl felt in the saddlebags and found a large flask of Hollands gin and water—half gin and half water—which he had placed there before the battle. He uncorked and gave it to me. I took a long pull at the stuff, that tasted like veritable nectar, then handed it to him, who did likewise. New life seemed to flow into my veins. Whatever teetotallers may say, alcohol is good at such a moment.

"Where are the Amawombe?" I asked.

"All dead by now, I think, Baas, as we should be had not your horse bolted. Wow! but they made a great fight—one that will be told of! They have carried those three regiments away upon their spears."

"That's good," I said. "But where are we going?"

"To Natal, I hope, Baas. I have had enough of the Zulus for the present. The Tugela is not far away, and we will swim it. Come on, before our hurts grow stiff."

So we went on, till presently we reached the crest of a rise of ground overlooking the river, and there saw and heard dreadful things, for beneath us those devilish Usutu were massacring the fugitives and the camp-followers. These were being driven by the hundred to the edge of the water, there to perish on the banks or in the stream, which was black with drowned or drowning forms.

And oh! the sounds! Well, these I will not attempt to describe.

"Keep up stream," I said shortly, and we struggled across a kind of donga, where only a few wounded men were hidden, into a somewhat denser patch of bush that had scarcely been entered by the flying Isigqosa, perhaps because here the banks of the river were very steep and difficult; also, between them its waters ran swiftly, for this was above the drift.

For a while we went on in safety, then suddenly I heard a noise. A great man plunged past me, breaking through the bush like a buffalo, and came to a halt upon a rock which overhung the Tugela, for the floods had eaten away the soil beneath.

"Umbelazi!" said Scowl, and as he spoke we saw another man following as a wild dog follows a buck.

"Saduko!" said Scowl.

I rode on. I could not help riding on, although I knew it would be safer to keep away. I reached the edge of that big rock. Saduko and Umbelazi were fighting there.

In ordinary circumstances, strong and active as he was, Saduko would have had no chance against the most powerful Zulu living. But the prince was utterly exhausted; his sides were going like a blacksmith's bellows, or those of a fat eland bull that has been galloped to a standstill. Moreover, he seemed to me to be distraught with grief, and, lastly, he had no shield left, nothing but an assegai.

A stab from Saduko's spear, which he partially parried, wounded him slightly on the head, and cut loose the fillet of his ostrich plume, that same plume which I had seen blown off in the morning, so that it fell to the ground. Another stab pierced his right arm, making it helpless. He snatched the assegai with his left hand, striving to continue the fight, and just at that moment we came up.

"What are you doing, Saduko?" I cried. "Does a dog bite his own master?"

He turned and stared at me; both of them stared at me.

"Aye, Macumazahn," he answered in an icy voice, "sometimes when it is starving and that full-fed master has snatched away its bone. Nay, stand aside, Macumazahn" (for, although I was quite unarmed, I had stepped between them), "lest you should share the fate of this woman-thief."

"Not I, Saduko," I cried, for this sight made me mad, "unless you murder me."

Then Umbelazi spoke in a hollow voice, sobbing out his words:

"I thank you, White Man, yet do as this snake bids you—this snake that has lived in my kraal and fed out of my cup. Let him have his fill of vengeance because of the woman who bewitched me—yes, because of the sorceress who has brought me and thousands to the dust. Have you heard, Macumazahn, of the great deed of this son of Matiwane? Have you heard that all the while he was a traitor in the pay of Cetewayo, and that he went over, with the regiments of his command, to the Usutu just when the battle hung upon the turn? Come, Traitor, here is my heart—the heart that loved and trusted you. Strike—strike hard!"

"Out of the way, Macumazahn!" hissed Saduko. But I would not stir.

He sprang at me, and, though I put up the best fight that I could in my injured state, got his hands about my throat and began to choke me. Scowl ran to help me, but his wound—for he was hurt—or his utter exhaustion took effect on him. Or perhaps it was excitement. At any rate, he fell down in a fit. I thought that all was over, when again I heard Umbelazi's voice, and felt Saduko's grip loosen at my throat, and sat up.

"Dog," said the Prince, "where is your assegai?" And as he spoke he threw it from him into the river beneath, for he had picked it up while we struggled, but, as I noted, retained his own. "Now, dog, why do I not kill you, as would have been easy but now? I will tell you. Because I will not mix the blood of a traitor with my own. See!" He set the haft of his broad spear upon the rock and bent forward over the blade. "You and your witch-wife have brought me to nothing, O Saduko. My blood, and the blood of all who clung to me, is on your head. Your name shall stink for ever in the nostrils of all true men, and I whom you have betrayed—I, the Prince Umbelazi—will haunt you while you live; yes, my spirit shall enter into you, and when you die—ah! then we'll meet again. Tell this tale to the white men, Macumazahn, my friend, on whom be honour and blessings."

He paused, and I saw the tears gush from his eyes—tears mingled with blood from the wound in his head. Then suddenly he uttered the battle-cry of "Laba! Laba!" and let his weight fall upon the point of the spear.

It pierced him through and through. He fell on to his hands and knees. He looked up at us—oh, the piteousness of that look!—and then rolled sideways from the edge of the rock.

A heavy splash, and that was the end of Umbelazi the Fallen—Umbelazi, about whom Mameena had cast her net.

A sad story in truth. Although it happened so many years ago I weep as I write it—I weep as Umbelazi wept.

CHAPTER XIV

After this I think that some of the Usutu came up, for it seemed to me that I heard Saduko say:

"Touch not Macumazahn or his servant. They are my prisoners. He who harms them dies, with all his House."

So they put me, fainting, on my horse, and Scowl they carried away upon a shield.

When I came to I found myself in a little cave, or rather beneath some overhanging rocks, at the side of a kopje, and with me Scowl, who had recovered from his fit, but seemed in a very bewildered condition. Indeed, neither then nor afterwards did he remember anything of the death of Umbelazi, nor did I ever tell him that tale. Like many others, he thought that the Prince had been drowned in trying to swim the Tugela.

"Are they going to kill us?" I asked of him, since, from the triumphant shouting without, I knew that we must be in the midst of the victorious Usutu.

"I don't know, Baas," he answered. "I hope not; after we have gone through so much it would be a pity. Better to have died at the beginning of the battle."

I nodded my head in assent, and just at that moment a Zulu, who had very evidently been fighting, entered the place carrying a dish of toasted lumps of beef and a gourd of water.

"Cetewayo sends you these, Macumazahn," he said, "and is sorry that there is no milk or beer. When you have eaten a guard waits without to escort you to him." And he went.

"Well," I said to Scowl, "if they were going to kill us, they would scarcely take the trouble to feed us first. So let us keep up our hearts and eat."

"Who knows?" answered poor Scowl, as he crammed a lump of beef into his big mouth. "Still, it is better to die on a full than on an empty stomach."

So we ate and drank, and, as we were suffering more from exhaustion than from our hurts, which were not really serious, our strength came back to us. As we finished the last lump of meat, which, although it had been only half cooked upon the point of an assegai, tasted very good, the Zulu put his head into the mouth of the shelter and asked if we were ready. I nodded, and, supporting each other, Scowl and I limped from the place. Outside were about fifty soldiers, who greeted us with a shout that, although it was mixed with laughter at our pitiable appearance, struck me as not altogether unfriendly. Amongst these men was my horse, which stood with its head hanging down, looking very depressed. I was helped on to its back, and, Scowl clinging to the stirrup leather, we were led a distance of about a quarter of a mile to Cetewayo.

We found him seated, in the full blaze of the evening sun, on the eastern slope of one of the land-waves of the veld, with the open plain in front of him. It was a strange and savage scene. There sat the victorious prince, surrounded by his captains and indunas, while before him rushed the triumphant regiments, shouting his titles in the most extravagant language. Izimbongi also—that is, professional praisers—were running up and down before him dressed in all sorts of finery, telling his deeds, calling him "Eater-up-of-the-Earth," and yelling out the names of those great ones who had been killed in the battle.

Meanwhile parties of bearers were coming up continually, carrying dead men of distinction upon shields and laying them out in rows, as game is laid out at the end of a day's shooting in England. It seems that Cetewayo had taken a fancy to see them, and, being too tired to walk over the field of battle, ordered that this should be done. Among these, by the way, I saw the body of my old friend, Maputa, the general of the Amawombe, and noted that it was literally riddled with spear thrusts, every one of them in front; also that his quaint face still wore a smile.

At the head of these lines of corpses were laid six dead, all men of large size, in whom I recognised the brothers of Umbelazi, who had fought on his side, and the half-brothers of Cetewayo. Among them were those three princes upon whom the dust had fallen when Zikali, the prophet, smelt out Masapo, the husband of Mameena.

Dismounting from my horse, with the help of Scowl, I limped through and over the corpses of these fallen royalties, cut in the Zulu fashion to free their spirits, which otherwise, as they believed, would haunt the slayers, and stood in front of Cetewayo.

"Siyakubona, Macumazahn," he said, stretching out his hand to me, which I took, though I could not find it in my heart to wish him "good day."

"I hear that you were leading the Amawombe, whom my father, the King, sent down to help Umbelazi, and I am very glad that you have escaped alive. Also my heart is proud of the fight that they made, for you know, Macumazahn, once, next to the King, I was general of that regiment, though afterwards we quarrelled. Still, I am pleased that they did so well, and I have given orders that every one of them who remains alive is to be spared, that they may be officers of a new Amawombe which I shall raise. Do you know, Macumazahn, that you have nearly wiped out three whole regiments of the Usutu, killing many more people than did all my brother's army, the Isigqosa? Oh, you are a great man. Had it not been for the loyalty"—this word was spoken with just a tinge of sarcasm—"of Saduko yonder, you would have won the day for Umbelazi. Well, now that this quarrel is finished, if you will stay with me I will make you general of a whole division of the King's army, since henceforth I shall have a voice in affairs."

"You are mistaken, O Son of Panda," I answered; "the splendour of the Amawombe's great stand against a multitude is on the name of Maputa, the King's councillor and the induna of the Black One [Chaka], who is gone. He lies yonder in his glory," and I pointed to Maputa's pierced body. "I did but fight as a soldier in his ranks."

"Oh, yes, we know that, we know all that, Macumazahn; and Maputa was a clever monkey in his way, but we know also that you taught him how to jump. Well, he is dead, and nearly all the Amawombe are dead, and of my three regiments but a handful is left; the vultures have the rest of them. That is all finished and forgotten, Macumazahn, though by good fortune the spears went wide of you, who doubtless are a magician, since otherwise you and your servant and your horse would not have escaped with a few scratches when everyone else was killed. But you did escape, as you have done before in Zululand; and now you see here lie certain men who were born of my father. Yet one is missing—he against whom I fought, aye, and he whom, although we fought, I loved the best of all of them. Now, it has been whispered in my ear that you alone know what became of him, and, Macumazahn, I would learn whether he lives or is dead; also, if he is dead, by whose hand he died, who would reward that hand."

Now, I looked round me, wondering whether I should tell the truth or hold my tongue, and as I looked my eyes met those of Saduko, who, cold and unconcerned, was seated among the captains, but at a little distance from any of them—a man apart; and I remembered that he and I alone knew the truth of the end of Umbelazi.

Why, I do not know, but it came into my mind that I would keep the secret. Why should I tell the triumphant Cetewayo that Umbelazi had been driven to die by his own hand; why should I lay bare Saduko's victory and shame? All these matters had passed into the court of a different tribunal. Who was I that I should reveal them or judge the actors of this terrible drama?

"O Cetewayo," I said, "as it chanced I saw the end of Umbelazi. No enemy killed him. He died of a broken heart upon a rock above the river; and for the rest of the story go ask the Tugela into which he fell."

For a moment Cetewayo hid his eyes with his hand.

"Is it so?" he said presently. "Wow! I say again that had it not been for Saduko, the son of Matiwane, yonder, who had some quarrel with Indhlovu-ene-Sihlonti about a woman and took his chance of vengeance, it might have been I who died of a broken heart upon a rock above the river. Oh, Saduko, I owe you a great debt and will pay you well; but you shall be no friend of mine, lest we also should chance to quarrel about a woman, and I should find myself dying of a broken heart on a rock above a river. O my brother Umbelazi, I mourn for you, my brother, for, after all, we played together when we were little and loved each other once, who in the end fought for a toy that is called a throne, since, as our father said, two bulls cannot live in the same yard, my brother. Well, you are gone and I remain, yet who knows but that at the last your lot may be happier than mine. You died of a broken heart, Umbelazi, but of what shall I die, I wonder?"[*]

[*—That history of Cetewayo's fall and tragic death and of Zikali's vengeance I hope to write one day, for in these events also I was destined to play a part.—A. Q.]

I have given this interview in detail, since it was because of it that the saying went abroad that Umbelazi died of a broken heart.

So in truth he did, for before his spear pierced it his heart was broken.

Now, seeing that Cetewayo was in one of his soft moods, and that he seemed to look upon me kindly, though I had fought against him, I reflected that this would be a good opportunity to ask his leave to depart. To tell the truth, my nerves were quite shattered with all I had gone through, and I longed to be away from the sights and sounds of that terrible battlefield, on and about which so many thousand people had perished this fateful day, as I had seldom longed for anything before. But while I was making up my mind as to the best way to approach him, something happened which caused me to lose my chance.

Hearing a noise behind me, I looked round, to see a stout man arrayed in a very fine war dress, and waving in one hand a gory spear and in the other a head-plume of ostrich feathers, who was shouting out:

"Give me audience of the son of the King! I have a song to sing to the Prince. I have a tale to tell to the conqueror, Cetewayo."

I stared. I rubbed my eyes. It could not be—yes, it was—Umbezi, "Eater-up-of-Elephants," the father of Mameena. In a few seconds, without waiting for leave to approach, he had bounded through the line of dead princes, stopping to kick one of them on the head and address his poor clay in some words of shameful insult, and was prancing about before Cetewayo, shouting his praises.

"Who is this umfokazana?" [that is, low fellow] growled the Prince. "Bid him cease his noise and speak, lest he should be silent for ever."

"O Calf of the Black Cow, I am Umbezi, 'Eater-up-of-Elephants,' chief captain of Saduko the Cunning, he who won you the battle, father of Mameena the Beautiful, whom Saduko wed and whom the dead dog, Umbelazi, stole away from him."

"Ah!" said Cetewayo, screwing up his eyes in a fashion he had when he meant mischief, which among the Zulus caused him to be named the "Bull-who-shuts-his-eyes-to-toss," "and what have you to tell me, 'Eater-up-of-Elephants' and father of Mameena, whom the dead dog, Umbelazi, took away from your master, Saduko the Cunning?"

"This, O Mighty One; this, O Shaker of the Earth, that well am I named 'Eater-up-of-Elephants,' who have eaten up Indhlovu-ene-Sihlonti—the Elephant himself."

Now Saduko seemed to awake from his brooding and started from his place; but Cetewayo sharply bade him be silent, whereon Umbezi, the fool, noting nothing, continued his tale.

"O Prince, I met Umbelazi in the battle, and when he saw me he fled from me; yes, his heart grew soft as water at the sight of me, the warrior whom he had wronged, whose daughter he had stolen."

"I hear you," said Cetewayo. "Umbelazi's heart turned to water at the sight of you because he had wronged you—you who until this morning, when you deserted him with Saduko, were one of his jackals. Well, and what happened then?"

"He fled, O Lion with the Black Mane; he fled like the wind, and I, I flew after him like—a stronger wind. Far into the bush he fled, till at length he came to a rock above the river and was obliged to stand. Then there we fought. He thrust at me, but I leapt over his spear thus," and he gambolled into the air. "He thrust at me again, but I bent myself thus," and he ducked his great head. "Then he grew tired and my time came. He turned and ran round the rock, and I, I ran after him, stabbing him through the back, thus, and thus, and thus, till he fell, crying for mercy, and rolled off the rock into the river; and as he rolled I snatched away his plume. See, is it not the plume of the dead dog Umbelazi?"

Cetewayo took the ornament and examined it, showing it to one or two of the captains near him, who nodded their heads gravely.

"Yes," he said, "this is the war plume of Umbelazi, beloved of the King, strong and shining pillar of the Great House; we know it well, that war plume at the sight of which many a knee has loosened. And so you killed him, 'Eater-up-of-Elephants,' father of Mameena, you who this morning were one of the meanest of his jackals. Now, what reward shall I give you for this mighty deed, O Umbezi?"

"A great reward, O Terrible One," began Umbezi, but in an awful voice Cetewayo bade him be silent.

"Yes," he said, "a great reward. Hearken, Jackal and Traitor. Your own words bear witness against you. You, you have dared to lift your hand against the blood-royal, and with your foul tongue to heap lies and insults upon the name of the mighty dead."

Now, understanding at last, Umbezi began to babble excuses, yes, and to declare that all his tale was false. His fat cheeks fell in, he sank to his knees.

But Cetewayo only spat towards the man, after his fashion when enraged, and looked round him till his eye fell upon Saduko.

"Saduko," he said, "take away this slayer of the Prince, who boasts that he is red with my own blood, and when he is dead cast him into the river from that rock on which he says he stabbed Panda's son."

Saduko looked round him wildly and hesitated.

"Take him away," thundered Cetewayo, "and return ere dark to make report to me."

Then, at a sign from the Prince, soldiers flung themselves upon the miserable Umbezi and dragged him thence, Saduko going with them; nor was the poor liar ever seen again. As he passed by me he called to me, for Mameena's sake, to save him; but I could only shake my head and bethink me of the warning I had once given to him as to the fate of traitors.

It may be said that this story comes straight from the history of Saul and David, but I can only answer that it happened. Circumstances that were not unlike ended in a similar tragedy, that is all. What David's exact motives were, naturally I cannot tell; but it is easy to guess those of Cetewayo, who, although he could make war upon his brother to secure the throne, did not think it wise to let it go abroad that the royal blood might be lightly spilt. Also, knowing that I was a witness of the Prince's death, he was well aware that Umbezi was but a boastful liar who hoped thus to ingratiate himself with an all-powerful conqueror.

Well, this tragic incident had its sequel. It seems—to his honour, be it said—that Saduko refused to be the executioner of his father-in-law, Umbezi; so those with him performed this office and brought him back a prisoner to Cetewayo.

When the Prince learned that his direct order, spoken in the accustomed and fearful formula of "Take him away," had been disobeyed, his rage was, or seemed to be, great. My own conviction is that he was only seeking a cause of quarrel against Saduko, who, he thought, was a very powerful man, who would probably treat him, should opportunity arise, as he had treated Umbelazi, and perhaps now that the most of Panda's sons were dead, except himself and the lads M'tonga, Sikota and M'kungo, who had fled into Natal, might even in future days aspire to the throne as the husband of the King's daughter. Still, he was afraid or did not think it politic at once to put out of his path this master of many legions, who had played so important a part in the battle. Therefore he ordered him to be kept under guard and taken back to Nodwengu, that the whole matter might be investigated by Panda the King, who still ruled the land, though henceforth only in name. Also he refused to allow me to depart into Natal, saying that I, too, must come to Nodwengu, as there my testimony might be needed.

So, having no choice, I went, it being fated that I should see the end of the drama.

CHAPTER XV

MAMEENA CLAIMS THE KISS

When I reached Nodwengu I was taken ill and laid up in my wagon for about a fortnight. What my exact sickness was I do not know, for I had no doctor at hand to tell me, as even the missionaries had fled the country. Fever resulting from fatigue, exposure and excitement, and complicated with fearful headache—caused, I presume, by the blow which I received in the battle—were its principal symptoms.

When I began to get better, Scowl and some Zulu friends who came to see me informed me that the whole land was in a fearful state of disorder, and that Umbelazi's adherents, the Isigqosa, were still being hunted out and killed. It seems that it was even suggested by some of the Usutu that I should share their fate, but on this point Panda was firm. Indeed, he appears to have said publicly that whoever lifted a spear against me, his friend and guest, lifted it against him, and would be the cause of a new war. So the Usutu left me alone, perhaps because they were satisfied with fighting for a while, and thought it wisest to be content with what they had won.

Indeed, they had won everything, for Cetewayo was now supreme—by right of the assegai—and his father but a cipher. Although he remained the "Head" of the nation, Cetewayo was publicly declared to be its "Feet," and strength was in these active "Feet," not in the bowed and sleeping "Head." In fact, so little power was left to Panda that he could not protect his own household. Thus one day I heard a great tumult and shouting proceeding apparently from the Isigodhlo, or royal enclosure, and on inquiring what it was afterwards, was told that Cetewayo had come from the Amangwe kraal and denounced Nomantshali, the King's wife, as "umtakati", or a witch. More, in spite of his father's prayers and tears, he had caused her to be put to death before his eyes—a dreadful and a savage deed. At this distance of time I cannot remember whether Nomantshali was the mother of Umbelazi or of one of the other fallen princes.[*]

[—On re-reading this history it comes back to me that she was the mother of M'tonga, who was much younger than Umbelazi. —A. Q.]*

A few days later, when I was up and about again, although I had not ventured into the kraal, Panda sent a messenger to me with a present of an ox. On his behalf this man congratulated me on my recovery, and told me that, whatever might have happened to others, I was to have no fear for my own safety. He added that Cetewayo had sworn to the King that not a hair of my head should be harmed, in these words:

"Had I wished to kill Watcher-by-Night because he fought against me, I could have done so down at Endondakusuka; but then I ought to kill you also, my father, since you sent him thither against his will with your own regiment. But I like him well, who is brave and who brought me good tidings that the Prince, my enemy, was dead of a broken heart. Moreover, I wish to have no quarrel with the White House [the English] on account of Macumazahn, so tell him that he may sleep in peace."

The messenger said further that Saduko, the husband of the King's daughter, Nandie, and Umbelazi's chief induna, was to be put upon his trial on the morrow before the King and his council, together with Mameena, daughter of Umbezi, and that my presence was desired at this trial.

I asked what was the charge against them. He replied that, so far as Saduko was concerned, there were two: first, that he had stirred up civil war in the land, and, secondly, that having pushed on Umbelazi into a fight in which many thousands perished, he had played the traitor, deserting him in the midst of the battle, with all his following—a very heinous offence in the eyes of Zulus, to whatever party they may belong.

Against Mameena there were three counts of indictment. First, that it was she who had poisoned Saduko's child and others, not Masapo, her first husband, who had suffered for that crime. Secondly, that she had deserted Saduko, her second husband, and gone to live with another man, namely, the late Prince Umbelazi. Thirdly, that she was a witch, who had enmeshed Umbelazi in the web of her sorceries and thereby caused him to aspire to the succession to the throne, to which he had no right, and made the isililo, or cry of mourning for the dead, to be heard in every kraal in Zululand.

"With three such pitfalls in her narrow path, Mameena will have to walk carefully if she would escape them all," I said.

"Yes, Inkoosi, especially as the pitfalls are dug from side to side of the path and have a pointed stake set at the bottom of each of them. Oh, Mameena is already as good as dead, as she deserves to be, who without doubt is the greatest umtakati north of the Tugela."

I sighed, for somehow I was sorry for Mameena, though why she should escape when so many better people had perished because of her I did not know; and the messenger went on:

"The Black One [that is, Panda] sent me to tell Saduko that he would be allowed to see you, Macumazahn, before the trial, if he wished, for he knew that you had been a friend of his, and thought that you might be able to give evidence in his favour."

"And what did Saduko say to that?" I asked.

"He said that he thanked the King, but that it was not needful for him to talk with Macumazahn, whose heart was white like his skin, and whose lips, if they spoke at all, would tell neither more nor less than the truth. The Princess Nandie, who is with him—for she will not leave him in his trouble, as all others have done—on hearing these words of Saduko's, said that they were true, and that for this reason, although you were her friend, she did not hold it necessary to see you either."

Upon this intimation I made no comment, but "my head thought," as the natives say, that Saduko's real reason for not wishing to see me was that he felt ashamed to do so, and Nandie's that she feared to learn more about her husband's perfidies than she knew already.

"With Mameena it is otherwise," went on the messenger, "for as soon as she was brought here with Zikali the Little and Wise, with whom, it seems, she has been sheltering, and learned that you, Macumazahn, were at the kraal, she asked leave to see you—"

"And is it granted?" I broke in hurriedly, for I did not at all wish for a private interview with Mameena.

"Nay, have no fear, Inkoosi," replied the messenger with a smile; "it is refused, because the King said that if once she saw you she would bewitch you and bring trouble on you, as she does on all men. It is for this reason that she is guarded by women only, no man being allowed to go near to her, for on women her witcheries will not bite. Still, they say that she is merry, and laughs and sings a great deal, declaring that her life has been dull up at old Zikali's, and that now she is going to a place as gay as the veld in spring, after the first warm rain, where there will be plenty of men to quarrel for her and make her great and happy. That is what she says, the witch who knows perhaps what the Place of Spirits is like."

Then, as I made no remarks or suggestions, the messenger departed, saying that he would return on the morrow to lead me to the place of trial.

Next morning, after the cows had been milked and the cattle loosed from their kraals, he came accordingly, with a guard of about thirty men, all of them soldiers who had survived the great fight of the Amawombe. These warriors, some of whom had wounds that were scarcely healed, saluted me with loud cries of "Inkoosi!" and "Baba" as I stepped out of the wagon, where I had spent a wretched night of unpleasant anticipation, showing me that there were at least some Zulus with whom I remained popular. Indeed, their delight at seeing me, whom they looked upon as a comrade and one of the few survivors of the great adventure, was quite touching. As we went, which we did slowly, their captain told me of their fears that I had been killed with the others, and how rejoiced they were when they learned that I was safe. He told me also that, after the third regiment had attacked them and broken up their ring, a small body of them, from eighty to a hundred only, managed to cut a way through and escape, running, not towards the Tugela, where so many thousands had perished, but up to Nodwengu, where they reported themselves to Panda as the only survivors of the Amawombe.

"And are you safe now?" I asked of the captain.

"Oh, yes," he answered. "You see, we were the King's men, not Umbelazi's, so Cetewayo bears us no grudge. Indeed, he is obliged to us, because we gave the Usutu their stomachs full of good fighting, which is more than did those cows of Umbelazi's. It is towards Saduko that he bears a grudge, for you know, my father, one should never pull a drowning man out of the stream—which is what Saduko did, for had it not been for his treachery, Cetewayo would have sunk beneath the water of Death—especially if it is only to spite a woman who hates him. Still, perhaps Saduko will escape with his life, because he is Nandie's husband, and Cetewayo fears Nandie, his sister, if he does not love her. But here we are, and those who have to watch the sky all day will be able to tell of the evening weather" (in other words, those who live will learn).

As he spoke we passed into the private enclosure of the isi-gohlo, outside of which a great many people were gathered, shouting, talking and quarrelling, for in those days all the usual discipline of the Great Place was relaxed. Within the fence, however, that was strongly guarded on its exterior side, were only about a score of councillors, the King, the Prince Cetewayo, who sat upon his right, the Princess Nandie, Saduko's wife, a few attendants, two great, silent fellows armed with clubs, whom I guessed to be executioners, and, seated in the shade in a corner, that ancient dwarf, Zikali, though how he came to be there I did not know.

Obviously the trial was to be quite a private affair, which accounted for the unusual presence of the two "slayers." Even my Amawombe guard was left outside the gate, although I was significantly informed that if I chose to call upon them they would hear me, which was another way of saying that in such a small gathering I was absolutely safe.

Walking forward boldly towards Panda, who, though he was as fat as ever, looked very worn and much older than when I had last seen him, I made my bow, whereon he took my hand and asked after my health. Then I shook Cetewayo's hand also, as I saw that it was stretched out to me. He seized the opportunity to remark that he was told that I had suffered a knock on the head in some scrimmage down by the Tugela, and he hoped that I felt no ill effects. I answered: No, though I feared that there were a few others who had not been so fortunate, especially those who had stumbled against the Amawombe regiment, with whom I chanced to be travelling upon a peaceful mission of inquiry.

It was a bold speech to make, but I was determined to give him a quid pro quo, and, as a matter of fact, he took it in very good part, laughing heartily at the joke.

After this I saluted such of the councillors present as I knew, which was not many, for most of my old friends were dead, and sat down upon the stool that was placed for me not very far from the dwarf Zikali, who stared at me in a stony fashion, as though he had never seen me before.

There followed a pause. Then, at some sign from Panda, a side gate in the fence was opened, and through it appeared Saduko, who walked proudly to the space in front of the King, to whom he gave the salute of "Bayéte," and, at a sign, sat himself down upon the ground. Next, through the same gate, to which she was conducted by some women, came Mameena, quite unchanged and, I think, more beautiful than she had ever been. So lovely did she look, indeed, in her cloak of grey fur, her necklet of blue beads, and the gleaming rings of copper which she wore upon her wrists and ankles, that every eye was fixed upon her as she glided gracefully forward to make her obeisance to Panda.

This done, she turned and saw Nandie, to whom she also bowed, as she did so inquiring after the health of her child. Without waiting for an answer, which she knew would not be vouchsafed, she advanced to me and grasped my hand, which she pressed warmly, saying how glad she was to see me safe after going through so many dangers, though she thought I looked even thinner than I used to be.

Only of Saduko, who was watching her with his intent and melancholy eyes, she took no heed whatsoever. Indeed, for a while I thought that she could not have seen him. Nor did she appear to recognise Cetewayo, although he stared at her hard enough. But, as her glance fell upon the two executioners, I thought I saw her shudder like a shaken reed. Then she sat down in the place appointed to her, and the trial began.

The case of Saduko was taken first. An officer learned in Zulu law—which I can assure the reader is a very intricate and well-established law—I suppose that he might be called a kind of attorney-general, rose and stated the case against the prisoner. He told how Saduko, from a nobody, had been lifted to a great place by the King and given his daughter, the Princess Nandie, in marriage. Then he alleged that, as would be proved in evidence, the said Saduko had urged on Umbelazi the Prince, to whose party he had attached himself, to make war upon Cetewayo. This war having begun, at the great battle of

Endondakusuka, he had treacherously deserted Umbelazi, together with three regiments under his command, and gone over to Cetewayo, thereby bringing Umbelazi to defeat and death.

This brief statement of the case for the prosecution being finished, Panda asked Saduko whether he pleaded guilty or not guilty.

"Guilty, O King," he answered, and was silent.

Then Panda asked him if he had anything to say in excuse of his conduct.

"Nothing, O King, except that I was Umbelazi's man, and when you, O King, had given the word that he and the Prince yonder might fight, I, like many others, some of whom are dead and some alive, worked for him with all my ten fingers that he might have the victory."

"Then why did you desert my son the Prince in the battle?" asked Panda.

"Because I saw that the Prince Cetewayo was the stronger bull and wished to be on the winning side, as all men do—for no other reason," answered Saduko calmly.

Now, everyone present stared, not excepting Cetewayo. Panda, who, like the rest of us, had heard a very different tale, looked extremely puzzled, while Zikali, in his corner, set up one of his great laughs.

After a long pause, at length the King, as supreme judge, began to pass sentence. At least, I suppose that was his intention, but before three words had left his lips Nandie rose and said:

"My Father, ere you speak that which cannot be unspoken, hear me. It is well known that Saduko, my husband, was my brother Umbelazi's general and councillor, and if he is to be killed for clinging to the Prince, then I should be killed also, and countless others in Zululand who still remain alive because they were not in or escaped the battle. It is well known also, my Father, that during that battle Saduko went over to my brother Cetewayo, though whether this brought about the defeat of Umbelazi I cannot say. Why did he go over? He tells you because he wished to be on the winning side. It is not true. He went over in order to be revenged upon Umbelazi, who had taken from him yonder witch"—and she pointed with her finger at Mameena—"yonder witch, whom he loved and still loves, and whom even now he would shield, even though to do so he must make his own name shameful. Saduko sinned; I do not deny it, my Father, but there sits the real traitress, red with the blood of Umbelazi and with that of thousands of others who have 'tshonile'd' [gone down to keep him company among the ghosts]. Therefore, O King, I beseech you, spare the life of Saduko, my husband, or, if he must die, learn that I, your daughter, will die with him. I have spoken, O King."

And very proudly and quietly she sat herself down again, waiting for the fateful words.

But those words were not spoken, since Panda only said: "Let us try the case of this woman, Mameena."

Thereon the law officer rose again and set out the charges against Mameena, namely, that it was she who had poisoned Saduko's child, and not Masapo; that, after marrying Saduko, she had deserted him and gone to live with the Prince Umbelazi; and that finally she had bewitched the said Umbelazi and caused him to make civil war in the land.

"The second charge, if proved, namely, that this woman deserted her husband for another man, is a crime of death," broke in Panda abruptly as the officer finished speaking; "therefore, what need is there to hear the first and the third until that is examined. What do you plead to that charge, woman?"

Now, understanding that the King did not wish to stir up these other matters of murder and witchcraft for some reason of his own, we all turned to hear Mameena's answer.

"O King," she said in her low, silvery voice, "I cannot deny that I left Saduko for Umbelazi the Handsome, any more than Saduko can deny that he left Umbelazi the beaten for Cetewayo the conqueror."

"Why did you leave Saduko?" asked Panda.

"O King, perhaps because I loved Umbelazi; for was he not called the Handsome? Also you know that the Prince, your son, was one to be loved." Here she paused, looking at poor Panda, who winced. "Or, perhaps, because I wished to be great; for was he not of the Blood Royal, and, had it not been for Saduko, would he not one day have been a king? Or, perhaps, because I could no longer bear the treatment that the Princess Nandie dealt out to me; she who was cruel to me and threatened to beat me, because Saduko loved my hut better than her own. Ask Saduko; he knows more of these matters than I do," and she gazed at him steadily. Then she went on: "How can a woman tell her reasons, O King, when she never knows them herself?"—a question at which some of her hearers smiled.

Now Saduko rose and said slowly:

"Hear me, O King, and I will give the reason that Mameena hides. She left me for Umbelazi because I bade her to do so, for I knew that Umbelazi desired her, and I wished to tie the cord tighter which bound me to one who at that time I thought would inherit the Throne. Also, I was weary of Mameena, who quarrelled night and day with the Princess Nandie, my Inkosikazi."

Now Nandie gasped in astonishment (and so did I), but Mameena laughed and said:

"Yes, O King, those were the two real reasons that I had forgotten. I left Saduko because he bade me, as he wished to make a present to the Prince. Also, he was tired of me; for many days at a time he would scarcely speak to me, because, however kind she might be, I could not help quarrelling with the Princess Nandie. Moreover, there was another reason which I have forgotten: I had no child, and not having any child I did not think it mattered whether I went or stayed. If Saduko searches, he will remember that I told him so, and that he agreed with me."

Again she looked at Saduko, who said hurriedly:

"Yes, yes, I told her so; I told her that I wished for no barren cows in my kraal."

Now some of the audience laughed outright, but Panda frowned.

"It seems," he said, "that my ears are being stuffed with lies, though which of these two tells them I cannot say. Well, if the woman left the man by his own wish, and that his ends might be furthered, as he says, he had put her away, and therefore the fault, if any, is his, not hers. So that charge is ended. Now, woman, what have you to tell us of the witchcraft which it is said you practised upon the Prince who is gone, thereby causing him to make war in the land?"

"Little that you would wish to hear, O King, or that it would be seemly for me to speak," she answered, drooping her head modestly. "The only witchcraft that ever I practised upon Umbelazi lies here"—and she touched her beautiful eyes—"and here"—and she touched her curving lips—"and in this poor shape of mine which some have thought so fair. As for the war, what had I to do with war, who never spoke to Umbelazi, who was so dear to me"—and she looked up with tears running down her face—"save of love? O King, is there a man among you all who would fear the witcheries of such a one as I; and because the Heavens made me beautiful with the beauty that men must follow, am I also to be killed as a sorceress?"

Now, to this argument neither Panda nor anyone else seemed to find an answer, especially as it was well known that Umbelazi had cherished his ambition to the succession long before he met Mameena. So that charge was dropped, and the first and greatest of the three proceeded with; namely, that it was she, Mameena, and not her husband, Masapo, who had murdered Nandie's child.

When this accusation was made against her, for the first time I saw a little shade of trouble flit across Mameena's soft eyes.

"Surely, O King," she said, "that matter was settled long ago, when the Ndwande, Zikali, the great Nyanga, smelt out Masapo the wizard, he who was my husband, and brought him to his death for this crime. Must I then be tried for it again?"

"Not so, woman," answered Panda. "All that Zikali smelt out was the poison that wrought the crime, and as some of that poison was found upon Masapo, he was killed as a wizard. Yet it may be that it was not he who used the poison."

"Then surely the King should have thought of that before he died," murmured Mameena. "But I forget: It is known that Masapo was always hostile to the House of Senzangakona."

To this remark Panda made no answer, perhaps because it was unanswerable, even in a land where it was customary to kill the supposed wizard first and inquire as to his actual guilt afterwards, or not at all. Or perhaps he thought it politic to ignore the suggestion that he had been inspired by personal enmity. Only, he looked at his daughter, Nandie, who rose and said:

"Have I leave to call a witness on this matter of the poison, my Father?"

Panda nodded, whereon Nandie said to one of the councillors:

"Be pleased to summon my woman, Nahana, who waits without."

The man went, and presently returned with an elderly female who, it appeared, had been Nandie's nurse, and, never having married, owing to some physical defect, had always remained in her service, a person well known and much respected in her humble walk of life.

"Nahana," said Nandie, "you are brought here that you may repeat to the King and his council a tale which you told to me as to the coming of a certain woman into my hut before the death of my first-born son, and what she did there. Say first, is this woman present here?"

"Aye, Inkosazana," answered Nahana, "yonder she sits. Who could mistake her?" and she pointed to Mameena, who was listening to every word intently, as a dog listens at the mouth of an ant-bear hole when the beast is stirring beneath.

"Then what of the woman and her deeds?" asked Panda.

"Only this, O King. Two nights before the child that is dead was taken ill, I saw Mameena creep into the hut of the lady Nandie, I who was asleep alone in a corner of the big hut out of reach of the light of the fire. At the time the lady Nandie was away from the hut with her son. Knowing the woman for Mameena, the wife of Masapo, who was on friendly terms with the Inkosazana, whom I supposed she had come to visit, I did not declare myself; nor did I take any particular note when I saw her sprinkle a little mat upon which the babe, Saduko's son, was wont to be laid, with some medicine, because I had heard her promise to the Inkosazana a powder which she said would drive away insects. Only, when I saw her throw some of this powder into the vessel of warm water that stood by the fire, to be used for the washing of the child, and place something, muttering certain words that I could not catch, in the straw of the doorway, I thought it strange, and was about to question her when she left the hut. As it happened, O King, but a little while afterwards, before one could count ten tens indeed, a messenger came to the hut to tell me that my old mother lay dying at her kraal four days' journey from Nodwengu, and prayed to see me before she died. Then I forgot all about Mameena and the powder, and, running out to seek the Princess Nandie, I craved her leave to go with the messenger to my mother's kraal, which she granted to me, saying that I need not return until my mother was buried.

"So I went. But, oh! my mother took long to die. Whole moons passed before I shut her eyes, and all this while she would not let me go; nor, indeed, did I wish to leave her whom I loved. At length it was over, and then came the days of mourning, and after those some more days of rest, and after them again the days of the division of the cattle, so that in the end six moons or more had gone by before I returned to the service of the Princess Nandie, and found that Mameena was now the second wife of the lord Saduko. Also I found that the child of the lady Nandie was dead, and that Masapo, the first husband of Mameena, had been smelt out and killed as the murderer of the child. But as all these things were over and done with, and as Mameena was very kind to me, giving me gifts and sparing me tasks, and as I saw that Saduko my lord loved her much, it never came into my head to say anything of the matter of the powder that I saw her sprinkle on the mat.

"After she had run away with the Prince who is dead, however, I did tell the lady Nandie. Moreover, the lady Nandie, in my presence, searched in the straw of the doorway of the hut and found there, wrapped in soft hide, certain medicines such as the Nyangas sell, wherewith those who consult them can bewitch their enemies, or cause those whom they desire to love them or to hate their wives or husbands. That is all I know of the story, O King."

"Do my ears hear a true tale, Nandie?" asked Panda. "Or is this woman a liar like others?"

"I think not, my Father; see, here is the muti [medicine] which Nahana and I found hid in the doorway of the hut that I have kept unopened till this day."

And she laid on the ground a little leather bag, very neatly sewn with sinews, and fastened round its neck with a fibre string.

Panda directed one of the councillors to open the bag, which the man did unwillingly enough, since evidently he feared its evil influence, pouring out its contents on to the back of a hide shield, which was then carried round so that we might all look at them. These, so far as I could see, consisted of some withered roots, a small piece of human thigh bone, such as might have come from the skeleton of an infant, that had a little stopper of wood in its orifice, and what I took to be the fang of a snake.

Panda looked at them and shrank away, saying:

"Come hither, Zikali the Old, you who are skilled in magic, and tell us what is this medicine."

Then Zikali rose from the corner where he had been sitting so silently, and waddled heavily across the open space to where the shield lay in front of the King. As he passed Mameena, she bent down over the dwarf and began to whisper to him swiftly; but he placed his hands upon his big head, covering up his ears, as I suppose, that he might not hear her words.

"What have I to do with this matter, O King?" he asked.

"Much, it seems, O Opener-of-Roads," said Panda sternly, "seeing that you were the doctor who smelt out Masapo, and that it was in your kraal that yonder woman hid herself while her lover, the Prince, my son, who is dead, went down to the battle, and that she was brought thence with you. Tell us, now, the nature of this muti, and, being wise, as you are, be careful to tell us truly, lest it should be said, O Zikali, that you are not a Nyanga only, but an umtakati as well. For then," he added with meaning, and choosing his words carefully, "perchance, O Zikali, I might be tempted to make trial of whether or no it is true that you cannot be killed like other men, especially as I have heard of late that your heart is evil towards me and my House."

For a moment Zikali hesitated—I think to give his quick brain time to work, for he saw his great danger. Then he laughed in his dreadful fashion and said:

"Oho! the King thinks that the otter is in the trap," and he glanced at the fence of the isi-gohlo and at the fierce executioners, who stood watching him sternly. "Well, many times before has this otter seemed to be in a trap, yes, ere your father saw light, O Son of Senzangakona, and after it also. Yet here he stands living. Make no trial, O King, of whether or no I be mortal, lest if Death should come to such a one as I, he should take many others with him also. Have you not heard the saying that when the Opener-of-Roads comes to the end of his road there will be no more a King of the Zulus, as when he began his road there was no King of the Zulus, since the days of his manhood are the days of all the Zulu kings?"

Thus he spoke, glaring at Panda and at Cetewayo, who shrank before his gaze.

"Remember," he went on, "that the Black One who is 'gone down' long ago, the Wild Beast who fathered the Zulu herd, threatened him whom he named the 'Thing-that-should-not-have-been-born,' aye, and slew those whom he loved, and afterwards was slain by others, who also are 'gone down,' and that you alone, O Panda, did not threaten him, and that you alone, O Panda, have not been slain. Now, if you would make trial of whether I die as other men die, bid your dogs fall on, for Zikali is ready," and he folded his arms and waited.

Indeed, all of us waited breathlessly, for we understood that the terrible dwarf was matching himself against Panda and Cetewayo and defying them both. Presently it became obvious that he had won the game, since Panda only said:

"Why should I slay one whom I have befriended in the past, and why do you speak such heavy words of death in my ears, O, Zikali the Wise, which of late have heard so much of death?" He sighed, adding: "Be pleased now, to tell us of this medicine, or, if you will not, go, and I will send for other Nyangas."

"Why should I not tell you, when you ask me softly and without threats, O King? See"—and Zikali took up some of the twisted roots—"these are the roots of a certain poisonous herb that blooms at night on the tops of mountains, and woe be to the ox that eats thereof. They have been boiled in gall and blood, and ill will befall the hut in which they are hidden by one who can speak the words of power. This is the bone of a babe that has never lived to cut its teeth—I think of a babe that was left to die alone in the bush because it was hated, or because none would father it. Such a bone has strength to work ill against other babes; moreover, it is filled with a charmed medicine. Look!" and, pulling out the plug of wood, he scattered some grey powder from the bone, then stopped it up again. "This," he added, picking up the fang, "is the tooth of a deadly serpent, that, after it has been doctored, is used by women to change the heart of a man from another to herself. I have spoken."

And he turned to go.

"Stay!" said the King. "Who set these foul charms in the doorway of Saduko's hut?"

"How can I tell, O King, unless I make preparation and cast the bones and smell out the evil-doer? You have heard the story of the woman Nahana. Accept it or reject it as your heart tells you."

"If that story be true, O Zikali, how comes it that you yourself smelt out, not Mameena, the wife of Masapo, but Masapo, her husband, himself, and caused him to be slain because of the poisoning of the child of Nandie?"

"You err, O King. I, Zikali, smelt out the House of Masapo. Then I smelt out the poison, searching for it first in the hair of Mameena, and finding it in the kaross of Masapo. I never smelt out that it was Masapo who gave the poison. That was the judgment of you and of your Council, O King. Nay, I knew well that there was more in the matter, and had you paid me another fee and bade me to continue to use my wisdom, without doubt I should have found this magic stuff hidden in the hut, and mayhap have learned the name of the hider. But I was weary, who am very old; and what was it to me if you chose to kill Masapo or chose to let him go? Masapo, who, being your secret enemy, was a man who deserved to die—if not for this matter, then for others."

Now, all this while I had been watching Mameena, who sat, in the Zulu fashion, listening to this deadly evidence, a slight smile upon her face, and without attempting any interruption or comment. Only I saw that while Zikali was examining the medicine, her eyes were seeking the eyes of Saduko, who remained in his place, also silent, and, to all appearance, the least interested of anyone present. He tried to avoid her glance, turning his head uneasily; but at length her eyes caught his and held them. Then his heart began to beat quickly, his breast heaved, and on his face there grew a look of dreamy content, even of happiness. From that moment forward, till the end of the scene, Saduko never took his eyes off this strange woman, though I think that, with the exception of the dwarf, Zikali, who saw everything, and of myself, who am trained to observation, none noted this curious by-play of the drama.

The King began to speak. "Mameena," he said, "you have heard. Have you aught to say? For if not it would seem that you are a witch and a murderess, and one who must die."

"Yea, a little word, O King," she answered quietly. "Nahana speaks truth. It is true that I entered the hut of Nandie and set the medicine there. I say it because by nature I am not one who hides the truth or would attempt to throw discredit even upon a humble serving-woman," and she glanced at Nahana.

"Then from between your own teeth it is finished," said Panda.

"Not altogether, O King. I have said that I set the medicine in the hut. I have not said, and I will not say, how and why I set it there. That tale I call upon Saduko yonder to tell to you, he who was my husband, that I left for Umbelazi, and who, being a man, must therefore hate me. By the words he says I will abide. If he declares that I am guilty, then I am guilty, and prepared to pay the price of guilt. But if he declares that I am innocent, then, O King and O Prince Cetewayo, without fear I trust myself to your justness. Now speak, O Saduko; speak the whole truth, whatever it may be, if that is the King's will."

"It is my will," said Panda.

"And mine also," added Cetewayo, who, I could see, like everyone else, was much interested in this matter.

Saduko rose to his feet, the same Saduko that I had always known, and yet so changed. All the life and fire had gone from him; his pride in himself was no more; none could have known him for that ambitious, confident man who, in his day of power, the Zulus named the "Self-Eater." He was a mere mask of the old Saduko, informed by some new, some alien, spirit. With dull, lack-lustre eyes fixed always upon the lovely eyes of Mameena, in slow and hesitating tones he began his tale.

"It is true, O Lion," he said, "that Mameena spread the poison upon my child's mat. It is true that she set the deadly charms in the doorway of Nandie's hut. These things she did, not knowing what she did, and it was I who instructed her to do them. This is the case. From the beginning I have always loved Mameena as I have loved no other woman and as no other woman was ever loved. But while I was away with Macumazahn, who sits yonder, to destroy Bangu, chief of the Amakoba, he who had killed my father, Umbezi, the father of Mameena, he whom the Prince Cetewayo gave to the vultures the other day because he had lied as to the death of Umbelazi, he, I say, forced Mameena, against her will, to marry Masapo the Boar, who afterwards was executed for wizardry. Now, here at your feast, when you reviewed the people of the Zulus, O King, after you had given me the lady Nandie as wife, Mameena and I met again and loved each other more than we had ever done before. But, being an upright woman, Mameena thrust me away from her, saying:

"'I have a husband, who, if he is not dear to me, still is my husband, and while he lives to him I will be true.' Then, O King, I took counsel with the evil in my heart, and made a plot in myself to be rid of the Boar, Masapo, so that when he was dead I might marry Mameena. This was the plot that I made—that my son and Princess Nandie's should be poisoned, and that Masapo should seem to poison him, so that he might be killed as a wizard and I marry Mameena."

Now, at this astounding statement, which was something beyond the experience of the most cunning and cruel savage present there, a gasp of astonishment went up from the audience; even old Zikali lifted his head and stared. Nandie, too, shaken out of her usual calm, rose as though to speak; then, looking first at Saduko and next at Mameena, sat herself down again and waited. But Saduko went on again in the same cold, measured voice:

"I gave Mameena a powder which I had bought for two heifers from a great doctor who lived beyond the Tugela, but who is now dead, which powder I told her was desired by Nandie, my Inkosikazi, to destroy the little beetles than ran about the hut, and directed her where she was to spread it. Also, I gave her the bag of medicine, telling her to thrust it into the doorway of the hut, that it might bring a blessing upon my House. These things she did ignorantly to please me, not knowing that the powder was poison, not knowing that the medicine was bewitched. So my child died, as I wished it to die, and, indeed, I myself fell sick because by accident I touched the powder.

"Afterwards Masapo was smelt out as a wizard by old Zikali, I having caused a bag of the poison to be sewn in his kaross in order to deceive Zikali, and killed by your order, O King, and Mameena was given to me as a wife, also by your order, O King, which was what I desired. Later on, as I have told you, I wearied of her, and wishing to please the Prince who has wandered away, I commanded her to yield herself to him, which Mameena did out of her love for me and to advance my fortunes, she who is blameless in all things."

Saduko finished speaking and sat down again, as an automaton might do when a wire is pulled, his lacklustre eyes still fixed upon Mameena's face.

"You have heard, O King," said Mameena. "Now pass judgment, knowing that, if it be your will, I am ready to die for Saduko's sake."

But Panda sprang up in a rage.

"Take him away!" he said, pointing to Saduko. "Take away that dog who is not fit to live, a dog who eats his own child that thereby he may cause another to be slain unjustly and steal his wife."

The executioners leapt forward, and, having something to say, for I could bear this business no longer, I began to rise to my feet. Before I gained them, however, Zikali was speaking.

"O King," he said, "it seems that you have killed one man unjustly on this matter, namely, Masapo. Would you do the same by another?" and he pointed to Saduko.

"What do you mean?" asked Panda angrily. "Have you not heard this low fellow, whom I made great, giving him the rule over tribes and my daughter in marriage, confess with his own lips that he murdered his child, the child of my blood, in order that he might eat a fruit which grew by the roadside for all men to nibble at?" and he glared at Mameena.

"Aye, Child of Senzangakona," answered Zikali, "I heard Saduko say this with his own lips, but the voice that spoke from the lips was not the voice of Saduko, as, were you a skilled Nyanga like me, you would have known as well as I do, and as well as does the white man, Watcher-by-Night, who is a reader of hearts.

"Hearken now, O King, and you great ones around the King, and I will tell you a story. Matiwane, the father of Saduko, was my friend, as he was yours, O King, and when Bangu slew him and his people, by leave of the Wild Beast [Chaka], I saved the child, his son, aye, and brought him up in my own House, having learned to love him. Then, when he became a man, I, the Opener-of-Roads, showed him two roads, down either of which he might choose to walk—the Road of Wisdom and the Road of War and Women: the white road that runs through peace to knowledge, and the red road that runs through blood to death.

"But already there stood one upon this red road who beckoned him, she who sits yonder, and he followed after her, as I knew he would. From the beginning she was false to him, taking a richer man for her husband. Then, when Saduko grew great, she grew sorry, and came to ask my counsel as to how she might be rid of Masapo, whom she swore she hated. I told her that she could leave him for another man, or wait till her Spirit moved him from her path; but I never put evil into her heart, seeing that it was there already.

"Then she and no other, having first made Saduko love her more than ever, murdered the child of Nandie, his Inkosikazi; and so brought about the death of Masapo and crept into Saduko's arms. Here she slept a while, till a new shadow fell upon her, that of the 'Elephant-with-the-tuft-of-hair,' who will walk the woods no more. Him she beguiled that she might grow great the quicker, and left the house of Saduko, taking his heart with her, she who was destined to be the doom of men.

"Now, into Saduko's breast, where his heart had been, entered an evil spirit of jealousy and of revenge, and in the battle of Endondakusuka that spirit rode him as a white man rides a horse. As he had arranged to do with the Prince Cetewayo yonder—nay, deny it not, O Prince, for I know all; did you not make a bargain together, on the third night before the battle, among the bushes, and start apart when the buck leapt out between you?" (Here Cetewayo, who had been about to speak, threw the corner of his kaross over his face.) "As he had arranged to do, I say, he went over with his regiments from the Isigqosa to the Usutu, and so brought about the fall of Umbelazi and the death of many thousands. Yes, and this he did for one reason only—because yonder woman had left him for the Prince, and he cared more for her than for all the world could give him, for her who had filled him with madness as a bowl is filled with milk. And now, O King, you have heard this man tell you a story, you have heard him shout out that he is viler than any man in all the land; that he murdered his own child, the child he loved so well, to win this witch; that afterwards he gave her to his friend and lord to buy more of his favour, and that lastly he deserted that lord because he thought that there was another lord from whom he could buy more favour. Is it not so, O King?"

"It is so," answered Panda, "and therefore must Saduko be thrown out to the jackals."

"Wait a while, O King. I say that Saduko has spoken not with his own voice, but with the voice of Mameena. I say that she is the greatest witch in all the land, and that she has drugged him with the medicine of her eyes, so that he knows not what he says, even as she drugged the Prince who is dead."

"Then prove it, or he dies!" exclaimed the King.

Now the dwarf went to Panda and whispered in his ear, whereon Panda whispered in turn into the ears of two of his councillors. These men, who were unarmed, rose and made as though to leave the isi-gohlo. But as they passed Mameena one of them suddenly threw his arms about her, pinioning her arms, the other tearing off the kaross he wore—for the weather was cold—flung it over her head and knotted it behind her so that she was hidden except for her ankles and feet. Then, although she did not move or struggle, they caught hold of her and stood still.

Now Zikali hobbled to Saduko and bade him rise, which he did. Then he looked at him for a long while and made certain movements with his hands before his face, after which Saduko uttered a great sigh and stared about him.

"Saduko," said Zikali, "I pray you tell me, your foster-father, whether it is true, as men say, that you sold your wife, Mameena, to the Prince Umbelazi in order that his favour might fall on you like heavy rain?"

"Wow! Zikali," said Saduko, with a start of rage, "If were you as others are I would kill you, you toad, who dare to spit slander on my name. She ran away with the Prince, having beguiled him with the magic of her beauty."

"Strike me not, Saduko," went on Zikali, "or at least wait to strike until you have answered one more question. Is it true, as men say, that in the battle of Endondakusuka you went over to the Usutu with your regiments because you thought that Indhlovu-ene-Sihlonti would be beaten, and wished to be on the side of him who won?"

"What, Toad! More slander?" cried Saduko. "I went over for one reason only—to be revenged upon the Prince because he had taken from me her who was more to me than life or honour. Aye, and when I went over Umbelazi was winning; it was because I went that he lost and died, as I meant that he should die, though now," he added sadly, "I would that I had not brought him to ruin and the dust, who think that, like myself, he was but wet clay in a woman's fingers.

"O King," he added, turning to Panda, "kill me, I pray you, who am not worthy to live, since to him whose hand is red with the blood of his friend, death alone is left, who, while he breathes, must share his sleep with ghosts that watch him with their angry eyes."

Then Nandie sprang up and said:

"Nay, Father, listen not to him who is mad, and therefore holy.[*] What he has done, he has done, who, as he has said, was but a tool in another's hand. As for our babe, I know well that he would have died sooner than harm it, for he loved it much, and when it was taken away, for three whole days and nights he wept and would touch no food. Give this poor man to me, my Father—to me, his wife, who loves him—and let us go hence to some other land, where perchance we may forget."

[*—The Zulus suppose that insane people are inspired. —A.Q.]

"Be silent, daughter," said the King; "and you, O Zikali, the Nyanga, be silent also."

They obeyed, and, after thinking awhile, Panda made a motion with his hand, whereon the two councillors lifted the kaross from off Mameena, who looked about her calmly and asked if she were taking part in some child's game.

"Aye, woman," answered Panda, "you are taking part in a great game, but not, I think, such as is played by children—a game of life and death. Now, have you heard the tale of Zikali the Little and Wise, and the words of Saduko, who was once your husband, or must they be repeated to you?"

"There is no need, O King; my ears are too quick to be muffled by a fur bag, and I would not waste your time."

"Then what have you to say, woman?"

"Not much," she answered with a shrug of her shoulders, "except that I have lost in this game. You will not believe me, but if you had left me alone I should have told you so, who did not wish to see that poor fool, Saduko, killed for deeds he had never done. Still, the tale he told you was not told because I had bewitched him; it was told for love of me, whom he desired to save. It was Zikali yonder; Zikali, the enemy of your House, who in the end will destroy your House, O Son of Senzangakona, that bewitched him, as he has bewitched you all, and forced the truth out of his unwilling heart.

"Now, what more is there to say? Very little, as I think. I did the things that are laid to my charge, and worse things which have not been stated. Oh, I played for great stakes, I, who meant to be the Inkosazana of the Zulus, and, as it chances, by the weight of a hair I have lost. I thought that I had counted everything, but the hair's weight which turned the balance against me was the mad jealousy of this fool, Saduko, upon which I had not reckoned. I see now that when I left Saduko I should have left him dead. Thrice I had thought of it. Once I mixed the poison in his drink, and then he came in, weary with his plottings, and kissed me ere he drank; and my woman's heart grew soft and I overset the bowl that was at his lips. Do you not remember, Saduko?

"So, so! For that folly alone I deserve to die, for she who would reign"—and her beautiful eyes flashed royally—"must have a tiger's heart, not that of a woman. Well, because I was too kind I must die; and, after all is said, it is well to die, who go hence awaited by thousands upon thousands that I have sent before me, and who shall be greeted presently by your son, Indhlovu-ene-Sihlonti, and his warriors, greeted as the Inkosazana of Death, with red, lifted spears and with the royal salute!

"Now, I have spoken. Walk your little road, O King and Prince and Councillors, till you reach the gulf into which I sink, that yawns for all of you. O King, when you meet me again at the bottom of that gulf, what a tale you will have to tell me, you who are but the shadow of a king, you whose heart henceforth must be eaten out by a worm that is called Love-of-the-Lost. O Prince and Conqueror Cetewayo, what a tale you will have to tell me when I greet you at the bottom of that gulf, you who will bring your nation to a wreck and at last die as I must die—only the servant of others and by the will of others. Nay, ask me not how. Ask old Zikali, my master, who saw the beginning of your House and will see its end. Oh, yes, as you say, I am a witch, and I know, I know! Come, I am spent. You men weary me, as men have always done, being but fools whom it is so easy to make drunk, and who when drunk are so unpleasing. Piff! I am tired of you sober and cunning, and I am tired of you drunken and brutal, you who, after all, are but beasts of the field to whom Mvelingangi, the Creator, has given heads which can think, but which always think wrong.

"Now, King, before you unchain your dogs upon me, I ask one moment. I said that I hated all men, yet, as you know, no woman can tell the truth—quite. There is a man whom I do not hate, whom I never hated, whom I think I love because he would not love me. He sits there," and to my utter dismay, and the intense interest of that company, she pointed at me, Allan Quatermain!

"Well, once by my 'magic,' of which you have heard so much, I got the better of this man against his will and judgment, and, because of that soft heart of mine, I let him go; yes, I let the rare fish go when he was on my hook. It is well that I should have let him go, since, had I kept him, a fine story would have been spoiled and I should have become nothing but a white hunter's servant, to be thrust away behind the door when the white Inkosikazi came to eat his meat—I, Mameena, who never loved to stand out of sight behind a door. Well, when he was at my feet and I spared him, he made me a promise, a very small promise, which yet I think he will keep now when we part for a little while. Macumazahn, did you not promise to kiss me once more upon the lips whenever and wherever I should ask you?"

"I did," I answered in a hollow voice, for in truth her eyes held me as they had held Saduko.

"Then come now, Macumazahn, and give me that farewell kiss. The King will permit it, and since I have now no husband, who take Death to husband, there is none to say you nay."

I rose. It seemed to me that I could not help myself. I went to her, this woman surrounded by implacable enemies, this woman who had played for great stakes and lost them, and who knew so well how to lose. I stood before her, ashamed and yet not ashamed, for something of her greatness, evil though it might be, drove out my shame, and I knew that my foolishness was lost in a vast tragedy.

Slowly she lifted her languid arm and threw it about my neck; slowly she bent her red lips to mine and kissed me, once upon the mouth and once upon the forehead. But between those two kisses she did a thing so swiftly that my eyes could scarcely follow what she did. It seemed to me that she brushed her left hand across her lips, and that I saw her throat rise as though she swallowed something. Then she thrust me from her, saying:

"Farewell, O Macumazana, you will never forget this kiss of mine; and when we meet again we shall have much to talk of, for between now and then your story will be long. Farewell, Zikali. I pray that all your plannings may succeed, since those you hate are those I hate, and I bear you no grudge because you told the truth at last. Farewell, Prince Cetewayo. You will never be the man your brother would have been, and your lot is very evil, you who are doomed to pull down a House built by One who was great. Farewell, Saduko the fool, who threw away your fortune for a woman's eyes, as though the world were not full of women. Nandie the Sweet and the Forgiving will nurse you well until your haunted end. Oh! why does Umbelazi lean over your shoulder, Saduko, and look at me so strangely? Farewell, Panda the Shadow. Now let loose your slayers. Oh! let them loose swiftly, lest they should be balked of my blood!"

Panda lifted his hand and the executioners leapt forward, but ere ever they reached her, Mameena shivered, threw wide her arms and fell back—dead. The poisonous drug she had taken worked well and swiftly.

Such was the end of Mameena, Child of Storm.

A deep silence followed, a silence of awe and wonderment, till suddenly it was broken by a sound of dreadful laughter. It came from the lips of Zikali the Ancient, Zikali, the

"Thing-that-should-never-have-been-born."

CHAPTER XVI

MAMEENA—MAMEENA—MAMEENA!

That evening at sunset, just as I was about to trek, for the King had given me leave to go, and at that time my greatest desire in life seemed to be to bid good-bye to Zululand and the Zulus—I saw a strange, beetle-like shape hobbling up the hill towards me, supported by two big men. It was Zikali.

He passed me without a word, merely making a motion that I was to follow him, which I did out of curiosity, I suppose, for Heaven knows I had seen enough of the old wizard to last me for a lifetime. He reached a flat stone about a hundred yards above my camp, where there was no bush in which anyone could hide, and sat himself down, pointing to another stone in front of him, on which I sat myself down. Then the two men retired out of earshot, and, indeed, of sight, leaving us quite alone.

"So you are going away, O Macumazana?" he said.

"Yes, I am," I answered with energy, "who, if I could have had my will, would have gone away long ago."

"Yes, yes, I know that; but it would have been a great pity, would it not? If you had gone, Macumazahn, you would have missed seeing the end of a strange little story, and you, who love to study the hearts of men and women, would not have been so wise as you are to-day."

"No, nor as sad, Zikali. Oh! the death of that woman!" And I put my hand before my eyes.

"Ah! I understand, Macumazahn; you were always fond of her, were you not, although your white pride would not suffer you to admit that black fingers were pulling at your heartstrings? She was a wonderful witch, was Mameena; and there is this comfort for you—that she pulled at other heartstrings as well. Masapo's, for instance; Saduko's, for instance; Umbelazi's, for instance, none of whom got any luck from her pulling—yes, and even at mine."

Now, as I did not think it worth while to contradict his nonsense so far as I was concerned personally, I went off on this latter point.

"If you show affection as you did towards Mameena to-day, Zikali, I pray my Spirit that you may cherish none for me," I said.

He shook his great head pityingly as he answered:

"Did you never love a lamb and kill it afterwards when you were hungry, or when it grew into a ram and butted you, or when it drove away your other sheep, so that they fell into the hands of thieves? Now, I am very hungry for the fall of the House of Senzangakona, and the lamb, Mameena, having grown big, nearly laid me on my back to-day within the reach of the slayer's spear. Also, she was hunting my sheep, Saduko, into an evil net whence he could never have escaped. So, somewhat against my will, I was driven to tell the truth of that lamb and her tricks."

"I daresay," I exclaimed; "but, at any rate, she is done with, so what is the use of talking about her?"

"Ah! Macumazahn, she is done with, or so you think, though that is a strange saying for a white man who believes in much that we do not know; but at least her work remains, and it has been a great work. Consider now. Umbelazi and most of the princes, and thousands upon thousands of the Zulus, whom I, the Dwande, hate, dead, dead! Mameena's work, Macumazahn! Panda's hand grown strengthless with sorrow and his eyes blind with tears. Mameena's work, Macumazahn! Cetewayo, king in all but name; Cetewayo, who shall bring the House of Senzangakona to the dust. Mameena's work, Macumazahn! Oh! a mighty work. Surely she has lived a great and worthy life, and she died a great and worthy death! And how well she did it! Had you eyes to see her take the poison which I gave her—a good poison, was it not?—between her kisses, Macumazahn?"

"I believe it was your work, and not hers," I blurted out, ignoring his mocking questions. "You pulled the strings; you were the wind that caused the grass to bend till the fire caught it and set the town in flames—the town of your foes."

"How clever you are, Macumazahn! If your wits grow so sharp, one day they will cut your throat, as, indeed, they have nearly done several times already. Yes, yes, I know how to pull strings till the trap falls, and to blow grass until the flame catches it, and how to puff at that flame until it burns the House of Kings. And yet this trap would have fallen without me, only then it might have snared other rats; and this grass would have caught fire if I had not blown, only then it might have burnt another House. I did not make these forces, Macumazahn; I did but guide them towards a great end, for which the White House [that is, the English] should thank me one day." He brooded a while, then went on: "But what need is there to talk to you of these matters, Macumazahn, seeing that in a time to come you will have your share in them and see them for yourself? After they are finished, then we will talk."

"I do not wish to talk of them," I answered. "I have said so already. But for what other purpose did you take the trouble to come here?"

"Oh, to bid you farewell for a little while, Macumazahn. Also to tell you that Panda, or rather Cetewayo, for now Panda is but his Voice, since the Head must go where the Feet carry it, has spared Saduko at the prayer of Nandie and banished him from the land, giving him his cattle and any people who care to go with him to wherever he may choose to live from henceforth. At least, Cetewayo says it was at Nandie's prayer, and at mine and yours, but what he means is that, after all that has happened, he thought it wise that Saduko should die of himself."

"Do you mean that he should kill himself, Zikali?"

"No, no; I mean that his own idhlozi, his Spirit, should be left to kill him, which it will do in time. You see, Macumazahn, Saduko is now living with a ghost, which he calls the ghost of Umbelazi, whom he betrayed."

"Is that your way of saying he is mad, Zikali?"

"Oh, yes, he lives with a ghost, or the ghost lives in him, or he is mad—call it which you will. The mad have a way of living with ghosts, and ghosts have a way of sharing their food with the mad. Now you understand everything, do you not?"

"Of course," I answered; "it is as plain as the sun."

"Oh! did I not say you were clever, Macumazahn, you who know where madness ends and ghosts begin, and why they are just the same thing? Well, the sun is no longer plain. Look, it has sunk; and you would be on your road who wish to be far from Nodwengu before morning. You will pass the plain of Endondakusuka, will you not, and cross the Tugela by the drift? Have a look round, Macumazahn, and see if you can recognise any old friends. Umbezi, the knave and traitor, for instance; or some of the princes. If so, I should like to send them a message. What! You cannot wait? Well, then, here is a little present for you, some of my own work. Open it when it is light again, Macumazahn; it may serve to remind you of the strange little tale of Mameena with the Heart of Fire. I wonder where she is now? Sometimes, sometimes—" And he rolled his great eyes about him and sniffed at the air like a hound. "Farewell till we meet again. Farewell, Macumazahn. Oh! if you had only run away with Mameena, how different things might have been to-day!"

I jumped up and fled from that terrible old dwarf, whom I verily believe— No; where is the good of my saying what I believe? I fled from him, leaving him seated on the stone in the shadows, and as I fled, out of the darkness behind me there arose the sound of his loud and eerie laughter.

Next morning I opened the packet which he had given me, after wondering once or twice whether I should not thrust it down an ant-bear hole as it was. But this, somehow, I could not find the heart to do, though now I wish I had. Inside, cut from the black core of the umzimbiti wood, with just a little of the white sap left on it to mark the eyes, teeth and nails, was a likeness of Mameena. Of course, it was rudely executed, but it was—or rather is, for I have it still—a wonderfully good portrait of her, for whether Zikali was or was not a wizard, he was certainly a good artist. There she stands, her body a little bent, her arms outstretched, her head held forward with the lips parted, just as though she were about to embrace somebody, and in one of her hands, cut also from the white sap of the umzimbiti, she grasps a human heart—Saduko's, I presume, or perhaps Umbelazi's.

Nor was this all, for the figure was wrapped in a woman's hair, which I knew at once for that of Mameena, this hair being held in place by the necklet of big blue beads she used to wear about her throat.

Some five years had gone by, during which many things had happened to me that need not be recorded here, when one day I found myself in a rather remote part of the Umvoti district of Natal, some miles to the east of a mountain called the Eland's Kopje, whither I had gone to carry out a big deal in mealies, over which, by the way, I lost a good bit of money. That has always been my fate when I plunged into commercial ventures.

One night my wagons, which were overloaded with these confounded weevilly mealies, got stuck in the drift of a small tributary of the Tugela that most inopportunely had come down in flood. Just as darkness fell I managed to get them up the bank in the midst of a pelting rain that soaked me to the bone. There seemed to be no prospect of lighting a fire or of obtaining any decent food, so I was about to go to bed supperless when a flash of lightning showed me a large kraal situated upon a hillside about half a mile away, and an idea entered my mind.

"Who is the headman of that kraal?" I asked of one of the Kafirs who had collected round us in our trouble, as such idle fellows always do.

"Tshoza, Inkoosi," answered the man.

"Tshoza! Tshoza!" I said, for the name seemed familiar to me. "Who is Tshoza?"

"Ikona [I don't know], Inkoosi. He came from Zululand some years ago with Saduko the Mad."

Then, of course, I remembered at once, and my mind flew back to the night when old Tshoza, the brother of Matiwane, Saduko's father, had cut out the cattle of the Bangu and we had fought the battle in the pass.

"Oh!" I said, "is it so? Then lead me to Tshoza, and I will give you a 'Scotchman.'" (That is, a two-shilling piece, so called because some enterprising emigrant from Scotland passed off a vast number of them among the simple natives of Natal as substitutes for half-crowns.)

Tempted by this liberal offer—and it was very liberal, because I was anxious to get to Tshoza's kraal before its inhabitants went to bed—the meditative Kafir consented to guide me by a dark and devious path that ran through bush and dripping fields of corn. At length we arrived—for if the kraal was only half a mile away, the path to it covered fully two miles—and glad enough was I when we had waded the last stream and found ourselves at its gate.

In response to the usual inquiries, conducted amid a chorus of yapping dogs, I was informed that Tshoza did not live there, but somewhere else; that he was too old to see anyone; that he had gone to sleep and could not be disturbed; that he was dead and had been buried last week, and so forth.

"Look here, my friend," I said at last to the fellow who was telling me all these lies, "you go to Tshoza in his grave and say to him that if he does not come out alive instantly, Macumazahn will deal with his cattle as once he dealt with those of Bangu."

Impressed with the strangeness of this message, the man departed, and presently, in the dim light of the rain-washed moon, I perceived a little old man running towards me; for Tshoza, who was pretty ancient at the beginning of this history, had not been made younger by a severe wound at the battle of the Tugela and many other troubles.

"Macumazahn," he said, "is that really you? Why, I heard that you were dead long ago; yes, and sacrificed an ox for the welfare of your Spirit."

"And ate it afterwards, I'll be bound," I answered.

"Oh! it must be you," he went on, "who cannot be deceived, for it is true we ate that ox, combining the sacrifice to your Spirit with a feast; for why should anything be wasted when one is poor? Yes, yes, it must be you, for who else would come creeping about a man's kraal at night, except the Watcher-by-Night? Enter, Macumazahn, and be welcome."

So I entered and ate a good meal while we talked over old times.

"And now, where is Saduko?" I asked suddenly as I lit my pipe.

"Saduko?" he answered, his face changing as he spoke. "Oh! of course he is here. You know I came away with him from Zululand. Why? Well, to tell the truth, because after the part we had played—against my will, Macumazahn—at the battle of Endondakusuka, I thought it safer to be away from a country where those who have worn their karosses inside out find many enemies and few friends."

"Quite so," I said. "But about Saduko?"

"Oh, I told you, did I not? He is in the next hut, and dying!"

"Dying! What of, Tshoza?"

"I don't know," he answered mysteriously; "but I think he must be bewitched. For a long while, a year or more, he has eaten little and cannot bear to be alone in the dark; indeed, ever since he left Zululand he has been very strange and moody."

Now I remembered what old Zikali had said to me years before to the effect that Saduko was living with a ghost which would kill him.

"Does he think much about Umbelazi, Tshoza?" I asked.

"O Macumazana, he thinks of nothing else; the Spirit of Umbelazi is in him day and night."

"Indeed," I said. "Can I see him?"

"I don't know, Macumazahn. I will go and ask the lady Nandie at once, for, if you can, I believe there is no time to lose." And he left the hut.

Ten minutes later he returned with a woman, Nandie the Sweet herself, the same quiet, dignified Nandie whom I used to know, only now somewhat worn with trouble and looking older than her years.

"Greeting, Macumazahn," she said. "I am pleased to see you, although it is strange, very strange, that you should come here just at this time. Saduko is leaving us—on a long journey, Macumazahn."

I answered that I had heard so with grief, and wondered whether he would like to see me.

"Yes, very much, Macumazahn; only be prepared to find him different from the Saduko whom you knew. Be pleased to follow me."

So we went out of Tshoza's hut, across a courtyard to another large hut, which we entered. It was lit with a good lamp of European make; also a bright fire burned upon the hearth, so that the place was as light as day. At the side of the hut a man lay upon some blankets, watched by a woman. His eyes were covered with his hand, and he was moaning:

"Drive him away! Drive him away! Cannot he suffer me to die in peace?"

"Would you drive away your old friend, Macumazahn, Saduko?" asked Nandie very gently, "Macumazahn, who has come from far to see you?"

He sat up, and, the blankets falling off him, showed me that he was nothing but a living skeleton. Oh! how changed from that lithe and handsome chief whom I used to know. Moreover, his lips quivered and his eyes were full of terrors.

"Is it really you, Macumazahn?" he said in a weak voice. "Come, then, and stand quite close to me, so that he may not get between us," and he stretched out his bony hand.

I took the hand; it was icy cold.

"Yes, yes, it is I, Saduko," I said in a cheerful voice; "and there is no man to get between us; only the lady Nandie, your wife, and myself are in the hut; she who watched you has gone."

"Oh, no, Macumazahn, there is another in the hut whom you cannot see. There he stands," and he pointed towards the hearth. "Look! The spear is through him and his plume lies on the ground!"

"Through whom, Saduko?"

"Whom? Why, the Prince Umbelazi, whom I betrayed for Mameena's sake."

"Why do you talk wind, Saduko?" I asked. "Years ago I saw Indhlovu-ene-Sihlonti die."

"Die, Macumazahn! We do not die; it is only our flesh that dies. Yes, yes, I have learned that since we parted. Do you not remember his last words: 'I will haunt you while you live, and when you cease to live, ah! then we shall meet again'? Oh! from that hour to this he has haunted me, Macumazahn—he and the others; and now, now we are about to meet as he promised."

Then once more he hid his eyes and groaned.

"He is mad," I whispered to Nandie.

"Perhaps. Who knows?" she answered, shaking her head.

Saduko uncovered his eyes.

"Make 'the-thing-that-burns' brighter," he gasped, "for I do not perceive him so clearly when it is bright. Oh! Macumazahn, he is looking at you and whispering. To whom is he whispering? I see! to Mameena, who also looks at you and smiles. They are talking. Be silent. I must listen."

Now, I began to wish that I were out of that hut, for really a little of this uncanny business went a long way. Indeed, I suggested going, but Nandie would not allow it.

"Stay with me till the end," she muttered. So I had to stay, wondering what Saduko heard Umbelazi whispering to Mameena, and on which side of me he saw her standing.

He began to wander in his mind.

"That was a clever pit you dug for Bangu, Macumazahn; but you would not take your share of the cattle, so the blood of the Amakoba is not on your head. Ah! what a fight was that which the Amawombe made at Endondakusuka. You were with them, you remember, Macumazahn; and why was I not at your side? Oh! then we would have swept away the Usutu as the wind sweeps ashes. Why was I not at your side to share the glory? I remember now—because of the Daughter of Storm. She betrayed me for Umbelazi, and I betrayed Umbelazi for her; and now he haunts me, whose greatness I brought to the dust; and the Usutu wolf, Cetewayo, curls himself up in his form and grows fat on his food. And—and, Macumazahn, it has all been done in vain, for Mameena hates me. Yes, I can read it in her eyes. She mocks and hates me worse in death than she did in life, and she says that—that it was not all her fault—because she loves—because she loves—"

A look of bewilderment came upon his face—his poor, tormented face; then suddenly Saduko threw his arms wide, and sobbed in an ever-weakening voice:

"All—all done in vain! Oh! Mameena, Ma—mee—na, Ma—meena!" and fell back dead.

"Saduko has gone away," said Nandie, as she drew a blanket over his face. "But I wonder," she added with a little hysterical smile, "oh! how I wonder who it was the Spirit of Mameena told him that she loved—Mameena, who was born without a heart?"

I made no answer, for at that moment I heard a very curious sound, which seemed to me to proceed from somewhere above the hut. Of what did it remind me? Ah! I knew. It was like the sound of the dreadful laughter of Zikali, Opener-of-Roads—Zikali, the

"Thing-that-should-never-have-been-born."

Doubtless, however, it was only the cry of some storm-driven night bird. Or perhaps it was an hyena that laughed—an hyena that scented death.

H. Rider Haggard – A Short Biography

Sir Henry Rider Haggard, KBE was born on June 22nd, 1856 at Bradenham in Norfolk, England.

More familiarly known as H. Rider Haggard, he was the eighth of ten children born to Sir William Meybohm Rider Haggard, a barrister (born, incidentally, in St Petersburg, Russia), and Ella Doveton, an author, poet and daughter of a merchant in the East India Trading Company.

Haggard was initially schooled at Garsington Rectory in Oxfordshire where he studied under the tutelage of Reverend H. J. Graham. His elder brothers, who seemed to find more favour with their father, graduated from various private schools whilst Haggard was sent to Ipswich Grammar School, saving his father a considerable sum in fees.

He failed his army entrance exam, and was therefore sent to a private crammer in London in preparation for the entrance exam to the British Foreign Office, which he appears never to have sat. However, it was during his two years in London that Haggard came into contact with a circle of people interested in the study of psychical phenomena and for which he too now developed a life-long interest together with a series of enduring friendships.

In 1875, Haggard's father used his family's connections to send him to Southern Africa to take up an unpaid position as assistant to the secretary to Sir Henry Bulwer, Lieutenant-Governor of the Colony of Natal. In 1876 he was transferred to the staff of Sir Theophilus Shepstone, Special Commissioner for the Transvaal. It was in this role that Haggard was present in Pretoria in April 1877 for the official announcement of the British annexation of the Boer Republic of the Transvaal. The official who had been nominated to read out the Proclamation lost his voice and Haggard was his replacement. It was a moment in history.

Haggard was to remain in the country for six years, during which time he served as Master of the High Court of the Transvaal and an adjutant of the Pretoria Horse.

It was here that he fell in love with Mary Elizabeth "Lilly" Jackson. He hoped to marry her once he obtained more certainty in his career path.

In 1878 he became Registrar of the High Court in the Transvaal and now the time seemed opportune to write to his father to tell him of his hope to marry. The reply from his father was uncompromising. He forbade it until his son had made a proper career for himself.

The following year, 1879, Lily married Frank Archer, a well-to-do banker.

Haggard returned briefly to England to marry a friend of his sister's, Marianna Louisa Margitson, a 21 year old, in 1880, and the couple travelled to Africa together. Haggard's years in Africa had proved, at least on a writing level, rich and inspirational for him, and while still in Natal he wrote two articles for The Gentleman's Magazine describing his experiences.

Moving back to England in (and accounts here differ as to whether it was 1881 or 1882) the couple settled in Ditchingham, Norfolk, Louisa's ancestral home. Later they moved to Kessingland and established connections with the church in Bungay, Suffolk. The marriage produced four children. A son named Jack (who tragically died at age 10 of measles) and three daughters, Angela, Dorothy and Lilias. (Lilias grew to become an author and her father's biographer.)

In England Law was to be the fulcrum of his career. However, although he studied, writing was growing in its appeal to him. His first book, Cetywayo and His White Neighbours, was an account and study of Britain's policies in South Africa.

From this point his career as a writer began to take substantial hold and with it a dramatic shift to fiction. Two years later he published his first fiction, Dawn followed in 1885 by arguably his most popular novel, King Solomon's Mines—detailing the life of the adventurer Allan Quatermain. This was followed the following year, 1886, by She: A History of Adventure, which introduced the female character Ayesha. Both characters, Quatermain and Ayesha, developed a series of books about their adventures.

The study of Law now fell away entirely. He appeared also to have a keen sense of his commercial appreciation. Rather than sell the copyright of his first best-seller, King Solomon's Mines, for a £100 fee he, instead, accepted a 10% royalty. This book is also generally accepted as the first of the Lost World writing genre.

Haggard obviously thought there were many further adventures to tell and it would be hard to find a publisher who would disagree given the start he had made. Sequels soon followed. Allan Quatermain continued his epic and swash-buckling adventures in Africa whilst the sequel to She entitled Ayesha played out her adventures in Tibet. Interestingly Haggard would later extend his characters adventures around the world with Eric Brighteyes, being the basis for an epic Viking romance.

The Haggard family lived at 69 Gunterstone Road in Hammersmith, London, from mid-1885 to mid-1888. It was here that he wrote his most famous works. His time in Africa had given him the experience and atmosphere as well as several observations and friendships of the people who would so influence his fictional characters. Chief among them were the larger-than-life adventurers Frederick Selous and Frederick Russell Burnham. Both were men of Empire and huge ambition as they helped uncover the great mineral wealth of Africa, as well as the ruins of ancient lost civilisations of the continent, such as Great Zimbabwe.

Three of Haggard's books, The Wizard (1896), Black Heart and White Heart; a Zulu Idyll (1896), and Elissa; the Doom of Zimbabwe (1898), are dedicated to Burnham's daughter Nada, the first white child born in Bulawayo; she had been named after Haggard's 1892 book Nada the Lily.

As is typical of the writing of the time his novels contain many of the stereotypes associated with colonialism, yet they also sympathise, to a degree, with the native populations. Africans often play heroic roles in the novels, although the protagonists are more often than not European. The time around the turn of the century was, after all, the great sprint to Empire by many European countries intent on gaining possessions of land, people and resources.

Three of Haggard's novels were written in collaboration with his friend Andrew Lang who shared his interest in the spiritual realm and paranormal phenomena and who was also a greatly admired editor.

Haggard's stories are still widely read today. Ayesha, the female protagonist of She, has been cited as a prototype by psychoanalysts such as Sigmund Freud (in The Interpretation of Dreams) and Carl Jung. Her epithet is, of course, "She Who Must Be Obeyed" and has for decades been used tongue-in-cheek to describe the presumed balance of influence between the sexes.

As a legacy it is easy to establish Haggard, and his pioneering work, as the author of the Lost World branch of writing and its influence of such other writers as Edgar Rice Burroughs, Robert E. Howard and Talbot Mundy. The Allan Quatermain character influenced many 'serials' in Hollywood during the 30s & 40s and can readily be seen as a template for Indiana Jones, the American archaeologist and explorer and huge box office film character.

Years later, when Haggard was a successful novelist, he was contacted by his former love, Lilly Archer, née Jackson. Lily had been deserted by her husband, who had embezzled funds and fled bankrupt to Africa. Haggard installed her and her sons in a house and saw to the children's education. Lilly eventually followed her husband to Africa, where he infected her with syphilis before dying of it himself. Lilly returned to England in late 1907, where Haggard again supported her until her death on April 22nd, 1909.

Haggard also wrote about agricultural and social reform, in part inspired by his experiences in Africa, but also based on what he saw in Europe. By the end of his life, he was adamantly opposed to Bolshevism, a position that he shared with his life-long friend Rudyard Kipling. The two had found friendship upon Kipling's arrival at London in 1889 largely on the strength of their shared opinions.

Haggard was extremely interested in the social affairs of the Country and eager to play a more active part in attempting reform. In 1895 he stood unsuccessfully for Parliament as a Conservative candidate for the Eastern division of Norfolk losing by 198 votes.

Also in 1895 he served on a government commission to examine Salvation Army labour colonies. This, and his heavy involvement in agriculture reform, led to him being a member of several further commissions on land use and related affairs, work that involved several trips to the Colonies and Dominions. This work, in part, helped lead to the passage of the 1909 Development Bill.

In 1911 he served on the Royal Commission examining coastal erosion.

He was an absorbed and dedicated writer of letters to The Times, nearly one hundred were published by them and the bibliography attached below reveals much in the range of subjects he wished to bring attention to.

He was made a Knight Bachelor in 1912 and a Knight Commander of the Order of the British Empire in 1919. Haggard was a member of several clubs including the Athenaeum, Savile, and Authors' clubs.

The district of Rider in British Columbia, Canada, was named in his honour.

Henry Rider Haggard died on May 14th, 1925 at the age of 68. His ashes were buried at Ditchingham Church. His papers are held at the Norfolk Record Office.

The first chapter of his book People of the Mist (1894) is credited with inspiring the 1912 motto of the Royal Air Force (formerly the Royal Flying Corps), Per ardua ad astra. "Through adversity to the stars" (or alternately "Through struggle to the stars") it is also used by other Commonwealth air forces such as the RAAF, RCAF, RNZAF, and the SAAF.

H. Rider Haggard – A Concise Bibliography

Novels
Dawn (1884) Published in three volumes
The Witch's Head (1884) Published in three volumes
King Solomon's Mines (1885) Allan Quatermain series
She: A History of Adventure (1886) Ayesha series
Allan Quatermain (1887) Allan Quatermain series
Jess (1887)
A Tale of Three Lions (1887) Allan Quatermain series
Maiwa's Revenge, or the War of the Little Hand (1888) Allan Quatermain series
Colonel Quaritch, VC (1889) Published in three volumes
Cleopatra (1889)
Beatrice (1890)
The World's Desire (1890) Co-written with Andrew Lang
Eric Brighteyes (1891)
Nada the Lily (1892)
An Heroic Effort (1893)
Montezuma's Daughter (1893)
The People of the Mist (1894)
Heart of the World (1895)
Joan Haste (1895)

The Wizard (1896)
Doctor Therne (1898)
Swallow: A Tale of the Great Trek (1899)
Lysbeth (1901)
Pearl Maiden (1903)
Stella Fregelius: A Tale of Three Destinies (1903)
The Brethren (1904)
Ayesha: The Return of She (1905) Ayesha series
The Way of the Spirit (1906)
Benita (1906)
Fair Margaret (1907)
The Ghost Kings(1908)
The Yellow God (1908)
The Lady of Blossholme (1909)
Morning Star (1910)
Queen Sheba's Ring (1910)
Red Eve (1911)
The Mahatma and the Hare (1911)
Marie (1912) Allan Quatermain series
Child of Storm (1913) Allan Quatermain series
The Wanderer's Necklace (1914)
The Holy Flower (1915) Allan Quatermain series
The Ivory Child (1916) Allan Quatermain series
Finished (1917) Allan Quatermain series]
Love Eternal (1918)
Moon of Israel (1918)
When the World Shook (1919)
The Ancient Allan (1920) Allan Quatermain series
She and Allan (1921) Allan Quatermain series / Ayesha series
The Virgin of the Sun (1922)
Wisdom's Daughter (1923) Ayesha series
Heu-Heu (1924) Allan Quatermain series]
Queen of the Dawn (1925)
The Treasure of the Lake (1926) Allan Quatermain series
Allan and the Ice-Gods (1927) Allan Quatermain series
Mary of Marion Isle (1929)
Belshazzar (1930)

Short Story Collections
Allan's Wife and Other Tales (1889)
Black Heart and White Heart: A Zulu Idyll (1900)
Smith and the Pharaohs (1920)

Publications in Periodicals and Newspapers
A Zulu War-Dance (July 1877) The Gentleman's Magazine
A Visit to the Chief (September 1877) The Gentleman's Magazine

Hydrophobia (letter) (3 November 1885) The Times
The Land Question (letter) (28 April 1886) The Times
About Fiction (February 1887) The Contemporary Review
Mr Rider Haggard and His Critics (letter) (27 April 1887) The Times
Our Position in Cyprus (July 1887) The Contemporary Review
American Copyright (letter) (11 October 1887) The Times
On Going Back (November 1887) Longman's Magazine
Delagoa Bay (letter) (17 December 1887) The Times
South African Policy (letter) (27 December 1887) The Times
Suggested Prologue to a Dramatised Version of She (March 1888) Longman's Magazine
Mr. Meeson's Will (18 June 1888) The Illustrated London News
The Wreck of the Copeland (18 August 1888) The Illustrated London News
Cleopatra (3 December 1888) The Illustrated London News
Hydrophobia and Muzzling (letter) (25 October 1889) The Times
The Annals of Natal (23 November 1889) The Saturday Review
Mummy at St Mary/Woolnoth's (letter) (25 December 1889) The Times
Mummies (letter) (27 December 1889) The Times
The Fate of Swaziland (January 1890) The New Review
In Memoriam (17 May 1890) Thompson's Seasons
American Copyright (letter) (5 June 1890) The Times
Mr Herbert Ward and Mr Stanley (10 November 1890) The Times
Nada the Lily (2 January 1892) The Illustrated London News
A New Argument Against Creation (19 December 1892) The Times
My First Book. Dawn. By H. Rider Haggard (April 1893) The Idler
The Tale of Isandlwana and Rorke's Drift (4 October 1893) The True Story Book
Lobengula (letter) (19 October 1893) The Times
The New Sentiment (letter) (6 November 1893) The Times
Wanted—Imagination   (25 December 1893) The Times
The Fate of Captain Patterson's Party (28 December 1893) The Times
The Three Volume Novel (letter) (27 July 1894) The Times
The Adventures of John Gladwyn Jebb (letter) (30 October 1894) The Times
Agriculture in Norfolk (letter) (30 October 1894) The Times
The Nelson Bazaar (letter) (16 February 1895) The Times
Everything is Peaceful (letter) (20 March 1895) The Times
Lord Kimberley in Norfolk (letter) (17 April 1895) The Times
The East Norfolk Election (letter) (23 July 1895) The Times
The East Norfolk Election (letter) (29 July 1895) The Times
Wilson's Last Fight (7 October 1895) The True Story Book
The Crisis in the Transvaal (letter) (2 January 1896) The Times
The Transvaal Crisis (letter) (13 January 1896) The Times
Jameson's Surrender (letter) (14 March 1896) The Times
The Rinderpest in South Africa (letter) (5 November 1896) The Times
Mr Rider Haggard and Dr Neufeld (letter) (9 January 1899) The Times
Shrinkage of Population in Agricultural Districts (letter) (9 May 1899) The Times
The South African Crisis—An Appeal (letter) (1 July 1899) The Times
Commandant-General Joubert and Mr H Rider Haggard (letter) (8 September 1899) The Times
Anglo-African Writers' Club (17 October 1899) The Times
The War (letter) (25 October 1899) The Times

Farming in 1899 (letter) (22 December 1899) The Times
Farming in 1899 (letter) (1 January 1900) The Times
Settlement of Soldiers in South Africa (letter) (5 May 1900) The Times
1881 and 1900 (letter) (2 October 1900) The Times
Farming in 1900 (letter) (1 January 1901) The Times
Central and Associated Chambers of Agriculture (letter) (6 November 1901) The Times
Small Holdings (letter) (8 November 1901) The Times
Rural England (letter) (4 February 1903) The Times
Mr Rider Haggard on Rural Depopulation (3 May 1903) The Times
Agricultural Distress (letter) (11 June 1903) The Times
The Motor Problem (letter) (24 June 1903) The Times
Fiscal Policy and Agriculture (letter) (16 December 1903) The Times
Telepathy Between a Human Being and a Dog (letter) (21 July 1904) The Times
Telepathy Between a Human Being and a Dog (letter) (9 August 1904) The Times
Mr Rider Haggard on Small Holdings (12 September 1904) The Times
Case L.1139 Dream (October 1904) Journal of the Society for Psychical Research
Mr Rider Haggard on Agriculture (22 October 1904) The Times
Mr Rider Haggard on Rural Housing (27 October 1904) The Times
The Deserted Village (letter) (25 August 1905) The Times
Decrease of Population and the Land (letter) (6 January 1906) The Times
Prevention of Cruelty to Children (3 February 1906) The Times
The New Land and Tenure Bill (letter) (12 March 1906) The Times
Garden City Association (17 March 1906) The Times
Mr H. Rider Haggard on the Zulus (19 May 1906) The Illustrated London News
To Be Proof against British Bullets: A Zulu Incantation (19 May 1906) The Illustrated London News
Housing of the Working Classes (26 June 1906) The Times
Mr Rider Haggard on Small Holdings (4 July 1906) The Times
The Unemployed and Waste City Lands (letter) (19 July 1906) The Times
Mr Rider Haggard on the Transvaal Constitution (7 August 1906) The Times
Vanishing East Anglia (1 September 1906) The Saturday Review
The Land Grabbing at Plaistow (5 September 1906) The Times
The Land Tenure Bill (22 November 1906) The Times
Publishers and the Public (letter) (19 February 1907) The Times
The Careless Children (2 March 1907) The Saturday Review
The Government and the Land (letter) (29 April 1907) The Times
Chambers of Agriculture (2 May 1907) The Times
The Government and the Land (letter) (8 May 1907) The Times
Miss Jebb on Small Holdings (15 June 1907) Country Life
Rural Housing and Sanitation Association (27 June 1907) The Times
St Thomas Hospital Medical School (28 June 1907) The Times
The Land Question (4 July 1907) The Times
A Plea for the Sitting Tennant (letter) (12 August 1907) The Times
A Literary Coincidence (letter) (19 October 1907) The Spectator
Town Planning Conference (26 October 1907) The Times
Dr Barnardo's Homes (16 November 1907) The Times
The Proposed Agricultural Party (5 December 1907) The Times
Mr Rider Haggard and Small Holdings (10 January 1908) The Times
Mr Haggard and Children's Legislation (13 March 1908) The Times

The Drink Trade and Common Sense (letter) (2 April 1908) The Times
The Zulus: The Finest Savage Race in the World (June 1908) The Pall Mall Magazine
Sparrows (letter) (18 August 1908) The Times
Sparrows, Rats and Humanity (letter) (5 September 1908) The Times
The Letters of Queen Victoria (letter) (26 November 1908) The Times
The Romance of the World's Greatest Rivers (December 1908) Travel Magazine
Afforestation. Mr Rider Haggard's View (1 March 1909) The Times
The Late Sir Marshal Clarke (letter) (13 April 1909) The Times
Mr Rider Haggard on Agriculture (27 November 1909) The Times
Mr Rider Haggard on South Africa (11 March 1910) The Times
Why? (letter) (25 April 1910) The Times
Mr Rider Haggard on Irish Agriculture (23 May 1910) The Times
Why Not? (letter) (12 July 1910) The Times
Mr Rider Haggard on Agriculture (16 September 1910) The Times
Mr Rider Haggard on Vermin (8 November 1910) The Times
Danish High Schools (21 December 1910) The Times
Sugar Beet Growing in Norfolk (6 March 1911) The Times
Rural Denmark (letter) (22 March 1911) The Times
Rural Denmark (letter) (3 April 1911) The Times
The Copyright Bill (letter) (6 June 1911) The Times
Mr Rider Haggard on Poverty. The Burden of Civilization (15 July 1911) The Times
Mr Rider Haggard and the Public Records (28 July 1911) The Times
The Farmers' Burden (1 December 1911) The Times
Egyptian Date Farm. The Financial Aspect (11 October 1912) The Times
Umslopogaas and Makokel. Sir H. Rider Haggard on Zulu Types (letter) (16 August 1913) The Times
The Death of Mark Haggard (letter) (10 October 1914) The Times
On the Land. Old Problems and New Ways. The War—and After. (15 March 1915) The Times
Soldiers as Settlers. After-War Problem for the Empire (20 August 1915) The Times
Raids by Air. Zeppelins and Zeppelins (letter) (22 October 1915) The Times
Women's Work on the Land. A Palliative in Hard Times (letter) (29 November 1915) The Times
Women on the Land. Town Girls' Unfitness for Farm Work (letter) (9 December 1915) The Times
Soldiers as Settlers. Sir Rider Haggard's Oversea Mission (2 February 1916) The Times
Soldiers as Settlers (letter) (7 February 1916) The Times
Soldier Settlers. The Future of Rural England (letter) (10 February 1916) The Times
Farewell Luncheon to Sir Rider Haggard (March 1916) United Empire
Soldier Settlers for the Empire. Offer from Victoria (18 April 1916) The Times
Sir R Haggard's Tour. Land for Ex-Service Men (22 July 1916) The Times
Sir H. Rider Haggard's Mission. Land for Ex-Soldiers (1 August 1916) The Times
Land for Ex-Soldiers. Outline of Sir R. Haggard's Report   (12 August 1916) The Times
Empire Land Settlement Deputation to the Secretary of State for the Colonies and the President of the
Board of Agriculture (September 1916) United Empire
Empire Land Settlement by Sir Rider Haggard (December 1916) United Empire
A Journey through Zululand by Sir H Rider Haggard (December 1916) The Windsor Magazine
Mr Wilson's Note. British Publicity (28 December 1916) The Times
Home Produce (letter) (22 February 1917) The Times
The Milk Supply (letter) (11 April 1917) The Times
Corn Production Bill. A National Measure (letter) (13 June 1917) The Times
A Protest and a Plea. Farmers and Meat (letter) (9 October 1917) The Times

Pig-Breeding. A Subject for Municipal Enterprise (letter) (22 February 1918) The Times
The German Colonies. Interests of the Dominions (letter) (5 November 1918) The Times
Light—More Light! (letter) (19 November 1918) The Times
A Great American. Tributes to the Late Mr Roosevelt (letter) (8 January 1919) The Times
Shut the Door (letter) (10 March 1919) The Times
Population and Housing. Emigration v Birth Control (25 March 1919) The Times
The Ex-Kaiser (letter) (11 April 1919) The Times
Empire Birth-Rate. Sir Rider Haggard on Emigration (17 April 1919) The Times
Ex-Service Men Abroad. Warnings from California (letter) (10 May 1919) The Times
Edith Cavell (letter) (16 May 1919) The Times
The Ex-Kaiser. Uncertainties of Trial (letter) (8 July 1919) The Times
Race Suicide Peril. Western Civilization Threatened (11 October 1919) The Times
The British Cinema. Production of Reputable Films (letter) (5 November 1919) The Times
Horrors on the Film. Limits of Publicity (letter) (19 November 1919) The Times
The British Museum (letter) (24 January 1920) The Times
Air Exploration and Empire (letter) (7 February 1920) The Times
The Liberty League. A Campaign Against Bolshevism (letter) (3 March 1920) The Times
Bolshevist Peril. Counter-Propaganda (4 March 1920) The Times
The Empire's Vacant Lands. Settlers and the Food Supply (14 April 1920) The Times
Films and Happy Endings. The Tyranny of a Convention (letter)   (21 April 1921) The Times
Land and its Burdens. Evil of Grinding Taxation (letter) (8 August 1921) The Times
Boy Emigrants (letter) (31 March 1922) The Times
Migration and Morals. Declining Birther Rate (7 April 1922) The Times
Labour Party's Programme. Confiscation and Class Hatred (letter) (28 October 1922) The Times
Efficient Denmark. Keeping the People on the Land (7 December 1922) The Times
The Egyptian Find. Tombs of Eighteenth Dynasty Queens (letter) (19 December 1922) The Times
King Tutankhamen. Reburial in Great Pyramid (letter) (13 February 1923) The Times
The Norfolk Dispute. A Truce while There is Time (letter) (3 April 1923) The Times
Rural Post and Telephone. Minister's Reply to Deputation (19 April 1923) The Times
Liberalism and Land Reform (letter) (1 May 1923) The Times
Small Holdings. Influence of Heredity (letter) (4 July 1923) The Times
Agricultural Parcel Post (26 July 1923) The Times
Country Houses for Sale. Empty East Anglian Mansions (letter) (14 June 1924) The Times
Plight of Agriculture (24 July 1924) The Times
Loans From the British Museum (letter) (30 July 1924) The Times
Zinovieff Letter. Mr MacDonald and a Political Plot (letter) (29 October 1924) The Times
Two Centuries of Publishing. Tributes to Messrs. Longmans (6 November 1924) The Times
Imagination and War (26 November 1924) The Times

Non-Fiction
Cetywayo and His White Neighbours (1882)
A Farmer's Year (1899)
The Last Boer War (1899)
A Winter Pilgrimage (1901)
Rural England (1902)
A Gardener's Year (1905)
The Poor and the Land (1905)

Regeneration (1910)
Rural Denmark (1911)
The Days of My Life (1926)

King Solomon's Mines

This novel has been adapted at least six times. The first version, King Solomon's Mines, directed by Robert Stevenson, premiered in 1937. The best known version premiered in 1950: King Solomon's Mines, directed by Compton Bennett and Andrew Marton, was followed in 1959 by a sequel, Watusi. In 1979 a low-budget version directed by Alvin Rakoff, King Solomon's Treasure, combined both King Solomon's Mines and Allan Quatermain in one story. The 1985 film King Solomon's Mines was a tongue-in-cheek parody of the story, with a 1987 sequel in the same vein, Allan Quatermain and the Lost City of Gold. Around the same time an Australian animated TV film came out, King Solomon's Mines. In 2008 a direct-to-video adaptation, Allan Quatermain and the Temple of Skulls, was released.

She

She has been adapted for the cinema at least ten times, and was one of the earliest films to be made, in 1899 as La Colonne de feu (The Pillar of Fire), by Georges Méliès. A 1911 version starred Marguerite Snow, a British-produced version appeared in 1916, and in 1917 Valeska Suratt appeared in a production for Fox which is lost. In 1925 a silent film of She, starring Betty Blythe, was produced with the active participation of Rider Haggard, who wrote the intertitles. This film combines elements from all the books in the series.

A decade later another cinematic version of the novels was released, featuring Helen Gahagan, Randolph Scott and Nigel Bruce. Unlike the book and the other films, this 1935 version was set in the Arctic, rather than Africa, and depicts the ancient civilisation of the story in an Art Deco style, with music by Max Steiner.

The 1965 film She was produced by Hammer Film Productions; it starred Ursula Andress as Ayesha and John Richardson as her reincarnated love, with Peter Cushing and Bernard Cribbins as other members of the expedition.

In 2001 another adaption was released direct-to-video with Ian Duncan as Leo Vincey, Ophélie Winter as Ayesha and Marie Bäumer as Roxane.

Dawn

The film Dawn was released in 1917, starring Hubert Carter and Annie Esmond.

Jess

This book was filmed in 1912, featuring Marguerite Snow, Florence La Badie and James Cruze, in 1914 with Constance Crawley and Arthur Maude, and in 1917 as Heart and Soul, starring Theda Bara in the title role.

Beatrice

The book was adapted into a 1921 Italian silent drama film called The Stronger Passion, directed by Herbert Brenon and starring Marie Doro and Sandro Salvini.

Swallow
The novel was adapted into a 1922 South African film.

Stella Fregelius
The book was adapted into a 1921 British film, Stella.

Moon of Israel
This novel was the basis of a script by Ladislaus Vajda, for film-director Michael Curtiz in his 1924 Austrian epic known as Die Sklavenkönigin (Queen of the Slaves).